*I am deeply indebted to a scientist
generously devoted hours of his p.
wonders of his particular field of scientific knowledge –
nanotechnology - to me. It is entirely thanks to him that my
imagination has not strayed into the realms of science fiction.*

*In light of the fact that this novel is a work of pure fiction
and a product of my imagination, I have called the city where
it is set Legano – a non-existant town in the South of Italy. One
departure from 'real life' is that the Stem Cell Research
department is a separate entity from the Nanotechnology
section. The role assigned to the 'Magnifico Rettore' in this
novel is, needless to say, entirely fictitious in every respect.*

*Since I completed this story, The Nanotechnology
Department of the University of Berkley, California, has
created a very small piece of 'invisibility material' which is
itself 'invisible' and thus cloaks what it is covering.   I am
pleased, if only because this story then becomes instantly more
authentic.*

*Please don't skip the Prologue – it is an integral part of the
story.*

*There is a glossary of the few Italian words and expressions
used in the narrative, with a translation into English, at the
end of the book. Where Italian expressions are used, I have
endeavoured to ensure that the meanings are made clear by
their context.*

*The front cover depicts the medieval town of Matera – in the
region of Basilicata, Southern Italy – where a crucial part of
the story unfurls. No, it is not a ghost – but an early attempt by
nanotechnologists at creating an 'invisibility cloak'. The*

silhouette of the man represents the presence of the mafia. The cover was designed by a sixteen year old student called Natalia Dalkiewicz.
Buona lettura! Happy reading! (Revised January 2018)

A dedication to Sophie and Matthew – two of my grandchildren – who inspired the brother and sister 'team' in this story, in which they become Italian and get called Anna and Riccardo.

Prologue

The sombre-looking girl was standing outside Legano railway station feeling abandoned. To make matters worse, it had begun to rain hard and she could hear menacing rumbles of thunder in the distance; the weather in Salento never did things by halves as she had already discovered. She ought to get moving before the worst of the storm arrived. And yet, she remained rooted to the spot, lacking the impetus to set one foot in front of the other. She simply did not want to return to the banality of her studio flat and face the unmade bed upon which they had both been curled up together in intimate contact such a short while ago. His train would be half way to Brindisi by now, but she had remained forlornly marooned on the concourse in front of the station. In the end, it was the realisation that he was not about to reappear before her eyes, by some form of teletransportation, that induced her to begin the trek in the gathering darkness back up the long avenue that led to the old part of the city. Her battered umbrella, a tiny carousel of sodden material poorly supported by a few flimsy struts of metal, was no protection against the rain cascading down around its sagging edges. The rain water had easily found out the weaknesses in the fabric of the umbrella and was now washing away her pointless tears as fast as they fell down her cheeks.

She had not felt so miserable and isolated since she had arrived two months previously to take up a research post in the Science Faculty here at Legano's university. It was not just a feeling of spatial isolation from the village where she had grown up, which involved two interminable train journeys to reach, but also the weird sensation that she was living in another time zone altogether. Her situation reminded her of a comedy film that she had laughed at a dozen times before. What was it called? Ah yes: 'Non ci resta che piangere'. She remembered it so vividly. It was about a couple of young men, who had driven down an isolated country lane one day only to find themselves catapulted back in time to the year 1492 – just in time, they vainly hoped, to prevent Christopher Columbus sailing off to discover America. The tragi-comedy finished up by their discovery that they were doomed never to return to modern times. It was a similarly despairing sensation of homesickness that she had been experiencing since she had arrived in Legano; she had the overpowering conviction that she would always be trapped in this baroque city in the deep south of an Italy which seemed, to her homesick soul, spiritually and morally stuck in a time warp from which she would never escape. Laughing at her own plight was the last thing she felt inclined to do at this moment of time. She might have felt that she existed in an unreal world, but the car, recklessly driven by some youth, who had images of himself as a latter-day Ayrton Senna, narrowly missing her as it jumped a red light, was alarmingly real. The potentially fatal near miss helped to restore a sense of grim reality.

'You're being pathetic!' she told herself when she arrived on the other side of the main road. She knew in her heart of hearts that she was allowing herself to be manipulated by this man, who certainly did not love her. She had become infatuated with him, seduced by his charm and his sense of purpose – not to mention his sexual prowess. 'You've got yourself involved in a situation which will almost certainly lead to losing a brilliant job and betraying your colleagues. And all for what? A couple more passionate sexual encounters before he has no further use for you! You really ARE pathetic!' she concluded and walked more purposefully towards her studio flat just off Via Cairoli. 'Forget him!'

Back in her apartment, she had a shower, put on some dry clothes and cooked herself something warm to eat. She turned on the tiny television and found herself watching a programme about children in Africa, who could never benefit from modern medical cures because of the complex and covert processes by which the developed world wrapped up its lucrative secrets behind a screen of bureaucratic procedures. Vested interests and petty restrictions prevented medical progress from reaching the children who had had the misfortune to be born in the Third World. It was precisely such arguments that HE had used to convince her that their secret undertaking was entirely morally justified.

When she was too tired to feel depressed, she went to curl up under the duvet on the unmade bed which still clearly bore the scent of their bodies. She was clutching her mobile phone, willing him to phone her so that she could tell him forcibly that she had decided not to go ahead with his dangerous and devious conspiracy.

She fell into a kind of reverie in which she was reliving the act of sex that they had indulged in before his untimely departure back to the north of Italy. She had behaved like a real sloven, she reckoned – and enjoyed the sensation immensely. She recollected that she had wrapped her legs around his back urging him onwards. She had never had an orgasm like it in her life. She had had the impression that she had left her body behind and was flying over cliff tops above a turquoise sea. Apparently, she had made a lot of noise too, although she had no memory of doing so.

Her lurid, pre-slumber fantasies were interrupted by the ringing of her mobile phone. A glance at the screen told her that it was HIM. Her heart beat had increased in anticipation of uttering the words that she knew would displease him.

But it was his voice that dominated the ensuing conversation, her contributions being reduced to monosyllabic responses echoing his words. In the end, she plucked up the courage to say:

'Dario, there is something I must tell you...'

'I must leave you now, mio amore. The taxi has arrived at my house. I'll come back and see you next weekend – or the weekend after that at the latest. In bocca al lupo for our project!' And he hung up leaving her feeling inadequate and defenceless in the bleak apartment.

When she woke up early the following morning and got ready to face the routine of a working week, she knew that her weaker 'self' had won the day. She would try to do what he wanted – merely to see if the risk was worth it; just to ascertain whether her conscience would let her get away with it. She could change her mind at any time, after all, and simply tell him that she did not want to run the risk of jeopardising her career. She could not face the thought of him returning in a week's time - if she was lucky - and being forced to tell him that she had achieved nothing. She ignored the insistent little voice within her that was plainly telling her that she was embarking on a journey to certain disaster.

1: Leonardo's Elusive Offspring

'What *is* going on here?' Professor Leonardo Molinari muttered to himself as he peered through the eyepiece of his powerful optical microscope. He should have been able to observe the tiny stem cells restructuring themselves into heart cells. He had had to leave his post for twenty minutes or so to take a phone call from his opposite number in the University of Padova. Now he was looking once again through the eyepiece of his microscope. But, inexplicably, there was nothing there to see – just a shimmering haze.

This was not the first occasion that his miniature structures had done a disappearing act. Last time, he had gone away to clean his spectacles properly, in the vain hope the explanation might be that simple. Then he had had to deal with an enquiry from a member of his team. When he had come back to look through the microscope lenses, fifteen minutes later, the missing cells had reappeared – as large as life, so to speak. With this, the latest manifestation, he went off in search of his second-in-command.

'I'm worried, Francesco, very worried indeed,' he said on finding his colleague.

Leonardo had been bottling up his anxiety for several weeks. Now he needed to unburden himself. Francesco Zunica was the one person whom he felt he could turn to.

The trouble was that, when one was dealing with objects, or rather entities, at the level of minuteness to which he was accustomed, it was difficult to keep track of where precisely their constituent parts were situated at any given moment of time. But over the last few months, it was quite apparent that some of their tiny creations were in the habit of disappearing for moments at a time, only to reappear mysteriously as if they had been transported in *Star Trek* fashion out of his university laboratory to an unknown destination and then back home again; always in the space of thirty minutes. On some occasions, it was even less than that.

It had been tempting to believe, rather fancifully he had to admit, that they had developed a life of their own and decided to explore their new environment on their own initiative, just like young children overwhelmed by a sense of curiosity and a growing realisation that they possessed that mysterious thing called identity.

Leonardo had been appointed to the post of professor in the already well-established Department of Nanotechnology and Bio-Science about a year ago. The Science Faculty as a whole was situated outside Legano in the satellite town of *Monteleone di Legano* and housed in a modern, purpose-built site called the *AltoTek*. Leonardo was fond of telling the frequent visitors to his department that the very un-Italian letter 'k' in the word *AltoTek* bestowed a kind of Teutonic seriousness on the name, thereby adding weight to the advanced research carried out under his auspices in this relatively unknown city, deep in the often politically neglected south of Italy. Most of the visitors smiled politely at his allusion to the letter 'k' but were not quite sure whether they had grasped the point he was trying to make. The work carried out by this department of the University had already achieved world-wide renown by the time Leonardo Molinari had taken over from his distinguished predecessor.

Leonardo's team of researchers had nicknamed their new leader 'Einstein' - despite the fact that his first name was already sufficiently imposing to conjure up images of Italy's historic genius, *Leonardo da Vinci*. Leonardo himself had modestly rejected his pseudonym, explaining that he merely possessed a certain ability to manipulate particles and things. 'Please just call me *Leonardo,'* he had requested. But, as his team consisted largely of men and women in their twenties or early thirties, they had felt too embarrassed to accept this invitation to familiarity with their leader. Thus, they called him simply *'capo'* when speaking to him in person. There was something vaguely old-fashioned about him which set him apart from most of the members of his team. His dress sense belonged to the twentieth century and he secretly smoked a pipe when he thought no one was looking. In point of fact, Leonardo was only in his mid-forties. He was married to Teresa Grassi, and they had a nine-year-old daughter called Emma whose intelligence led her, on frequent occasions, to correct her primary school teachers in public - much to her mother's secret pride but public reproof.

Only one member of Leonardo's team was marginally older than he was. Francesco, his deputy, had been working there throughout the reign of the previous Head of Department. His face was the kind of face that you were happy to look at from one day to the next. He had soft grey eyes and the lines around them were wrinkled from constant smiling. He 'cultivated' an unkempt moustache which rose up at the extremities every time he smiled. His inherent good humour coloured almost every word he spoke. It was Francesco who cemented the team together even if everybody deferred to their official *capo* over matters technical. It was not that Leonardo was unapproachable, quite the contrary, but most of the team turned instinctively to Francesco with any day-to-day matters that cropped up. Leonardo himself did not have a resentful cell in his body and he was delighted to accept the evenly distributed balance of power and influence within his team. If the arrangement furthered the cause of science, then that was all that mattered. He believed in leading by example.

'I suspect we might have a really serious problem,' continued Leonardo, talking to his deputy that morning. 'Although for the life of me I cannot put my finger on it.'

'You are right, *capo*,' replied Francesco immediately. 'I expect you are trying to say that we suffer from having an over-qualified bunch of geniuses working on our behalf, with so many brilliant ideas spilling out of their collective brain that we simply do not know which direction to take next,' he concluded with a totally serious expression on his face.

As usual, his chief looked at him as if trying to evaluate the gravity of the words being uttered. After five seconds, which was as long as the frown lasted, Leonardo's face broke into a pensive smile.

'Ah! You're joking, aren't you, Francesco?' he said solemnly, as if he had just found the missing element which provided the solution to a complex equation.

'Yes, and no, Leo. What is worrying you, *amico mio?*'

Leonardo looked up and down the public corridor where members of his team and the administrative staff were coming and going, carrying folders or coaxing the coffee machine into life. Leonardo took his colleague by the elbow and led him towards his office.

'Real cloak-and-dagger stuff, *capo!*' he said teasingly. As soon as his door was closed behind them, Leonardo explained to his second-in-command what was troubling him.

'It has only happened three or four times that *I* have noticed, Francesco, but it seems that some of our stem cell cultures are disappearing from our 'nursery' only to reappear some minutes later – as if they had been on a brief trip somewhere.' Leonardo had only been in office for a few days when he coined the phrase *asilo nido* for the laboratories where all their precious stem cell creations were lovingly brought to life – as if they were tiny human beings that were being nurtured under the scientists' attentive ministrations. The phrase had caught the imagination of the team.

Francesco was thoughtful. Looking at his senior colleague's expression and knowing that his *capo* was not likely to have imagined the phenomenon that he was describing, he felt disinclined to make light of his concerns.

'How could this happen, Francesco? I am puzzled and a little concerned.'

'Well, I don't think we can evoke Heisenberg's Uncertainty Principle in this instance, Leo. Our tiny molecular structures should be far too stable to be affected by the vagaries of their quantum constituents; at least, we would assume that to be the case. So it *ought* to be possible to know where they are at any given time.'

Leonardo nodded sagely. What his colleague was saying seemed indisputable; it should not be possible for something as 'concrete' as a cell structure to disappear into thin air.

'Has anybody else reported similar occurrences – or *anything* unusual?' asked Leonardo, clutching at straws. He was not sure whether the anxiety he was experiencing was caused by a possible flaw in one of their most important projects or by the challenge to his firmly held scientific convictions. Either way, it produced a nagging sensation in his mind which he took home with him at the end of his working day. Francesco had a more down-to-earth explanation, which, if correct, would be far more threatening to the safety of *all* their projects, including the infinitely more sensitive nano-sized creations in their adjoining laboratories. But he did not want to exacerbate his chief's state of mind without being more certain of his suspicions.

'I'll look into it for you, Leo, and ask around our colleagues to see if they have noticed anything amiss. Meanwhile, we have tomorrow's public conference to think about.'

Leonardo sighed audibly. He hated appearing in public and had been very happy when his second-in-command had offered to be the main protagonist on this occasion. Francesco positively enjoyed performing in front of an audience and he was much more adept at explaining the work carried out by the science faculty in simple layman's terms. He managed to charm and entertain his audience – at the same time as being informative. All Leonardo would have to do would be to introduce Francesco formally and then sit on the podium in his role as figurehead. The conference was important for the department's future funding and renown. It would be attended by a number of local politicians, industrialists, bankers, academics and medical researchers - not to mention the media and the democratically compulsory student representatives. Even the Minister of Education had indicated her intention of being present – which would, at least, guarantee the attendance of their controversial *Rettore,* Fabiano Mela, who usually managed to be involved in some scandal, whether political or personal. The presence of the minister – a deceptively mild-looking, bespectacled lady in her forties whose brief was to make spending cuts wherever possible – was also guaranteed to attract banner-waving university students outside the *Hotel Europa* where the conference was to be held. The *'Magnifico Rettore'*, Fabiano Mela, had appeared on the local TV station, *Telenorba*, the previous morning, proclaiming that any disturbance outside the conference venue would be quickly and severely dealt with and that students involved should 'think carefully about their continued presence at the University'. His confrontational declaration ensured that the student protest would double in size and vociferousness whilst alienating ninety per cent of the teaching staff in the same breath.

'*Bravo* yet again, *Signor Mela!*' was the bitterly ironic comment on the majority of academic lips.

* * *

The following morning, Leonardo was driving Francesco from the *AltoTek* along the city's ring road towards the *Hotel Europa*. The broad, tree-lined avenue, where most of the University buildings were situated in all their decaying fascist splendour, led straight to the hotel. Banner-bearing students thronged the pavements along the avenue, supported by a number of teaching staff.

'Ah, they've done us proud, Leo,' stated Francesco. To Leonardo's discomfort, his second-in-command wound down his window and stuck an arm out, thumb enthusiastically raised, as they drove past the rows of protestors.

'Francesco, have a care!' said Leonardo fearfully. In deference to his chief's anxious protestation, he withdrew his arm immediately and contented himself with reading the slogans painted on the banners. They were mainly improvised affairs with the words roughly painted on to sheets of paper supported on poles held by a slogan-chanting student on each end. The banners expressed protests against the impossible education cuts imposed by the government in almost equal measure to those deriding the *Rettore* and his despicable attempts at threatening the students' rights to manifest their discontent. His surname, *'Mela'*, meaning 'Apple', explained the frequency with which this simple image was daubed over so many of the banners. One banner in particular, which amused Francesco, had an arrow, in William Tell mode, piercing the fruit balanced on the head of an accurate, if rough-and-ready sketch of the Minister for Education. 'Thus killing two birds with one stone,' suggested Francesco in jest to his chief. Leonardo smiled a nervous smile. As the car slowed down just before the roundabout at the end of the avenue, Francesco's attention was drawn to another banner held in place by two girls. Unlike most of the banners they had seen, this one had been carefully planned and executed. A highly amused Francesco drew Leonardo's attention to the wording on the banner at the same time as he took out his smartphone to take a photo of it - just as if he had been out on a sight-seeing tour of the city. The caption read:

Una *'Mela'* al giorno –
Toglie la cultura di torno.

The banner had also been translated into English, so Francesco presumed that it was the work of *Legano's* modern languages students, whose faculty was under threat of losing all its mother-tongue teachers through the cuts imposed by their *Rettore*. **An 'Apple' a day, keeps learning at bay**, he read out to his chief in a very passable English accent. Leonardo, in his state of pre-conference nerves, managed another fleeting smile and an acknowledgement of the cleverness of the slogan before he turned left and drove into the concourse of the *Hotel Europa,* parking the car in a reserved space near the main entrance.

* * *

The conference was ready to start. Leonardo was amazed that the large, luxurious conference room was full. A TV reporter from *Telenorba*, the local TV network stood up, shoulder camera ready to shoot. Leonardo got reluctantly to his feet to make his brief introductory comments into the microphone. He had got no further than clearing his throat nervously into the microphone when the *Magnifico Rettore* himself stood up from where he had been sitting in the front row of seats. He had obviously taken one look at Leonardo's mode of dress and hesitant manner and decided instantly that his own 'magnificent' impact was required to initiate proceedings. Like a Roman Emperor, he stepped with pompous authority on to the podium, waving one of his most important members of staff to one side with an imperious hand as he took his colleague's place in front of the microphone. Leonardo looked disconcerted in the extreme. He had been building himself up for the moment when he would introduce his second-in-command and, despite his deferential attitude to the authority which emanated from their Rector, he felt a stab of anger and humiliation as he sat down again, having been made to look like an inadequate pupil who had just given a wrong answer in front of the class. Francesco stared in utter scorn at the Rector's back and turned to look in Leonardo's direction with hands parted in a gesture of resigned disbelief. 'Typical of the man!' he mouthed to Leonardo, not caring whether the assembled audience noticed or not. The arrangement had been for the *Magnifico Rettore* to address the delegates at the end of the presentation. Francesco vowed to redress the balance when it was his turn to stand up and begin his presentation.

'*Signori, signore,*' began the emperor in the richest and deepest timbre of voice that he had been at pains to cultivate for such public occasions; '*It is our pleasure to welcome you all here today. Our special thanks to the Minister of Education who has given up her valuable time to grace our city and this important gathering with her presence today. I am sure you will all be enthralled by the words and scientific demonstrations of our Professor, Leonardo Molinari, who heads a team of international scientists at our university. I will leave you in the hands of the Professor and his second-in-command, euh, Dottore...?*' The Rector turned round to look quizzically at Francesco Zunica, realising belatedly that he could not remember the man's name. Francesco looked at the Rector with an engaging smile, but did not deign to enlighten him, leaving their grand leader to curtail his brief interruption of proceedings awkwardly as he descended from the podium to regain his seat, slightly ruffled but unrepentant. The audience, who had at first looked on slightly perplexed at the minor drama they had witnessed, allowed themselves a titter of cynical amusement as Francesco Zunica made encouraging gestures in his chief's direction for him to stand up and go over to the microphone. The *Magnifico Rettore* looked sorely displeased – a fact that did not escape Francesco. The *Telenorba* reporter did not quite know in which direction to point his camera. The private cameraman belonging to the University's science faculty had no such doubts; it was the expression of outrage on the Rector's face that he caught for posterity.

The head of the Science Department reluctantly stood up and walked towards the abandoned microphone. Uncharacteristically, he wore a slightly belligerent expression.

'In the first place,' he began; *'I would like to welcome all the students present today and secondly correct an impression that might have been inadvertently created in your minds. Our team cannot be properly called an 'international' team as might have been suggested.'* The audience – especially the students representing their fellow undergraduates - were exchanging meaningful glances with inordinate glee, totally intrigued by the obvious rift that had been revealed like a fault line running through the structure of the University's upper echelons. *'We are a very national team. Indeed, with only two exceptions, we are proud that our colleagues are all from Puglia. We are a close knit community between whom rank and ability are equally shared. Our goal is to ensure that our beloved Salento remains at the hub of these important fields of developing knowledge.'* This comment earned Leonardo a brief round of applause and a muted cheer.

Francesco had calculated correctly that his normally reserved *capo* would be on his mettle after the untimely intervention of their Rector who, Francesco noted with pleasure, was seething in the front row unseen by the rest of the audience.

'And now, ladies and gentlemen, it is my pleasure to introduce my totally indispensable friend and colleague, Francesco Zunica, who is about to introduce you to the magic world of our tiny creations. Do you believe in magicians – and

magic?' asked the head of the University's advanced science department to this gathering of stony-faced bankers and industrialists. The *Magnifico Rettore* tutted loudly in disapproval. Francesco was delighted that his reserved *capo* was obviously warming to the task. *'In the words of one of our founding fathers, Eric Drexler,'* continued Leonardo, studiously ignoring the Rector, **'To the layman, the manifestations of nanotechnology will appear to be nothing less than magic,** *were the words he used. The renowned physicist, the late Richard Feynman, was present when these words were spoken and this perceptive scientist did not deny the truth of them. Nanotechnology is the Alchemy of modern times,'* concluded Leonardo. *'And now, I will leave you in the hands of my colleague, friend - and magician, Francesco Zunica!'* There was a burst of applause as Francesco stood up and walked to the microphone.

To the amusement of all – even the bankers – Francesco pointed suddenly up to the conference room ceiling, shouting the word *'LOOK!'* Instinctively, all eyes rose to the ceiling. When they looked down again, Francesco was wearing a black magician's hat with silver stars all over it. There was a round of applause accompanied by a degree of good-natured laughter. Only the *Magnifico* Emperor in the front row was looking like thunder due to the facile direction this vital fund-raising conference appeared to be taking. Francesco noticed that their *Rettore* was stirring uncomfortably in his chair – which ensured that he, Francesco, would take an even greater pleasure in delivering his lecture.

'A classic case of misdirection,' said Francesco to his now fully attentive audience. *'I hereby promise that everything else you hear and see this morning will not be a trick – an illusion,*

possibly, because so much of what we perceive with our poor earthbound brains does not really correspond to the reality of the physical universe around us. But the 'magic', from now on, will be the magic of pure science.

I want to start my brief presentation by challenging your imaginations. I am about to ask you to think about your own perception of reality.' Francesco took off his magician's hat, as if to get down to serious business, and placed it carefully on the table. There was a gasp of surprise when, before their eyes, the black hat seemed to turn blue and the silver stars turned gold. It was not a trick of the light because the change in appearance of the hat spread progressively over the surface like a ripple; furthermore the only artificial lighting consisted of an array of imbedded ceiling lights. What they had witnessed was clearly visible in the rays of sunlight streaming through the windows.

'Ah, you've noticed our chameleon hat!' said Francesco mysteriously. *'No, it is not a trick of the light but a property of the material which is coated with photon-emitting nano-particles. Don't forget – our perception of colours is really nothing other than a wonderful trick of nature; a change in the wavelength of the light striking our eyes! One day in the not too distant future, ladies, it should be possible for you to put on a red dress in the morning and finish up with a blue dress by the evening, according to your change of mood. Furthermore, you will never have to iron it again! But now, where was I?'* resumed Francesco. He knew, from that moment on, that his audience would be listening avidly to every word he spoke. *'Ah yes - my question to challenge your own perception of reality! Do you find it easier to imagine the vastness of space, stretching to infinity, or does your mind find it simpler to*

picture the tiniest of all known particles – a quark? In other words, can you manage to visualise travelling at 300 000 kilometres every second for a million years and still be nowhere near the limits of the universe? Or would you find it easier to imagine you are the size of a molecule – totally invisible to the naked human eye - and be faced with the stark reality that you are gigantic in size compared to the quarks that make up your atoms? Their unimaginable tininess is worth dwelling upon from time to time. And, as a mere molecule, you are surrounded by huge amounts of SPACE filled with energetic forces of such strength that we simply cannot conceive of them with our limited perception of physical reality. The only force that we perceive is that of gravity, which is dwarfed by the forces that hold particles together. That is a fundamental fact of our incomprehensible existence in the cosmos.' Francesco paused for five seconds to allow what he had said to sink in before adding: *'It's enough to make one believe in God!'* There was a subdued burst of laughter and a few people applauded briefly. Francesco asked for a show of hands. About a third of those present voted for the gigantic universe, a third for the tiny quark and the rest admitted that both concepts were unimaginable. *'And hands up those who did not commit themselves at all?'* asked Francesco who had noted that the *Magnifico Rettore* had not participated. As expected, the Rector's hands remained firmly clasped in his lap as he appeared to be looking hard at a point somewhere beyond the confines of the conference room with an expression on his face that suggested he was contemplating where to make the next spending cuts. Even the Lady Minister had voted good-naturedly – in favour of infinite space. 'Good!' thought Francesco. 'At least, I've embarrassed the man.'

'*And now, down to business!*' he announced to his audience. The *Telenorba* reporter was pointing his camera exclusively at the speaker. The members of the press started taking notes and switching on their recording devices.

2: The Francesco Zunica Road Show

'Just one of the fields of activity with which we are concerned, as I am sure you are all aware,' continued Francesco enthusiastically, *'is all about the cultivation of stem cells with a view to transforming them into other cells such as liver, heart or any other cell structure that is needed to mend damaged parts of the human body. Our modest genius directly in charge of this field of research is our colleague, Luana Palomba, who was born, raised and educated in this city. I hope you will have a chance to meet and talk with her after I have finished. She is at the moment very much tied up with a three month old baby son and has entrusted us with the task of explaining our unique approach to the creation of specialised cells from stem cells. Indeed, we currently have a very special little patient whom we are treating in the maternity ward of the 'Andrea Marconi' hospital. We hope we are about to make medical history.'*

Francesco made a generous sweeping gesture with his left hand to include his *capo* sitting on the podium behind him. Leonardo nodded modestly.

'We are all very conscious in our team of the fact that we are privileged to be dealing with a very precious commodity – the very elements of life itself. I am happy to say that, as the days go by, we become ever more in awe of the miraculous nature of creation. As a team, we shall never be able to claim that we have 'invented' anything new. All we can ever do is to learn how to harness the tiny particles to which everything owes its existence, and transform our already more substantial stem cells into specific body cells - in the hope that we are serving humankind and performing the miracles that, tomorrow, will become an accepted part of knowledge.

It is a startling and humbling fact of our lives that stem cell structures – invisible to the naked eye – appear to KNOW how to set about the task of transforming themselves into the different structures that enable them to take on the function of looking after our bodies. One of our missions in life is to help overcome the small, but potentially fatal, malfunctions that occasionally happen in infancy but which occur with increasing frequency as men and women live to a greater age; malfunctions which risk destroying the lives of ordinary people. Ours is not merely a scientific quest but also a moral crusade. We are all acutely aware that we are, to some extent, 'playing God'. So we endeavour to cultivate humility as well as cultivating stem cells. The same sense of wonder applies to our many nano-sized creations – which I shall also be demonstrating for you this morning.

Francesco's words had been spoken with such passion that a few of his audience broke into spontaneous applause. Francesco acknowledged the applause with a bow and a whimsical smile which turned up the ends of his moustache as if to emphasize his pleasure.

'And now we come to the important part,' he continued, modifying his tone of voice as if he was about to share an intimate secret with all those present. 'A real orator!' thought Leonardo in admiration of his colleague.

What we have succeeded in doing, here in our very own university, is unique in the world. Not even the Americans, with all the financial means at their disposal, have achieved what we have managed to do in our modest laboratories.' Francesco paused for dramatic effect. *'We nurture stem cells – the basic structures from which all cells are eventually born. Stem cells are able to assume any cellular form we wish, enabling them to* repair damaged human tissue and organs, without resorting to the use of any artificial, chemical or biochemical stimuli. We have created 'nurseries' – a term coined by Leonardo here – where stem cells can be nurtured as if they were our own offspring and be allowed to grow up naturally. They can then be transformed into any kind of master cell that we wish – be it liver, heart or skin cells - without any artificial inducement. This is the miracle that we are privileged to witness on a daily basis and this is the reason why the eyes of the world are upon us.

American efforts have been shown to suffer from unwanted side effects because they have made the mistake of inducing cell development by artificial chemical or bio-chemical means. As usual, they are in too much of a hurry to see scientific results that can be turned instantly into dollars!' A ripple of appreciative laughter ran round the assembled gathering accompanied by the sage nodding of heads as people updated their hurriedly scribbled notes.

'Needless to say,' continued Francesco with a note of quiet irony in his voice that did not go by undetected by his audience, 'there is a price to pay for our patient and benign approach to this vital field of medical research. By a historical accident and by our good fortune, we happen to share our beloved Peninsula with the Holy Roman See. Although the State is a separate entity from the Vatican, our moral values and our deeply held Christian beliefs are inextricably bound up with our civil laws. As you are all aware, I trust, the only legal grounds for extracting stem cells from the placenta – where such cells are in pristine abundance – is conditional on the cells being used on the donor patient, or her immediate family. Naturally, this is a restriction that we are very happy to abide by.'

Francesco Zunica paused meaningfully as if he was inviting a reaction from his attentive audience. Sure enough, a smart looking young man who was unknown to Francesco broke the brief and expectant silence.

'You seem to be implying, *professore,* that any future sponsors of this particular project are likely to be seen as charitable benefactors in the eyes of the nation. Due to the legal restrictions which apply in our country as to the exploitation of stem cells, potential investors can hardly expect a huge return. Am I right?'

Francesco Zunica gave one of his most engaging smiles which sent the tips of his moustache more than half way up his cheeks.

'What price are we prepared to pay to keep stem cell research in Italy? Do we want to suffer the humiliating prospect of our best brains leaving our Peninsula for America – or, even worse, China – thereby handing over our unique achievements to nations who are not held back by the same moral considerations as we are?' A murmur of assent ran round the assembly. *'But, signore, all is not lost! In a short while, I hope to demonstrate the wide scope of our other research projects – like the material used in the magician's hat – where there are no legal restrictions in force; including, I should mention, a nano-toothpaste which will obviate the need for fillings. LUANA...!'* said Francesco looking to the back of the conference hall, his arms opened in welcome to the leader of their stem cell research team, before anyone had really taken in what he had said about toothpaste. The *Telenorba* camera swung round, if only because the bearer instinctively turned to see whom the speaker was addressing.

There was much discussion among the audience after the event as to whether the arrival of this modestly pretty woman in her mid-thirties had been carefully staged by some pre-arranged signal or whether the timing of her entrance was merely fortuitous. Either way, Francesco's greeting was genuinely warm. Leonardo stood up and walked down the aisle between the seats and ushered their colleague towards the podium at the front. They were seen to be whispering urgently as they walked towards the front of the conference room. 'La Dottoressa Palomba has an important announcement to make,' said Leonardo to the audience. The Magnifico Mela was frowning in disapproval again at the degree of informal egalitarianism indulged in by his senior staff. The lady Minister of Education, sitting next to the Rettore, continued to peer dispassionately at the proceedings through spectacles whose lenses were as thick as the plate glass used to house an aquarium full of sharks; her lack of passion was, in this case, a positive sign decided Francesco.

There were a few seconds of comedy as Luana went up to the microphone and began talking, only to find that her mouth was well below the level of the microphone. To everybody's amusement she made a show of standing on tip-toe to make up for her lack of height until Francesco ran over, all smiles, to readjust the level of the stand. Her voice was surprisingly soft and feminine as she began talking almost shyly.

'I am not sure what my colleague has already told you, but I suspect you know by now that our greatest achievement in this field has been to avoid using chemical means to trigger off the differentiation of stem cells to become, let us say, heart cells. With our system, the cells that we develop already have their *own miniscule geometry and structures inbuilt so as to achieve the differentiation between cell types.'* Luana paused and turned round to Francesco who nodded with a smile to indicate that he had covered this aspect of their work. The audience was visibly relieved, since Luana's way of explaining this aspect of her work already sounded as if it was going to become too technical for them.

'Good. So I can tell you all right away that I have just returned from the city hospital where I have had the most heart-warming experience of my life so far – apart from the birth of my son three months ago.' In true Italian style, she was spontaneously applauded by everyone - including the *Magnifico Rettore,* who managed to pat his hands together limply three times before his patrician principles got the better of him.

'This is the case of little Mariangela. Working in close collaboration with the Andrea Marconi hospital, we discovered the case of a mother who was about to give birth to a baby girl suffering from a life-threatening heart defect. I won't go into all the medical details right now. We were legally allowed to use stem cells from the mother's placenta at the time of birth since the person who would benefit was her own daughter.' Luana had to pause in her narrative to overcome the tears of emotion that threatened to overwhelm her. *'Well, I am so happy to be able to tell you that, four weeks after the baby's birth, Mariangela now has a healthy heart, thanks to the intervention of our unique process of converting her mother's shared stem cells into cells that have successfully repaired her baby's heart. You will be able to read all about it in tomorrow's edition of 'Il Quotidiano' and, with any luck, see a report on 'Telenorba' this evening.'*

This time the applause was universally unrestrained and the student body let out a cheer. Luana earned herself a standing ovation a few seconds later. She modestly gestured towards her two colleagues and went to sit down on the chair graciously vacated by Francesco, who was still applauding as he approached the microphone to resume the proceedings. He performed a sort of levitation gesture with his right hand above the microphone which distracted the audience's attention while with his left hand he slowly and smoothly raised the microphone stand off the ground. The illusion was quite convincing for just a couple of seconds. The audience loved him by now and gave him a mock round of applause as he readjusted the height of the stand.

'Thank you,' he said. 'I should tell you that, in my spare time, I do conjuring tricks at kids' parties. It's something to do with our meagre academic salaries, I suppose,' he added ruefully. The audience obligingly laughed and the *Magnifico Rettore* obligingly scowled once again. The lady Minister for Education continued to look impassively through her thick-lensed spectacles, ignoring all provocation.

'I apologise,' said Francesco to his audience. 'I did promise that there would be no more tricks, didn't I! Francesco looked serious again as his moustache settled down to its horizontal position once more. 'What Luana Palomba has just told us is indeed the most gratifying and deeply satisfying piece of news that our team could ever have hoped for. But I would like to take up the point that the gentleman in the audience raised earlier on. It is true that one of our most vital and important fields of research concerns stem cell culture. The research that we are doing strikes at the heart of all that sentient human beings believe in – how to alleviate human suffering and help *to create a better future for the human race. But we are involved in a wide variety of projects, of which stem cell research is only one aspect. Much of what we do can be regarded as highly marketable. I am saying this in case some of you have come here today with a mind to sponsor our University's research programmes. You may be reassured that your rewards need not be entirely in heaven!'*

Once again, there was an appreciative reaction from the audience – especially from the business men and bankers in the front rows. The Minister of Education directed a meaningful glance in the Rector's direction. The gentleman in question was looking noticeably more relaxed as the mention of potential sources of income had come to the forefront of proceedings.

Francesco made a sign to two men standing at the back of the conference room. First of all, they wheeled in what looked like a miniature solar panel measuring about a half a square metre which was placed on a table on the podium facing the windows down the side of the hall.

'This will only take a minute to set up,' he explained.

A second trolley was then wheeled into position half way down the centre aisle. On it there was an electric motor that was attached to a model of a carousel with coloured lights and miniature horses, the whole apparatus being no more than 30 centimetres in height. While the audience's attention was distracted by this apparatus, Francesco was plugging something in to the side of the solar panel.

'Now, before I begin this demonstration,' he announced in his magician's voice, *'I need a couple of volunteers.'* Several hands at the back of the room shot up notably from amongst the students. Those sitting at the front of the conference

room turned round or stood up in their places so they could see what was happening.

'I wonder if I may enlist your aid, Onorevole Signora,' asked Francesco deferentially of the Lady Minister of Education. *'Would you be so kind as to select a couple of volunteers for me – so that there can be no suspicion of skulduggery on my part!'* Two volunteers were duly chosen at random by the Lady Minister who looked as if she was beginning to enjoy herself in as much as she did not appear to be vexed by the invitation.

'Thank you, signora. Now, I would like you two young people... What are your names?' asked Francesco.

'Chiara,' replied the girl in her early twenties.

'And what are you studying, Chiara?'

'Physics and maths, *professore*,' she replied.

'Pierluigi, *professore*,' said the young man, 'studying law here at Legano.'

'All I want you to do, Chiara, Pierluigi, is to walk round the carousel and the electric motor, and reassure the audience that there are no wires or cables attached to the apparatus. Va bene? Can you confirm that?'

'No cables or wires attached,' the two students confirmed.

'Now may I ask you to come up to the front? Here is a big switch attached to the solar panel. Would you put it into the ON position, please? Both of you together - that's right - like cutting a wedding cake.'

Nothing happened and the audience reacted with a sigh which was a mixture of amusement and embarrassment. Francesco was, of course, unperturbed. *'Oh dear! Turn it off again will you, my friends - I forgot to attach the solar panel to the motor,'* he apologised to the audience in general with a gesture of mock impatience at his careless oversight.

What happened next produced a stir of conversation and suppressed laughter around the conference room. To all appearances, Francesco seemed to be performing a mime of walking down the aisle towards the carousel whist unfurling a length of something invisible. He wore a happy smile as if thoroughly enjoying the effect he knew he was having on his audience. He paused briefly when he reached the table and seemed to be inserting something into the terminal of the electric motor. Those sitting nearest to the aisle had caught sight of *something* in his hand – and the connection to the terminal was definitely metallic.

'Alright, Chiara and Pierluigi, you can switch us on now!'

There arose a general gasp of amazement as the little carousel sprang to life, the solar panel apparently connected to the carousel by thin air. It lit up with minute coloured lights while a musical box began to play a tinkling fairground tune as the carousel began to revolve round and round. The audience was mesmerised and then began to applaud enthusiastically at this further display of the wizard's tricks.

Francesco brought his audience back to earth.

'Well, ladies and gentlemen, we warned you at the outset that the new technologies would appear to be like magic! I feel you must be convinced of that by now. Behind the magic, lies a whole new field of research. We need to continue to develop these very advanced technologies before they are ready to be manufactured on a large scale. But we already have several major Italian companies interested in these products.'

'But what ARE these products exactly?' asked someone from the audience obviously feeling confused and frustrated by the inexplicable nature of what they had witnessed. Francesco reassured the questioner with a calming gesture and a smile.

'I was coming to that, signore. The first, of course, is an example of a fourth generation solar panel, coated with nano-sized elements which are so sensitive to light that they can generate power even by starlight. That is barely an exaggeration. Solar energy will almost certainly become our main energy source in the future – even if, by drawing on the sun's energy, we will be fractionally shortening its life span – and, consequently, that of all living creatures, including us.'

This revelation was greeted by a general gasp of shocked surprise.

'I'm afraid there really IS no such thing as a free lunch in our universe. The second product is my own pride and joy; an electron bearing super-conducting cable made of nano-carbon strands. The material is practically two-dimensional and able to assume the colour of the background against which it is set. In a few years' time, newly built houses will no longer have their electric cables buried in the plaster but will run along the interior walls and be virtually unnoticeable. I need hardly tell anybody here who has had to rewire an old property what a huge benefit such an invention as this will mean to the construction industry. We have a website where you can view all our research projects – or you can even come in person to our department. And now, a couple more demonstrations and then you can ask any one of us all the questions you like!' said Francesco.

His helpers reappeared and wheeled out the apparatus that he had used in his demonstration. One of them placed a framed photograph on the table where, previously, the solar panel had stood. Those at the back of the room could just make out the well-known face of the much respected President of the Republic, Giorgio Napolitano. Most of the audience supposed that the ritual presence of a photograph of the President was a simple recognition of tradition; after all, there is a legally binding obligation to display the current President's image in every single public institution in the land. Nobody present could have anticipated the transformation that the President was about to undergo. Francesco was preparing to use the 'joker card' that he had up his sleeve.

Without a word, Francesco walked behind the table, took out from his pocket a square piece of material barely larger than a folded table napkin. At a sign from the scientist, the lights were dimmed, leaving only the natural daylight that filtered in through the window blinds. He shook the material open and held it up in the air for a couple of brief seconds. The material had an unusual shimmering quality about it. The scientist, acting just like a magician about to astound his audience, draped the material over the photograph of Giorgio Napolitano and stood to one side of the table so as not to obstruct the audience's line of vision. One could hear a pin drop in the conference room. Seconds later, there was a collective intake of breath, as if they had witnessed some supernatural phenomenon. Before their very eyes, the material had begun to melt away as if a film of fog was spreading from the top working downwards. But what provoked the second shockwave of disbelieving voices, all saying 'NO' in protest against this travesty of the accepted order of the laws of nature, was the realisation that the President of the Republic had vanished. Nobody applauded this time. They were in a state of total bewilderment. Francesco solemnly plucked at empty space and the photograph of Giorgio Napolitano instantly reappeared as did the square of misty material that Francesco folded up and tucked back into his pocket.

'Now, if you have any questions...?' he asked with a broad grin that sent the tips of his moustache up level with his ears. There was, of course, an instant reaction to his invitation as a sea of hands began waving in the conference room demanding that their curiosity be satisfied.

'As I assume you all want to ask the same question, let me say something now about our Harry Potter cloak of invisibility. Without becoming too technical, we have developed a material coated with millions of specially engineered nanoparticles which are able to act as a cloaking device by deforming the grid of space around the object. Light rays are bent as they travel round the cloak. They exit as if they have travelled through empty space, thus hiding an object from an external observer. At certain wavelengths of light, the effect is to create the ultimate optical illusion of invisibility.

'But what practical use could this be put to?' asked one member of the audience innocently. His question provoked subdued laughter as people's imaginations got to work.

'I have to say that the effect is partial and only convincing on a small scale at present – but I suppose it could spell the end of marital infidelity,' suggested Francesco quite seriously. His audience had become so attuned to his voice that their immediate reaction was to laugh without reflecting on what he meant. As the implications of what he had said sunk in, the laughter became more conspiratorial as images of an invisible bedroom *voyeur* sprang to mind.

'I do not think it would be wise to dwell too much on the Harry Potter cloak,' continued Francesco seriously. *'It is only a tentative and imperfect exploration into the possibilities as to where the field of nanotechnology might lead us. With your help and support, we can continue to research into overcoming the diseases and malfunctions that our earthly bodies are prone to; heart disease, liver disease, cancer and even degenerative disorders such as Alzheimer's. The potential of this field of research is almost without limits. But I would also like to tell you something about the many other projects with which we are concerned. As well as advanced solar panels and conductors of electricity that are almost invisible, we have created nano-sized robots which can detect impurities during the production of wine and olive oil, materials which can deflect lightning strikes – the aeronautical industries are particularly interested in this. We are engaged in research into the behaviour of the brain without the use of clumsy electrodes fitted on to a patient via sticky pads. We hope such projects will help to get to the bottom of brain malfunctions – such as dementia. In collaboration with other universities, we have created a fish that can swim under water and detect the slightest of movements – this could be invaluable in searching for survivors or sunken aircraft wrecks when the sea is too deep for divers. We have built a little humanoid robot who thinks and reacts like a six-year-old child – who is learning as he goes along. Look on our website when you have a chance. Even better, come to our Open Day, which we are organising in the near future. But right now, I would like to invite you all to put questions to us about any aspect of our work that interest you. We are at your disposal.'*

Francesco had redirected the audience's attention to more serious considerations, whilst the residual impression that they had just witnessed something unique in their lives still remained uppermost in their minds. The audience's questions were directed mainly at Francesco and Luana, who both went into greater details about aspects of their research – including the nano-toothpaste, which had struck a chord in some of the more attentive listeners' minds. There were one or two unexpected questions addressed to Francesco from the back of the conference room by younger people who seemed more interested in the man than his research:

'Are you a practising Catholic, *professore?*' asked one serious, bespectacled girl - obviously a student of theology, thought Francesco.

'I believe in God, if that is what you are asking me, signorina,' replied the *maestro* seriously. *'And yes, I hope I abide by Christian principles in my research. It is difficult not to believe in a creator in our line of work.'* The girl seemed satisfied with his answer. Francesco was pleased that this particular question had been asked. He was certain that many others present would have been reassured by his answer. He had discovered from his contact with the students he taught just how many Italians secretly clung to their traditional beliefs in a soulless, technological world.

'And now,' stated Francesco amidst the silence of an audience still too pensive to think of applauding, 'the three of us are ready to answer individually any queries you may have about aspects of our work which you might have been hesitating to ask in public.'

He turned to Leonardo inviting him to round off the official proceedings. The head scientist was quite happy to let his two members of staff steal the limelight. He was about to breathe a sigh of relief at the obvious success of the conference. He had been mentally preparing himself to say a few closing words of thanks to his colleagues before they mingled with the audience. Suddenly, out of the blue, a lady journalist from the newspaper *Il Mezzogiorno di Legano*, well-known for her trenchant observations and searching questions, stood up and spoke in a clear, articulate voice. Everybody stopped their private conversations to listen to her.

'I have a question for *you, Professore Molinari*, before this meeting comes to an end,' she began ominously. The TV reporter from *Telenorba*, who had been on the point of packing away his video camera, decided at the last moment that a potential confrontation was in the offing and hastily shouldered his video camera once again.

3: Forza Leonardo!

Leonardo was looking nervously at the lady journalist. Something about her tone of voice and aggressive stance alerted him to the fact that she was determined to put a spanner in the works if it was in her power to do so.

'That woman is a man-eater,' thought Francesco, already on his guard and ready to leap to the aid of his *capo*. 'She is the last person we want around at the moment.'

'What would you like to know, *signora?*' asked Leonardo warily.

'It is what I know already, *professore,* which should concern you,' she replied.

Francesco decided that the wearing of kid gloves was not going to be helpful in this instance. He launched immediately into counter attack mode.

'If you would be so good as to come to the point without delay, *cara Costanza,* we shall be glad to satisfy your curiosity. But we do have a number of people here who wish to talk to us privately – about serious matters.'

'I would suggest that the present assembly should hear what I have to say publicly before they talk to you in private,' countered the lady journalist who had been only momentarily thrown off track by Francesco's use of her first name. 'And I am addressing my question to the *professore*, not you, *dottore,*' she added caustically.

'She knows instinctively that Leonardo is a softer target,' thought Francesco.

With the morbid playground curiosity engendered by the prospect of a public fight, everybody in the room waited in silent anticipation to see how the ensuing verbal duel would evolve. Most of those present felt a degree of sympathy for Leonardo and Francesco rather than for this local journalist well known for her acerbic tongue and reputation-destroying prose.

'I understand, *professore,* that you do not have in place any measures to ensure the security of your research projects. I believe that there have been one or two unreported incidents in recent weeks of certain vital elements of your most important projects... how shall I put it... that have gone missing. It hardly inspires the confidence of would-be investors,' concluded the lady journalist in triumph.

'Well, *signora,* I am at a loss to ...' began Leonardo, visibly perturbed by the direction that events had taken – especially as he suspected there might be an element of truth in her words. 'But where did you get this information from?' he asked innocently. It had been too late for Francesco to step in to avoid his chief's tactical *faux pas,* which showed his vulnerability above all else.

'From someone claiming to be an acquaintance of one of your own staff, *professore* - and before you ask, no, I cannot reveal my sources.'

Whereas Leonardo accepted the words of the journalist at face value, Francesco had instantly seen red.

'I see. You have picked up some detail which has been taken out of context, possibly a scrap of conversation that one of your junior reporters has misheard in a local bar, and you have decided to try and make a story out of it without a shred of evidence or knowledge about our security system – for which, incidentally, I am responsible, not my Head of Department,' retorted Francesco with controlled anger.

'I hate to disappoint you, *dottore...*' began the reporter called Costanza. At this juncture, after a rapid word from the Lady Minister of Education, the *Magnifico Rettore Mela* leapt on to the podium and seized the abandoned microphone.

'Ladies and gentlemen, and students of this splendid university,' he intoned in his most imperial voice. 'I would like to thank our three professors for what, I am sure you will all agree, has been the most enthralling experience that we have witnessed for a long time – if not indeed the most remarkable display of scientific knowledge that it has ever been our privilege to see.'

For once, the students in particular, felt it appropriate to cheer their generally despised and aloof leader. The bankers, businessmen and women applauded loyally. The reporters made rapid additions to their notes.

'I myself have all too often been a victim of the excessive liberties taken by the press,' the *Rettore* continued, rashly exposing himself to a sudden loss of audience sympathy. 'And so I would advise the lady journalist against the risk of jumping to unfounded conclusions.'

It was well known that the *Magnifico Rettore* had, on one occasion, threatened to sue this journalist over an allegation of some sexual misdemeanour. The paper had published a retraction of the accusation so as not to become embroiled in a protracted law suit rather than because they believed the accusation to be ill-founded.

Francesco led a round of applause in the hope of forestalling any further embarrassing revelations from the *Rettore,* who had caught sight of a stern frown directed at himself from the Lady Minister. 'So, I would like to thank our team once again for all their efforts and the insight that they have given us into the wonderful world of nanotechnology,' concluded the *Rettore* hurriedly before standing down.

'Three cheers for our *capo,* Professore Molinari,' intervened Francesco, 'without whom we would be like a rudderless ship. Hip hip...' Fortunately, the audience joined in with enthusiasm so great was the sympathy that Francesco had elicited in the minds of his audience.

The damage limitation exercise was over with no clear indication as to which side had come out best. But Costanza De Santis, the journalist, stalked out giving Francesco a hard and very disdainful look, which held the promise of revenge. But with the timely appearance of complimentary buffet food and glasses of *Prosecco,* the unpleasant interruption seemed to lose its impact as a shaken Leonardo, a relieved Francesco and a frankly bewildered Luana made moves to mingle with their audience.

Francesco took one look at his head of department and knew that he had taken the accusations to heart. Leonardo hardly looked in the right frame of mind to win support from potential financial backers. Francesco went up to his chief and spoke in a low, urgent voice:

'*Forza Leonardo!* This accusation is without foundation. You must talk to these people as if nothing had happened. Reassure them. Come on, *capo,* you can do it!' he said gripping his arm tightly. 'We'll talk about all this on the way back. Just remember, *capo,* there is no truth in what that journalist said.'

'But, Francesco, we don't have a security system in place, do we?' asked Leonardo rather desperately.

'Yes, of course we do, *capo,*' lied Francesco with a beatific smile on his face. 'It's infallible, I can assure you.'

Leonardo appeared to be reassured. Only Francesco had any inkling, since his chief's revelation of the previous day, that there might be something amiss in their laboratories. But he needed to play for time whilst he thought through the implications of what Leonardo had told him about their 'disappearing stem-cells'. He could make no sense of it at all at present. Meanwhile, there were people who were waiting to talk to him: bankers, industrialists, doctors, representatives from pharmaceutical companies, reporters – even students who had been fascinated and inspired to discover what had been achieved within the precincts of their very own university. He had to reassure many of the men and women that he spoke to that the journalist's accusations were totally unfounded, but that he would continue to be very watchful at all times.

'After all,' said one of the more astute bankers, 'if I have understood correctly, the material that you are dealing with is so minute that it would fit into a man's wallet.'

'Or into a lady's mascara dispenser,' joked Francesco.

Francesco and Luana were equally besieged by numerous individuals whose curiosity had been aroused by the revelations of these ultra-modern fields of research. Leonardo was congratulated by the lady Minister for Education who made her get-away after having a few words with Francesco, Luana and, naturally, the *Magnifico Rettore.* The rector of the university had an intense and private talk with Leonardo leading him by the elbow away from the people thronging round Francesco and Luana.

Finally, it was over and Francesco was driving his *capo* back to the *AltoTek* campus buildings on the outskirts of

Legano. 'Well?' asked Francesco. 'What did our esteemed leader have to say to you?'

'I have a meeting with him tomorrow morning where I shall have to reassure him about the security procedures that we have in place,' explained Leonardo with a wry smile. 'He did deign to say that the Minister was very impressed indeed; she almost promised not to make further cuts to our science budget. In addition, it was hinted that we may have found new sponsors, but I shall know a bit more about that possibly later on today. Apart from that, he berated me for contradicting him in public until I told him that he should be proud of the fact that all our team is Italian rather than 'international' as he announced. I told him that we were a team of scientists – not an Italian football team.'

'Well done, Leo!' exclaimed Francesco with a broad smile at his chief's topical touch of wit.

'Thank you, Francesco - your presentation was superb and your moral support a life-saver,' added Leonardo.

After a lull in their conversation, Leonardo, the distinguished holder of the Chair of Science at Legano's university, turned to look at his colleague and said quietly: 'But we do not have any security procedures in place do we, Francesco.' It was not a question.

* * *

The team had been summoned to an urgent meeting by Leonardo that same afternoon at 5 o'clock in a classroom that doubled up as a meeting room when the occasion arose. They were gathered around a couple of conventional plastic topped tables pushed hurriedly together and seated on functional, moulded plastic seats. They were nearly all clutching small bottles of mineral water rather than the usual tiny brown disposable coffee cups since the day had become particularly humid. Leonardo was doing a mental roll call to see which of the team was still missing. Apart from Francesco and Luana, there was Andrea Calvano, Alessandro Agostino, Giovanna Binetto, (*'A pretty girl!' thought Leonardo. 'It's a pity that she always looks so solemn.'*) and Mariastella Russo – who preferred to be called simply Stella, he recalled.

'Where's Micaela De Giorgi?' asked Leonardo, identifying the missing person.

'Miky's just finishing something off,' replied Stella. 'You know how involved she becomes when she's in the middle of an experiment. She can't tear herself away. She's always working overtime.' The comment was made entirely without malice by Stella about the team's newest appointee.

* * *

Leonardo and Francesco had already had a lengthy and confidential discussion earlier in the afternoon about a potential leak of information from their laboratories, during which Francesco had confessed to his head of department that he and most of his team had gone out the previous evening after work at Francesco's invitation.

'We just went to our normal bar in Monteleone,' explained Francesco. 'I wanted to find out if anybody else apart from yourself had noticed anything out of the ordinary, Leo. There *was* someone else sitting on a table nearby who could have overheard what we were saying. Our people all denied vehemently that they had ever knowingly discussed our work to any outsider. But I suppose one can't be a hundred per cent certain...'

'Which members of our team *weren't* with you yesterday evening?' asked Leonardo.

Francesco looked at his *capo* half amused.

'Well, chief inspector,' he answered with a half-smile that sent only the left side of his moustache up in the air. 'Luana went home to rescue her parents who were baby-sitting for her. And Stella excused herself because she had arranged to meet a friend. Miky stayed for a while but had to catch the last coach back to Sannicola...'

'And *had* anybody noticed?' interrupted Leonardo who seemed not to have realised that his second-in-command was gently chiding him for his interrogation tactics. The abruptness of the question threw Francesco for a second before he caught up with his chief's train of thought. After a significant pause, Francesco looked squarely at his *capo* and said:

'In a word, Leonardo, *yes* - both Miky and Alessandro have noticed exactly what you were describing. Miky is a very smart girl, by the way, Leo. She was the first one to suggest that the temporary absence of our stem cell structures might indicate that somebody is tampering with them. You know what a clear voice she has. Maybe someone overheard...'

'Or somebody had a directional listening device on them,' added Leonardo to Francesco's surprise.

'I didn't know you were an expert in that kind of thing, Leo,' said Francesco respectfully.

'Don't forget that I am married to Judge Grassi's daughter, Francesco! I learnt all about modern electronic spyware during that episode in our lives.'

The disappearance of Leonardo's father-in-law a few months previously had hit the national news before Amedeo

Grassi had become a local hero for his valiant defiance of the local mafia boss.

'Ah,' said Francesco, 'that explains your insider knowledge then!'

'Why did you address that journalist by her first name this morning, Francesco?' asked Leonardo, who had been worrying about this ever since that morning.

'The interrogation continues I see, *mio capo!* Honestly, Leo, I just wanted to disconcert her. Everybody in Legano knows Costanza De Santis – and what damage she can inflict on people's reputations. It's a positive feature when she is attacking corrupt politicians, but I was not prepared to let her capitalise on some error of judgement committed by us. I don't know, Leo, it just came out. It was probably a tactical error, I admit.'

During the rest of their discussion, they had both agreed that it would be a very dangerous move to imply in their public staff meeting that they suspected anybody in the team of passing on reserved information to an outside agent. But to say nothing at all would equally be a mistake.

'We may need outside help to get to the bottom of this,' said Francesco. To his great surprise, his *capo* had replied:

'I agree with you Francesco. And I believe I know just who to ask for help. Leave it with me for a day or so.'

Leonardo Molinari had refused to be drawn any further. Francesco smiled with both ends of his moustache and their intimate *tête-à-tête* came to an end.

* * *

Leonardo, looking nervously at his watch, was on the point of sending someone to fetch the missing 'Miky' when she burst enthusiastically through the door all of her own accord. She looked genuinely horrified that the whole team was already assembled and embarrassed that everyone was looking in her direction with various expressions of amusement and mock indignation on their faces.

'I'm sorry *capo,*' she said to Leonardo. 'I was so involved in what I was doing that I didn't realise what time it was. Excuse me everybody! I'll set the alarm clock on my mobile next time, I promise.'

'Don't worry, Micaela,' said Leonardo kindly. 'I just hope you managed to finish what you were so involved in.'

'I DID!' she exclaimed enthusiastically 'I really think I've got the hang of using the SPM now. *(Scanning Probe Microscope)* It is so fascinating, isn't it! I just can't believe that I'm looking at elements that have been magnified one million times.'

'And being able to manipulate them, too,' added Alessandro.

'Yes, it's quite scary, isn't it?' added Miky thoughtfully.

Of all the team members, Francesco was thinking, Miky had the kind of face that spells out 'honesty and genuineness' in capital letters. She wore glasses which made her look scholarly. She was not what one would call beautiful but each individual one of her features was attractive and the whole effect was to give her an open and appealing countenance, especially when she smiled – which was frequently.

'Some man is going to snap her up quickly,' thought Francesco, the *sciupafemmine,* the lady-killer. 'I just hope she finds the right one.'

Leonardo coughed politely to bring the assembled scientists to order.

'I am sure you are all aware why we are here,' he began.

Nearly every member of the team except Luana and Francesco shook their heads.

'Not exactly, *capo,*' said Giovanna Binetto without a smile.

Leonardo explained simply why he had become worried over the last few weeks. He went on to explain what had happened at their conference that morning and outlined the accusations that they had had to face from the journalist, Costanza De Santis. He implored his team to be very wary about discussing the details of their work outside the confines of their laboratories.

'I am sure we never said anything that could constitute a breach of security,' commented Andrea Calvano, who worked directly under Francesco. 'You can bear me out, surely, Francesco. What we talked about would not even be understood by anyone listening casually.'

Francesco contented himself with a shrug of his shoulders adding only that the journalist from *Il Mezzogiorno* had picked up some titbit of information from somewhere.

Leonardo changed the subject and concentrated the discussion on the strange phenomenon of the cellular structures that had vanished only to reappear some minutes later. It transpired that nearly everyone present whilst working on stem cells had noticed this but had put it down to a temporary fault or power cut affecting the microscopes. The team discussed the issue animatedly for several minutes until Francesco said what nobody wanted to think or say:

'Leonardo and I are worried that somebody might be tampering with our work,' he said simply. 'We could be faced with the eventuality that the fruits of our labours are being leaked to the outside world. But for the life of us, we cannot understand exactly how.

There followed a protracted silence while the assembled scientists digested this disturbing piece of information. It was their newest recruit, Miky De Giorgi, who broke the silence.

'But...forgive me if I am being obtuse, everyone. Surely this would imply that it is one of *us* who is responsible for what is happening? Only a scientist with our particular skills and knowledge would know how to set about achieving such a thing. And if there was an outsider involved, we would have noticed the presence of a stranger.'

There followed a silence that was even more disconcerting than the first, so much so that Miky began to blush to the roots of her hair. 'I'm sorry. I expect I'm being stupid,' she stammered.

'No, Miky, that is the point. You would appear to be right,' said Francesco to reassure her. 'You are the one who had the courage to say it out loud, that's all.'

There followed an outbreak of dismayed protests from several members of the team which, in true Italian fashion, involved each person talking over everyone else. Francesco wondered, not for the first time, how Italians ever managed to reach a consensus of opinion about *anything* - when even a discussion about what type of pasta a particular dish required could provoke a vociferous debate. The only member of the team who did not join in the general outcry was Giovanna Binetto, who remained seemingly aloof. She wore a thoughtful frown throughout the tirade of words that had ensued.

It was Leonardo who brought the meeting quietly back to order as the outburst began to subside.

'We mustn't jump to premature conclusions,' he said in a calming voice. 'We have no proof that anything is amiss as yet. I would just urge you all to be careful what you talk about outside these four walls. And, please, be vigilant in our research labs! Feel free to report any unusual occurrence to me in complete confidence. Now, I want to tell you that there is some good news as well. I have been informed this afternoon that, as a result of Francesco's brilliant presentation this morning – as well as Luana's wonderful achievement with our little patient – we have had a promise of on-going sponsorship from a local bank and, I am delighted to say, from the newspaper *Il Sole 24 Ore...*'

'And I was approached by the online scientific journal *Tecnoscienza* who want to include us on their website every week,' added Francesco.

'What about our beloved lady Minister for Education?' piped up Mariastella Russo.

'She was very complimentary indeed,' replied Leonardo making a wry face.

'I bet she was!' stated Andrea Calvano. 'Paying compliments does not require her to loosen the purse strings.'

'How could you be so cynical, Andrea!' exclaimed someone else ironically.

And so the meeting broke up with a semblance of unity restored. It would only be afterwards that members of the team began to air their suspicions in private to those they trusted most. As usual, Giovanna Binetto kept her own council. Only one member of the team left the room pervaded by a deep sense of guilt; she determined once again that she would no longer go down the treacherous route she had embarked upon.

* * *

Leonardo's wife, Teresa, always knew when something was troubling her overly intellectual husband. She also knew that she would have to tackle him head on in order to make him talk openly about what was bothering him. The moment seemed ripe while she and her daughter, Emma, were sitting round the table at supper time. Leonardo had, with obvious relish, drunk a whole glass of his favourite red wine – a locally produced *Salice Salentino* – and, thus mellowed, was obviously willing to share his anxieties with his little family.

He told them every minute detail of what had happened on that seemingly endless but eventful day.

'I just don't know how to set about solving this problem,' he said as if the events of the day had already defeated him. 'The last thing I want to believe is that one of our team is a traitor capable of smuggling details of our projects out of the laboratories.'

'Well, it would be better to face up to that possibility rather than let the suspicions linger on indefinitely,' replied his wife firmly.

'*Sì, forza papà!*' interjected Emma, his daughter, barely understanding what was troubling her father. 'You can do it!' she added with a look of such faith in her father's abilities that Leonardo felt moved. It was the second time that day that Leonardo had had the word '*forza*' directed at him to exhort him to find the courage to act decisively – something which did not come naturally to him. He preferred avoiding confrontational situations until the very last minute, after which he tended to over-react.

'There, *caro!*' exclaimed Teresa. 'Even your own daughter is giving it to you straight down the line!'

There was a reflective pause before Teresa added: 'Just think of my father, Leo! It took him far more courage to defy the local mafia than it will take you to confront one of your staff who is despicable enough to betray the whole team and put all your hard work in jeopardy. *Forza* Leo!' she added for good measure. 'Besides which, we have already discussed with Rosaria Miccoli and Alessandro Greco the idea of giving Rosaria – I should use her professional name, Elena Camisso – a temporary administrative post in your department. If anyone can winkle out the truth of what is going on, it is her. We already know she's an excellent private investigator because of how she set about solving the mystery of my father's abduction. And you spoke to them a couple of weeks ago when you first noticed something unusual going on. It's the obvious answer, Leo!'

'Well, as it happens, one of the admin staff is due to take maternity leave next week,' said Leonardo thoughtfully. 'Will you get in touch with Rosaria – sorry, Elena – tomorrow, Teresa? I'll discuss it with the Rector in the morning.'

* * *

'It is all highly irregular, *professore,*' stated the *Magnifico Rettore,* pontificating from behind his polished mahogany desk, which struck Leonardo more as an altar to vaulting human ambition than a necessary piece of office equipment.

'We are faced with an irregular situation, *Magnifico,'* countered Leonardo, 'and one which we cannot afford to ignore.'

'But you *do* understand my position, *professore,* do you not? You are asking me to sanction not only the compulsory maternity benefit for a member of your secretarial staff but, on top of that, to pay an extra full time salary for this...*signorina* whom you wish me to employ as a private investigator in the hope that she will unearth something that you are not even sure is happening; and all this, at a time when I am under extreme pressure to reduce our wages bill. Do you feel that I have summed up the situation correctly *professore?'*

Under normal circumstances, Leonardo might easily have capitulated under the weight of the Rector's authority, but the insistent voices of Francesco, his wife and daughter all exhorting him to show courage, gave him the mettle to battle on.

'You have overlooked the fact that we shall also have to pay the investigative agency of Alessandro Greco a moderate fee to cover the temporary absence of his valued assistant,' added Leonardo with some internal trepidation. 'But since our department is about to receive considerable financial backing from various sources...' continued Leonardo, who was puzzled to see what appeared to be a look of frustrated annoyance flash briefly across the academic emperor's face, '...it would seem entirely acceptable to fund this investigation – as a precaution – to counter the serious risk of a breach in our security,' said Leonardo forcefully; 'a breach which all of my team feel is a real likelihood. It would be very counter-productive, would it not, *Magnifico,* to be spending sponsorship money on research which is being leaked out of our University to an agent operating unscrupulously, with the aim of capitalising on my team's extraordinary talents. I am sure that you do not want to be instrumental in *that, Magnifico!'*

The Rector looked as if a complicated internal struggle was taking place behind the imperial mask of the face that he daily presented to the outside world. He was, no doubt, balancing the pros and cons of some devious line of reasoning, thought Leonardo.

'Very well, *professore*,' he said reluctantly. 'I shall sanction this very unusual request for a maximum of two weeks – and no more - but only because I respect you as a valued member of the team.'

The interview was terminated. The professor of the science faculty stood up and, rather than uttering the words 'thank you', contented himself with a slight inclination of his head in the Rector's direction. *'Arrivederla, Magnifico,'* he said as he turned round and left the room without a backward glance. The muscles in his shoulders relaxed visibly as he closed the door behind him and walked into the courtyard under the suspicious eye of the Rector's unsmiling secretary, who had deigned to give a curt nod as he walked past.

He felt an immense sense of relief that the weight of his trouble with their microscopic structures would be shifted on to an extra pair of shoulders. He might have felt less relieved had he been able to foresee the path that events would take as soon as Rosaria Miccoli, alias 'Elena Camisso' took up her unusual post in his department.

4: Cat among the Pigeons

Rosaria Miccoli's first feeling on walking into the university was one of sheer pleasure at finding herself back in the environment where she had spent four deeply engrossing years studying for her degree in Economics and Banking at the end of which she had emerged with a grade of 105/110. She was only alarmed at how many years had elapsed since that glorious day when her family, cousins, aunts and uncles included, had all turned up to honour her at her graduation ceremony. As she walked down the familiar-looking corridors of the modern campus at Monteleone, she reflected equally on the unexpected paths that her life had taken since that day nearly twenty years ago.

Rosaria had entertained no illusions about the nature of this her latest investigation on behalf of the 'Greco Private Investigation Agency', whose new plaque outside the old building in Legano's historical centre boasted the snazzy logo **GIP** standing for *'Greco Indagini Privati'*, which happened to be the same initials as for an Examining Magistrate. She had discussed in detail with her official boss, Alessandro Greco, the founder of the agency, the pitfalls and frustrations that she would encounter by accepting this challenge; but it was the element of 'challenge' that had finally persuaded her to accept the assignment. Since she had been closely involved in the unusual events surrounding the abduction of Judge Amedeo Grassi, Rosaria had been pining for a case that offered a greater intellectual stimulus than the run-of-the-mill investigations into banal cases of suspected marital – or even pre-marital – infidelities, which had become the standard fare of the Greco agency. Here was something that she could get her teeth into once again.

During the dramatic events surrounding the Judge Grassi case, she had become good friends with the judge's daughter, Teresa Grassi. It had been Teresa who had persuaded Rosaria to talk to her husband, Leonardo Molinari, about his suspicions that all was not as it should be in his university department. The financial side of things having been settled to Alessandro Greco's entire satisfaction, Rosaria was free to take up her temporary secondment within the university faculty of Bio-medical and Nanotechnology research in order to initiate her covert investigation into the potential leaking of their projects. She knocked reverentially on the door where the department's administrative personnel were housed. Receiving no answer to her discreet signal, she opened the door, calling out *'Permesso?'* in a forthright voice, as she stepped over the threshold with a confidence that she did not feel.

'Buongiorno. I'm Elena Camisso,' she announced to the three people who had barely bothered to look up as she entered. When working on a case, Rosaria had adopted the precautionary strategy of using a professional pseudonym, a ploy which she had frequently found to be indispensable in this line of work, as it often involved digging into the private lives of other people, who resented the intrusion. The three people – two women and a man – continued to sit in front of their computer screens without giving 'Elena' more than a cursory glance. She had time to study them each in turn; the woman who was presumably in charge was in her late forties, an austere looking lady who had an expression of studied disapproval on her face. The second person was

much younger; a pretty, dark-haired girl in her twenties. She gave Rosaria what looked as if it was about to become a smile but ended up with a slight shrug of her shoulders, which might just have been by way of an apology for the indifferent welcome that she had received. To judge by the young man's graceful movements as he stood up and walked over to a filing cabinet, Rosaria assumed that he was gay. 'Good,' she thought casting her mind back over the unwanted attention she had frequently attracted during her working life. 'There won't be any distractions from *that* quarter, at least!'

She stood there for another thirty seconds before deciding that it was time to assert her presence more forcibly.

'If you prefer, *signora,*' she said addressing the older women in a firm voice but with a sweetly accommodating smile on her face, 'I can go and introduce myself to Professor Molinari, as you seem to be so busy.'

That did the trick. She caught a fleeting, surreptitious smile on the face of the younger woman as the uncongenial lady deigned to stop doing whatever it was that had been occupying her, the interruption accompanied by a perceptible tut of impatience. 'That won't be necessary, *signorina.* I was in the middle of sorting out a consignment of equipment that we had ordered,' she added in a tone of voice suggesting that dealing with a new member of staff was the last form of distraction she needed at that particular moment in her life.

'I understand perfectly,' countered Rosaria. 'And it's *signora,* by the way,' she added to remove the notion that she was some junior clerk who had been picked up from the streets. If the unwelcoming secretary had heard the pointed correction by Rosaria concerning her social status, she failed to register any change of facial expression as she pointed out 'Elena's' desk to her.

'This is where you will be working, *Signora Camisso*. This is where your predecessor, Valentina Rolandi, used to sit...'

'But I understood that this Valentina is on maternity leave, *signora*,' stated Elena calmly. 'You sound as if you consider that I am in some way usurping her position here.'

'Nonsense!' retorted the senior secretary impatiently.

'May I know *your* name, *signora* – before we go any further?'

'Marchetti Livia,' replied the lady stiffly, giving her surname first and given name afterwards; a clear indication that she wished to distance herself from the newcomer. She could not quite understand why *la Signora Marchetti* was reacting to her presence in this manner, but imagined she would find out sooner rather than later.

Elena was aware that the computer key-board noises had ceased in the background. A surreptitious glance over the lady's shoulder revealed that the other two members of the admin team were listening intently to what was going on whilst appearing to be concentrating hard on their silent screens.

'When I have finished what I was doing,' continued Livia Marchetti, 'I shall tell you what your duties will be. You seem to know *il professore* already, *signora*,' pursued Livia Marchetti, with a hint of disagreeable suspicion in her voice which alerted Elena to a possible explanation for her temporary boss's resentment towards her.

'I have never met him before in my life,' lied Elena with the smoothness of a professional actress. 'And now, *signora*, as you are busy, I would like to introduce myself to my other colleagues.' By the expression on Livia Marchetti's face, she had been quite taken aback by the forthright manner in which her new underling had asserted her presence. Tight lipped, Livia Marchetti returned to her seat and continued with whatever task she had been involved in.

As Elena made to approach her other colleagues, the sound of computer keys being smartly tapped simultaneously resumed their robotic chatter. Elena went over to the young woman in her twenties whose desk was the nearer of the two.

'Elena Camisso,' she said receiving the briefest of handshakes before the slender hand was withdrawn.

'Renata Colombo,' said the girl. Now that Elena was close up to her, she was struck by the furtive way in which Renata had supplied her name, as if she was frightened of giving something away. She had a similar sensation when she introduced herself to the young man, whose soft skin and delicate handshake seemed to confirm her first impressions – reinforced by the slightly feminine timbre of his voice as he replied with a lesser degree of reticence to Renata's:

'Stefano Pellegrino, *signora*... Elena,' he added as an afterthought. With him, at least, there was an almost apologetic look in his eyes. Elena had the intuitive impression that her arrival had been discussed at length by these three people, no doubt dominated by the chief secretary, who obviously seemed to resent her intrusion in some inexplicable way.

An awkward hiatus in proceedings was averted by the arrival of a cheery looking man with a moustache that looked too big for a face that tapered gracefully down to a pointed chin. But as soon as he spotted Elena, his face lit up with a delighted smile that sent the tips of his moustache several centimetres into the air. Elena instantly recognised Francesco Zunica from the description given to her by Leonardo a couple of days beforehand.

'Ah! You must be our newcomer!' said Francesco cordially. 'Welcome to our world, *Signora Elena!*'

Elena knew that Francesco was the only other member of the team aware of her true role, so she was careful to feign ignorance of his name until he had formally introduced himself. A meaningful frown in his direction prompted Francesco not to stare at the newcomer before he remembered to introduce himself formally.

'Come and have a cup of coffee, Elena,' he said sensing the atmosphere in the room. 'As long as you don't mind, of course, Livia,' he added with a sweet smile in the chief secretary's direction. Her only response was an indifferent shrug of the shoulders as Francesco led Elena out of the room and down the corridor.

'I imagine you had a frosty reception just now,' began Francesco. 'But I have the impression that you stood up to the lady very well.'

'Well, Francesco. I suspected that I would not have an easy ride when I came here. But I didn't think that the difficulties would arise from that particular quarter,' stated Elena.

'I think she put in a request that Valentina Rolandi should be replaced by a niece of hers during the maternity leave. I suspect that the lady is suffering from a bit of thwarted nepotism!' replied Francesco with a confidential smile. 'And I don't suppose that our chief secretary is reassured when a beautiful woman like yourself descends upon her,' added

Francesco with such simple candour that Elena could not feel embarrassed – or compromised.

'Thank you Francesco,' she replied simply.

'Are you thanking me for the explanation or for the compliment?' he added with a mischievous smile.

'Both, of course,' replied Elena smoothly looking directly into his face.

'Ah, I can see why Leonardo was impressed by you,' added Francesco in a wistful voice as he ushered Elena into a laboratory where Leonardo was working with two of the girls from his team.

'Buongiorno signora,' said Leonardo stiffly, formally shaking Elena-Rosaria by the hand as Francesco introduced her. Later, he apologised through his wife, Teresa, for overdoing the formality. 'I was so concerned about convincing the two girls that I did not know her,' he explained to Teresa, 'that I must have seemed quite unfriendly.'

'I'm sure she understood perfectly well. Stop being over-sensitive, Leo!' his wife would reply.

'This is Elena Camisso who is replacing Valentina while she is having her baby,' said Francesco to the two girls, stepping in quickly when he realised that his *capo* was having difficulty pretending that he had never met Elena before. 'This is Stella, who has been with us for now for a few months. And this is Giovanna Binetto. They are both very versatile – but they are working with me in the Innovative Materials and Nanodevices Section at present.'

Stella, raven haired and darkly beautiful, smiled broadly at Elena as she shook her hand briefly by the finger tips since her hands were enveloped in surgical rubber gloves. '*Benvenuta da noi, Elena,*' she said warmly.

Giovanna had an intense expression on her face, looking directly into Elena's eyes as she shook her hand – after removing her protective gloves. She did not smile but gave the impression she was mentally summing up the newcomer. Elena found it mildly disconcerting but was at pains to conceal her discomfort with her brightest smile. Giovanna, too, was quite attractive, thought Elena, although less obviously so than Stella. She radiated an internal calm that rendered her solemnity appealing.

'I wish I understood what Innovative Materials and Nanodevices meant,' added Elena after the introductions had been made.

'Oh, I'll give you an introductory lesson if you like,' offered Francesco laughing.

Elena had the distinct impression that Leonardo's second-in-command had taken a liking to her. She reckoned that the advantages would almost certainly outweigh the drawbacks if she was to get anywhere with her new assignment. The very language used to designate the team's job descriptions had sounded baffling to her – and, she noticed, the job descriptions were in English, not Italian.

'I suppose I had better get back to my desk and begin to earn my living,' said Elena to the group apologetically. 'I'll take up your offer of a coffee a bit later, Francesco,' she added. As she turned round to leave them, she caught an appealing look in Giovanna's eyes. Elena's intuitive impression was that Giovanna had something that she wanted to say to her in private. It was so fleeting as to be unnoticeable to anyone else. Elena, attuned to such subtleties, registered the covert signal immediately. The briefest nod of her head in the girl's direction was enough to let her know that she had understood. Elena was escorted back to the admin office by a gallant Francesco, who placed a hand under her elbow for a fleeting instant, as he said to her in a confidential whisper:

'*In bocca al lupo, Elena!* Best of luck!'

'Don't worry, Francesco. I can cope with the lady in question. And thank you,' she said as they parted company – Francesco, with obvious reluctance, thought Elena. She would have to tread delicately along that particular path; but she would need all the help she could get from this man with the mobile moustache and the kind, humorous eyes.

Back at her desk, Elena managed to dispatch the tasks that she had been assigned by the chief secretary by mid-morning coffee time. Without saying a word, she left the room and went once again in search of Francesco, making an ambiguous gesture in the general direction of Livia Marchetti, supposedly to convey the personal nature of her departure from her desk. She wanted to request a list of the official university e-mail addresses of all those employed in the department. It would require time, patience and perhaps even a degree of good fortune to acquire their personal e-mail addresses and the numbers of everybody's mobile devices, which might possibly aid the process of discovery of a *talpa* within Leonardo's team of scientists. The set-up seemed to be so normal that it was difficult to believe in the presence of a mole in their midst. She reminded herself that she had not yet met the other members of this team of researchers. No, her task was not going to be straightforward. Elena sighed audibly as she went off in search of Francesco – and the promised dose of espresso coffee.

Francesco was not immediately to be tracked down. In the end, Elena stopped a young man in his late twenties in the corridor. He looked like a thousand other southern Italian men; swarthy complexion, shortish in stature, unsmiling, and a black five o'clock stubble covering most of his face, despite it only being mid-morning. Elena's English partner, Adam, who taught English at the University, always said jokingly that if the typical southern Italian was to walk down a street in suburban England, it would immediately be assumed by passers-by that he was some kind of shady drug dealer – or even a member of a mafia clan. As soon as Elena asked him where she might find Francesco Zunica, the underlying good nature of so many Italian men transformed his expression into one of kindness and interest – helped, no doubt, by Elena's openness and the brilliance of her smile.

'I'm Elena Camisso,' she explained. 'I'm standing in for Valentina during her maternity leave.'

'Ah yes,' replied the man. 'My name is Andrea Calvano. I'm the Soft Matters Nanotechnology Divison Leader. Welcome to our troubled department!' he added unexpectedly.

The last comment took Elena totally by surprise. She remembered just in time that she should register surprise at this startling comment.

'Why troubled?' she asked. 'Everything seems to be so highly organised here.'

Andrea Calvano realised that he might have expressed an inner anxiety too readily. He back-tracked hurriedly, saying that he had encountered a technical problem that morning.

He had not meant to sound negative about the whole department.

'I was actually looking for Francesco,' said Elena, mentally storing away the scientist's apparent slip of the tongue.

'I'll take you to him, Elena,' he said smiling and led her further down the corridor than she had previously ventured – past the welcoming sight of a drinks and snacks dispenser and a little bar where a middle-aged barmaid was making a cappuccino for a solitary woman in her thirties sitting at one of the little metal tables waiting for her coffee. Elena was impressed by the fact that almost all the staff she had seen so far looked so young. The woman was busy reading a document spread out on the table in front of her. Elena was taken to another laboratory which, Andrea Calvano explained, was their stem-cell 'nursery'. She found Francesco in deep conversation with a woman whom he introduced as Luana Palomba. The name rang a bell with Elena. She had seen her on the local television a couple of days ago in connection with a baby girl who had been treated for a heart defect which had saved her young life.

'I don't understand what you do exactly, *professoressa*, and even less do I understand the processes involved,' said Elena to Luana, 'but congratulations on what you have all achieved here. It is nothing short of miraculous.'

'Yes,' replied Luana with true humility, 'it seems that way to us most of the time. But, please, call me Luana,' she added, sensing that her colleague liked and trusted their temporary secretary.

'I've got a video DVD of our press conference for you, Elena,' said Francesco. 'It will give you some idea of what we are attempting to do here.'

Francesco gave Elena a brief guided tour during which she was introduced to two more researchers whom she had not yet met; 'Miky' De Giorgi, a pleasant, bright young woman who let Elena look into the amazing world of nano-sized structures through a highly sophisticated electron microscope.

'But they're *alive!*' exclaimed Elena in genuine amazement, peering at what looked like a headless toy creature driven by an invisible battery.

'Yes, precisely, Elena - we are dealing with minute structures imbued with energy of their own. We assume they are not consciously aware of their own existence – but I wouldn't like to swear to that!'

'It's astounding, and quite daunting!' added Elena.

The two women had a brief conversation during which Miky told her that she had studied biomedicine and robotic engineering at a university in Rome. 'But I come from Sannicola, a village just south of Legano. I'm living with my parents at the moment.'

'I know Sannicola well, Miky,' said Elena. They parted company with the promise that they would talk again soon. Elena-Rosaria thanked her lucky stars that she had been given the gift of inviting confidentiality and forming bonds easily with people she met. The second person whom she was introduced to, Alessandro Agostini, was a man in his early thirties, who wore thin, metal-framed spectacles and whose arched eyebrows gave him a permanent air of astonishment. He gave the impression of being shy and slightly embarrassed at meeting Elena.

'Alessandro is our Robotics Division Leader,' explained Francesco. Elena had the distinct impression that the scientist blushed slightly at the important sounding title. He shook Elena's hand very briefly whilst looking quizzically at Francesco as if to ask why he was being introduced to a temporary member of the admin staff. But, Elena felt, the reaction had been one of puzzlement; there had been no hint of animosity there at all.

'Come on Elena,' said Francesco. 'Let's go and have that coffee.'

* * *

'I think I had better spend the rest of the day doing my job as secretary,' Elena told Francesco over coffee. 'Or else my cover will be blown in no time at all.'

'You are probably right, Elena, although I shouldn't worry too much. We always make newcomers feel welcome whatever their rank, so to speak. I probably overdid it a bit by introducing you to the team in the space of one morning, though,' he admitted. 'But it is important for you to know who is in the team as early as possible. You've only been granted a couple of weeks by our esteemed Rector, I understand.'

'But, Francesco – having met everybody in the team, it seems impossible that it could be anyone of them. Are you really sure that someone is tampering with your research material? It all seems so unlikely.'

'Oh yes. Something has been going on Elena – even if it appears that the interference has been restricted to the stem cell research unit so far. And then,' Francesco added, 'someone tipped off that journalist from *Il Mezzogiorno.* You are bound to know of her. She's called Costanza De Santis, the most inquisitive lady journalist in Italy...'

Elena was looking puzzled.

'Yes, I've heard of her, of course, Francesco. But how does she...?'

Francesco realised that Elena would not have known about the incident at their press conference presentation and he quickly outlined the events regarding the journalist's very public accusations.

'We are being very heavily sponsored by local and national businesses. They are all insisting that we have, as they call it, 'proper mechanisms in place' to ensure the security of projects which they are financing. Now, we can say that we have taken steps to ensure that there will be no further leaks,' concluded Francesco smiling disarmingly. 'That's *you* of course, Elena!'

'That is an awesome responsibility to place on one person's shoulders, Francesco. I'm not sure whether I'm up to this.'

'Don't underestimate yourself, *mia cara*. You are smart, I can see that. I bet that, after a week, you will know what direction to take.'

At this point, Francesco fished out a DVD from his pocket and handed it to her.

'Here you are, Elena. Have a look at this when you get home. It will put you in the picture a bit as to what we do in this department. And over the days to come, I'll explain to you all our major projects and take you on a complete guided tour of the whole building. Then you will see why we are worried about information being leaked to the outside world. A lot of what we do is literally ground-breaking stuff that would be worth a fortune to any unscrupulous person willing to sell information to an outside agent.

'I had better be getting back to my desk,' said Elena apologetically. She had just begun to feel intrigued by what she was learning from this engaging man. But other members of the Faculty were descending on the bar for their morning coffees, among them Giovanna Binetto, who gave them an appraising look as she headed for the bar.

'I'll e-mail you the official contact details of the whole team this afternoon, Elena,' he promised.

She escaped with a smile as if very reluctant to leave the bar and his company; it was not too difficult a subterfuge to perform.

Elena spent lunchtime on her own. She went to the canteen and ate a plate of *penne* and tomato sauce; passable for such an institutionalised meal, she considered. She whiled away the time sitting on a bench outside in the sunshine, phoning first of all her partner, Adam, who was about to take their two children back to school for the short afternoon session.

'I think this undertaking is going to be a bit fraught, Adam!' was her only comment followed by a promise that she would unburden her woes on him later on that evening.

'Ah well, Rosy,' replied Adam, naturally using the abbreviation of her real name. 'That will be something to look forward to, *amore.*'

After the years that they had been together, Rosaria was well attuned to English irony and took comfort from it. She also phoned her *capo*, Alessandro, who was having a sandwich in their *studio*, wishing to share her concerns about this case with another person.

'It's only your first day, Elena! You can't expect to have your *eureka* moment so soon!' Out of habit, Alessandro Greco used her 'official' name even though he was well aware of her real name. It had become a professional habit. He knew from past experience that his associate was always impatient to see immediate results. This time, the game would require a lot more subtlety, he told her.

'But I don't even understand their job descriptions, Sandro!' she snapped back at him. She was aware that she was taking out her feelings of inadequacy on her *capo* and she regretted letting her emotions get the better of her - still the passionate southern Italian woman despite her apparent maturity of years. Her boss was accustomed to her occasional outbursts and, with deliberate calm, sought to reassure her.

As Elena stood up to return to work, a familiar face drew level with her. *'Ciao…* Signora Camisso,' said the face. Elena recognised the scientist to whom she had been introduced earlier – the shy one with the surprised eyebrows. She was annoyed with herself because his name escaped her.

'Alessandro Agostini,' he said, obligingly saving her the embarrassment of having to ask. Another Alessandro, she thought. They walked back together in an awkward silence which Elena was desperately trying to break with some trivial topic of conversation. Alessandro Agostini did not do small talk, she reckoned. In the end it was the scientist himself who broke the silence.

'I'm afraid you have come to us while we are under a bit of a cloud,' he said shyly. 'You must forgive us if we seem offhand.' Elena had to feign surprise as she waited for the man to elaborate. Alessandro, however, was not the kind of person to go in for elaboration, so it seemed. So she felt she should add that, on the contrary, she had been made to feel very welcome. As they parted company with little else being said, Elena wished him *'buon lavoro'* and watched the retreating steps of this lanky scientist as he disappeared down the corridor.

'Well, *something* unusual is obviously going on!' she thought. 'I suppose I should be pleased that there is a purpose to my being here.'

She was assigned the task of sorting out student applications for the rest of the afternoon. Livia Marchetti had obviously decided that her new administrator needed to be kept busy to stop her wandering off to fraternise with 'her' *professori*.

It was well past five o'clock when Elena had finished her appointed task, which had proved to be time-consuming but not mentally taxing. Livia looked disappointed that she had finished so soon, having entertained the hope that the task would occupy her the following morning too. Stefano and Renata had both just left for the day deigning to give Elena a brief smile and an almost imperceptible gesture of goodbye with the hand which could not be seen by Livia as they walked past Elena's desk.

Elena had turned off her computer and picked up her handbag in a decisive way. 'Children to collect,' she said firmly before the chief secretary could find an excuse to give her extra work. In fact, it was her partner, Adam, who was due to do the school run that afternoon. But it was a pretext that could not easily be argued with, even by Livia Marchetti.

Elena headed for the exit door. There was no sign of any of the scientists, not even Francesco whom she had half expected to see again that evening. As she walked across the campus to the car park, she noticed a waiting figure which looked familiar, loitering nonchalantly a few paces ahead of her. As Elena drew nearer, the girl turned to meet her face on. It was Giovanna Binetto.

'Ah, there you are at last!' were Giovanna's unexpected opening words, as if they had had a prearranged meeting time and place. Giovanna fell into step with Elena and walked with her towards the car park. Elena was struck by the feeling of familiarity that the young scientist managed to convey unintentionally; she appeared to be able to dispense with all the conventional opening gambits that one normally employs on making a new acquaintance. Giovanna's next words stopped Elena in her tracks as she looked at her in open-mouthed astonishment.

'You're far too intelligent to be a secretary, Elena. You're here to find out who our *talpa* is, aren't you?' The words emerged as a statement of fact rather than a question.

5: Giovanna's Perspective

The sensation of surprise was such that Elena found herself incapable of finding suitable words either to confirm or deny Giovanna's unheralded pronouncement. Instead, she linked an arm through the younger woman's and began walking towards her car. Giovanna was evidently content to accompany her since she showed no sign of resistance.

It took Elena a good thirty seconds to regain some measure of mental composure and reassess how she should react to her companion's startling and perspicacious deduction.

'You're not exactly lacking in intelligence yourself, Giovanna,' she said respectfully.

'I know,' replied Giovanna, surprising Elena all over again. She had spoken these two words modestly, in a matter-of-fact tone of voice. 'It's my blessing and my curse,' she added with a hint of ironic sadness in her voice. Elena had more than an inkling of what Giovanna meant, largely because she had often had to face a similar paradox in her own life. She wanted to encourage Giovanna to open up a little more but they had already reached Elena's fairly new Lancia Ypsilon, which had, nevertheless, a layer of city dust covering it. Preoccupied with her own thoughts or merely wondering how she might prolong her conversation with Elena, Giovanna subconsciously ran a finger over the side of the car, revealing a neat strip of clean burgundy-coloured paintwork where her finger had been. Realising what she had done, Giovanna blushed slightly and apologised with a self-conscious grin.

'That's my security camouflage you're removing!' said Elena laughing. 'The theory is that thieves see a dirty car and don't have the same desire to steal it.'

Giovanna gave a brief, hesitant laugh and added: 'Well, your theory seems to have held good so far, Elena.'

Elena noted the use of her first name and was pleased.

'Where's your car, Giovanna?' she asked.

'I don't have a car. I just take the bus normally. Or my father gives me a lift sometimes.'

'Where do you live?' asked Elena, hoping that the young woman was not going to say Gallipoli or anything else more than thirty kilometres away.

'Lequile,' she said. Elena breathed an inner sigh of relief; it was only a short distance from where she lived.

'But there's no need to…' continued Giovanna hurriedly. 'I just wanted to talk to you for a while.'

'It will be a pleasure, Giovanna.'

A silence fell as Elena drove off at a sprightly pace taking little heed of speed restrictions. She understood that Giovanna was a naturally reticent person and realised that she would have to initiate proceedings delicately if she was to get her to open up.

'Do you have a boyfriend, Giovanna? Or a *fidanzato?*' It was usually a fairly safe question but Elena held her breath nevertheless.

'Not at the moment,' she replied almost abruptly. Elena was afraid that she had touched on a raw nerve and was about to apologise. But after a pause, Giovanna continued under her own steam, obviously wanting to unburden herself, thought Elena.

'It's one of the problems of being intelligent, I find. Too many young men from these parts prefer their women to be pretty but compliant. They find brains a bit of a challenge,' she said with a characteristic touch of wry humour. 'I've lost three boyfriends like that,' she added, looking sideways at Elena. 'Don't you find that, too?'

Elena knew exactly what she meant and told her so. Giovanna, visibly more relaxed, let out something resembling a contented sigh – as if she had finally found someone to whom she could relate.

'So, what about you, Elena – I mean, have you managed to find someone who is right for you?'

Elena laughed. 'Well, I got round the problem by finding an English partner,' she said, omitting to mention that her partner was some twenty years older than she was. 'I can recommend it, Giovanna. Their idea of gender equality is far better developed. One day, I'll tell you how it all happened.'

They had already taken the exit road off the *superstrada* that goes all the way down to Gallipoli and beyond. Giovanna was giving her companion vague manual directions to her house which Elena seemed to have no trouble following even though they both continued to chat. They pulled up in front of a large, detached, flat-roofed house surrounded by a two metre high wall and a wrought iron security gate under an elaborate porch, which suggested the shape of a boat riding the crest of a wave. 'Standard middle class residence for professional parents,' thought Elena. Giovanna made no move to get out of the car. She seemed much more relaxed and Elena wondered if she dare broach the subject of security breaches within their faculty. Again, to her surprise, Giovanna took the initiative in her own direct manner.

'You almost certainly feel out of your depth at this moment in time, don't you Elena?' she began. Those words, spoken by anyone else, would have sounded discouraging to say the least. From Giovanna's lips, they emerged as a simple statement of the truth, thought Elena. She looked at her companion sitting next to her in the car, her brown eyes reflecting a kindness that was rare after so brief an acquaintance. Elena smiled and nodded: 'Just a little bit,' she admitted.

'Well, it isn't surprising. So I'll tell you what I think, if you have the time, Elena?' The statement sounded like a question, so Elena nodded enthusiastically. 'Of course, I have time Giovanna,' she answered, thinking about her partner, Adam, and their two children, who were probably beginning to wonder where she was. After five minutes, Elena was very glad she had not rushed off, even if she was unsure if she had been enlightened or whether the waters had become even more muddied.

'What makes me suspicious,' began Giovanna, 'is that the temporary disappearance of our little cellular structures is just that - temporary. It makes no sense. So far, the oddness has been confined to the stem cell research area of our research projects – our 'nurseries' as we like to call them. I don't know whether you know about what other projects we are researching?' Elena shook her head and showed her the DVD which Francesco had given her. 'I was going to watch it this evening,' she said.

'Well, you will discover how easy it is to make things 'disappear' into thin air,' continued Giovanna. 'We have managed to develop a material which can deflect the light particles that strike it from behind so that the light is not reflected back to the eye of a human beholder...'

Elena coughed politely. Giovanna understood that she had lost her companion already. 'It's OK, Elena,' she said reassuringly. 'You don't need to understand the science. What I am saying to you is this: in my opinion, making stem cell structures disappear for a few minutes, only to reappear later, is just a red herring, a distraction from the main purpose of the operation. If I wanted to 'steal' our secrets and pass them on to a third party, it is exactly the kind of ruse that I might have employed. The 'invisibility' material is just one aspect of what we do. But even that one creation is the kind of invention that some outide agencies would pay millions of euros, dollars or even Chinese Renminbi to acquire.

'This is frightening stuff, Giovanna,' began Elena as the implications of what the young scientist was saying began to sink in.

'But that is only one of our projects, Elena. I cannot tell you too much myself because *I* would be betraying a trust too! It is up to Einstein – sorry, it's the nickname we have given Professor Molinari – or more likely Francesco, to go into further details if that is what they see fit to do. I don't mean to sound secretive, Elena, because I feel that I can trust you implicitly. I'm good at judging people,' added Giovanna. It was not said boastfully, thought Elena, just a modest statement reflecting her own self-awareness. Elena laid a hand on her companion's arm:

'I quite understand, Giovanna,' she reassured her. 'And I probably would not understand what you were talking about anyway!'

After a brief pause, Elena added, almost reluctantly, afraid to shatter the fragility of their growing trust by pushing Giovanna too far:

'Do you mean, Giovanna, you have an idea who might be behind this elaborate deception?'

Giovanna sighed before replying and frowned as if she was debating internally what words she should use in answer to this pertinent question.

'The simple answer, *mia cara Elena,* is 'yes', I do. But I really have nothing other than instinct to go on at the moment. I just don't want to come out with someone's name only to find out later that I have maligned the wrong person. It's a really delicate issue, isn't it? I would be so deeply embarrassed if I accused an innocent person that I would feel obliged to look for a post somewhere else – maybe even in America!' She had spoken without apparent irony.

'I understand completely, Giovanna, and I promise not to push you for any more information,' Elena reassured her. 'But...' she continued with a rueful smile, 'Can't you just tell me if you suspect a man or a woman?'

Giovanna's right hand was reaching for the door handle. She smiled broadly at Elena and said teasingly: 'You're the detective, my dear. You'll work it out soon. But...' she added as she began to get out of the car, '... look out for a person who smiles whilst talking to you, but who looks nail-bitingly anxious when they think they are not being observed; someone who might have a secret, hidden agenda.'

By now, Giovanna was on the pavement. She bent down to address Elena through the open window. 'You are a good person, Elena. I liked you the moment I saw you. We'll talk again soon, won't we?' It was hard to decipher whether this was a simple statement or whether there was a note of appeal in her voice. 'Thank you for the lift, by the way. It was really sweet of you.'

'It was a pleasure, Giovanna. See you tomorrow.'

'And I'll be on the look-out for an English boy-friend,' she added with a big grin. How pretty she looks when she is smiling, thought Elena. A final quick wave and Giovanna was keying in a code to open the gate, which seemed to be at least twelve digits long. She did not turn around again and Elena drove home in the gathering gloom of rain clouds, attempting to assimilate what she had just heard. She was trying to remember Giovanna's exact words because there had been a fleeting image that had crossed her mind whilst her new ally had been speaking. But the memory of it eluded her. Stop! It would come to her if she didn't try to force it to the forefront of her mind.

When she got home after a ten minute drive, her long-suffering partner, Adam, looked at her in mock reproach, which concealed the relief that he felt that the invisible circle that encompassed their little clan had been safely closed for the night.

'Well, I trust you have managed to solve the case in a single day, Rosy,' said Adam half sarcastically, half hopefully. By way of response, she came close up to him and hugged him tightly, knowing from experience that the contact of her body always mollified him. Adam returned the hug knowing full well that he ought, by rights, to resist a little longer. Rosaria could forget she was Elena from that moment on. She went over and hugged the two children in turn.

'You look pretty, *mamma*,' said Riccardo beguilingly.

'You look tired, *mamma,'* said Anna from her superior vantage point of the elder sibling.

'Anna!' interjected Adam. 'Your mum has been working all day long. She deserves a few kind words from you, doesn't she?'

'*Mamma*, you look very beautiful...but a little tired,' corrected their daughter not wanting to relinquish her hold on what she felt had been a fair and mature observation.

'It has been a very long day indeed,' conceded Rosaria.

Adam knew better than to ask questions. He knew that his partner always bottled up her feelings, sometimes for days at a time, before the words that expressed her inner anxieties would tumble out, but only after her thoughts had formed some coherent, manageable pattern in her mind.

After a light evening meal, during which a great quantity of salad was eaten, the family of four sat down together on a sofa in front of the television screen. Riccardo was thwarted in his desire to devour large servings of cartoons on the *Rai 'Gulp'* channel. He protested but was overruled by his mother. When Rosaria was set on watching something that she wanted to watch, her son knew that his objections would be pointless. Rosaria slipped a DVD into the player. In a matter of seconds, Adam, Rosaria and Anna, who had decided to continue to play at being mature, were engrossed by what they were witnessing. Even Riccardo began to forget about his cartoons as soon as he witnessed the magician's hat changing colour. By the time they all saw the photo of the President shimmering before it disappeared under the 'invisibility cloak', they were agog. Even Riccardo wanted a replay.

'I just love that funny man's moustache, *mamma,*' exclaimed Anna. 'Do you know him?'

'He's called Francesco Zunica,' answered Rosaria, who went on to point out the other people whom she had met. When Leonardo appeared on the screen, Riccardo had a moment of recognition. 'We saw him, didn't we *mamma,* at that garden party we went to.'

'Well recognised, Riccardo!' said Adam. 'So we did!'

Rosaria's attention was caught the second time round by a figure briefly captured by the video camera. The cameraman must have gone up on to the podium to film the episode of the lady journalist, Costanza De Santis, when she had accosted Leonardo Molinari. As Rosaria was engrossed by this brief exchange, she almost failed to spot the other figure in the audience. It was a girl in her twenties and she had seen her that day – one of the scientists she had been introduced to. She had to stop the DVD and wind the film backwards frame at a time. Even so, it was difficult to be sure. Yes, it was one of the other scientists to whom she had been introduced. What was her name? 'Stella something,' said Rosaria to herself. She mentioned this to Adam. 'I suppose there is nothing strange about a fourth member of the team being there,' he commented vaguely.

'That's what I want to do when I grow up,' said Anna decisively after they had watched the DVD a third time. 'Be a nano... nano... person!' she concluded, her young mind truly inspired by what she had seen.

Later on that evening, Adam and Rosy were sitting on the bed together. It took Rosaria the best part of an hour to replay everything that had happened to her since she had arrived at the university that morning. Adam was always enthralled by the vivid manner in which she 'relived' her experiences during their narration; she never looked straight at him when she was in that particular mode. Instead, it was exactly as if the scenes and the conversations that she was describing were taking place in an abstract space that she could visualise, step by step, as her words brought events to life. Adam could almost see Francesco Zunica or Giovanna Binetto materialising in their bedroom so intense was her description of them.

'And I have just begun to wonder,' she concluded as the narrative reached the point where she had left Giovanna at the entrance to her house, 'whether Giovanna singled me out for her own purposes! Heaven forbid but I have to consider the possibility that she is playing a very subtle game to throw me off the true scent. I hope and pray that it will not turn out to be her who is the traitor in the camp. She did say something about going to America if she was wrong about the identity of their *talpa.* Do you think I am being paranoid, Adam? Please tell me what you think.'

Adam was always a bit alarmed that she displayed such blind faith in his intuitive abilities, but he usually considered that it was better to give his opinion even if he turned out to be wrong in the end. In addition, declining to offer his opinion would mean that they would never get any sleep.

'Well,' he began after a lengthy interval, wishing to weigh his words carefully. He had once overruled Rosaria's choice of curtains for their bedroom. The style and colour had turned out to be disastrous. It had thrown Rosaria into a depression that lasted over a week. The only solution had been to spend another fortune on a new set of curtains.

'It seems to me very unlikely that Giovanna would have opened up to you to such an extent on such a short acquaintance if she had anything to hide. If she is as intelligent as you say it would have been an easy matter to cover her tracks before you had a chance to discover anything. No, I think she is the kind of person who is totally devoted to her work. She does not strike me as being two-faced. In fact, it sounds as if she is a bit lonely and in need of a friend who thinks like she does. You should be guided by your first impressions in my opinion. That is what I honestly think, Rosy.'

That earned him a kiss and a loving hug. Adam was not sure if it was because he had said what she wanted to hear or whether it was the precursor to greater intimacy.

* * *

Sometime later, before they fell asleep Rosaria sighed. 'It is strange how, whenever I get caught up in a case, it is quite impossible not to become personally involved with those around me. You know - just as I did with Teresa, the judge's daughter.'

'It's the secret of your success, I suspect,' replied Adam yawning.

'And, do you know... it's still bothering me that Giovanna slipped a little clue into the conversation – right at the very end. I'm sure it was a subtle hint. I wish I could remember...'

Those were her last words before she fell soundly asleep until the morning. As usual, Adam was left turning things over in his mind before he followed her into the land of slumber some time afterwards.

6: Another Day – Another Question Mark

Rosaria, becoming Elena once again, arrived at work fifteen minutes late the following morning. She had had to take the children to school first as Adam had an early morning English lesson at the University. Anna and Riccardo were more relaxed when their mother took them to school, allowing her to accompany them right up to the school gate rather than abandoning their father somewhere on the outskirts of the circle of mums crowding around the immediate vicinity of the entrance. The children were of an age when they had become self-conscious about comments from other children suggesting that their father looked more like their grandfather. Their staunch defence of their father had led to an increase in the malicious teasing which children of that age seem to delight in. Despite the closeness of the family, Adam was becoming poignantly aware that the disparity between his and Rosaria's age might one day prove to be an obstacle to their seemingly unshakable unity. He would banish the negative thought firmly from his mind as he gave Anna and Riccardo a rapid *bacio* on their cheeks before they ran off towards the school gate without a backward glance in their father's direction or a final wave of goodbye.

When Elena arrived at her desk, she was relieved to find that Livia Marchetti was not present to show her frowning disapproval of Elena's late appearance. Her co-workers were marginally warmer towards her today, she noticed. She put it down to the absence of the secretary in charge. Stefano glided gracefully past her desk and asked her whether she wanted a coffee. Although common politeness was being observed, Elena had the impression that he expected she would decline the offer.

'That's very kind of you, Stefano,' she said smiling sweetly. 'Espresso with no sugar please.' She accompanied the words with the gesture of opening her handbag as if to look for her purse. Stefano waved aside the suggestion of money and continued his smooth progress out of the office. Elena really had not felt like drinking a third coffee so soon after the other two cups that she had drunk at breakfast time, but tactics were all important at this stage. Once the offer had been made, it would seem discourteous to continue ignoring her as they had tended to do during the previous day.

'Where is... *la Signora Livia* this morning, Renata?' asked Elena as soon as Stefano had disappeared. 'I can't imagine her ever allowing herself to be late for work,' she added with pointed irony.

Elena was rewarded by a smirk, rapidly suppressed, on the face of her colleague.

'I believe she's attending a union meeting this morning,' replied Renata guardedly. 'She's the CGIL representative here. She takes her responsibilities quite seriously,' added Renata with a half-guilty look, loaded with significance, in Elena's direction.

'Ah!' said Elena in a knowing manner which implied that she had discovered another reason behind the attitude of their chief administrator towards the new arrival. Renata turned to her computer screen and began to concentrate on the task in hand, fearful that she might have revealed more than it was diplomatic to do.

'Don't be concerned, Renata,' said Elena. 'I am very aware of the delicacy of my present situation.'

Renata gave Elena a brief smile of gratitude as Stefano returned with three cups of coffee, one of which he placed delicately on Elena's desk as if it had been an offering of Italian *haute cuisine.* Elena smiled her appreciation as much to conceal her amusement at the grace of his gesture as to acknowledge his small act of kindness.

Wondering how on earth she was going to make any progress in this nebulous case that she had become involved in, whilst she remained stuck behind a desk pretending to be an administrative assistant, Elena switched on her computer.

She had two e-mails. The first was from Francesco and contained a list of the research team members accompanied by their official e-mail addresses. The list also contained the personal mobile phone numbers and private e-mail addresses of all but four of the scientific team. The missing ones belonged to Leonardo Molinari, Miky De Giorgi, Mariastella Russo and Giovanna Binetto. The list also contained the official e-mail addresses and personal mobile numbers of Elena's 'colleagues' in the admin section – even Livia Marchetti's. Francesco had been very diligent. Elena speculated as to the possible reasons why the four people whose personal electronic data was excluded might have withheld this information. Many people prefer to keep their private lives separate from their professional lives, reasoned Elena. She could well imagine Giovanna falling into this category. But, in the present situation, other motives for concealment could not be ruled out. She would have to use her ingenuity to discover the missing bits of information; it could prove to be vital. If only she had a more concrete notion as to what she was up against! Elena sent the e-mail to her own iPhone so that she had a record of the information to hand whenever it was needed whilst simultaneously printing off a hard copy for immediate reference.

She turned her attention to the second e-mail. Her suspicions were aroused in advance. She knew that something was not quite as it should be since the e-mail bore no recognisable sender's name. Her reactions on reading the brief, but vitriolic, text were mixed; her initial feeling was one of mild despair followed by growing irritation. But her rational side prevailed and she saw how the unexpected arrival of this electronic missive might well work in her favour. It would certainly give her the impetus necessary to force the pace of her investigation. The message read:

Signora Camisso – having connections in high places does not make your employment in a public institution tenable or legal. Hand in your notice or be prepared to defend yourself in public.

The message merely informed her that the e-mail had been 'sent from my iPhone'. Whoever the sender might be, they had severely underestimated her ability to use modern technology. Within minutes she had the sender's number on her screen. It looked familiar. She checked the number against the list which Francesco Zunica had supplied her with and was not surprised to discover that it corresponded to Livia Marchetti's. Elena knew that she would enjoy the rest of the morning and took a perverse pleasure in contemplating her act of revenge. Rosaria-Elena, when crossed, was a force to be reckoned with. Her fiery, Mediterranean temperament was struggling to escape from under the veneer of conventional good manners that daily social intercourse demanded. A more calculating Rosaria decided to wait until the hapless head secretary was seated opposite her. The results would be more dramatic.

She stood up without a word and walked out of the office in search of an ally – any ally. She would certainly have to tell Leonardo about the e-mail and how being stuck at her desk under the orders of Livia Marchetti was going to make it difficult to find out anything useful. She would not say anything to Leonardo until she had confronted *la signora* in person. She went into the first laboratory hoping that she would find Francesco. Instead, she met Alessandro Agostini, the lanky scientist whom she had met outside the previous day. He straightened himself up from his position of peering at a large screen connected by cables to some machine resembling an unmanned satellite and smiled shyly at Elena. On the screen, there was a 3D image of something that looked precisely like a length of entwined knitting.

'What's that, Alessandro?' asked Elena, after another brief mental search to recall the scientist's name.

'It's a carbon nano-tube,' stated Alessandro. 'We are experimenting with the aim of increasing its efficiency even more.'

'And what's this machine exactly?' asked Elena, none the wiser. She was bewildered by the size of the contraption into whose innards the scientist had been peering.

'Oh, it's our new Scanning Electron Microscope,' he answered. 'It cost about a million euros.'

'Well, at that price, it should be able to magnify by about the same amount!' stated Elena, who could think of very little else to say by way of conversation.

Alessandro smiled shyly as if he had never considered the connection between price and magnification. As it appeared that Alessandro was not going to add any further information, Elena asked him if he had seen Francesco.

'He was walking around with Einstein… sorry, I mean *Professore* Molinari. I think they were heading back to the professor's office,' suggested Alessandro. Elena smiled warmly and thanked him as she headed back the way she had come, feeling even more mystified by this brave new world being created by such ordinary looking mortals. She had the impression that this building was much bigger than had first appeared. She could imagine a whole maze of corridors leading off in other directions. Leonardo's office door was open but of its occupant or Francesco Zunica there was no sign. She headed reluctantly back towards her office. Through its glass panel, she could see that Livia Marchetti had arrived. Good! Now Elena felt she was back in a world that she could cope with.

She treated Livia to a defiant stare as she entered the office, a look which did not escape the notice of Stefano or Renata. Livia's eyes shifted from side to side, as a fleeting hint of guilt crossed her face, quickly replaced by her habitual expression of haughty severity. Elena sat down composedly and with great deliberation retrieved her phone from her handbag. At some point during the previous day, Livia Marchetti had intimated to Elena that making and receiving phone calls in the office was severely discouraged. Thus, Elena hoped, her gesture would appear to be an act of flagrant disobedience. She calmly entered a number on the keypad whilst looking defiantly at her boss whose incipient frown of disapproval had begun to form. Elena was gratified to see the sudden start of surprise when the chief secretary's phone began to ring shrilly in the subdued atmosphere of the office.

'*Pronto,*' said Livia severely. '*Chi è?*'

As on the previous day, the sound of computer keys hard at work had inexplicably fallen silent as Renata and Stefano strained to listen to how their boss would cope with this unaccustomed interruption to the routine which she herself had imposed. To their complete astonishment and secret delight, it was their new colleague who initiated the conversation in a clear voice which filled the office.

'*Signora Marchetti,*' began Elena, 'I should be grateful, on any future occasion that you have some personal matter to convey to me, if you did it to my face rather than sending me anonymous e-mails.'

La Signora Marchetti looked as if she was about to protest her innocence but one look at Elena's face told her that the game was up. Quite deflated, she covered her embarrassment by switching off her phone and continuing to look angrily at something on her computer screen. Behind her, Elena was amused to see Renata and Stefano silently applauding her performance by a discreet and soundless clapping of their hands.

There was no longer any need for pretence on Elena's part. She left the office determined to find Francesco or Leonardo and tell them that they must find some solution that would allow her to pursue freely the task for which she had been unofficially appointed.

Fortuitously, she found both of them together in Leonardo's office, heads bent together in earnest discussion. The door was half open.

'*Disturbo?*' she asked politely. Judging by the beatific smile she received from Francesco, accompanied by the elevation of the tips of his moustache, she gathered that her interruption was not unwelcome. Even Leonardo smiled and indicated that she should pull up a third chair and join them round the desk. She beat Francesco to the chair in his noble attempt at a gallant gesture to fetch the seat for her.

'We have a problem,' stated Elena who went on to relate her *contretemps* with the head secretary. The two men looked at each other meaningfully.

'Interesting,' said Francesco. 'We were just discussing the fact that Leonardo has already received a phone call from the *Magnifico Rettore* this morning about your presence among us.'

Francesco looked at his chief as if to confirm that he could go into further details. Leonardo waved a hand to show that he was free to say whatever he wanted.

'It seems that our esteemed leader has been contacted by the union – the CGIL – concerning your appointment, Elena. He was at great pains to point out that he does not want a confrontation with *other social parties,* as he put it.'

'But I am only here for two weeks. Surely the Rector knows that!' said Elena, amazed at the political furore that her temporary appointment had caused.

'It would appear that the *Magnifico Signor Mela* is more concerned about his own position than any risk to the security our research projects,' said Francesco. 'In fact, Leonardo was under the distinct impression that the Rector thought we were making a fuss over nothing.'

'That is strange,' commented Elena. 'He ought to be erring on the side of caution, surely!'

Leonardo sighed and nodded in agreement.

'I don't suppose you've had enough time to...' began Leonardo with a hint of desperate optimism in his voice.

'Well,' began Elena who wanted to offer some crumb of comfort to him, 'I seem to have found an ally.'

The two men looked at her with interest.

'You mean...?' began Leonardo.

'Let's just say that this person has a shrewd idea as to who your mole might be. At the moment, this person does not wish to reveal identities.'

'Neither do *you*, it seems!' said Francesco with a smile. Elena shrugged her shoulders and said simply: 'Give me a day or so.'

It was agreed that Leonardo would tackle Livia Marchetti and reassure her that her complaints had been heeded.

'If I tell her that you are only here for two more weeks then she won't lose face. Only we know that your appointment was for that period of time anyway,' said Leonardo. It was agreed that Elena should continue working in the main office but that she would be free to do so without interference from the chief secretary.

'I'll say you are engaged on a special assignment,' explained Leonardo.

'Come on, Elena,' offered Francesco. 'I'll give you a proper conducted tour of our laboratories. And, with Leonardo's permission, I'll tell you about some of the research projects that we really do want to protect from prying eyes – or colleagues with evil intent,' he added. Leonardo nodded his consent.

Elena was conducted along 'corridors' lined with heavy black curtains rather than solid walls – to reduce light pollution and unwanted reflections, Francesco explained. The scientists whom she had met briefly the day before were all peering at computers showing pin-pricks of light dancing across their screens or were manipulating controls whilst peering into complex-looking microscopes.

Each member of the team, Elena noticed, was wearing a pair of surgical rubber gloves as if they were performing some delicate medical intervention.

'We need to reduce contamination to the minimum,' explained Francesco. 'In a moment, I'll show you the 'Clean Room', as we call it – where the atmosphere is kept as near to being dust free as is possible. It's almost like breathing in pure mountain air - without the scenery,' he added smiling.

At one point, they came across Miky De Giorgi and Giovanna Binetto, who paused and smiled knowingly at Elena. She raised one eyebrow slightly as if to ask: 'Have you found out who it is yet?' Elena gave her a wry look and shook her head imperceptibly. The exchange did not escape Francesco's notice.

'Your new ally, I presume?' he asked with a wicked grin. Elena looked at him non-committedly and was careful not to react.

'You must have a real knack of inspiring confidence, Elena,' he added with a hint of envy in his voice. 'Giovanna is renowned for her discretion.'

'What are Giovanna and Miky working on exactly?' Elena asked with sudden intense interest. She did not want to give Francesco the satisfaction of knowing he had guessed correctly.

'This morning, they are working on a very important *'Bottom Up'* project – as we call it,' ventured Francesco. The quizzical look on Elena's face was a picture. 'As opposed to a *'Top Down'* project, I suppose?' she enquired with a touch of irony.

'You are a clever person, Elena,' replied Francesco seriously. Elena had wanted to sound intelligent yet sarcastic in the same breath. It seemed that she had inadvertently supplied the correct answer.

'You will still have to explain,' she said.

'Put simply,' Francesco began, *'Top Down* means that we take a chunk of material – silicon, say – and begin to chip away at it until we have created the object we want, such as a microchip. Whereas...' Francesco paused to give Elena a chance to elaborate. She, however, just looked blankly at him.

'Whereas...a *Bottom Up* project means that we start with basic nanoparticles and gradually build them up into the size, shape and function that we need.'

'What does *nano* mean exactly, Francesco?' asked Elena embarrassed by her own ignorance.

'A *nanometre* measures ten to the power of minus nine. That is to say ....'

'...a ten with nine noughts added,' interrupted Elena who did not want to appear totally ignorant. 'So it's invisible to the naked eye, isn't it?'

'Correct!' said Francesco. 'Now, as to what Miky and Giovanna are doing...well, I'm sure they will want to tell you themselves.'

Giovanna gave her colleague a friendly nudge and said: 'Go on Miky! *You* tell Elena what we are concocting!'

'What is Giovanna up to?' thought Elena. 'Why doesn't she tell me herself?'

As Miky launched into an enthusiastic explanation of Optogenetics – an entirely new field of discovery in which their institution was a world leader, she was saying – Elena looked at Miky's animated features and into her honest brown eyes, alight with scientific passion. Suddenly, Elena understood Giovanna's motives.

'She's telling me that Miky is above suspicion. She doesn't want me to waste time on the wrong person,' thought Elena, enlightened and impressed at the subtle manner in which Giovanna's mind worked.

'It means we can do away with clumsy and inaccurate electrode probes,' Miky was saying. 'It will help us to understand better how the human brain works – something which we know surprisingly little about.'

Before Francesco led Elena off on the next leg of their journey through this land of marvels and mysteries, she thanked Miky warmly and managed fleeting eye contact with Giovanna. Elena was yet again struck as to how well they communicated with one and other. It was almost telepathic. Giovanna smiled a smile of complicity – pleased that Elena had picked up the correct signals.

They came across Stella Russo in the next division, parting the black curtains which divided one section from another. Stella had her back turned to them as they stood some metres behind her. The young scientist was seemingly totally absorbed in what she was doing. Her latex covered fingers were nimbly manipulating the controls of a complex looking machine as she peered into its inner workings.

'She's one of the most able people we have here,' Francesco whispered in Elena's ear. 'A natural scientist with a real flair for what she does. And she's about the most versatile of all of us; she can turn her hand to almost any one of the projects we are engaged in.'

Elena looked at him straight in the eye - without uttering a word. Francesco understood in an instant the significance that her glance carried with it.

'No,' he said as emphatically as he could manage whist still talking in a stage whisper. 'That's so unlikely as to be...absurd.'

'She's a very attractive young woman, Francesco. But that fact alone does not place her above suspicion.'

It was quite apparent to Elena from the expression on Francesco's face that he had never once questioned his own judgement regarding Mariastella Russo.

'Besides which, it was me that appointed her,' he added lamely, thinking that this woman standing discreetly by his side was decidedly not to be underestimated.

Elena took a step forward and gently tapped Stella on the shoulder. The effect was sudden and startling. Stella's head swung round as if she had been branded with a hot poker, a look of shocked surprise on her face. Elena instinctively recoiled. A split second later, there was a frantic smile on Stella's face as she apologised with a mixture of relief and embarrassment although the look in her eyes still registered shock.

'I'm sorry, Elena...Francesco! I got so absorbed in what I was doing that I was literally in another world.'

Stella held up her gloved hands as if to indicate that she could not shake Elena by the hand but, instead, planted a quick *bacio* on either cheek.

'We are sorry to disturb you, Stella,' said Francesco. 'I was giving Elena a proper guided tour of our laboratories.'

'Can I know what it was you were doing that you were so engrossed in, Mariastella?' enquired Elena. 'I warn you, though, that I may well not understand a thing!'

'Come and have a look into the 'nano' world, Elena!' suggested Mariastella. 'And please call me Stella.'

'Because she really *is* our star!' added Francesco pointedly from somewhere behind Elena's shoulders. He had a tell-tale grin on his face which did not go unnoticed by Elena as she sat down where, a few seconds previously, Stella had been crouched over her work in such profound concentration.

What Elena could see was not quite believable. She felt as if she was looking at some alien life form. It looked like a tiny set of gear wheels attached to something that was a cross between a miniature robot and an insect. Its miniscule parts were moving.

'Is it alive?' asked Elena incredulously.

'I suppose you would say so,' replied Stella. 'But I am not sure whether it *realises* this or not!'

'But it must be *tiny!*" exclaimed Elena.

'Yes, Elena, it's minute. Its elements measure about a ten millionth of a metre, to be precise,' said Francesco from behind them.

'You are seeing a highly magnified version of it,' explained Stella. 'It's only because we can magnify things that we can see what we are doing to create it.'

Elena stood up looking as totally confused as Stella had been startled a minute or so previously. 'But what does it *do?*' she asked bewildered.

'It's part of our MEMS project,' replied Stella.

'Mems?' repeated Elena. 'What is a Mems?'

'It's not a word, Elena,' explained Francesco laughing at Elena's mystification. 'It's a *sigla* – an abbreviation. It stands for Micro Electro-Mechanical Systems.'

Elena assumed that these two people were under the delusional impression that they had clarified the matter for her.

'*E poi...?*' she added almost aggressively, inviting further explanation.

'It's a bio-sensor,' continued Stella. 'This particular one will be able to detect unwanted bacteria during the process of wine production. One of Puglia's most important wine producers is going to put this tiny gadget to good commercial use.'

'Other bio-sensors like this can do the same to detect impurities in the production of olive oil, for example,' added Francesco.

Elena could only express her admiration as she took leave of Stella and her tiny, living nano-sized machine. 'I hope we shall be able to meet again soon, Stella,' she said. Stella's reaction to this invitation seemed inexplicably ambiguous, thought Elena. The momentary flicker of movement of her eyes was replaced by what sounded convincingly like genuine pleasure at the prospect as she replied:

'I would like that very much, Elena. Whenever you like...'

Francesco was walking slightly ahead of Elena as they continued their tour round the maze created by the rows of heavy black drapes. He did not see the frown of concentration on her face. 'Stella is hiding *something,*' Elena was thinking. She had also arrived at the startling conclusion that Stella was one of those women who needed regular, energetic sex. There was a hungry look about her beautiful, even features that demanded the attention of the opposite sex. She gave off that tell-tale aura of physical desire which cannot be disguised. Elena knew from personal experience how these internal desires betray themselves without the person in question being aware that they are sending out signals of invitation. It worked like a subtle scent. Decidedly, it must be a priority to become better acquainted with Stella. She also understood clearly that Francesco had been captivated by the invisible pull of Stella's physical presence. 'No impartial judgement from *that* quarter!' she concluded ominously.

Keeping the true nature of her opinion to herself, she spoke quietly to Francesco as they walked away.

'Whatever you might think, Francesco, Stella is expending a lot of emotional energy suppressing some kind of personal problem.'

Francesco looked at Elena with open disbelief.

'You cannot possibly have deduced that in such a short space of time. She was her usual ebullient self, Elena! Full of enthusiasm for her work and ...'

Francesco's voice trailed off as he caught the look of mischievous amusement in Elena's eyes. After a brief flash of irritation, his good humour reluctantly returned to alleviate his embarrassment.

'But seriously, you cannot *possibly* have enough to go on to justify such a conclusion! Can you...?' he added, a note of doubt in his voice.

'Call it woman's instinct,' replied Elena. 'But, I'm telling you, Francesco, there is *something* bothering our Stella!'

By the time they had completed their tour and stopped to talk at some length to Andrea and Alessandro, Elena's mind was overwhelmed with new knowledge. She had learned about – or at least been told about – carbon nanotubes that were able to improve conductivity tenfold, a 3D photocopier that could be programmed to replicate a human bone, a genetically modified mosquito called a *Drosofila* which shares 60% of its DNA with human beings and 50% of its protein with mammals in general.

'It is a living organism which we have cultivated to detect the presence of nano-toxicity,' explained Francesco to an Elena whose brain was just beginning to reel. 'Sometimes, substances like gold which are harmless to human beings in normal sized quantities become toxic when they are nano-sized. This can become a problem when nanotechnology is applied to the production of the latest cosmetics, industrial paints – or toothpaste,' he added. At least, Elena-Rosaria felt she had acquired a dawning knowledge of what went on in her new environment.

By the time she had learnt about research on self-healing tissues, materials that could disperse lightning strikes – applicable to the aeronautical industry, Francesco explained – cloaking techniques and artificial tendons which were soft and flexible for use in the prosthetic limbs of the future, Elena's brain was reeling. She held up her hands in protest.

'No more for now, *please* Francesco! *My* brain has ceased to function!'

But her protest turned to silent admiration for what miracles were being performed between these walls – or, rather, black curtains.

At this point, she turned to Francesco and said: 'You don't know this, but the DVD which you lent me of your presentation at the *Hotel Europa* the other day has become my children Anna and Riccardo's favourite TV viewing of all time. They want to become nano-scientists just like you.'

'In that case, I shall give you two more DVDs about our wonderful, life-sized fish and our engaging little robot called RIC6 – both projects shared with other universities.'

'Better still, Francesco, why don't you come round to dinner tomorrow evening and you can give the DVDs to them in person. Anna is fascinated by your moustache. I had better forewarn my partner, Adam. He does the cooking for us,' added Elena. 'I take it your wife will not object?'

The smile of pleasure that had lit up Francesco's face at the prospect of an invitation clouded over at the mention of the word 'wife'.

'I'm separated,' he explained. 'My two teenage daughters live with Amelia, my wife. *'Colpa mia,'* he said striking his breast with clenched fist. 'The result of a single rather tumultuous indiscretion a short while ago.'

'I'm sorry, Francesco,' she said simply.

Francesco looked at his watch. Elena, who never wore a watch, was surprised to learn that it was already 12.30. 'Let's have lunch in the canteen,' he suggested. Elena, who would rather have contrived a meeting with Mariastella, nevertheless accepted his invitation. It was during their short lunch break that Elena learnt that, because of his separation, he was living on a very tight budget. 'I even have to drive a 15 year old FIAT *Tipo*,' he told Elena sadly.

'Just like Montalbano!' said Elena brightly. 'No shame in that!'

After they had eaten their plate of *fave e cicoria* and pronounced it well cooked by the canteen's chef, Francesco led Elena back towards the laboratories. Despite her protests that she could not absorb anything else scientific that day, Francesco promised that there was only one more laboratory that he wanted her to see; without even going inside it, he had promised.

Elena was peering through thick, darkened glass into a room containing yet more sophisticated scientific equipment whose uses she could not begin to guess at. The whole laboratory was bathed in a soft yellow light.

'*This* is what we call the 'Clean Room', Elena,' he explained. 'The air inside is maintained at a constant temperature and is constantly filtered to reduce contamination to the minimum. The ambient light is yellow because at this wave length the photons are less likely to affect the research experiments. Blue light is the most damaging. This room is even ultra-violet proof – the glass acts like a pair of gigantic sun-glasses.'

Francesco showed her the hospital-like plastic suits and masks hanging on hooks round an antechamber that served as the changing room. Access could only be gained by an electronic identity card which had to be checked and validated before entry was permitted.

Elena was about to ask Francesco what kind of experiments were conducted in the Clean Room. Despite her earlier declaration that her brain had reached saturation point, her curiosity had got the better of her. At that moment, Francesco had a summons from Leonardo whose muffled voice sounded anxious.

'Come on, Elena. You come too,' insisted Francesco.

They found Leonardo in the company of Andrea Calvano, whose swarthy features were covered not only with a five o'clock shadow but with a glistening layer of sweat. They both looked anxious.

'What's up?' asked Francesco.

'Andrea is convinced that someone has been into the Clean Room during lunch time,' stated Leonardo.

Francesco explained rapidly to Elena that an unwritten rule required that whoever went inside the Clean Room had to mention it either to Leonardo or himself.

'As an additional measure of security,' Francesco added to Elena. 'It's alright, Andrea. You might as well know that Elena is not a secretary. She is here as an undercover investigator.' Francesco had caught the quizzical expression on the scientist's face as they broached matters of a possible security breach. Andrea looked at Elena with a slightly disbelieving look in his eyes. In the end he just went: 'Ahh!' as if he had known beforehand that there had been something about her that did not add up.

'It was such a small thing,' said Andrea. 'But one of the suits had been hung up hurriedly and had fallen on to the floor. It wasn't like that before lunchtime, I could swear to it.'

'Did you authorise anyone to go in there, Francesco?' asked Leonardo, hoping that the answer would be in the affirmative. But Francesco shook his head. 'Nobody asked me,' he said quietly.

Elena excused herself and left them to discuss the significance of this event. She could catch up on developments later. She needed the toilet – and an after lunch coffee. There was a familiar figure sitting at one of the metal tables. It was Mariastella Russo. She was on her mobile phone talking in an urgent, anxious whisper with her hand cupped around the mouth-piece of the phone.

'No, I can't. No, I won't do it. I don't want to go on like this,' Elena heard her say. She went to buy two coffees and deliberately sat down at the same table, her most engaging smile directed at Mariastella. With an embarrassed and frightened grin on her face, Mariastella brought the conversation to a rapid close with words: *A dopo! C'è una collega!'*

'I'm sorry, Stella. I didn't realise you were on the phone,' lied Elena smoothly. 'Trouble?' she asked in a sympathetic tone. 'You look a little flustered.'

'My boyfriend – he's becoming very demanding of late,' said Stella simply. Elena understood immediately that this was a severe understatement of the truth.

'You're not from Puglia, are you, Stella?' continued Elena in a conversational manner as she pushed the second cup of coffee across the table towards Stella. She picked up the cup and swallowed the liquid in two gulps, not bothering to add the sugar. She grimaced at the bitterness of the drink.

'No, I'm from a village outside Bologna, in the distant North. I don't really have any friends down here. It's been very hard.'

'I would like to be your friend, Stella,' said Elena simply, with her heart in her mouth at the gamble she had just taken. 'I have a feeling that we would get on well together.'

Elena had correctly concluded that Stella was in sore need of a kindred spirit, a companion whom she could talk to outside working hours. The look of relief on Mariastella's face was unmistakable. The two women had exchanged phone numbers and, like two new schoolgirl buddies, had tried ringing one and other to make sure the numbers were correct. Stella promised to phone her later on that evening and said that she should get back to work. 'I really love this place,' she confided to Elena. 'It has been the only thing that has enabled me to endure my homesickness – until I met you, that is,' she added plaintively.

Elena remained sitting at the table - after Stella had returned to her laboratory. Elena was fingering her coffee cup in deep meditation. She was pleased on a social level that she had begun to build the bridge of friendship with this young woman whom she genuinely liked. But one thing puzzled and intrigued her. Why, oh why, had Stella phoned her boyfriend and drunk her coffee whilst still wearing her latex gloves?

7: Out of the Mouth of Babes ...

Elena, still in investigative mood, decided there was one more useful avenue to explore that day, before she left to pick up Anna and Riccardo from school. She went back to the desk in the main office, where she was studiously ignored by Livia Marchetti but smiled at in a conspiratorial manner by the other two occupants of the room. She sat and thought carefully about how she should approach the notorious lady journalist, Costanza De Santis, who had made such a disconcerting appearance at the *Hotel Europa* on the day Francesco had given his famous presentation. What Elena wanted from the journalist was some kind of hint as to who had tipped her off about the lack of security measures within the science faculty. She would hardly have risked such a public confrontation on the basis of a mere hunch, Elena argued. She debated with herself as to whether she should make this phone call within earshot of Livia Marchetti and company but decided that, despite the background noise, it would be safer to go and find a public telephone kiosk; there were two – almost redundant - just outside the main entrance, she had noticed. Yes, that would be a sensible move, she considered.

With some trepidation, she rang up the local offices of the newspaper, *Il Mezzogiorno,* and asked to be put through to the desk of the lady journalist in question.

'May I tell her who is calling?' asked the receptionist.

Elena-Rosaria had anticipated being asked this question. She hesitated for a fraction of a second before replying: 'Well, it is a bit delicate. Could you tell her that it is to do with the mole in the science faculty at the University? I have some further information for her.' Elena crossed her fingers that the journalist was there. After a short delay, she heard a strident female voice on the other end of the line.

'*Sì?*' said the voice in a peremptory manner.

'I am the person who phoned you before about the leaking of information from Legano University's science...'

Elena was stopped short by a burst of harsh laughter.

'Please do not waste my time or take me for a fool, *signorina!*'

'No, you're right, *Signora De Santis – Costanza.* I should not have underestimated you.'

'No, you should not, *signorina.* Now will you give me your name and tell me why you are really phoning me?'

'May we meet up tomorrow morning, *Signora* Costanza? I really do have some very specific information that I believe the public ought to know about. I would really rather not tell you anything over the phone. I'm sure you understand,' said Elena in her most conspiratorial voice. 'I was there at the conference at the *Hotel Europa,*' she added as a subtle hint as to the authenticity of her identity.

It was enough to catch the lady journalist's thirst for scandal. A time and a bar near the newspaper's offices were agreed. Elena assured the journalist that she would have no difficulty recognising her the following morning. The flattering implication that Costanza was such a celebrity in the public eye was sufficient to remove any remaining shadow of doubt from the journalist's mind.

Changing her tone of voice to something between flattery and intrigue, Elena asked Costanza how she had picked up on the fact that the caller was not the same person that had contacted her before. There followed the same brief outburst of harsh laughter.

'Well, *signorina,* apart from the first caller's very pronounced Bologna accent, the person I spoke to was fairly obviously a young man!'

'Really, *signora!* That does surprise me! I'll tell you why tomorrow morning. *Arrivederla, signora e grazie mille.'* And Elena hung up. She waited outside the kiosk for a while longer and was gratified to hear the phone ringing, unanswered, for twenty seconds or more. Elena was very glad that she had not telephoned from her own office.

Elena looked at her watch. It was time to go and pick up the children. She walked thoughtfully towards her car, digesting the information that she had gleaned. She was unsure whether it confirmed her suspicions or detracted from them. Time would tell, no doubt.

As soon as she got into her own car, she thought of herself quite instinctively as Rosaria again, the mother of two young children and lifelong partner to 'her' Englishman.

Nevertheless, the latex gloves bothered her all the way to the children's school. She had to shelve her speculative thoughts while she listened to an enthusiastic catalogue of all that Anna and Riccardo had done – plus the usual accounts of how the teachers were always nagging the other children for being too noisy or too lazy.

'Only the *other* children, I suppose. Never you two!' teased Rosaria.

'No, *mamma,* never me! *My* teacher tells me to slow down to give the others a chance to catch up,' declared Anna.

'She's such a show off and a teacher's pet!' chipped in Riccardo happily. 'Her teacher wants to promote her up one class just so she can become bottom of the year above!' From the mouth of a boy who had just turned seven, it was really quite a witty comment. Even the intended victim, his sister, found the assumption behind the words flatteringly amusing.

'How would you feel about having a special dinner guest tomorrow?' asked Rosaria.

'It depends who it is,' said Riccardo, who tended to consider that he got less to eat when other people came round to share their food.

'Is it a man or a woman, *mamma?*' Anna wanted to know.

'It's a man. He's called Francesco. He wants to show you another DVD and he is looking forward to meeting you.'

'Has he got a funny moustache, *mamma?*'

'That's right, Riccardo. You've guessed!'

There was an enthusiastic outbreak of approval from the back seat at the news that their hero was going to come and see them in their house.

'But first of all, we have to ask your father.'

'Oh, *papà* won't mind,' declared Anna. 'He likes strange people coming to dinner.'

'But it's polite to ask first, Anna. Isn't that so, *mamma?*'

'*Bravo* Riccardo! So let me ask your father first – *d'accordo?*'

'*D'accordo!*' they chorused.

Just as Rosaria suspected would happen, Anna and Riccardo rushed to greet their father as soon as they heard his car turn into the stony drive in front of the house. He was accosted by two excited children as soon as he stepped out of the car. After the usual hug, they both enthusiastically informed Adam that the scientist with the funny moustache was coming to dinner the following evening.

'Oh really? We had better not give him minestrone soup then, in case the bits get stuck in his whiskers!' said Adam. The comment got an obliging laugh. He went indoors, kissed Rosaria and gave her a hug.

'I'm sorry Adam. I *was* going to ask you first, I promise.'

'Our two little bearers of good news are obviously pleased! It should be interesting, Rosy. It never takes you long to break the ice whenever you meet new people. It's admirable, in fact,' complimented Adam.

'I felt sorry for him, Adam.' Rosaria went on to explain about Francesco's separation from his wife and daughters. Adam found it amusing that the rejected husband was concerned about having to drive an old FIAT Tipo.

'Just like that Sicilian detective, *Montalbano!*' he commented.

'That's just what I said to him!' laughed Rosaria. 'The idea didn't seem to make him feel any better though.'

'I wonder if he had his costly fling with one of the scientists who work under him,' commented Adam wryly. The look on Rosaria's face told him that this thought had not occurred to her. The memory of little things she had noticed during that long day came back to her. She went up to Adam and hugged him again with a look of admiration in her eyes.

'Most extra-marital affairs usually happen in the workplace,' he added. 'Or so I am told, Rosy...' he added rapidly on seeing the accusatory expression of suspicion on her face. He considered risking an additional ironic comment to the effect that it could not apply to them since they were not married, but he thought better of it. Trust was re-established with a warm kiss on her mouth before they went about their usual routine of cooking, eating, homework, television and, eventually, the children's bedtime – this final ritual inevitably being shared by both of them.

While Adam was drying his son's hair after his shower, Riccardo had pretended to be a tiger, or some such animal. He was performing a mock claw-scratching gesture in front of his father's face. Adam took one look and went to fetch the nail scissors from the bathroom cabinet. Riccardo instantly regretted his game since he hated the ritual of sitting still for the tedious two minutes that it took to have finger and toe nails trimmed. Adam went to carry out the same check on Anna's nails but found to his surprise that her finger nails were bitten down to the quick. He pointed this out to Rosaria. *Mamma* was full of concern and asked if she was worried about something at school. Anna looked a bit sheepish but decided to come clean. Just like her mother, she tended to bottle up her inner feelings for days on end before revealing what was troubling her.

'I get teased at school by some of my classmates,' she confessed in a subdued little voice.

'But what do they tease you about, *amore mio?'* asked Rosy, visibly concerned.

'It's only two or three of the girls,' said Anna. 'They make fun of me being the teacher's pet and...' She looked embarrassed in her father's direction and burst into tears.

'Ti voglio bene, papa...!' she said between sobs.

Rosaria comforted her until she had stopped crying a few seconds later, feeling better that she had let out her pent up emotions. She explained that the girls kept teasing her about her dad really being her granddad.

'But Anna, *tesoro mio*,' said Adam kindly, kneeling down to be on her level. 'I don't want you to bite your lovely fingers off because of a silly thing like that!'

In a rare display of true affection for her father, she ran up to him and put her arms round his neck. Riccardo had remained silent for a surprisingly long time for him, quietly impressed by his big sister's sudden display of emotional vulnerability.

'Yes, Anna,' he piped up. 'Please don't bite your fingernails anymore, or else we shall have to make you wear rubber gloves.'

Nobody could understand why Rosaria had a huge smile on her face at that juncture. She was looking in awe at her younger child, amazed how children often inadvertently reveal truths that adults have failed to register.

'Why are you hugging *me, mamma?*' asked Riccardo. 'It's Anna who needs hugging at the moment, isn't it? I'm fine!'

'No bedtime story tonight, *ragazzi*,' stated Rosaria to her family. 'I'll tell all of you about my day at university instead.' Adam was as puzzled and intrigued as the children by his partner's reaction to Riccardo's innocent comment. After she had got to the bit about Stella wearing her surgical gloves while she had been drinking her coffee and talking furtively to her *fidanzato* on the phone, all became clear to them – well, almost clear.

When the children had finally settled down to sleep, it was past ten o'clock. Adam and Rosaria were sitting next to each other on the long sofa in their sitting room. Rosaria put her head on Adam's shoulder.

'You remember I told you about giving one of the other girls, Giovanna Binetto, a lift home, don't you Adam? I remembered what it was she said just before I drove off. She wouldn't tell me the name of the person she suspected of being our *talpa*. But she said something about this person being 'nail-bitingly anxious'. As soon as Riccardo came out with that comment to Anna, it all fell into place.'

'Now I understand what you are getting at, Rosy. Thank God for our children's inadvertent perceptions!'

'It also confirmed what I had been thinking about this girl, Stella. I knew there was something serious troubling her.'

'So you've probably solved the mystery after only a couple of days,' said Adam hopefully.

'I hope so. But the real problem is how to deal with what we have just discovered, Adam.' After a moment's thought, she added: 'That's a point. Our Stella said she would phone me this evening. I wonder if she will?'

Stella's call to Rosaria was not absolutely on cue, but happened while Adam and Rosaria were discussing what they would cook for Francesco's visit the following evening. Rosaria's mobile device rang suddenly. The sound startled them both. 'It's *her!*' mouthed Rosaria. Adam made a gesture of cupping his hand round an ear, so she put the device on loudspeaker mode before answering the call.

'Buonasera Elena. I hope I'm not disturbing you.'

'No, Stella. You aren't disturbing me at all. I was hoping you would call me.'

It struck Adam immediately that Stella's crystal clear voice was charged with tension.

'I would have called you earlier but my fidanzato has been on the phone for the past half an hour.'

'Still putting pressure on you, is he Stella? You sound very nervous,' commented Rosaria, choosing her words carefully.

She did not want to alert Stella that she suspected anything other than simple boyfriend problems.

'I told him that I didn't want to go along with his...I mean, I told him I didn't want to see him anymore, Elena.'

'And how did he react to that, Stella? I suppose he became very angry, didn't he?'

'No, Elena,' she said close to tears. *'That's just the problem. He didn't get angry at all. He simply refused to accept that I was being serious. He was kind and considerate and told me I didn't really mean what I was saying. He's going to come down from Bologna on Thursday night. So he'll be here on Friday. He says he's got something special to show me. Elena, I'm scared. I know that when I see him, he'll try to persuade me to carry on with...'* There was a significant pause as she realised she was on the point of revealing more than she intended in her pent up emotional state.

Elena did not wish to get into this sensitive area over the telephone, so she said in a consoling voice:

'Don't be anxious, Stella. He can't do anything to you tonight. We'll meet up first thing tomorrow morning, I promise. I'm on your side – don't forget that.'

'Va bene, Elena. Grazie. Ci vediamo domani. Scusami...'

It was plain from her voice that she wanted to go on talking but Rosaria knew that any further discussion would be counter-productive. So she added a few more words of consolation before she brought the conversation gently to a conclusion.

'There Adam – it couldn't be clearer, could it?'

'No, Rosy. It was very clear. Twice she was on the verge of telling us more than she intended to say.'

There was a long, thoughtful silence before they both decided to take the matter to the bedroom. They went upstairs and looked at their two children fast asleep in the bedroom which they still shared. Years ago, when Adam had first arrived in Puglia, he used to make a mental list of the 'cultural differences' that existed between this country and his now long-abandoned, middle-class English life and assumptions. One of the many differences that had struck him forcibly during his English speaking sessions with his university students was that many of them still shared a bedroom with brothers and sisters well into their technically 'adult' life whenever they went back home at weekends. His oft repeated question: 'Wouldn't you rather have a room to yourself?' left his students perplexed. It was obvious that many of them derived comfort from the fact that they were not sleeping on their own. There is no native word for 'privacy' in the Italian language – they use the English word, albeit pronounced the American way, Adam would observe on many occasions.

Rosaria often teased Adam about his practice of asking his students questions about their personal lives. His habitual response was that the educational necessity of encouraging students to speak English gave him licence to ask them about a host of semi-personal matters concerning the way they lived and thought. Thus the subjects of religion, politics and even personal relationships, usually taboo in their own language because of the furore of disagreement that would ensue, could quite safely be broached in a foreign language.

At that particular moment, he was looking at Anna sleeping like an angel. But inside her complicated nine-year-old mind, there was a place for anxious thoughts just as in any other human soul. He kissed them both gently on the forehead and left them, hand-in-hand with Rosaria, to their happy state of oblivion.

In bed, lying close to each other, Rosaria began talking about Stella.

'At least I am happy about one thing,' Rosy was saying. Adam knew what she was going to say in advance because he had already worked out the one important discovery that they had made as a result of Stella's tensed up phone call. Instead of spoiling her moment of insight, he said simply: 'Go on Rosy.'

'We know now that Stella is not filching secrets from her workplace out of selfish motives. She is under severe pressure from this...boyfriend. She is obviously scared of him, under some kind of spell...'

'Yes, you are right,' said Adam. 'I was thinking along the same lines.'

He went on talking quietly about the conclusions that he had come to. As had so often happened in their life together, he asked Rosy a question in the darkened room but got no response. She had fallen asleep within seconds. They had not even decided what they would cook for dinner the following evening. 'Ah well,' thought Adam, 'I'll just have to ask the children what they want to eat tomorrow during breakfast time.'

* * *

Breakfast the following morning was the usual clamorous, hurried affair during which intelligent conversation was replaced by competitive disputes as to what constituted a fair dosage of the favourite cereal of the day, the clattering of spoons scraping round bowls and the crunching of jaws dealing with pieces of toast and jam. Adam only had coffee. His pivotal question about the evening meal seemed so remote to Anna and Riccardo that, at first, he had difficulty in getting a meaningful reply.

'Antipasti,' said Anna between mouthfuls, 'like we had last time.'

'Fusilli with sausage sauce,' stated Riccardo, 'but without porcini mushrooms this time – *che schifo!*'

'*Sì papà,*' added Anna. 'I'm quite sure Francesco won't like his pasta with bits of mushroom in it!'

'And what makes you so sure of that, Anna?' asked Adam, curious to know how she would justify her assertion.

'Well, he spends all his time messing around with tiny particles so I would think he will feel more relaxed with chunky bits of sausage!'

Anna was genuinely surprised and very gratified to find that the rest of her family burst into spontaneous laughter and applause. Had she really said something clever? It made her feel much better about facing the day at school.

'Followed by chicken pieces cooked in breadcrumbs,' stated Riccardo, doubting whether anyone would bother to contradict him at this stage. 'And then lemon *sorbetto.*'

Thus, the evening meal was decided. Anna and Riccardo looked from parent to parent – a wordless, ritual interrogative to discover which one was doing the school run that day.

'I'll take you this morning,' stated Rosaria decisively. 'We're going early this morning.' Anna gave a sort of apologetic shrug in her father's direction and ran off to clean her teeth and pick up her pink school satchel. Both children sensed that *mamma* was on the warpath this morning after the previous evening's revelations.

'Watch out someone!' said Riccardo as if to himself, big brown eyes alive with mischief. '*Mamma* means business.'

'You won't do anything to embarrass me, will you *mamma?*' asked Anna anxiously.

'I can't promise *tesoro mio.* But it would be wrong of me to do nothing about it.'

Anna shrugged resignedly. All three of them knew that once Rosaria was faced with a challenge, nothing short of divine intervention would deter her from seeking a solution to whatever problem it was.

'It's not really all that serious, *mamma.* I've got friends as well you know.'

'Look at your poor finger nails, Anna. I don't call that *nothing serious,* do you?'

When they arrived at the school gate, there was hardly anyone else there. As more and more parents arrived and deposited their offspring at the school gate, which was manned by a severe, middle-aged woman teacher, Rosaria let Riccardo run off into the school yard to join his friends. To Anna's dismay, Rosaria walked through the school gate holding her firmly by the hand.

'You can't come in with your child, *signora,*' barked the teacher on gate duty. Rosaria gave her one withering look and replied: 'This is a public, state-owned establishment, *signora.* I have every right to be here.' Anna cringed inwardly. 'How does *mamma* manage to find it easy to be so brave?' she wondered. After a few brief minutes, Rosaria felt Anna's hand tighten involuntarily in hers at the appearance of a slightly overweight girl with untidy hair, who had just been released through the gate by a harassed looking woman not much taller than her daughter.

'What's her name, Anna?' asked Rosaria in an urgent whisper.

'Sofia,' replied Anna resignedly.

'She doesn't deserve such a pretty name,' muttered her mother walking smartly over to intercept the plain-looking girl. Like all bullies, the girl was easily scared. She looked desperately around for help. On finding no-one, she was forced to stand in awe of this forthright woman, who launched into a quiet tirade of words. Sofia looked cowed. She enjoyed a brief second's hope when the severe teacher on guard at the gate came over to intervene.

'*Signora...?*'

'Miccoli,' stated Rosaria.

'I will not have you intimidating pupils in this manner. You either leave or I shall call the head teacher.'

'I should be very grateful if you did just that, *signora* – unless, of course, it is the practice in this school to condone bullying.'

The harridan walked away, deflated, her repertoire of counter-arguments exhausted. 'You can go now, Sofia,' said Rosaria. 'But remember what I have just told you.' Sofia ran off looking suitably chastised.

Rosaria walked back towards where Anna was standing looking at her mother with a mixture of reproach and admiration. Rosaria hugged her daughter and sent her on her way.

'If you have *any* trouble from Sofia, be sure to tell me, *tesoro.*'

'*Grazie mamma,*' said Anna under her breath and ran off.

Outside the school gate, Sofia's mother had been standing looking on in bewilderment at the scene. Rosaria stopped and had a quiet conversation with the woman. What Rosaria learnt revealed what she had suspected to be the case; Sofia's father worked in Milan and hardly ever came home; a simple case of envy, maybe? She would try to explain this to Anna at some stage.

Now, Rosaria would have to drive quickly to the university. She wanted to be sure that she was already there to greet Stella. Rosaria was feeling tense about this encounter. It would undoubtedly be very painful for Stella. On the way, she remembered belatedly that she had made an appointment to meet the lady journalist, Costanza De Santis. Never mind! It would not do the woman any harm to be stood up for once. Furthermore, Elena had already found out what she had wanted to know. Costanza would not be able to trace the person who had called her the previous day. No, it was more important to reach the university in Monteleone and catch Mariastella as soon as she arrived. Elena parked her car and walked towards the building. The morning sunshine already felt uncomfortably hot on her face. She was not altogether surprised to find that Stella was already hovering nervously near the entrance.

'Oh, Elena!' she began. 'I'm so glad you're here. I haven't slept all night. I have something so awful to confess to you and I know you are all going to hate me when you find out how stupid I have been.'

'Stella, please relax. You will worry yourself to death. I know what you've done – perhaps not in detail but certainly in essence. Come on! We'll sit down somewhere quiet so you can tell me all about it.'

'But Elena…You cannot possibly know…'

But it was obvious from 'Elena's' self-assured manner that she *did* know. Stella looked at her companion with an immense sense of gratitude and relief.

'There's a little garden beyond the car park,' said Elena. 'Let's go and sit in the shade and you can tell me how you got yourself into this mess.'

Before they had taken a step away from the main entrance, Stella's mobile phone rang.

'It's him!' she said, obviously petrified.

'Give me the phone, Stella,' ordered Elena-Rosaria. She took one look at the name on the screen. 'Dario? Is that his name?'

Stella nodded. Rosaria had to react quickly as it was evident that Stella was not in a fit state to think clearly.

'Answer it, Stella,' Rosaria insisted. 'He must not be suspicious that anything has changed. But tell him you're with colleagues and you can't talk freely. Keep it very brief.'

It was not a very convincing performance but it would give them time to work out what steps would need to be taken. As they started walking away from the building, they met Giovanna Binetto arriving for work.

'Buongiorno Stella, Elena,' she said with a brief smile. But her eyes glowed with admiration, conveying a message which clearly said: 'Well done, Elena! *Bravissima!'*

8: La Talpa

'I don't know where to begin, Elena,' said Stella shamefacedly after they had sat down side by side in the shade of a gnarled old olive tree that pre-dated its modern surroundings by more than four centuries. Somebody in the dim and distant past had thoughtfully provided a rudimentary stone bench which was just about wide enough to seat the two women. Stella was gripping her knees tightly with her un-gloved hands. Rosaria noticed that her nails were indeed bitten right down – just as Anna's had been.

'How did you know it was *me* who...?' began Stella haltingly. 'I mean, I'm so relieved that someone has stopped this nightmare I've been living but...'

Was it perhaps that the glamorous Stella had persuaded herself that the role she had been playing had been totally convincing? Was there just a hint of self-delusion and pride at work here? Rosaria decided that it was not the moment to analyse Stella's undoubtedly complex psychological make-up. She had just decided that she would shatter any self-congratulatory notions that Stella might be harbouring about her conduct since her appointment when Stella herself revealed a level of self-awareness which belied any negative impression that she might have given.

'*O mio Dio!* I've just realised how terrible that must have sounded, Elena. I'm so sorry! You must think I'm some sort of drama queen whose performance has not measured up to her own expectations. I didn't mean it to sound like that at all. It's just that I've been living out this ghastly pretence so long and so intensely that I had almost convinced myself it was reality. Please ignore everything I just said, Elena.'

At least the ice had been broken, thought Elena-Rosaria.

'It was the latex gloves that gave you away, Stella,' she contented herself by saying enigmatically. Stella smiled without understanding the significance of the comment. Not for the first time in her working life, Rosaria was tempted to abandon her pseudonym and tell Stella that her real name was Rosaria – not only because she liked Stella but also because it seemed so important to gain her complete trust. She occasionally felt that using a false name smacked of deceit rather than self-protection. But some instinct warned her that events might still take an unexpected, or even sinister, turn. She resisted the temptation to abandon her professional 'disguise'.

'Tell me first of all about this boyfriend of yours – Dario,' began Elena back in her business frame of mind. 'He's from Bologna too, I assume.' It was a shot in the dark but Elena was working on the assumption that he would hail from the same region of Italy as Stella herself. And then, there had been the telephone call to Costanza, the journalist, from a 'young man with a Bologna accent'. If Giovanna Binetto's theory was correct that the leaking of supposedly vital information concerning the security in the stem cell division had been a red herring to cover up the real purpose of the scheme, then this Dario was a prime suspect.

Stella looked at her sympathetic inquisitor with surprise and a renewed sense that this woman already knew all about her hidden life as the Judas in the camp. However, Stella's answer almost immediately muddied the waters again in a disconcerting way.

'Yes, Dario is from Bologna,' Stella confirmed, 'although I am not sure how you knew that, Elena.'

'Elena' merely waved a dismissive hand in the air as if to imply that the deduction was obvious. She did not wish to interrupt the flow of Stella's revelations.

'But I met Dario quite by accident down here in Legano,' she added almost inconsequentially. Rosaria's internal ear pricked up immediately. This *was* an unexpected piece of information.

'Oh really, Stella?' she said, wishing to sound only mildly curious. 'How *did* you meet him then?'

'I was outside my flat in *Via Cairoli.* I had just been to the supermarket and was carrying two fully-laden plastic bags with my provisions for the week – I hate food shopping, Elena, and I try to get it done all in one go.'

Rosaria smiled encouragingly.

'Well, I was trying to find the key to open the front door and had one of the plastic bags wedged between my legs to stop it tipping over, when this guy who was passing by stopped and asked me if I needed a hand.'

'Go on Stella,' encouraged Rosaria.

'Well, he was well-spoken, handsome I thought and, wonder of wonders, he spoke with a Bolognese accent. He offered to carry the bags up to my flat. He was friendly – even charming. He didn't seem like the typical man from down here – you know, Elena, the type of man who undresses you with his eyes in the first minute of acquaintance. Well, it all kind of stemmed from that moment, I suppose.'

'Just one question, Stella; how long had you been down here before you met this man – I assume we are talking about Dario.'

Stella nodded and thought about the question before replying. 'I don't remember exactly. I had been feeling so alone and homesick down here. I suppose it was about a month, maybe five weeks.'

'And before you met Dario...?' asked Rosaria quietly. 'I know it's none of my business but...' Rosaria allowed her voice to trail off apologetically. She had the satisfaction of seeing Stella blush.

'It was nothing really. Just a passing thing,' she muttered. 'I'm dreadful about sex, Elena. I don't know why I am like I am, but I seem to need it...well, often.'

Rosaria permitted herself a conspiratorial smile. 'Don't worry, Stella. I know exactly what you mean!' Elena-Rosaria wanted to ask Stella if it had been with someone from the university department. But she realised that this was merely to satisfy her own curiosity. It had little or nothing to do with subsequent events, she was quite certain.

'At first, our relationship seemed perfect in every way,' continued Stella. 'He told me he was a representative for the pharmaceutical company, Menarini – you've heard of it, of course.' Elena-Rosaria nodded, encouraging her to continue. 'He told me he's responsible for sales in Puglia and Molise and that he had to come to Legano every week or so. We started a relationship after his second visit. He was older than me – about thirty-one, I believe. I prefer older men, for sex, I mean. They know what they are doing...' She tailed off in embarrassment when she saw that Rosaria was smiling secretly.

'Carry on, Stella. I'm with you all the way,' said Rosaria without enlightening her.

'Well, I began to spend my whole life just waiting for him to come back to Legano. It was pathetic... *I* was pathetic, Elena. I was becoming dependent on him – for company, conversation and above all, sex. It was like a concoction of drugs that I had to take every week. He could see that I needed him mentally, emotionally, physically... Yet, he never took advantage of me in the early days. He was an ideal boyfriend, or so I thought.'

'But Stella, excuse me interrupting you. Didn't it ever occur to you that your first meeting with him – with your shopping bags, outside your own apartment in a backstreet of Legano – was just a little bit too good to be true? Didn't you think it was stretching good fortune and coincidence too far?' Rosaria had spoken in a kindly voice without the slightest hint of criticism.

Stella considered this aspect of her relationship as if for the first time.

'I suppose so,' she said after due thought. 'Oh, Elena, you must think I am so stupid and naïve!'

Rosaria laid a hand on Stella's bare arm. Stella started suddenly as she had done the day before, showing how tensed up she still was.

'Here I am with a first class degree in particle physics and I can't even think straight when it comes to basic common sense. What must you think of me, Elena?'

'It's alright, Stella. You mustn't be so hard on yourself. Your eyes are open now, aren't they? That's what is important from now on.'

Stella was looking thoughtfully at some spot on the ground in front of her, seemingly fascinated by the random patterns created by the dried up olives and the silvery-green leaves at her feet. She was unconsciously rearranging them with the tip of her sandals as if she was manoeuvring nano-sized structures in the laboratory.

'Forgive me for still being blind, Elena, but why does the way I met Dario seem important to you? It doesn't change how irresponsibly stupid I've been, does it?'

'Dear Stella, I haven't been quite straight with you,' began Rosaria. She went on to enlighten Stella as to her true role in the department. Stella merely nodded, unsurprised by what she had learnt.

'You never really came across as a secretary replacing someone on maternity leave,' she added simply.

Once again, Rosaria had to stop herself revealing her true name to this girl who, she had to remind herself, had fallen victim to her own emotional vulnerability whilst running the risk of taking a whole scientific research faculty down with her. Rosaria was sure that nothing Stella had done was motivated by calculated self-interest but she, Rosaria, needed to remain detached for the time being.

'In answer to your question, Stella, I think the way you met Dario does have a far greater significance than you realise. It changes the whole focus of the affair in point of fact.' Rosaria paused to let her words sink in before continuing.

'In the first place, I think you can safely dismiss the idea that your meeting Dario was accidental. I'm sure you will agree with *that* in the light of what he tried to get you to do – but more of that in a minute. No, this is the scary aspect of it - if Dario knew where to find you, it was because someone here in Legano told him, and that implies it is somebody at the university who is behind the conspiracy. How did you find your apartment, Stella? Was it through an estate agent?'

Stella shook her head silently. 'No, it was the personnel department at the university,' she answered in a hushed voice. 'But you surely don't suspect that it's one of our team of scientists who...?'

Rosaria sighed audibly. She had felt so elated that she had managed to identify Stella as the immediate culprit that the deeper implications which lay behind the plot to steal the university's scientific secrets had not occurred to her.

'No, I don't think it is anyone from the department, Stella,' Rosaria said finally. 'But this means that there is some shadowy figure in the background who has been manipulating you for their own ends; somebody who is known to Dario, probably...but certainly a man – or a woman – who is familiar with the workings of the University.' Her voice trailed off as she realised that there was a long way to go before the roots of this conspiracy would be unearthed.

'Stella,' she said more abruptly than she had intended. 'I want you to give me a contact number for Dario before we go any further. He is the only lead we have got for now. Please show me the number on your phone.'

Rosaria could see the resistance building up by the expression on Stella's face.

'Come on Stella, *please!* You have simply got to put all this behind you if you want to have any chance at all of keeping your post at this university – or anywhere else for that matter,' she added darkly.

That was sufficient to persuade Stella. She showed Rosaria her contact number for Dario, which she immediately transferred to her own phone.

'What's Dario's surname, Stella?' she asked.

Stella was looking very sheepish and kept her head lowered.

'Don't tell me! You never asked him! Am I right?'

The briefest of nods from Stella, her face still lowered as she looked at the ground beneath her feet, confirmed what Rosaria had suspected. There was nothing to be gained by criticising the girl – she would leave that to Leonardo. Instead, she put a comforting arm round Stella's shoulders and hugged her. This simple gesture was enough to open up the flood gates of emotion. Stella's shoulders began shaking as the tears ran down her cheeks and fell softly on the leaf-strewn ground at her feet. Stella knew from that moment that her relationship with Dario was over. She would have to face once again the emotional and sexual void that his absence would create. She began to cry out loud in the little hidden olive grove which provided her with a fleeting refuge from the grim reality which awaited her in the real world. Rosaria waited patiently until the tears subsided before she began to probe a little deeper.

'When did you realise that he was interested in what you were doing at the university, Stella?'

'Oh, he was very patient. We had lengthy conversations about what the Legano team was doing. He seemed genuinely interested, especially in the stem cell research projects – just generalities at first. We had long discussions as to how secretive it all was, how he believed that such knowledge should be in the public domain. He was very persuasive.'

'And he was a good lover, I presume,' said Rosaria almost inaudibly. Stella blushed and looked at her companion, smiling at the memories of the total sexual abandon that she had indulged in so recently. Rosaria was struck anew by the beauty of her face, her shapely, pouting mouth thrust forward by the perfect symmetry of her bone structure, wide open eyes full of the sensual passion that drove her. Yet there was an aura of innocence about her face as a whole. It was so difficult to realise that this self-same face concealed a highly intelligent scientific brain. A dangerous concoction, Rosaria reckoned.

'It was after one of his particularly vigorous fucks one evening that he must have reckoned I was softened up enough for him to let me in on 'a brilliant idea' he had just dreamed up.' At first, Rosaria had been shocked by Stella's unexpectedly vulgar turn of phrase, until she realised it was her way of putting her own gullibility into perspective. Her narrative came to a complete standstill as a series of conflicting emotions crossed her face. Rosaria was on the point of prompting her to start talking again but, after a pause that went on for a long time, Stella began speaking of her own accord.

'He never said in so many words that he would leave me if I didn't go along with his scheme, but he knew I was hooked by then. He let me understand plainly how important his idea was to 'some people' that he knew,' Stella said bitterly. 'Oh Elena, I so did not want to lose him that I agreed to give it a trial run – on the understanding that I would stop if my job was at risk.'

'Go on Stella,' encouraged Rosaria.

'It was his idea to film the stem cell research experiments to begin with. He gave me a kind of advanced memory stick device that could be inserted into the microscope and record what was going on. It was easy to disguise what was going on. I inserted a tiny filter on the camera – so to all intents and purposes, it appeared that the stem cell structures had vanished. It meant I could film for a bit longer without anyone guessing what was happening.'

'A very intelligent colleague of yours called Giovanna Binetto had a shrewd idea that the disappearing stem cells were just a decoy to conceal the real purpose of this conspiracy. Was she right?' asked Rosaria.

Stella looked genuinely shocked at the idea that another colleague had come so close to the truth.

'Not at first, Elena. But after a time, that was the plan...*his* plan. He began to want me to steal the other projects we are engaged in. He said the disappearing stem cells trick would distract everyone from what I was doing.'

'Was it Dario who phoned that lady journalist, do you know?'

Stella looked bewildered. She had obviously not made the connection with the incident at the conference. Elena-Rosaria changed tack.

'Is there a particular project that Dario is interested in, Stella?'

Stella was beginning to look very uncomfortable again.

Dai! Forza, Mariastella! You can't hold back now.'

'He wants to know about everything we are doing, Elena. But the ultimate prize – the project he wants to winkle out of me at the moment – is the Encryption Machine.'

'The *what?*' exclaimed Rosaria suspecting she would soon be out of her depth yet again.

'It's in the Clean Room, Elena. It's based on the quantum notion of one photon of a particular value only being able to occupy a unique state...'

Rosaria held up her hands in surrender.

'You had better save up the technical stuff for when you speak to Leonardo, *mia cara* Stella. By the way, I presume it *was* you who went into the Clean Room yesterday lunchtime?'

Stella nodded, looking guilty. A cloud passed over her features and the tears began to gather again as she realised she was about to be exposed for what she was before her *capo* – a traitor and a deceiver.

'I know that Dario has been using me. I know how stupid I've been,' she sobbed. 'But I just want *you* to know for the record that, over the last few weeks, I've not really been cooperating with him. I just couldn't continue with the deceit any longer. So I've been feeding him with incomplete information and with false algorithms. Luckily, Dario is no physicist. Nothing that I've given him is of any use to anyone...'

'Do you *know* who he is passing all this information on to, Stella?'

She shook her head. 'He's very vague and secretive about that side of things. But that's why I'm so afraid of his next visit - somebody is bound to have twigged by now that I've been feeding them incomplete information about everything...' Stella's voice trailed off again.

'Come on, Stella. It's time you got all this out in the open with somebody who will understand the implications of what you have done. I haven't a clue what an algorithm is! You are a very bright person Stella – and far too attractive to waste your life on a man who is using you for his own ends.'

'What a pity I am so stupid in every other way!' she said, realising the enormity of what she had done now that she would be forced to reveal to Leonard the full extent of her duplicity.

'I know it is of little concern to me, Stella. But how did you pass the information on to Dario?' asked Rosaria.

'Usually on a USB device,' admitted Stella sheepishly. 'Otherwise in words and mathematical symbols on a piece of paper in a brown envelope,' she added. 'Towards the end, the information I gave them was increasingly sketchy – if not downright meaningless. I preferred not to think about what happened after it had fallen into Dario's hands.'

'Out of curiosity, Stella, why did you go to Francesco's presentation at the *Hotel Europa?*'

Rosaria noticed the slight blush again. 'It was Francesco's idea, Elena. I think he wanted to impress me,' she said with a touch of irony. Rosaria did not comment but linked her arm through Stella's as if they were old school buddies and led her resolutely in the direction of Leonardo's office. 'When you've finished, Stella, we must talk about where you are going to live. After tomorrow, we must find you a place where you can hide from Dario when he comes down to Legano. You'll no longer be safe where you are now.'

'*Grazie* Elena. Thank you for saving my life!' said Stella and gave Rosaria a warm, sisterly hug.

'*In bocca al lupo!*' said 'Elena' as they arrived at Leonardo's office. 'Stella has something very important to tell you, Leonardo.'

The look of puzzlement on his face told Rosaria that, despite his illustrious nickname, he had no inkling as to why Stella was there.

'Thank you, Rosaria...I mean Elena,' stammered Leonardo trying to cover up his blunder. Stella seemed too nervous to have attached any significance to his slip of the tongue. She had a look of intense appeal on her face as if she was willing her saviour to stay. Rosaria shook her head sadly and gave Stella an encouraging smile as she turned to leave the room.

* * *

The first person Rosaria ran into was Francesco, who gave her his most engaging smile and told her how much he was looking forward to coming to dinner that evening – he hoped it was still on.

'Yes, of course, Francesco. At eight o'clock. I must tell you how to get there although it's very easy. The children are very excited.'

'What about your partner? Is he excited too?' added Francesco mischievously. 'What's his name?'

'Adam…the first man in my life,' she added pointedly.

The tips of the moustache rose to unprecedented heights. He appeared to find the comment entertaining.

'Adam is looking forward to meeting you too,' she added smiling. Rosaria hesitated before delivering the blow which, she suspected, would rapidly bring the level of the moustache down to ground level again. But there was no point in concealing the news from Leonardo's second-in-command.

'I have to tell you with the deepest regret that your shining star, Mariastella, is at this very moment in Leonardo's office making a full confession, Francesco. I'm as sorry as you are, but Stella is your *talpa.*'

Francesco looked with open incredulity at Rosaria, shaking his head in denial of this inconceivable notion.

'I'm sorry, but it's true. She told me everything this morning. I suggest you go to Leonardo's office – I think your boss might need some moral support.'

'I wouldn't want to embarrass Stella. Maybe I should wait until they have finished talking?' replied Francesco, his usual *brio* deflated like a punctured balloon.

'Well, I can understand your reluctance – in light of your little fling with Stella when she first arrived.' Rosaria had spoken so quietly that Francesco was not sure whether he had caught the words or not. It had been a shot in the dark, of course. She could not be sure that she had read the signs correctly. The accuracy of her deduction was confirmed immediately. Francesco was too honest a man to try and bluff his way out of the situation with fatuous denials. A guilty smirk spread over his face.

'And I thought you were brought here to discover the identity of our mole! But you've managed to unearth all our guilty little secrets to boot! You really are a remarkable lady. May I call you Rosaria this evening?' he added appealingly. His fragile self-confidence had taken a knock. 'Are you sure I am still welcome in your home?'

'Of course, you are. I couldn't stand the children's disappointment if you didn't come,' she added with deliberate cruelty. 'Now, go to Leonardo's office. Both of them need your support.'

'Leonardo was right! You are a woman to be reckoned with!' he added ruefully.

'And don't judge Stella too harshly. She's not the main culprit in all this, believe me. There is something – or someone – very nasty behind all this, Francesco. I think we have only scratched the surface,' Rosaria added ominously. Francesco reluctantly headed off in the direction of Leonardo's office.

After the stress of her encounter with Stella, Rosaria gravitated by some natural instinct towards the coffee bar. She had noticed Giovanna hovering in the background while she had been talking to Francesco. Rosaria was not surprised, therefore, to see Giovanna heading as nonchalantly as she possibly could towards the little metal table where she was sitting. In Giovanna's case, such was her self-control that she almost managed to carry off the act of studied indifference as she approached Rosaria's table – empty-handed because she had omitted to go and buy even a bottle of mineral water. She sat down opposite Rosaria and looked quizzically at her without saying a word. So much had transpired since she had given Giovanna a lift home two evenings previously that Rosaria had forgotten she was dealing with a woman who had made reticence into an art form.

'*Ciao* Elena,' she said. 'I noticed you were talking to Mariastella just now. Was she helpful?'

Two could play at this game, thought Rosaria.

'She managed to throw some light on matters, yes, Giovanna.'

'So, was I right, Elena?'

'About what exactly, *cara* Giovanna?' said Rosaria innocently.

'You know perfectly well what I mean,' she replied coolly. 'I thought we two could dispense with unnecessary explanations. We think along the same lines.'

Rosaria gave up with a good grace. It was impossible to beat Giovanna at her own game – and quite pointless in the circumstances. She leant forward over the table and told Giovanna everything that had transpired. Giovanna was highly amused by the account of Riccardo's chance comment about the rubber gloves. By the end of the narrative, Giovanna seemed devastated by Stella's plight.

'We have to find somewhere for Stella to live, Giovanna. We've got one day left before this Dario comes down to Legano. I'm quite certain if he ever catches Stella on her own, she won't be strong enough to resist.'

Giovanna was thoughtful for a minute before she said simply:

'She can stay with me at my parents' house, Elena...' Rosaria had become tired of being called by a false name and decided on the spur of the moment to take Giovanna into her confidence.

'My name is really Rosaria. But please don't tell anyone. I use the name Elena when I'm working – just as a precaution.'

As usual, Giovanna seemed to absorb this piece of information without a hint of surprise. She used no pointless words such as: 'Trust me. I won't tell anyone.' Instead, she just carried on without a pause.

'Our house is like a fortress, Rosaria. My parents change the entry code every five minutes. My father was a police officer until he retired. She would be safe with us. I hope she won't mind...'

'Stella is not in a position to mind anything, Giovanna, not for quite some time, I would imagine. *E grazie infinite!*'

'Just give me time to talk to my parents this evening – just out of respect. They won't say no, I promise you. And don't worry about Stella and Leonardo. I know that he will do all he can to keep her. She's a born scientist, Rosaria.'

These were Giovanna's parting words, uttered with her usual unruffled calm. They went their separate ways with the undertaking that they would keep in constant touch over developments.

Rosaria was left wondering what else she could do for the rest of the day when she was startled by her smartphone ringing somewhere in the depths of her handbag. She rummaged around and retrieved the device some ten seconds later. It was Alessandro Greco calling her. She felt a pang of guilt because she had not been in touch with her boss since her first day at the University.

'*Pronto, Sandro.* I'm sorry I haven't called you but…'

'Don't worry, Elena. I'm sure you are well on the way to solving their little problem.'

'Oh yes, I've found out who is responsible for…'

'I've just had a strange phone call, Elena. That's why I am phoning you.'

'Go on, Sandro…' Rosaria had detected the tension in his voice and listened more attentively.

'It was a phone call from that lady journalist called Costanza De Santis.'

Rosaria froze. She suddenly felt exposed, vulnerable and extremely mystified.

'Elena?' queried Alessandro, not receiving any reaction to his words. 'She claimed that you were supposed to be meeting her this morning in a bar somewhere near *La Piazza Sant'Oronzo…*'

'Sandro, what did you say to her?'

Alessandro detected the panic in her voice and tried to reassure his partner.

'I didn't tell her anything – merely that you were out of the office at the moment.'

'Are you sure she asked for Elena Camisso? She didn't know my real name, did she?'

'No, she asked for Elena Camisso. Why, what's the matter, Ros... Elena? Are you in some sort of trouble?'

'I hope not, Sandro. I'll explain everything when I next see you. What worries me is how she traced me back to our agency. It means that *somebody* who is intimately associated with my appointment at the University has been very free and easy with what should be a closely guarded secret.'

'What are you going to do, Elena?'

It was a very good question indeed! What *was* she going to do about this disturbing development?

'I don't know, Sandro. I really don't know,' said an anxious Rosaria. She cursed her moment of hasty weakness in revealing her real first name to Giovanna. 'I hope to goodness she really is trustworthy.'

Rosaria was feeling inexplicably unsettled and insecure after Sandro's phone call.

9: Shifting Sands

What Rosaria decided to do was dictated by diplomacy rather than by any great desire to confront the lady journalist. After the traumatic revelations of the morning, she would dearly have liked to go home and surround herself with familiar objects and, above all, her family. But it wasn't even lunchtime and the nagging uncertainty as to how Costanza De Santis had found it so easy to track her down needed to be faced up to as a matter of urgency. Even allowing for the possibility that the journalist had traced her call to the phone booth outside the *AltoTek* science facility, it should have been totally impossible to identify her as the anonymous caller of the previous day. Unless...! Rosaria feared she might be becoming paranoid.

She called Alessandro Greco again and asked him if they could arrange to meet Costanza De Santis together. She knew that the antagonism she felt towards the journalist would only serve to make matters worse. She needed Alessandro's diplomatic presence to compensate for her tendency to be too outspoken. He phoned back about fifteen minutes later to say that he had arranged the meeting for midday. That would just give Rosaria time to see Francesco about dinner that evening and check up on Stella who, Rosaria noticed through the glass-panelled office door, was still in earnest conversation with Leonardo. Francesco was sitting diplomatically in the background. He looked unusually pale and a deep frown furrowed his brow. When it was obvious that the conference was not going to come to an immediate end, she tapped discreetly on Leonardo's office door. He gestured for her to come in. She gave Francesco a piece of paper with her address and direction to their home and took one smiling look at Stella, who was looking humbled but considerably more relaxed.

'I'll be back in about an hour's time,' explained Rosaria. 'I can look after Stella when I get back, if you want.' She went on to explain briefly where she was going and who she was going to meet.

'Don't worry, *capo,*' she said. 'I won't tell her anything.'

Rosaria explained about her anonymous phone call and how the journalist had managed to find out her name seemingly without difficulty. Francesco was frowning even more. He had picked up immediately on the implications of what Rosaria had just said. He excused himself for a minute or so and came out of Leonardo's office with Rosaria. He was looking very concerned.

'You must be really wary of that woman, Ros...Elena,' he corrected himself on seeing the stern frown on her face as soon as he had uttered the first syllable of her real name. 'She's worse than a poisonous serpent – she lets you die slowly.'

'Don't worry, Francesco. I'm meeting her with my boss, Alessandro.'

'What boss, Elena?' he asked puzzled.

Rosaria realised that Francesco would not know about the Greco Private Investigation Agency, which she officially worked for. 'I'll tell you tonight,' she promised.

'I'm sure you'll be able to cope with her, Elena. Her Achilles Heel is her massive ego – keep flattering her and she'll be as happy as a lark.

Rosaria felt like smiling for the first time that day – before Francesco's next words:

'But you realise, don't you, that there is only one source that she could have got your name from?'

'Livia Marchetti?'

'No, I think you can rule her out. She's as grumpy as a bear before breakfast – but she would rather be stretched on the rack than give information out to a stranger.'

She looked at Francesco expectantly. But Leonardo called out his deputy's name from the office. He obviously thought it better to have a witness present throughout this crucial talk with Stella.

'Think about it Elena. I don't want us to jump to conclusions.'

But Rosaria was afraid that Francesco had just confirmed her own very tentative suspicions. She would have to allow her brain cells to work on the problem on their own. It was nearly midday – time to go and meet the lady journalist.

Rosaria was so pleased to see her partner in crime, Alessandro – who had arrived before the appointed time – that she planted a warm *bacio* on each of his cheeks. There was little opportunity to discuss strategy, since the lady journalist had also had the idea that arriving early would give her a tactical advantage. Alessandro and Rosaria both spotted her well before Costanza De Santis spotted them – if only because she was looking out for a woman on her own whom she had never seen before. When making the appointment for midday, Alessandro had carefully omitted to say that he would be present as well. 'Tactics,' he said succinctly to his partner.

Neither of them had ever seen the journalist close up before. But her physical appearance corresponded alarmingly to the preconceived image that they had of her.

She was in her fifties and, in common with many Italian ladies of a certain age, had dyed her hair a carroty red colour to hide the onset of the greying process; a pointless gesture of defiance to the world at large, Rosaria's partner, Adam, had once observed. Costanza De Santis had a square-shaped face sitting atop a portly figure, which she nevertheless carried off well – in the mode of a retiring sergeant major who has just finished drilling her recruits into submission for the last time. Alessandro stood up and beckoned the journalist over to the table where they were sitting. The semblance of a smile on her face was belied by the hard look in her eyes. They shared the instant impression that the smile was intended merely to act as a disguise to lull the unwary into a false sense of security; it vanished as soon as she had sat down. Her first act was to stare down both her interlocutors, who continued to look at her as if waiting deferentially for her to speak first. This had been the one element of their opening gambit that Alessandro had had time to convey to his partner. It worked. Costanza was forced to speak when she mistakenly assumed that this 'young' couple were in awe of her.

'Thank you for wasting my time this morning, *signorina,*' she began, looking at Rosaria accusingly. If she had expected an abject apology, she was disappointed to find that neither Rosaria nor Alessandro offered one. She was obliged to continue.

'I was expecting to be meeting you alone,' she continued brusquely, singling out Rosaria with a cold stare.

Alessandro spoke for the first time, with the hint of a sardonic smile on his face.

'Only a *very* foolhardy person would hold a crucial meeting such as this might prove to be with nobody else present, Costanza. Wouldn't you agree?'

It had been beautifully executed, with just a hint of flattery and grudging respect in his tone.

'Well, I hope at least you have something of interest to tell me about this business?' The journalist was maintaining the aggressive stance with which she usually succeeded in intimidating her intended victims.

'What business might *that* be, *signora?*' Rosaria said sharply. There followed the harsh, barking gust of laughter which Rosaria had been treated to during her phone call.

'Oh come now! We're not going to pretend there's nothing going on behind the scenes in the science faculty of this city's university, are we?'

'No, *signora,* we are not going to pretend anything!' snapped Rosaria.

Alessandro thought it might be an appropriate moment to intervene.

'*Signora* Costanza, before we divulge anything, I think it would be a very sound move on your part to explain how you managed to discover my colleague's name and link it unerringly to the investigative agency which we run. Because, *signora,* in our opinion, you have already overstepped the boundaries which journalistic etiquette demands.'

'I must have friends in high places, *signore!*' Costanza retorted haughtily.

'Very indiscreet friends, *signora* – whatever their status might be!' continued Alessandro with studied calm.

'I cannot divulge my sources,' replied Costanza, who was nevertheless beginning to sound as if she was attempting to bluff her way out of a corner.

'In that case, *signora,* I fear we have nothing more to say to you,' said Alessandro quietly, moving his chair back as if he was about to stand up.

'You've been talking to the Rector, Fabiano Mela, haven't you?' stated Rosaria boldly, throwing caution to the winds.

Alessandro had been about to place a restraining hand on Rosaria's arm, but the fleeting expression of surprise that crossed the journalist's face told him plainly that the shot had found its mark. The waiter arrived at their table at the crucial moment and they ordered mineral water and coffees because they could think of nothing else. Costanza De Santis appeared to be calculating the effect of Rosaria's words and decided that it would further her own ends better if she admitted the truth of the accusation.

'More precisely, to his secretary, *signorina,'* Costanza replied with the first hint of respect for this alarmingly forthright woman, 'although she put me on hold and consulted the Rector privately a couple of times during the course of our conversation. It would appear that the *Magnifico Rettore* finds you something of a political embarrassment. I gather, reading between the lines, that he would rather see the back of you. Can you think of any reason why, Elena?'

Rosaria was startled by the use of her first name – even if it was only her assumed name. Francesco's warning words about serpents sprang to mind in timely fashion. 'No idea,' she replied noncommittally. After a protracted silence while the waiter placed the drinks on the table, she added:

'In point of fact, there is no longer a security problem within the department. There is no story to make public.'

'Now I simply do not believe you, young woman.' The journalist's patronising manner was making Rosaria's blood boil anew. Alessandro intervened once again.

'What I believe my colleague is saying, *signora,* is that any revelation to the press at this stage would be premature. Am I right, Elena?'

'Somebody's life may be at risk. It's as simple as that.'

'May we shelve this discussion for now, *signora?* We undertake faithfully to contact you personally as soon as we feel that the moment has arrived to make the matter public. I think there might well be national or even international implications behind all this.'

Alessandro spoke convincingly enough, even though he had no idea what had transpired over the three days during which his partner had been at the University. Costanza De Santis was astute enough to sense that there were a number of angles to this story that she might well be able to exploit in the near future. She took her leave without touching her drinks and with only the minimum of words. She did not offer to pay her share of the bill.

'Thank you, Alessandro,' said Rosaria with a huge sigh of relief after the journalist's departure. 'You were great!'

She promised to fill him in on the details as soon as she could but decided she should get back to look after Stella.

'Things really came to a head today,' she explained to her boss. 'But you know, Sandro, there is something sinister about the Rector's stance in this affair. It's as if he agreed to allow me in to investigate the leaking of information to placate Leonardo Molinari, but now he can't wait to sabotage the whole enquiry. I know he's under pressure from the Union, but he knows perfectly well I won't be there after next week...'

'Who knows, Elena? He's a very devious individual, as we've seen in the past. I suppose he *could* have his own agenda. Maybe he's just scared of adverse publicity.'

* * *

A contrite, paler-looking Stella was waiting for Rosaria when she returned to the *Altotek* campus. Rosaria was sure that Stella had shed a kilogramme in weight over the last twenty-four hours.

'Well, Stella – are you feeling better now?'

'I feel less contaminated than before,' she replied after a thoughtful pause. 'Leonardo and Francesco say I must go back to my flat and pack. I don't know where I can go but I must be out of that flat by tomorrow – before *HE* arrives on Friday.'

'We'll take care of you, Stella. Don't worry. What have they decided about your job?'

'*Il Professor* Molinari says he doesn't want to lose me,' replied Stella with tears of emotion in her eyes. 'But he needs time to think things over and discuss everything with Francesco...*Il Professor* Zunica, I mean,' she added blushing slightly at her minor *faux pas.* Rosaria looked at her and wagged an admonishing finger in Stella's direction. There was a knowing twinkle in her eyes. Stella looked at Rosaria, shocked that her 'saviour' seemed to know about her brief and abortive affair with the man with the moustache.

'He promised he wouldn't tell anyone, Elena. How could he be so feckless?' She was more disturbed by Francesco's supposed betrayal than by the memory of their transient act of passion.

'Don't think ill of Francesco, Stella. He didn't say anything. I worked it out for myself. You must stop believing that you can go through life concealing the truth from people. There are a thousand little signs every day that give our secrets away to anyone who is looking closely. It was Giovanna Binetto who worked out that it was you who... I don't want to rub salt in the wound. But she guessed it was you just because you bit your fingernails all the time. You see what I'm getting at, don't you Stella?'

'Oh, Elena...' began Stella, about to become maudlin again.

'Come on Stella. Let's go into town and have some lunch before we go back to your flat.'

'I so wish I didn't have to go there at all, Elena. I have been so tormented and depressed in that place...'

'We'll find you somewhere special to live when all this is over, Stella. Just for now, you'll have to keep a low profile. I'll come and help you pack your suitcase. You'll only be there for one more night, won't you?'

* * *

By late afternoon, Rosaria was able to leave everything behind her and drive back to her home and her family. Tired out at this stage of the day, she was regretting her act of hospitality in inviting Francesco to dinner, although she seriously doubted he would prove to be anything other than an entertaining guest.

Apart from the emotional intensity of the day's events, Rosaria had spent a physically exhausting hour or so cleaning and tidying Mariastella's flat. She had been shocked at the state of the small studio flat. Stella never put clothes back in the single tiny wardrobe with its inadequate number of drawers. Jeans, blouses, underwear in an exotic assortment of colours and styles, lay strewn over the floor, the spare chair and on the unmade bed. Other items of underwear were dangling over the top of the shower cubicle. She opened the washing machine door only to find that it served as an extension of the available storage space. It wasn't that her clothes were soiled in any way Rosaria noted with relief – just that that they had never been stowed away. Rosaria found Stella's shoes and boots flung haphazardly under the bed, gathering dust.

'I'm sorry it's a bit untidy, Elena,' Stella ventured to say. Rosaria thought it was the understatement of the year. She had to remind herself that she had to some extent showed the same tendencies at Stella's age before the necessity of bringing up children had forced her to organise her living space efficiently. Bearing in mind the confusion and uncertainty in Stella's working life, it was not surprising that the chaos was reflected equally in her day-to-day living, Rosaria thought.

'Come on Stella! Let's get you organised! You deal with the clothes and I'll clean up the flat a bit.' When Rosaria began cleaning, she devoted the same dogged determination to the task in hand as she did when investigating a case. Adam, who had occasionally turned his hand to housework, had given up almost completely when he discovered that Rosaria would subject areas that he considered already spotless to the same rigorous attention.

After an hour and a half, Stella's flat looked habitable. Stella thanked her companion sheepishly and promised she would be ready to vacate the flat the following day. Rosaria made sure Stella had stored her smartphone number on her own mobile device.

'You call me whenever you like, Stella – day or night! And if *he* phones you, don't answer it. Better still, leave it switched off altogether.' Rosaria had made her promise on everything and everybody she held dear that she would phone her for whatever reason. During the course of the afternoon, Rosaria had discovered that Stella was an only child. Her parents were already in their late fifties and had remained mystified that they appeared to have given life to a beautiful girl whose academic brilliance had left them feeling they belonged in the Middle Ages. This was Rosaria's interpretation of what Stella had told her rather than the literal sense of the description that she had given of her home life.

Stella hugged 'Elena' warmly before she left, full of the immense gratitude that she felt towards the woman who had helped her through this traumatic day.

'Thank you, Elena. You have saved my life,' she said simply and sincerely.

'I'll pick you up tomorrow morning, Stella. About half past eight, OK? And phone me if you are feeling worried about *anything.*

Despite having done all she could, Rosaria felt inexplicably concerned about leaving Stella on her own. She knew what havoc nocturnal fears could wreak on someone in such a vulnerable state of mind.

Rosaria drove back home with an ominous sense of impending doom which she could not explain rationally. 'I must be tired!' she told herself in an attempt to assuage the sense of unease at leaving Stella in the lurch.

What a glorious sense of relief it was to be home again! Preparations for the evening meal were well under way. Anna and Riccardo were helping their father. They had already laid a table for five people in the big kitchen and were in the process of peeling and cutting potatoes to make *patate al forno.*

'They've been great,' said Adam hugging Rosaria before sending her off to have a shower. 'Anybody would think we had a member of the English Royal Family coming to dinner.'

'*Il Principe Francesco!*' joked Anna.

'Your *Principe Azzuro,* Anna – your knight in shining armour!' Riccardo taunted his sister and got a dig in the ribs for his pains.

Any worries that the evening would be awkward were dispelled as soon as Francesco arrived – ten minutes early. The children were in awe of their dinner guest for all of thirty seconds. After that, Francesco had no peace. During that half minute, Francesco gave Rosaria a *bacio* on each cheek, asked if he could call her Rosaria throughout the evening, shook Adam by the hand and said, in English: *'It's a pleasure to meet you, A-damn.'*

'Should we watch the DVDs before or after dinner?' Francesco asked the adults.

'Now!' replied Anna and Riccardo in unison.

Adam and Rosaria merely shrugged their shoulders in resignation, while the children prepared to lead Francesco off in the direction if the living-room.

'Dinner will be ready in twenty minutes,' said Adam.

'Why don't we watch one DVD before dinner and one after?' suggested Francesco to the children. They agreed.

'Which one shall we watch before dinner - the one about RIC6 – the boy robot – or the fish robot that swims in the deep oceans?' asked Francesco.

'You decide, Francesco,' said Anna in her mature, don't-ask-my-little-brother voice.

Riccardo protested.

'Don't worry, Riccardo. In any case, I'm going to give you the DVDs to keep, so you can watch them whenever you like.'

'*Grazie di cuore,* Francesco!' said Riccardo, smiling in gratitude as they led their new-found friend off to the living room.

'How do you grow your moustache so big, Francesco?' asked Riccardo.

'I sprinkle fertiliser on it every morning.' Subdued giggles!

'What does your wife say when you kiss her?' This, from an innocent Anna, who wished to get down to the essential consequences of possessing such an appendage.

'Off to a good start,' whispered Rosaria to Adam in the kitchen, embarrassed for Francesco. She need not have worried.

'She tells me that, even if she were to emigrate to Australia, she still wouldn't be out of range of my whiskers.' A chorus of laughter this time.

Back in the kitchen, Rosaria came close up to Adam and kissed him full on the mouth. She was glad Adam had refused to grow a moustache when she had launched the idea early on in their relationship.

If either Adam or Rosaria had been anxious about the success of the evening, their fears would have been groundless. It was one of those meals where communication was more important than the food. Francesco had

155

complimented Rosaria on her cooking skills only to be told that he should be directing his praise towards Adam. Francesco had made a permanent friend of Adam because he had brought two bottles of *Selvarossa* from *Le Cantine Due Palme* as well as a bottle of white wine called *Santa Caterina* from the same wine producer.

The children had come to the table enthralled by what they had learnt about the little robot called RIC6.

"They've invented a robot who's called after ME!' exclaimed Riccardo proudly.

'How much would it cost me if I wanted a RIC6 for my birthday, Francesco?' Anna asked seriously.

'Oh, let me see, Anna. It would set your parents back about €250 000, I would think!'

There were gasps of surprise at this revelation. Francesco went on to talk about the development of A.I. – 'Artificial Intelligence,' he explained. 'It's a scary concept, but they reckon, by the middle of this century, robots like RIC6 will be twice as intelligent as a human being – and it won't stop there either. RIC6's mental age is increasing by leaps and bounds.'

'What's the significance of the 'six', Francesco?' asked Adam.

"It represents his mental age,' explained Francesco. 'By next year, we will probably have to re-baptise him RIC7.'

For the rest of the meal, Riccardo, who was seven, pretended to be an intelligent six-year-old robot child modelled on RIC6. He had decided that, as the sum of a quarter of a million euros was probably out of his parents' reach, he would mimic the robot boy himself. To everybody's amusement, he made all his movements look exactly like the automated gestures of the little robot. Anna fed him lines: 'Pass me the Parmesan cheese please, RIC6' 'Can I have another glass of water, RIC6?' When he succeeded in imitating the appealing, doe-eyed, slow blinking facial gestures of the miniature humanoid, he got a round of applause.

'What is 42 plus 173, RIC6?' Francesco asked him to test the limit of his robotic abilities.

Riccardo had fluttered his eyelids engagingly just as RIC6 had done and answered in his robot's voice: 'Not while I'm eating, master, *please!*' Riccardo had been so gratified by the universal outburst of laughter from his audience that he kept up the act even when he was dispatched to bed at 11 o'clock – too tired to watch the second video about the robotic fish which could swim in the blind ocean depths.

'Would you all like to meet RIC6 in person?' Francesco had suggested. He explained that the version of RIC6 which they had worked on in collaboration with their colleagues from other universities would be on display in a few days' time. The invitation was greeted with enthusiasm all round.

Even when the children had gone to bed, Francesco only touched briefly on the matter of Stella's passing on of sensitive materials.

'It's difficult to assess the damage she has done – she has been very clever at only passing on snippets of information. But if, as we suspect, there is some powerful organisation behind all this, then her life might well be in danger now she has been stopped.' Rosaria had been right to be fearful about leaving Stella on her own, even for one night.

Rosaria had filled in Adam rapidly as to what had happened during that long day. She ended up with her description of Stella's flat. Rosaria talked about her job at the Greco Investigation Agency to satisfy Francesco's curiosity. At one point, she received a text message from Giovanna Binetto confirming that her parents had agreed to put Stella up for as long as it was necessary.

Francesco made a serious proposition to Adam that he should come to the *AltoTek* and teach English to the research team. 'Word has got around about your teaching abilities, Adam.' Rosaria had corrected his pronunciation of her partner's name. 'You should spread your wings a bit instead of sticking exclusively to the *Beni Culturali* faculty for the rest of your working life. I'll put forward your name to Professor Molinari if you are interested.' Adam thought it was a great idea and thanked Francesco.

'Where do you come from, Francesco?' asked Adam, who was curious to know more about their guest's background.

'Me? I'm from Bologna – just like Mariastella, in fact.'

This was something of a surprise to Rosaria. She vaguely remembered that Leonardo Molinari had told the audience at the conference that only two members of their research team were not from Puglia. So, Francesco was the other 'foreigner' in the team! She entertained the private hope that this revelation would not open up another dimension in an already complicated situation.

Francesco took his leave just before midnight. They all agreed they had spent an entirely pleasant evening in each other's company.

'Drive carefully down to Galatone, won't you Francesco,' said Rosaria anxiously.

'Ah, I didn't tell you, did I, Rosaria? I'm allowed back to my home tonight – the first signs that my transgressions might be forgiven.' He grinned mischievously and the tips of his moustache joined in the smile.

'That is really good news, Francesco,' said Rosaria, who was holding Adam's hand as they waved him off into the night.

'Good night, master!' came a robotic voice from a first floor window. 'Drive carefully.' Riccardo and Anna had been too excited to fall asleep despite their tiredness.

* * *

Rosaria had fallen asleep as soon as her head touched the pillow – just as Adam had expected. They were both deeply unconscious at six o'clock the following morning when Rosaria's phone woke them up with its insistent ringing. She struggled into wakefulness as her finger touched the icon on the screen.

'*Pronto,*' she mumbled automatically. Within ten seconds, she was sitting up alert, taking in what Stella was saying.

'Elena, help me! He's outside my flat sitting in a blue Ferrari sports car, for God's sake! What shall I do?' she wailed, desperate panic in her voice.

10: Evasive Action

Rosaria's first slumber-induced reaction had been to dismiss what Stella was saying – simply on the grounds that, in her view, Ferraris must always be red.

'He's arrived a day earlier than he told me, Elena! Tell me what to do!'

Whatever her doubts about the colour of Ferraris, Rosaria could not ignore the terror in Stella's voice. *That* was quite unequivocal.

'It's alright, Stella. Please don't panic. Give me a second to think. Listen, Stella. Has he phoned you yet?'

'Yes, he must have done. There's been one incoming call. It has to be from him. But I did as you told me and switched the phone off all night. I've just switched it on to call you. What am I going to do, Elena? I'm scared stiff. Elena? Are you still there?'

Adam, who was always wide awake as soon as sleep had deserted him, touched Rosaria's arm and indicated that he would go and make the coffee, even though he was waiting, all agog to hear how she would deal with this crisis. Adam was already certain in his mind that there would be an extra body in the house that evening. As he was leaving the bedroom, he heard Rosaria say to Stella:

'Right, Stella, this is what you do. Send him a text message saying that you are staying with one of your colleagues...in Sannicola. He won't know where that is. Say you will be coming to work mid-morning – that'll give us some time to think. I'm going to come over and pick you up as soon as I'm dressed. Don't leave the flat whatever you do. I'll send you a text message when I arrive – Dario will almost certainly have driven off by then. Are you sure it's a Ferrari?' she asked despite herself.

But Stella just begged her not to be too long. She clearly had not heard the question.

Fifteen minutes later, two bleary-eyed children were standing in the kitchen anxiously watching their mother drinking a cup of coffee standing up.

'Are you on another mission, *mamma?*' asked Riccardo. A break in their family routine usually meant that his mother was involved in another of her investigations.

'You're not going to do anything dangerous, are you *mamma?*' enquired Anna, clearly uneasy.

'No, I promise. I just have to pick up a lady called Stella from her flat in town. I shall be back soon,' Rosaria reassured her children – and her partner, who had been looking equally concerned at the unexpected turn of events.

'Good,' said Adam. 'In that case, we'll all come along just as we are.'

Rosaria protested but Adam insisted. Rosaria secretly welcomed their company despite her protestations. Her intuitive feeling that there was an element of threat behind the sudden appearance of Dario was a persuasive argument.

So two adults, and two children with dressing gowns wrapped round them, set off to Legano at speed. There was very little traffic about as dawn broke over the lofty *campanile* rising above the ancient city.

'When we get there, keep an eye open for a Ferrari sports car with a man in it,' said Rosaria. 'Stella tells me that it's a blue one, but there's no such thing as a blue Ferrari...'

'Yes there *is, mamma!*' stated Riccardo. His precocious passion for expensive Italian cars was well-known within the family circle. 'It's called a Ferrari *California*. You can get it in blue. It's got a hard-top roof that comes off,' he concluded informatively.

Adam smiled. 'There, Rosy – now we know. Stella was right.'

The blue Ferrari was parked in the narrow street opposite Stella's flat making it easy to spot from the window above. Rosaria parked her Lancia Ypsilon behind the Ferrari – wanting to get a look at the man in the car, emboldened by the presence of her little family. The young man in the car had his phone pressed to his ear. He was gesticulating in frustration. As Rosaria was about to get out, the man – presumably Dario – startled by the arrival of another car, switched off his phone and pushed the ignition button on the car. The engine roared angrily into life and the Ferrari swerved into the road at speed, shooting off down the street towards the periphery of the city.

Mannaggia la miseria!' exclaimed Rosaria, annoyed with herself. 'I should have looked at the number plate!'

'AN579RC' stated Anna, who had undone her seat belt the instant her mother had pulled up so that she could get a good look at the car.

'What?' said Rosaria. 'How did you…?'

Adam laughed. 'Now aren't you glad we came along too!'

'Are you sure, Anna?' asked Rosaria in admiration. 'You could only have had the briefest of glances…'

'AN for Anna, **579** is easy and **RC** for Riccardo!' she said triumphantly.

Rosaria leant over the seat and kissed both her children loudly on the cheek.

Thus it was that Stella, emerging pale and scared-looking from the main entrance to her apartment block, was escorted by the whole family to the comparative safety of their home. She sat, tensed up, wedged tightly between Anna and Riccardo in the back seat. Her suitcase, stowed in the boot, almost filled the space completely. She had been too preoccupied to display surprise at the discovery that Rosaria was the mother of two children. She had smiled a brief, nervous smile as she had been introduced, shaking each member of the family mechanically by the hand without taking in their names.

Breakfast was, for once, a silent affair. They were all sitting round the kitchen table. Stella was clutching a large cup of milky coffee in both hands as if to keep her fingers warm on a cold day. Anna and Riccardo munched their way through a plate of cereal without a word – stunned into silence by the presence of this uneasy stranger in their midst. The silence was broken in an unexpected manner – certainly from Adam's point of view.

'It's time to go to school, papà.' It was Riccardo who had spoken but, for the first time in his life, he had said the words in perfect English – even if he kept the word *papà* in Italian. Anna, who was never to be outdone by her younger brother, added:

'Are you taking us to school today, papà?'

Adam looked delighted. He had religiously spoken English to his children since they were born but had failed to evince a single word of English from his son or daughter despite his strenuous efforts. It was odd – almost as if they had suddenly wanted to create an intimate family space which set them apart from this strange girl that their mother had unexpectedly introduced into the household.

'*Bravi Anna, Riccardo!*' said Rosaria. 'What has brought this on all of a sudden?'

'It was Francesco, last night,' explained Anna.

'He told us that if we wanted to be nano...nano-technogilists,' said her brother, not quite coping with the word, 'we should start to speak English as soon as possible!'

'Thank you, Francesco!' said Adam, ironically thinking how unfair it was how the scientist had achieved in one evening what he had been trying to do for years.

'Has Francesco been here?' asked Stella jolted out of her reverie by the mention of Francesco's name.

'Yes, he came to dinner yesterday,' said Riccardo.

'He gave us a DVD about RIC6,' added Anna.

'I'm working on that project too,' Stella informed them enthusiastically.

From that moment on, Stella was no longer an alien in their home. They went off to school thinking that this dark-haired girl was not so bad after all.

Adam was allowed to take his son and daughter right up to the gates and give them a goodbye *bacio* without their faces clouding over with embarrassment. Anna told him that '*mamma* had sorted out that other problem'. In addition, Adam guessed, his status had been unexpectedly enhanced in his children's eyes by dint of being an Englishman.

'*See you later, papà,*' they said and shot off, leaving Adam wondering about the mysteries of language acquisition.

* * *

'Stella, I have to tell you something important and I have to trust you too.' Mariastella looked fearful again at the forthright manner in which she had been addressed.

'What haven't you told me, Elena?'

'Simply this, Stella – my name is not Elena. It's Rosaria. Even if I prefer 'Elena' to my real name,' she added.

'Oh, that's wonderful. I like the name Rosaria – it's *my* middle name,' she declared with the first genuine smile in twenty-four hours. It was short-lived, however, as the full realisation dawned that she would have to face up to the threat of Dario's premature arrival.

'You mustn't put yourself in *any* danger because of me, El...Rosaria. You have two such beautiful kids. I couldn't bear it if anything happened to you because of my involvement with *him.*'

'Do you think he could be dangerous, Stella?'

'Yes, I'm sure of it. He is going to hound me down until he gets me back in his grasp,' she stated bluntly. 'It might be better for you and your family if I just disappeared. You must be careful...Rosaria.'

Stella's words shed a new light on her character – she was not simply concerned about her own safety.

'Have you any particular reason for supposing this?' asked Rosaria.

'It's that car,' Stella stated enigmatically. 'I know how much he earns by being a pharmaceutical rep. His annual salary is a fraction of what one of those Ferrari's would cost – even second hand. That means he has got money from another source...'

There was no need to delve into what Stella meant. There was silence between them while they both thought through the implications of this revelation.

'I don't suppose you have any idea who...?' Rosaria asked tentatively.

Stella shook her head. 'All I know is that, while I was with him, he frequently had phone conversations with a man whom he always called *zio*. I don't know whether it was a real uncle or just a nickname – but they certainly never talked about family matters! If the subject of conversation became sensitive, Dario always walked away from me so I couldn't hear what they were saying.'

'So you never heard this *uncle's* voice?'

'Yes, because once, he accidentally left it in loudspeaker mode.'

'Did you notice anything particular about his voice, Stella? Was it a young man, an old man...?'

'It wasn't a young man's voice – educated middle-class, I guess.'

'Was there *anything* else you picked up? A voice you recognised perhaps?'

Rosaria noted with interest that Stella's eyes moved rapidly from side to side before she answered the question.

'No, not really, Elena... I mean Rosaria. Only that... No, it's silly but...' Frustratingly, she left the sentence unfinished.

Rosaria wanted to press the point home but did not wish to force Stella into declaring what she was thinking. She would ask her again later on in the day.

Rosaria told Stella about Giovanna Binetto's offer to give her a 'safe house' in which to stay until the danger was over.

'Giovanna's parents' house is like a fortress. Her father's a retired policeman. You'll be safe there for a few days.'

'Giovanna must despise me for what I've done, Rosaria. I shan't be able to look her in the face.'

'You'll find everyone is on your side, Stella. Stop worrying about what the others think.' Rosaria had spoken reassuringly, hoping rather than being entirely convinced by her own words. 'Now I need to go to the University for a few hours.'

Stella looked alarmed at the prospect of being left on her own. She need not have worried. Rosaria had thought of the obvious solution to ensure Stella would not be left exposed.

'Come on!' she said. 'I'm taking you into town and you are going to spend the morning with my colleague, Sandro. You'll like him.' Rosaria had to explain that she worked for a sophisticated private investigation agency in Legano. 'Sandro could do with some company, Stella. I've abandoned him all this week... Don't look so worried – he won't bite!'

Stella was greeted warmly by Alessandro Greco. She looked instantly reassured by his appearance.

'Let's see what you can learn about marital infidelity today, Stella,' he joked. 'It's not particle physics, but it can be equally intriguing.'

* * *

With that anxiety removed, Rosaria drove quickly back to the *AltoTek* complex. When she arrived there, she found there was a meeting in full swing. All the scientists were present, bar one, listening to Leonardo's account of Stella's misdemeanours. There was a look of profound shock and disbelief on their faces. Leonardo was at pains to explain that

Mariastella had been coerced into passing on information. They looked relieved when he told them how astute she had been at 'feeding' incomplete data to the, as yet, unidentified recipients of their more sensitive projects. When Rosaria arrived, he explained her role in the investigation to those who did not know already.

'We have Ros...Elena to thank for saving the situation from disaster.' He had stopped himself just in time before calling her by her real name.

'I don't think it matters any longer, *capo*. I told Stella this morning that my real name is Rosaria,' she informed everyone present. 'By the way, where is Micaela?' She had just noticed the recently appointed scientist's absence.

'Miky is always late for meetings,' declared Andrea Calvano with an indulgent smile. 'She'll be here any moment, you can bet on it. But it is unusual for her to be this late. She probably missed the coach from Sannicola.'

True to form, Miky arrived breathless almost as soon as Andrea had finished his sentence. She was greeted with tolerant laughter and a few well-meant wisecracks about her unearthing some new species of molecule. Miky, however, continued to look sombre and a little unnerved.

'I have something to tell you all – it's the reason why I'm so late. There's something odd going on. When I came out of my house this morning, there was a blue Ferrari parked just up the road...'

'WHAT!?' exclaimed Rosaria in horrified astonishment. She had instructed Stella to tell Dario that she was staying with a colleague in Sannicola – thinking this would throw him off the scent. 'Go on Miky! What happened next? This is very serious. I'll tell you all why in a minute.'

'Well, I was walking towards the car with some curiosity – as you can imagine, a Ferrari is not a common sight in Sannicola! Then the man in the car spoke to me as I drew level. His exact words were: *'Haven't you got Stella with you? I'm her fidanzato. She told me she was staying with you last night.'* I was so shocked that I just looked at him with my mouth open. But what I didn't like was the fact that he was wearing dark glasses so I couldn't see his eyes.'

Miky had stopped talking while she recovered her breath.

'Go on, Miky,' said one of the men. 'Then what happened?'

'Well, he wasn't smiling at all and he came across as a bit threatening, or nervous. He offered to give *me* a lift into Legano. I just shook my head and decided to go back into my house where my parents were. It was my dad who drove me here – I had missed the coach. By the time we left, the Ferrari had disappeared.' Miky was looking white with shock as she related her morning's experiences. 'What does it mean, Elena?' she concluded.

Miky could not understand why muted laughter followed her question. Luana, who was sitting next to Miky, quietly gave her a shortened version of events – and the 'name change'.

'I'm sorry, Miky. It was my fault,' said Rosaria. She went on to explain her attempt at shielding Stella from Dario, for the benefit of everyone present as well as for Miky's sake. Leonardo and Francesco had already outlined the crucial elements of the crisis to the group at large.

'What is alarming about Dario's role,' continued Rosaria with a nod from Leonardo and Francesco, 'is that he seems to know who each one of you is, what you look like – and where you live. Now, Stella might have talked about each one of you, but it is unlikely that she would have given him your personal details too...'

'Which means,' cut in Francesco, 'that he has got the information from someone higher up the ladder in this University.'

'Specifically, from the Rector's office,' said Rosaria. 'Dario has either got the information by hacking into the system or, which is worse, with somebody's complicit cooperation. There is a murky side to all this that should put all of us on our guard.'

The group discussed Stella for the rest of the session. Leonardo said that they would have to delay a decision about Stella's future until the danger to her was over. Nobody wanted to lose her from the team if it could be avoided. Giovanna's offer to take on the task of looking after Stella from the following evening was talked about at length. 'She'll be safe in my house,' said Giovanna. 'My father will be there all the time. He's kept his old police pistol,' she added without a hint of a smile – to everyone's amusement.

'There is one more thing I should say,' continued Rosaria. 'I would urge everybody to keep an eye out for this Dario. But, it has to be said, he cannot be all that intelligent - anyone who drives around in a car like his can hardly be possessed of much common sense. He is giving away his whereabouts wherever he goes. No, there is someone much bigger and more sinister than Dario behind all this.'

There were nods of agreement all round from the group of scientists.

'We must all stick together over the next few days,' exhorted Leonardo. 'Please report every little thing to myself or Francesco...'

'Or to Rosaria!' added Francesco, smiling for the first time that morning.

Rosaria knew whom she had to contact next. She had a long-standing ally in Legano; a high-ranking officer in the *carabinieri* whose name was Marco Scarpa. Apart from wanting his moral support, there was one very specific piece of information she needed from him.

* * *

'This Dario doesn't appear to be very astute – even for a minor criminal!' exclaimed *Colonnello* Marco Scarpa after Rosaria had finished her account of events at the University's science faculty.

'He's young and, I suspect, a bit spoilt. He's got himself involved with people whose ruthlessness he has totally underestimated,' replied Rosaria.

'You must be careful, Rosaria Miccoli,' said the *colonnello*. Even as he uttered these words, he knew he was wasting his breath. 'I have a shrewd idea we shall have to keep a professional eye on you over the next few weeks,' he added with mock reluctance.

'I don't think *I* am directly under threat,' she said. 'I'm far more worried about the risk of something happening to Mariastella Russo. She is very vulnerable and liable to do something impulsive over the next few days. If I have read her correctly, she is suffering from a deep sense of guilt at the moment. She might attempt to make amends for her act of professional betrayal, as she sees it. She's also very vulnerable sexually, at present. I fear she might act rashly in response to her situation.'

'Well, I'll certainly have my team keep an eye out for the Ferrari – and we can rely on the help of the local police, too.'

There was a discreet knock on Marco Scarpa's office door and a young, uniformed *carabiniere* stepped in holding a sheet of printed paper. He saluted his senior officer and said: 'We've traced the car registration plate that you requested, *colonnello*. It's a blue Ferrari California registered to someone called Dario Fabbro from Bologna. He's the second owner of the car.'

Rosaria looked pleased with herself. 'There – the enemy has a traceable name!' she said to Marco Scarpa.

'Thanks to your very smart daughter, it seems.'

Rosaria was delaying the moment when she took her leave of this man – only a few years her senior. She could never understand why this handsome police officer was not married. But she was always hesitant to cross the threshold of familiarity that asking such a question would entail. The colonel seemed to sense what was going through her mind.

'I think I shall make a point of contacting the *Guardia di Finanza* over this matter. I smell the odour of greed and large sums of money. I have a nephew who is in the *Guardia di Finanza* – he's the son of one of my sisters.'

Rosaria could not find an excuse to stay in this man's reassuring presence any longer. Besides, she should go and rescue Stella from her boss, Alessandro Greco – or *vice versa,* she thought cynically.

'Keep in touch, Rosaria,' said Marco Scarpa. Rosaria was appalled to find that she had blushed when this man planted a *bacio* on each cheek. She took her leave hurriedly. Adam had always teased her that, if anything should happen to him, she would have another admirer to fall back on. She drove her *Lancia Ypsilon* even faster than usual round Legano's ring road to reach the Greco studio in an attempt to dispel the onset of such perilous emotions.

It was obvious, as soon as she stepped through the door of the Greco offices that Sandro and Stella had been getting on like a house on fire. She looked at her boss with mock reproach and sarcastically apologised that she would have to take Stella home. 'We have to pick up the children from school,' she said in matter-of-fact tone of voice to bring them both down to earth.

'See you tomorrow, Stella,' said Sandro, looking defiantly at his partner. He added pointedly: 'Stella will be safer here.' Rosaria could not deny the truth of this but raised a mocking eyebrow in Sandro's direction – just for good measure.

* * *

'Don't get too excited, Stella,' said Rosaria cruelly, as they were driving to pick up Anna and Riccardo. 'Sandro's got a *fidanzata.* I don't want you to get hurt again.'

'Thank you, Rosaria,' replied Stella tartly. 'Sandro told me about Isabella. I think you'll find they broke up about two months ago.'

Rosaria felt a rush of jealousy. Why would Sandro tell Stella about splitting up with Isabella and not her? She would tackle him about that the next time she saw him on his own. Rosaria had only met Isabella once or twice and on each occasion had been struck by Isabella's reserved, unadventurous nature. She had never been convinced about her boss's choice of lifelong partner.

'You be careful, Stella,' she said more kindly.

'I will, I promise. Besides which, I am still in deep trouble, aren't I?' It was not really a question.

Some minutes later, the children were sitting in the back seat talking to Stella as they drove home. If Stella had been feeling more relaxed, Anna's next words reminded her of the perilous situation she was in.

'I bet that Ferrari's outside *our* house this time!'

Whether it was pure guesswork or childlike intuition on the part of her daughter, Rosaria's reaction was to slow down as they turned into their road.

'*Dio santo,* Anna! You're right!' Rosaria looked at Stella's face, expecting to find the terrified look in her eyes again. She had turned paler, but there was an expression of defiant anger on her face too.

'Let me get out, Rosaria. I don't want you involved in this,' she said resolutely.

'It's not the moment to show your hand yet, Stella. Quick, get down on the floor. Anna, Riccardo, throw that blanket over her.'

Stella did as she had been ordered. Rosaria drove the car up the short drive to the house.

'Right, children, get out quickly and go into the house. Stella, I'm sorry. Stay where you are for another few minutes.'

Rosaria walked determinedly towards the road. Anna and Riccardo, like little guardian angels, had disobeyed their mother and walked one on each flank towards the Ferrari and its occupant, each holding their mother by the hand. Dario looked up as they approached, his mouth set in an expression of thwarted anger. His Gucci sunglasses reflected the little family group standing defiantly on the pavement. He must have recognised Rosaria's car from that morning, if not its occupants. Stella was right, Rosaria was thinking. Dario was a very unpleasant specimen of humanity. There was a ruthless self-confidence about him coupled with an undeniably virulent male presence. Disconcertingly, he said nothing.

'I like your car, *signore*. How much did it cost?' It was Riccardo who had spoken. His boldness shocked Rosaria.

'You don't ask strangers questions like that, Riccardo!' chided his sister.

Dario was looking suddenly nonplussed. Rosaria thought she should stand her ground. It might shake this man out of his arrogant self-assurance.

'The person you are looking for is not here,' she said, wondering if she would have sounded so sure of herself had it not been for the presence of her two children. 'She is in a safe place where you will never find her. I advise you to go home, Dario Fabbro – or shall I call the police?'

Hearing his name spoken achieved more than a hundred carefully chosen words. He attempted to cover up his shock by treating the group to a nasty sneer. But he pressed the ignition button and roared off at speed.

Rosaria hugged her two children all the way back to the house where they rescued Stella from the car floor. It was Rosaria who looked the paler of the two women.

'Now you know what he's like!' said Stella quietly to her rescuer.

Rosaria nodded. 'Yes, I don't think he will give up so easily, Stella.

* * *

175

Friday dawned with a summer thunder storm which swept majestically over the whole of Salento in the early hours of the morning. Anna and Riccardo emerged from their bedroom looking tired and wan. Riccardo loved thunder storms whereas they merely kept Anna from falling asleep.

'Stella was talking in her sleep last night,' Anna told her parents as they sat round the breakfast table. 'I think she had a nightmare too.'

'I wouldn't be surprised,' said Rosaria. 'She has enough problems at the moment to give her more than her fair share of disturbing dreams.'

'And Riccardo kept getting up in the middle of the night to look out of the window,' added Anna.

'Were you watching the lightning, Riccardo?' asked Adam kindly.

'I was keeping an eye out for the Ferrari – in case it came back,' replied Riccardo, as if it had become his own personal mission in life to stand on guard for his family.

Stella had arrived in the kitchen as Riccardo was speaking. She looked embarrassed but gave Riccardo a grateful hug, which he endured without protest. Rosaria felt secretly relieved that she would be able to take Stella round to Giovanna's house later that day and restore peace to her family.

Rosaria did the school run with Stella, who seemed to be in a quietly determined mood. She had loaded her suitcase into the boot.

'Thank you all very much,' she said. 'When all this is over, I would love to come back and see you again.'

'Of course you will, Stella. You'll always be welcome,' Rosaria reassured her. Anna and Riccardo had the good grace to murmur their agreement.

After depositing Stella into Alessandro's safe-keeping – and briefly glaring meaningfully in his direction – Rosaria was at a loss to know what to do. She had meant to ask Stella what she had been about to say about Dario's uncle's voice overheard on his phone. But the stresses of the previous day had put it out of her mind. In the end, she decided to go back to the *AltoTek* to see if there had been any new developments. Everybody seemed subdued. The scientists were all going about their work as if they were attempting to restore a sense of normality. Rosaria had a word with Giovanna about bringing Stella round to her house that evening. Giovanna had an unaccustomed gleam in her eye, thought Rosaria.

During the course of the morning, Rosaria accepted an invitation to have coffee with the two assistant secretaries, Renata and Stefano, who had got wind of what was happening. Somehow, they had gleaned what Rosaria's role had been and were eager for gossip. They still called her Elena, but Rosaria could not be bothered to correct them. Stefano talked a bit about a documentary he had seen on Rai Uno about the University of Beijing, which had just opened a nanotechnology department. 'I bet they copy us!' he said in his usual flamboyant manner. Rosaria frowned. His words rang an alarm bell somewhere in the back of her mind. One of the scientists had mentioned China at some stage of this long week.

'I'm sorry you won't be staying with us, Elena,' Renata was saying. 'We love the way you deal with Lady Livia!'

The comment lightened the atmosphere and they joked about Rosaria's first impressions of their workplace.

Rosaria spent time with Francesco and Leonardo. She filled them in on her visit to the *Carabinieri* and the appearance of Dario and his blue Ferrari outside their family home. They were all hoping that their problems would melt away over the weekend. Rosaria doubted that matters would be resolved so easily.

It was about three o'clock in the afternoon when Alessandro Agostini burst into Leonardo's office where Rosaria, Francesco and Leonardo had been talking casually about Adam coming to teach them English. For the lanky scientist to burst in anywhere was so out of character that the three people sitting round the desk started in surprise.

'*Capo,*' he said breathlessly. 'I've just been into the Clean Room. Our big piece of the photon-deflecting material has gone!'

'You mean the invisibility cloak?' asked Rosaria.

'If that's the misnomer by which you refer to it, Rosaria. Yes, it's disappeared,' he stated, too shocked to appreciate the irony of his words.

The men looked too stunned to speak. But Rosaria remembered something that Stella had said earlier. She had more than an inkling as to the whereabouts of this piece of invaluable material. But why would Stella run the risk of losing all credibility and the final vestige of her colleagues' trust by stealing such an important item?

'Leave this to me, *signori,*' said Rosaria with enough conviction in her voice to stem any demands for an explanation from the three scientists.

11: On the Brink of the Abyss

Such was the authority in Rosaria's voice that nobody present thought of questioning what she intended to do. In point of fact, she went straight home, threw herself on the bed and fell soundly asleep for three hours. She woke up with the problem of the missing piece of material partly resolved; she would tackle Stella directly as soon as she was alone with her. There was little other alternative. She was convinced that Stella had hatched some devious scheme which she was keeping to herself.

Adam, Anna and Riccardo, returning from school, found Rosaria in deep meditation on the bed.

'Mamma, I saw you biting your nails just now! Is there something you wanted to talk to me about?' asked Anna in her grown-up voice, enjoying the role reversal. Anna's words produced a smile. Rosaria managed to expel the mysterious workings of Mariastella's thought processes from her mind for a while.

'You might be jumping to conclusions, Rosy,' suggested Adam later on as the family were having tea-time snacks round the kitchen table and discussing Stella.

'No, instinct tells me I am right, Adam,' she replied in total seriousness. 'She admitted she went to the Clean Room yesterday but she never really explained why. And then, it was something she said to me yesterday...'

Rosaria stopped herself from putting into words what she was thinking. It would sound naïve – or downright absurd. 'I'll tell you all this evening after I've taken Stella round to Giovanna's house,' she promised.

* * *

Rosaria had been obliged to witness the lingering farewells between Stella and Sandro. They were obviously smitten with each other. She could not understand why she felt piqued at the sight of her boss enjoying the company of another woman.

'Give me a few weeks, Sandro,' Stella was saying as she stood gazing into his eyes. 'I'll be back soon, I promise.' Rosaria had to admit grudgingly that Stella was far better suited to Sandro than Isabella had been. Nevertheless, she did not wish to spend the remainder of the evening waiting for the pair of them to prolong their dramatic leave-taking until dusk fell. She coughed pointedly from the doorway. 'I do have things to do this evening,' she said with heavy irony. The pair had finally managed to overcome the strong magnetic force that drew them together.

In the car, Stella had a beatific look in her eyes. Rosaria considered it her duty to bring Stella back down to earth. She still could not escape the nagging suspicion that her *protégée* had a secret agenda all of her own. True to character, Rosaria did not calculate what she would say next. She simply found herself saying:

'When you told me yesterday that you thought it might be better for you to 'disappear', I didn't imagine you meant it so literally, Stella.'

It took Stella roughly fifteen seconds to work out that Rosaria had accurately deduced that it had been her who had taken the piece of light deflecting material – the 'invisibility cloak' – from the Clean Room. She had hoped that its absence would not have been detected so soon.

Rosaria had expected a guilty reaction from Stella, sitting next to her in the passenger seat looking radiantly attractive.

'It's not what you think, Rosaria. I'm sorry if it appears that I wanted to deceive everyone. I have the instinctive conviction that my life might be in danger in the near future. I may have behaved in a despicable manner towards my colleagues – and I do feel deeply guilty about it. But I would prefer to make amends for what I have done rather than end up a corpse. That will help nobody. That piece of material might just save my life.'

Rosaria was amazed at Stella's complex analysis of the risks she was running as a consequence of her own catastrophic misjudgement. She felt inadequate and just a mite overwhelmed by this girl's resolve. From being a repentant, manipulated young woman, she had been transformed into a crusader possessed with the will-power and purposefulness of a latter-day Joan-of-Arc.

Thus, instead of reproving her for her subterfuge, Rosaria asked meekly: 'But do you think it will work, Stella?' They had just pulled up in front of Giovanna's house.

At the end of a tumultuous week, with more twists and turns in it than a corkscrew, the reaction that she had least expected from Stella was for her to let out a tinkling burst of laughter as she thrust her breasts forward in a warm embrace and puckered her sensuous lips into a kiss that she planted warmly on Rosaria's right cheek.

'You've been a true friend to me over the last few days, Rosy. How heart-warming that your parting words show you are worried about my safety instead of condemning my rash stupidity! *Grazie di cuore. Ti voglio veramente bene.'*

Rosaria could still feel the pressure of Stella's breasts on her arm. There was no other response possible after such a spontaneous gesture of affection. She hugged her tightly and said: 'Please be careful, Stella.'

They both became aware of a third presence. Giovanna had emerged through the security gate and was standing on the pavement looking at them through the car window. The first few seconds of this meeting of three women was like a *tableau vivant.* Rosaria's fleeting reaction was one of frozen surprise at the intense expression on Giovanna's usually impassive face; she read a mixture of envy and longing that was quite unmistakable. The tableau instantly sprang to life and resumed the aspect of normality.

'Leave your phone on please, Rosy,' Stella was saying. 'I'll keep in touch with you whenever possible. And don't worry! I promise to be careful.'

As she drove home, Rosaria's overwhelming sensation was the realisation that this rapidly unfolding story had far more to do with the complexities and vagaries of human nature than the scientific intricacies of nanotechnology.

* * *

The 'truce' was short-lived. Rosaria was surprised that she and her little family got through the whole of Saturday and a late breakfast on Sunday before the peace was shattered. On a beautiful, sunny Saturday morning, Adam had driven the family south out of Legano, down towards Sannicola, where they had headed for their favourite stretch of sandy beach. Even in late May, the beach was deserted apart from a handful of hardy families from the local villages. Adam was always astounded that most of the local population considered May too early to sunbathe and swim in the sea. To him, it was already summer compared to his native Britain.

Rosaria had warned her family on Friday evening that there might be trouble brewing before too long. The peace was broken at half past eleven on Sunday just as the last crumbs of the last jam-filled *cornetto* had been swept into Riccardo's mouth.

It was Giovanna who was calling. Her habitual calm had been abandoned. There was panic in her tearful voice. At Adam's insistence, Rosaria had promised to leave her phone in loudspeaker mode so that they all knew what was happening. Thus, silence fell in the family kitchen as Rosaria, Adam, Anna and Riccardo remained spellbound by the turn of events.

'Rosaria... it's me, Giovanna. A terrible thing has happened and it's my fault, my own stupid fault...'

'I'm sure it is *not* your fault, Giovanna. Just tell us what happened.'

'That blue Ferrari turned up outside *my* house this morning at ten o'clock. Stella could see it from her bedroom window. I... It *was* my fault, Rosaria. I only wanted to comfort her last night because she had been calling out in her sleep. But I...I only meant to...' She could not bring herself to finish the sentence.

'Calm down, Giovanna. You haven't done anything wrong,' said Rosaria calmly. 'Please tell me what happened to Stella.'

'When she saw the car, she grabbed a shoulder bag and stuffed a few things inside it. Then she just said: 'All this is my doing. I have to go and put a stop to this once and for all.' I begged her not to go. I tried to stop her physically but it just made matters worse. My parents had gone out to church, but I don't think it would have made any difference. Oh, Rosaria! What have I done?'

At this point, Giovanna broke down and her words became punctuated by sobs followed by a real outburst of tears.

Anna and Riccardo were looking shocked and upset, riveted to the spot by what they were hearing. Adam took them into the garden with his arms around their shoulders.

'Don't worry. She'll be alright,' he said consolingly.

'But, *papà,*' said Anna quietly. 'It's not this Giovanna. It's Stella we're worried about. I suppose she got into that man's car and he's driven her off somewhere...'

'She could be in danger,' said her brother.

Adam hugged them both, full of emotion that two young people, *his* two young people, had read and instantly understood the situation.

'Come on,' he said. 'Let's go back inside.' They did not need shielding from reality, he thought. They too were involved in these events.

Rosaria was talking quietly to Giovanna, reassuring her that this development was something that Stella had planned and was not a reaction to Giovanna's gestures of affection.

'It was more than a gesture of affection, I promise you, Rosaria,' Giovanna was saying with self-condemnatory sarcasm.

'You mustn't blame yourself, Giovanna. There is nothing wrong with having those kinds of feelings...'

To Adam and Rosaria's surprise, Anna had let out a quiet snigger, instantly silenced by a look from her mother. They were shocked – but half amused – that Anna had appeared to understand the implications of the words she had heard.

After the phone call had been brought to an end, neither Adam nor Rosaria would have considered it necessary to comment on Anna's reaction. But Anna herself said in a matter-of-fact voice: 'I can understand Giovanna. Stella is really very pretty, isn't she?' Anna's declaration deserved some kind of sympathetic response but Giovanna's closing words had taken Rosaria completely by surprise and her attention switched to more sinister matters.

'By the way, Rosaria, I nearly forgot,' Giovanna had said making an effort to overcome her distress. 'Stella had a message for you. She said to tell you that the voice on the phone sounded just like our Rector. Does that make any sense to you?'

* * *

Rosaria, Adam, Anna and Riccardo sat round the table in silence. Rosaria was frowning in concentration. None of the other three wanted to be the first to break into Rosaria's meditations. In the end, it was Rosaria herself who said quietly:

'Oh Stella! What have you done?'

'She's got into that man's car and he's driven her off somewhere,' Anna whispered fearfully.

'What's he going to do to her?' asked Riccardo with innocent concern.

'What was all that about the Rector's voice?' asked Adam. 'It didn't make any sense to *me*, Rosy. *Did* it make any sense to you?'

Rosaria nodded.

'Yes, I'm afraid it did.' She went on to explain about Dario's constant calls to someone whom he referred to as *'zio'* and the mounting evidence that Fabiano Mela had been very free with information regarding the personal details of those working within the science faculty.

'This Dario and his blue Ferrari have been turning up with inexplicable precision outside the homes of three people working at the *AltoTek* – including *our* home! It isn't just somebody in the Rector's immediate entourage involved in this affair. It looks as if it's the Rector himself.'

'But that would imply...' began Adam, feeling a frisson of excitement at the prospect of scandal surrounding their notorious leader.

'...that he is corrupt and guilty of deception, fraud and maybe something much worse too! He is almost certainly involved with some outside agent to whom he is passing on scientific information,' Rosaria completed the sentence for him. 'Dario, nephew or not, is just the messenger boy doing the dirty work for him. Furthermore, we can be sure that the Rector will be diligently covering his tracks by now.'

'Then the matter should be in the hands of the *Carabinieri* and *La Guardia di Finanza,*' stated Adam categorically before Rosaria could entertain any notion of pursuing her own line of enquiry.

But Rosaria nodded and said: 'It will be, don't worry.'

Rosaria's fingers had unconsciously been toying with her smartphone. The obvious thing to do would be to call Stella, but Rosaria could imagine all too readily the drift of such a phone call.

'Hello Stella. Where are you?'

'Oh I'm sitting in my boyfriend's blue Ferrari. We're doing 150 kilometres an hour down the superstrada to...' In any case, by phoning Stella, Rosaria might well alert Dario that the extent of his involvement was in the open. That, in its turn, could bring the situation to a head and precipitate some drastic gesture which might endanger Stella's life. No, she

would have to exercise self-control and trust that Stella knew what she was doing. Maybe she *hadn't* got into the blue Ferrari; not even Giovanna knew that for certain. She explained her thoughts to her family. Adam looked dubious.

Rosaria's restraint was eventually rewarded in a totally unexpected manner just as they were sitting down for lunch at one o'clock. They all jumped out of their skins when Rosaria's phone sprang to life like an injured wasp spinning senselessly round on the table top in vibration mode.

'It's Stella,' stated Rosaria. Their plates of pasta remained untouched as the four family members laid their forks down on top of the food.

'Don't say anything straight away, *mamma,*' warned Anna. 'Let her speak first.'

Rosaria was becoming acutely aware that her children understood as much, if not more, about this affair than she did. In hindsight, Anna's words yet again took on an almost prophetic significance – as with the arrival of the Ferrari outside their house. The whole family realised, as soon as Rosaria touched the green icon on the screen that they were eavesdropping on a heated dispute between Stella and Dario. Stella's voice was as clear as crystal whereas they had to strain their ears to pick out Dario's words over the noise of the travelling car. Stella had called Rosaria's number to enable her to listen in on the conversation. Rosaria prayed fervently that their respective batteries had sufficient charge in them - a perennial problem with her. Stella's voice was high-pitched with tension and apprehension.

Where the hell are you taking me, Dario?
(Silence)

Come on! This isn't a game. I want to know.

(Silence)

If you don't tell me, I shall start screaming at the top of my voice.

(Reply difficult to decipher)

BASILICATA? Where in Basilicata?

(Matera)

MATERA! Why there?

(Business…Monday morning. Thought you'd like the ride. We need to talk.)

I've said all I want to say to you. It's over, Dario.

(…not that simple…they know…they'll be after us…disappear)

I don't want to disappear. I've got a new life in Legano.

'I wonder if she means her job – or Sandro?' thought Rosaria despite herself.

(…in this together, mia cara.)

Oh no we are not! You are the one who's in trouble!

(muttered words)

Besides, I shall be reported missing and the police will be on the lookout for this stupid car. They probably already ARE! Not even your UNCLE will want to help you now, Dario.

(Che cazzo stai dicendo, Stella? Puttana!)

Oh yes, Dario. I know who your uncle is!

The connection was broken. Anna and Riccardo had turned white.

'Where's Matera, *mamma?*' asked Riccardo in trepidation.

'I know about Matera,' said Anna. 'We learnt about it at school. It's an ancient town cut out of the rock. People used to live in caves in the hillside above the ravine. You can still see them. And there's a big church cut into the rocks now. A real church hollowed out of the hillside...'

'That's where they filmed Mel Gibson's *The Passion of the Christ,* isn't it?' said Adam. 'It's supposed to look just like the Holy Land must have looked two thousand years ago.'

'But how far away is it from Legano?' Riccardo wanted to know. 'Is it near enough for us to go and rescue Stella?'

Even Anna was too moved by events to make any disparaging comment about her brother's innocent suggestion.

'Stella has just given us a very clear message,' said Rosaria. 'Whatever else we do, we must contact the *carabinieri* immediately.'

Adam took one look at Rosaria and shook his head. He had immediately latched on to the significance of the words 'whatever else we do'.

'No, Rosy. We must leave this matter entirely to the police. By the time we could get to Matera, anything could have happened. Your *colonnello* will get things done more rapidly than we can.'

Their faith in the ability of Marco Scarpa to set the wheels of rescue in motion was thwarted by the fact that, however many times Rosaria tried to contact him, all she got was that irritating, matter-of-fact female voice stating that *'La persona desiderata non è al momento disponibile'.*

Rosaria's frustration and Adam and the children's alarm increased with every attempt she made. Telephoning the city's *Carabiniere* station made matters worse. The officer on the end of the line showed a stubborn disinclination to take any action at all until Monday when, he explained, *Il Colonnello Scarpa* would be back and their missing person would have been gone for more than a day.

'The colonel gave specific instructions not to be disturbed today, *signora,*' the male officer continued doggedly. Rosaria cursed him and threatened that she would be standing in front of him within twenty minutes and then he would regret his refusal to take action.

'As you wish, *signora,*' he replied with lazy indifference. He had had too many incidents of hysterical women on the end of the line to feel the necessity to be goaded into action, only to be reprimanded afterwards by his colleagues for wasting police time.

Twenty minutes later, he was surprised to see a forceful woman of about forty standing in front of him. The look of determined rage on her face was daunting. She even had her family in tow by way of reinforcement.

'Do you understand the implications of a single word that I have told you?' she was saying. 'A woman's life is in danger. You have a car registration number on your records that you are supposed to be looking out for. If you don't do your job *now, Il Colonnello* Scarpa will boil you in oil tomorrow morning, believe me!'

The annoying officer decided he should take the threat seriously and began, with annoying calm, to take down the details of this woman and her complaint. Things might have gone from bad to worse when, just as Rosaria was giving her name, there emerged from a frosted glass-fronted office, a young, uniformed police woman who looked up alertly at the sound of the familiar name.

'Rosaria Miccoli?' she said. 'That name rings a bell. Weren't you involved in the investigation of the abduction of Judge Grassi? My name is Adriana Galante. I was assigned to look after the judge by *Il Colonnello* Scarpa – the judge always commented ironically that my initials were the same as his; it seemed to amuse him for some reason! Colonel Scarpa often sings your praises, *signora!* It's alright, Bruno,' she said dismissively to the now sulking male officer. 'I'll deal with this.'

And so, thirty minutes later, they drove home breathing a deep sigh of relief. Police officer Galante had ensconced all four family members in her cramped office while Rosaria began relating the story of Maristella Russo. At one point, Adriana Galante held up a hand and said: 'It's alright, Rosaria. We are all – well, nearly all – aware of the basic details of this affair.' She had resignedly waved a hand in the direction of the front desk. 'Just tell me about the latest development.'

Not only had Adriana Galante telephoned a colleague in Matera but she had also contacted the ordinary *polizia* in that town.

'The officer in charge of the *polizia* in Matera is a lot brighter than his opposite number in the *Carabinieri,*' she had explained without mincing her words.

On the way home, Riccardo looked almost happy – his faith in the police's ability to save Stella restored.

But the delay inadvertently caused by Marco Scarpa's absence that day had allowed time for darker forces to muster. Even as Rosaria and family pulled up in their driveway, a modest-looking, black FIAT Brava with three men inside it, shrouded in dark suits and sunglasses, had arrived in Matera on the look-out for a blue Ferrari.

***

The *Magnifico Rettore,* Fabiano Mela had become increasingly disgruntled during the course of the previous weeks. His unease had been rapidly transformed into outright concern as it became increasingly obvious that his 'nephew' was an inept bungler who had fallen prey to the allure of easy cash and the false trappings of wealth. He never dreamt that his idiotic illegitimate son would blow such a large proportion of the relatively modest sum of €250 000, which he had bestowed on him by way of encouragement, on such a ridiculously ostentatious motorcar.

'It's alright, *zio,'* Dario had ingenuously reassured him. 'It's only a second hand one!'

Just this week, Dario had been flashing around Legano, announcing his presence wherever he went. The Rector had just come to the conclusion that the fruits of his unwise involvement with a beautiful violinist all those years ago had now become a severe liability. Dario could, quite unintentionally, publicly expose him for what he really was – an important man in Italian society in a position of public trust who was skilfully and painstakingly ensuring a secure and comfortable retirement for himself in a few years' time.

And then, he had had to bow to pressure from his chief scientist, Leonardo Molinari, to hire someone to investigate the very leaking of the University's advanced technological projects thanks to which he had begun to have access to funds which could never be directly traced back to the University. He would have to be content with channelling smaller sums of 'public' money into his own accounts over a much longer period of time. It was truly galling!

Never had he ever dreamt that this woman, from some private investigation agency in the city, would succeed in laying bare the source of the leaks from the science faculty in the space of under a week. To cap it all, he had received an anonymous text-message which stated bluntly that the sender 'knew what he was up to'. He could not even begin to guess at the identity of this person – some trouble-maker obviously!

Fabiano Mela suddenly felt vulnerable. He sighed deeply as he came to the inevitable conclusion that he must risk disastrous public exposure – or take the step of eliminating the problem at source. He had dreaded the moment when he would be forced to contact *those people* again and admit that their plans had been seriously compromised. But there was no point in delaying the evil moment. He had just been informed by his 'nephew' that he was heading for Matera and that he had the girl with him. Two birds with one stone, he thought as he dialled the private number of the one man in Salento who could settle his problems for him. Fabiano Mela had no compunction about being instrumental in the elimination of two human souls if it meant saving his own skin – but he did not want to know the gruesome details. He was a man who loved to enjoy the delicacies of eating high class meats but who would always leave the bloody labour to those who worked in the slaughter houses.

* * *

Dario had been shocked into a sense of full awareness by Stella's words. For the first time since he had seduced her six months ago, he realised he was dealing with a woman who was considerably smarter than had first appeared. He had to face the distinct possibility that she was smarter than *he* was. The realisation undermined his so far unshaken belief in his own superior male ego. He had spent most of his life manipulating and exploiting girls and even fully-grown women for his own sexual and financial ends. Now he was faced with a beautiful, sexually awakened woman who had seen right through him and a scheme – admittedly devised by his father – which he had considered fool-proof. This 'girl' had even had the gall to refer to his car as 'stupid'! He was feeling angry and defenceless against forces suddenly beyond his control. But he had not quite lost his sense of self-preservation. He sat in silence as he drove speedily along the highway towards Matera. He needed time to think how to deal with this new situation. He would have to make a supreme effort to sound reassuring to Stella, sitting by his side feeling increasingly uneasy as they sped towards their unfamiliar destination. The flat countryside of Puglia gave way to the rugged foothills of the *Appennini*, which run down the spine of Italy, petering out as soon as they reach Italy's heel.

'It's alright, Stella,' he began in a conciliatory tone. 'I'm not angry with you at all. Our scheme did not work out. Let's forget it.'

He was treated to a sidelong glare from Stella whose eyes and sensuous, pouting mouth expressed derision. He took his eyes off the nearly deserted road for three seconds, his stare fixed on the swell of her breasts.

'LOOK OUT!' shouted Stella.

A squat, unshaven man was lurching out into the road about fifty metres in front of the car, forcing Dario to apply the brakes.

'DON'T STOP!' shouted Stella. 'It's a trap!' At the last moment, Dario swerved out into the middle of the road, missing the man by no more than thirty centimetres.

'Sicilian highwaymen,' explained Stella with a note of hysteria in her voice provoked by the suddenness of the apparition. 'I've been told by so many people to be wary along these roads. They have been known to steal people's cars and leave the occupants stranded penniless in this wilderness.'

The shared shock had, for the time being, re-established a sense of familiarity between them – more dangerous than outright enmity, Stella realised. She would have to be very strong-willed if she was to maintain her resolve.

The approach to Matera through its twentieth century slums was depressing. Their first sighting of the old city was, by contrast, nothing less than breathtaking. It was as if they had suddenly been caught up in a New Testament story which made the baroque streets of Legano seem like recent history. Instead of wearing flowing robes as they should have been, the few inhabitants emerging from their siesta looked out of place – dressed in jeans, skirts and T-shirts. Stella was fascinated despite being in the presence of this man whom she had hoped to lure away from her friends and colleagues. In one way, she had succeeded in achieving this, but not at all in the manner which she had envisaged.

'We'll find a nice hotel,' said Dario with now only one objective in mind.

'I don't want to…' began Stella.

'I need to be here overnight, Stella. I've been given Basilicata to cover by my company. I have an early morning appointment in town. I'll take you back to Legano afterwards…and that will be the end of it, I promise.'

Stella's reluctance to share a bed with Dario was mitigated when she saw the hotel room. They had driven down a road with a camera, mounted on a pillar, which had briefly flashed as they drove by. Good! Someone official would know where they were heading. She was hoping desperately that Rosaria would have acted on the information that she had relayed to her friend earlier in the day. But she had no way of knowing whether Rosaria had been able to hear what she had said since she had had to cut the call short before Dario became suspicious.

Dario had picked one of the hotels in Matera whose bedrooms were carved out of the solid rock. It was an ancient cave with all the modern amenities to hand, dimly lit by concealed lights around the stone walls. To Dario's frustration, Stella insisted on going for a walk round the ancient town. She needed a drink and something to eat, she said. She was playing for time – hoping that she would be 'rescued' before she had to succumb to his inevitable sexual advances. When they arrived back at the hotel later on, twilight was falling. Just as well, she thought. The blue Ferrari was parked in a makeshift car park opposite the hotel entrance. Stella noticed there was a black FIAT *Brava* with tinted windows parked a few spaces away. She could make out three motionless figures sitting in the car smoking cigarettes. Dario did not appear to notice anything untoward. He was more concerned about the safety of his Ferrari and the prospect of an anger-releasing, vengeful bout of violent sex.

Stella had all but given up hope that the police would arrive in time to rescue her. It was more than six hours ago that she had called Rosaria. She was not to know that, due to a technical fault, the video surveillance screens in Matera had all gone down. Being a Sunday, the police stations had only a skeleton staff operating them. To make matters worse, the *carabinieri* had been called out to investigate reports that a gang of Sicilian highway robbers were operating again on the deserted stretch of road to Taranto. The police officer whom Adriana Galante had alerted received the message very late on in the day and had been obliged to get his two officers to phone around all the hotels in Matera one by one to find out in which hotel a certain Fabbro Dario had registered – along with his blue Ferrari *California.* There was a list of well over one hundred to get through. So far, they had drawn a blank.

* * *

Stella read the unmistakable signs of lust on Dario's face the minute she had stepped out of the shower with only a fluffy white bath towel round her body. The swelling beneath his trousers was unmistakable as he walked deliberately towards her. Already she felt that powerful urge growing inside her which defied resistance and banished all rational thought processes from her mind. *'Animale'*, she thought as he began to remove his shoes, jeans and the shirt which covered his taut muscular body. *'Animale'*, she said again and was thrilled by the power of the word. She felt the wet warmth spreading in anticipation between her legs as he guided her none too gently towards the bed. This was how she liked it – the feeling of utter powerlessness to do anything to stop what was going to happen; the inevitable breaching of her body's defences as he pushed into her with all his rigid strength.

Dario deftly turned her over so she was face down on the soft bed. He found the curvature of her buttocks pushed up towards him in deliberate and provocative invitation the most exciting sensation he knew. He put his hands roughly between her thighs and felt the warm, moist flesh demanding that he enter her. No pretence at fore-play this time. He just wanted to experience the raw pleasure of unbridled libido. She gasped as she always did when he plunged deep inside her.

Stella was at first disconcerted to find that his hand on the back of her neck was pushing her face into the bedclothes, making it difficult to breathe. Then she felt the onset of panic and the cold realisation that, this time, he was punishing her. Why had she been so impulsive? She thought of Alessandro in that instant of growing pain in her lungs. How could she ever face him again after this act of betrayal? Then more pain as her lungs began to be starved of oxygen. She just had time to pray once more as the pain in her chest was far greater than any sensation of sexual pleasure she had felt a brief moment beforehand. He was trying to kill her. At least, he would go to jail for murder...

Dario releasing her neck was a reflex action in response to the violent and insistent banging on the bedroom door.

'*Polizia! Apra la porta, Signor Fabbro.* It's about your car,' shouted a coarse voice.

In the same instant as Stella was drawing life-giving oxygen into her lungs, she knew that it was not the police outside the door.

'*Un attimo!*' Dario called out. 'Get dressed, Stella! Quickly!'

Stella got into her jeans and pulled a warm sweater over her head. Shoes... She dived for her shoulder bag as Dario, already fully dressed, walked towards the door. She just had time to hit the switch that extinguished the main lights in the bedroom, leaving only the subdued wall lights which cast ghostly shadows on the rocky walls.

Three dark-suited men wearing sunglasses grabbed Dario. He saw and felt the revolver pushed against his temple. 'We're going for a ride in your car, *signore.* I hope you've remembered the ignition-card.' Dario nodded in terror. The sudden contrast between his strong erotic urges and the cold reality of the revolver left him numb. As they frog-marched him outside into the darkness, the man with the revolver spoke to one of the other two mobsters.

'You - go inside and get the girl!' he ordered tersely.

The man did as he was told. He came out again after a minute just as Dario was being bundled into the driving seat.

'She's not there, *capo.'*

He was treated to a blow around the head. 'You're a blind fool, Antonio. You, Manny, go and get the girl. Look everywhere – even under the bed and in the wardrobe.'

Dario was sitting petrified in the driving seat of his Ferrari. The man with the revolver was sitting in the passenger seat. He shoved the barrel of the revolver between Dario's legs. They waited. The mobster called Manny emerged from the darkness and crossed the narrow street to the car park.

'He's right, *capo.* There's no sign of her – just a bra and a pair of knickers on the floor. Oh yeah, and a broken vase.'

'Cazzo puttana!' swore the leader of the gang pushing the revolver hard into Dario's genitals. 'Where the fuck is she?'

'I don't know,' croaked Dario in terror. The sound of a police siren higher up in the city coming ever nearer galvanised the group into action. 'We'll come back and get her later. She can't get very far. *Adesso muoviamoci!* You drive exactly where I tell you to go,' said the gang leader to Dario. 'You two, follow us closely.'

They swept off in a noisy cloud of dust into the dark countryside, taking a road that led out of Matera and deeper into the rugged countryside of Basilicata. They were following the road that skirted the deep ravine where the water flowed only in the winter and the early springtime.

* * *

The two uniformed policemen, who had finally tracked down the hotel San Martino, found the bedroom door wide open and the room light blazing. They remarked on the cheap, plaster vase lying smashed on the floor near the door. Of the two occupants whom they expected to find, there was no sign.

'Nothing looking remotely like a blue Ferrari either, *capo,*' one of the policemen told his senior officer over his mobile phone.

'*Merda!*' exclaimed the senior police officer under his breath. He hated loose ends.

12: A Time of Suspense

'It's been such an awful shock to me, Rosaria. But at the same time, I'm relieved because now I understand myself so much better. It's as if I've been keeping a guilty secret locked up in a dungeon in my brain all this time – so deeply buried that I didn't even know it was there. Suddenly, I can see myself as I really am. I hope you don't think any the worse of me, Rosaria.'

A very different Giovanna was sitting next to Rosaria Miccoli in the passenger seat of her car being driven to the University campus outside Legano. Rosaria's waking thoughts had been for Stella; not surprisingly, because she had not been able to stop herself worrying about Stella's fate since she had overheard her disturbing exchange of words with Dario.

But later on, Rosaria had thought how Giovanna must be feeling that Monday morning, believing that she had been instrumental in provoking Stella's flight into the unknown the day before. Giovanna would need reassuring or else she would probably refuse to show her face in front of her colleagues.

'I was just wondering exactly how *affectionate* she really was!' said Rosaria ironically to Adam as they lay side by side in bed.

'Perhaps you should offer to give Giovanna a lift into the University this morning, Rosy,' Adam had suggested.

'Good idea!' she had replied.

Rosaria had taken Anna and Riccardo to school. Anna had had vivid dreams about Stella wandering around scantily dressed through the deserted countryside trying to find her way back to Legano on foot. Riccardo had anxiously plied his mother with questions that she was unable to answer.

'I know as much as you do, Riccardo,' she said. 'I hope we'll have some news when you get home after school.'

Rosaria had already called Giovanna and went to fetch her after kissing her children a hurried goodbye at the school gate.

In the car, on their way to the *AltoTek* campus, Rosaria drew a deep breath and summoned up the mental strength to choose the words which would reassure Giovanna. Rosaria reckoned that she would not have to stretch the truth too far.

'Of course I don't think any the worse of you Giovanna. You're the same person as you always have been – but with a much clearer idea as to where your true self lies. That is something very positive...'

'I don't want anyone at work to know just yet, Rosaria. You won't...'

'If you didn't trust me, Giovanna, you wouldn't have told me all this, now would you?'

'No. Thank you for being so understanding. You're a good friend, Rosaria.'

'As for Stella, I can tell you without a shadow of doubt that she had a personal mission in life to become a sort of *capro espiatorio* – a scapegoat – for all of us. She felt she had to make amends for betraying you all. I think she wanted to safeguard *me* as well.'

'Safeguard *you!* How do you mean, Rosaria?'

'She is convinced that there is some malign force at work behind all this. I believe she is right. She wanted to protect me and my family from any involvement in this affair. She has been very courageous – if not downright foolhardy.'

'But where is she right now?' asked Giovanna anxiously.

Rosaria let out a profound sigh. 'I really wish I knew, Giovanna. I'm hoping for some news today. Whatever has happened to her, she has switched off her phone...or somebody else has,' concluded Rosaria ominously.

They pulled into the *AltoTek* car park. Rosaria was not sure how she was going to occupy her day. She did not want to be at home on her own waiting on tenterhooks for a phone call about Stella. Technically, she was supposed to be employed by the University for one more week. She would be freer to do what she had in mind back in the *studio* of the Greco Agency, but it seemed essential to come in and tell Francesco and Leonardo about Sunday's alarming turn of events. She would also have to warn them about the potential involvement of their leader, *Il Magnifico Rettore,* Fabiano Mela, in this affair, which was beginning to show all the hallmarks of a criminal conspiracy, led by a corrupt public official.

On arriving at the University entrance, Rosaria gave Giovanna a reassuring hug and left her to live out her working day with her secret discovery tucked away inside her. Or so she thought! Her colleagues commented to each other and to Rosaria that they had been surprised that Giovanna had actually smiled broadly at them all and wished them a pleasant day.

'What's come over her?' some of them commented, quite taken aback by the sudden change in her hitherto reserved attitude towards them.

As soon as she was on her own, Rosaria remembered that there was now another interested party whom she had not contacted; her boss, Alessandro knew nothing about the disappearance of the new love of his life. She overcame the fleeting, sadistic desire to keep him in the dark and phoned him once she knew that he would have arrived at the *studio.* As expected, Alessandro bombarded her with questions much as Riccardo had done.

'We will have to be patient, Sandro – and pray she is safe.' Rosaria promised she would find the time to come into the agency later that day; Alessandro sounded as if he might need her moral support.

* * *

It was reassuring to be back in the familiar world of scientific research. The whole team went about its daily business, peering through the lenses of giant microscopes at minute, living entities of which the vast majority of the human race has no clear concept. Other white-coated figures were studying screens covered with dancing spots of light representing a cosmos that remained meaningless to Rosaria. It was the casualness with which the team treated all these wonders, thought Rosaria, which was reassuring; to them, it was all as natural as preparing a cup of coffee in a Moka pot. She was content to see Giovanna sharing one of these *séances* with her colleagues. She *was* being unusually talkative today.

Rosaria reluctantly headed for Leonardo's office. At her suggestion, their *capo* summoned Francesco away from his work in the Clean Room. They had decided to put the encryption project at the top of the priority list. Nobody had commented on Stella's absence because she had not been expected to be there until the problem had been resolved

'How's the project going, Francesco?' asked Leonardo.

'I wish Stella was here to help me. She had an amazing grasp of the complex maths and physics involved,' replied his deputy nostalgically.

This comment did not make it any easier for Rosaria to tell them the bad news that she had to impart.

'I just wanted to bring you two up to date,' began Rosaria tentatively. As she was relating the incidents of the previous day, the men's faces grew increasingly concerned.

'I hope Stella isn't really relying on that 'invisibility cloak' to protect her,' Leonardo said at one stage during Rosaria's narrative. 'It doesn't really make a person disappear! At best it might blur what other people can see.'

'I'm sure she's aware of that, *capo,*' Francesco reassured him.

Rosaria was half way through telling them about Stella's overheard dialogue with Dario on the way to Matera when her phone rang. It was the *colonnello,* Marco Scarpa.

'This could be important,' she said excusing herself as she went out into the corridor outside Leonardo's office, leaving the two scientists deep in conversation.

'*Buongiorno,* Rosaria. I just wanted to say how sorry I am about letting you down yesterday,' he began. 'I spent the day with my father in the hospital at Tricase. He's just had a big operation...'

'I'm sorry to hear that, Marco,' she said. Had she really called him by his first name?

'I'm just very worried that the delay might have put your colleague's life in danger. It's the first time in years I've had to switch off my phone,' he continued after the briefest of pauses.

'Are you aware of what has happened?' asked Rosaria.

'Only what I've been told by my colleague, Adriana, whom you met yesterday.'

'So, you haven't got any news about Stella and...the man with her?'

'I've been in contact with the *commissario* in Matera. He's a good man – really on the ball. He'll be back in touch with me later today.'

'I'll come and see you later, Marco,' offered Rosaria. Once she had called him by his first name, it was easier the second time.

'No, I'll try to come over to see you this time. I owe you that favour after letting you down yesterday.'

Rosaria protested quietly that it wasn't his fault.

'As soon as I know anything, Rosaria, I'll phone you.'

When Rosaria stepped back inside Leonardo's office, he was just ending a phone call on his desk phone.

'*Sì, Magnifico. Certo...a prestissimo allora.* I've got to go and see the Rector in an hour's time,' said Leonardo with a look of displeasure on his face. 'He sounds a little rattled about something, to say the least.'

Rosaria took a deep breath and looked meaningfully at both Francesco and Leonardo.

'I know what you are about to say, Rosaria,' said Francesco. '*Capo,*' he continued, turning to face Leonardo. 'Rosaria is about to tell you that we suspect – although there is no concrete proof – that our Magnificent Rector is deeply involved in this business.'

Speaking rapidly, Rosaria told him everything they knew – including the fact that they strongly suspected that Dario had been manipulated by the Rector, who was seemingly his 'uncle'. Leonardo's face turned paler as she was speaking.

'You'll have to tread very carefully, Leonardo,' said Francesco.

'Yes, Leonardo. You simply must not alert him to the fact that we know about the possible Dario connection. And please, I beg of you, *capo,* remember he thinks my name is Elena Camisso – should I come up in the course of conversation.'

'Apparently, he wants to talk to me about funding,' said Leonardo, letting out a profound sigh. 'I'm really not cut out to deal with all this subterfuge...'

'*Forza,* Leonardo!' Francesco and Rosaria said in unison, provoking a burst of laughter from them both and bringing a rueful smile to Leonardo's face.

'So everybody keeps telling me!'

* * *

Instead of sitting behind the solid defences of his vast mahogany desk so he could look down disdainfully on his interlocutor, as was his wont, the Rector came round to Leonardo's side of the desk and sat down on the second armchair. This gesture in itself made Leonardo instantly suspicious, providing clear evidence that Fabiano Mela's habitual arrogance had been deflated by some change of outlook. 'Interesting how changes in behaviour can betray a shift in the inner workings of a man's mind,' mused the scientist inconsequentially. Leonardo did not have much time to ponder on the philosophy of behaviourism, however. The Rector had begun talking earnestly, adopting a tone of sycophantic sincerity, leaning forward in Leonardo's direction to emphasise the intimate importance of their discussion.

'I'm happy to tell you, *Professore*...may I call you Leonardo, by the way...that we have received some quite considerable donations from the organisations present at your excellent presentation at the Hotel Europa a week ago. I wished to interrupt your vital efforts for our university, nay, for our great nation, to assure you that the promised funds will be at your immediate disposal.'

Leonardo was instantly alerted by the Rector's complete volte-face. He was by now quite convinced that Francesco and Rosaria were right in their assumption that the *Magnifico Rettore* was involved in some dubious manipulation of public funds. *'Peculato'* is a dirty word in Italian but, the truth had to be admitted, embezzlement was rife in his country.

'It would help me, *Magnifico,* if you could give me a precise idea as to the amount of funding we might expect,' said Leonardo with heart in mouth. It was clean against his nature to think that anyone in a position of public trust could possibly be anything other than white as snow in their handling of public money. He was at once disturbed but not surprised by the Rector's evasive reply. His colleagues' suspicions appeared to be vindicated.

'I'm afraid I am not in a position to be so precise at the present moment,' Fabiano Mela smoothly avoided committing himself to a definite figure. 'The final sums are being worked out by our financial department even as we speak. Besides which, we have not yet received all the donations indicated. What I want from you today, Leonardo, is an estimate, a global figure if you will, that will cover your research needs. I can assure you that there will be sufficient funds available to cover your most forward-looking projects.'

Leonardo tentatively mentioned a figure close to five million euros. He was sure he detected a fleeting expression of relief on the Rector's face – quickly covered up by one of his reassuring smiles.

'Why don't you give me some idea of what your main project involves, Leonardo?' continued the Rector standing up and walking round to the other side of his desk once more. He sat down assuredly in his swivel chair. 'I'm fascinated by what is going on in your department.' He was evidently under the impression that his chief scientist had been appeased by the prospect of receiving such generous funding.

Leonardo was mindful of the injunction laid upon him by Francesco and Rosaria not to arouse the Rector's suspicions. Nevertheless, he took some pleasure in blinding this man with a science he was convinced would leave him totally in the dark.

'It's the world's most advanced encryption machine, *Magnifico*...'

'So, it codes and decodes information, I suppose. But what makes this particular invention so important?'

'Do you really want to know, *Magnifico?* The explanation is really quite technical...'

'Yes, *Professore,*' replied the Rector tartly, his former pretence at amicability discarded like an unwanted garment. 'I really do want to know!'

'Very well then, *Magnifico,* I'll make it as simple as possible for you,' said Leonardo looking pointedly at his superior. 'The device depends entirely on the peculiar properties of quantum mechanical behaviour. I expect you have heard of Pauli's Exclusion Principle, which in simple terms states that a particle can only occupy one quantum state at a time?'

Leonardo was warming to his task as he saw a glazed look appear in the Rector's eyes.

'Of course!' said Fabiano Mela, nodding furiously.

'Well, we have succeeded in attaching a tiny part of a message to a single photon – that's a light particle, of course – using simple binary logic.

But the amazing part of it is,' he continued, 'that if anyone attempts to intercept and observe the photon on its way to a recipient, the message will become corrupt. The system relies on the fact that, as soon as you measure quantum data, you simultaneously perturb this data. Thus any eavesdropper – whom we nickname Eve – will instantly be detected by the recipient of the message. So wonderfully simple, isn't it *Magnifico?*'

Leonardo knew that he had lost the Rector. He boldly decided to fire one parting shot that should find its mark very accurately. He was astounded at his own temerity.

'Just imagine, *Magnifico,* how much such an invention would be worth if it ever fell into the wrong hands!'

Leonardo was gratified to see a shifty look briefly appear on his leader's face, quickly covered up by some comment that it was just as well he had employed 'that woman' from the detective agency.

'Well, thank you *Professore* for your time. I'll let you carry on with your work in the knowledge that you have our full backing. *Buon lavoro!'*

The audience was at an end. Leonardo stood up and left the room as deferentially as he could. He was amazed at the Rector's capacity to reassume his public *persona* with such ease. Leonardo was quite convinced that Rosaria and Francesco had been right in their suppositions; their Rector was deeply involved in this affair and, Leonardo suspected, he had almost certainly corrupted someone working in the University's financial department too.

'I'm glad it isn't up to me to unravel this web of intrigue,' he thought as he was driving back to the *AltoTek* campus in pensive mode.

* * *

As soon as he was back, he called Francesco and 'that woman' from the agency into his office and asked them to close the door behind them. He treated them in a hushed whisper to an account of what had transpired between himself and the Rector.

'*Bravo*, Leonardo!' Francesco complimented his *capo* in admiration.

'I'll be talking to my *colonnello* later today, I hope,' said Rosaria. 'I'll tell him what happened with the Rector. I suspect he will want to get the *Guardia di Finanza* involved as soon as possible. This has obviously become far too complex for us to handle. With your permission, Leonardo, I would like to go back to my office at the *studio* now. I want to try and track down a connection between Dario Fabbro and the Rector...' Rosaria's mobile phone rang – as it always seemed to whenever she was in Leonardo's office.

'It's the *colonnello!*' she said with a look of fear in her eyes. 'He might have some news about Stella or...'

As she listened to Marco Scarpa's voice, her face turned white.

'I'm going back to the Greco agency now, Marco. Come and see me there if...'

She left the sentence unfinished. Marco Scarpa was still speaking, reassuring Rosaria about something. The call came to an end.

'The police in Matera have spotted the burnt out remains of a Ferrari at the bottom of a gully,' she explained. 'They've sent for a crane to pull it out. We shall just have to wait and see...'

The three people in the room stood silent, each praying fervently for the same outcome.

* * *

Rosaria was driving back towards the centre of Legano. She wanted to spend the rest of the day doing some research on her *own* computer, at her *own* desk, back in her *own* office. She needed to find something to occupy her in order to keep her mind from dwelling endlessly on the fate of Stella. When she went up the stairs to the third floor and entered the familiar office, she found Alessandro pacing restlessly around with his mobile phone pressed to his ear, hoping vainly that Stella would answer his calls.

'Stella's phone has been switched off all day, Sandro,' she said simply. 'I've been trying ever since I woke up this morning.'

Rosaria had never seen her official boss looking so distraught. Any vestige of envy she might have felt that she was no longer the centre of his daily attention had been dispelled. They were both equally anxious about Stella's fate. Rosaria felt bound to tell Alessandro about the burnt out Ferrari which the local police had discovered in Matera - if only because she needed to share this disturbing development with another living soul. Alessandro immediately expressed the thought that had also been worrying Rosaria.

'Burnt out? At the bottom of a ravine did you say? But that sounds as if the mafia has had a hand in this business,' he said puzzled. This discovery did nothing to alleviate his fears.

'Rosaria, I can't bear the thought that I could lose Stella just as I seem to have found my true soul-mate. That would be too tragic.'

Rosaria noticed that Sandro, too, had begun calling her by her real name. She would have to remonstrate with him when all this was over, or at least remind him to keep to her pseudonym in matters of business. She went up to him and laid her hand on his arm.

I'm sorry, Sandro. We shall just have to wait until Marco Scarpa phones. Meanwhile, let's keep ourselves as busy as we can. Will you help me try and find a connection between the Rector and this man Dario Fabbro? It could be useful – if only to tie up loose ends. At the moment, the Rector's involvement in this business is little more than suspicion and conjecture.'

'You mean, go into the Rector's past life, Rosaria? I'm sorry. I can't go on calling you Elena Camisso. But don't worry, it's only while we are on our own.'

Rosaria made a noise to indicate that she would allow this only because circumstances were exceptional, giving him her stern look with which he was all too familiar.

'I bet that journalist, Costanza De Santis has already dug up some dirt from Fabiano Mela's past!' declared Alessandro.

'We can't get her involved yet, Sandro. If she has even the slightest suspicion that there might be a scandal in the air, it will be in the public domain before tomorrow evening.'

'No, I know. That would ruin any official investigation before it even got underway. I was merely speculating, Ros…Elena,' he said smiling briefly for the first time since she had arrived.

By early afternoon, they had unearthed a mass of information about Fabiano Mela's past history. He was born in Bologna and had grown up in that far away city in the north. But what puzzled them was the fact that he was an only child. They spent a long time discussing the fact that Dario's 'uncle' could not, after all, be the Rector of Legano's university. The discovery was disconcerting.

'That's odd, Sandro. Stella seemed so positive that there was a connection between Dario and the Rector. She wasn't being fanciful, I'm certain.'

'Sometimes people call older men 'uncle' as a term of endearment, Elena. By the way, I prefer 'Elena' to 'Rosaria' any day!' laughed Alessandro. 'I'll stick to Elena, I think.'

'So do I, if the truth be told, Sandro,' smiled Rosaria.

They fell silent for several minutes as they both inevitably began to think about Stella again. Rosaria looked at her watch and started in surprise.

'*O Dio!* I've got to pick up my kids, Sandro. They will never forgive me if I'm late – and neither will the head teacher. She already disapproves of working mothers. Listen, Sandro. Can I bring them back here for a while? I don't want to leave you on your own.'

'Of course - I haven't seen your children for ages. They must be quite grown up by now. I'll try and dig up something useful on Mela while you're away.'

* * *

'But please, *mamma!* Why don't *you* phone the *colonnello?*' pleaded Riccardo from the back seat of the car as they sped back towards the agency ignoring as many red lights as possible. 'Maybe he's just forgotten to call you back.'

'*Non dire sciochezze, Riccardo!*' interjected Anna decisively. 'The *colonnello* would *never* forget to phone *mamma.* He likes her too much! But don't repeat what I just said when *papà* is there!'

Rosaria was listening to every word as she pretended to be concentrating hard on the city traffic. She had debated with herself whether or not to tell them about the discovery of the burnt out Ferrari. She decided that they were already sufficiently aware of the fragility of life - there was no need to shield from the precariousness of Stella's situation. Anna's last words had revealed a degree of emotional awareness which was becoming increasingly apparent as the days went by. They arrived at the Greco agency and the children clambered upstairs to be greeted by Alessandro, who had heard their voices on the stairwell.

'Anna! Riccardo! How tall you've grown! The last time I saw you two was when your mum and I left you eating a pizza while we went off to rescue Judge Grassi from the mob. Do you remember that?' asked a smiling Alessandro.

'Of course we remember, Sandro,' said Anna indignantly.

'We wanted to come too!' said Riccardo.

'Come on in, *ragazzi!* Make yourselves at home.'

'You're looking pleased with yourself, Sandro,' commented Rosaria.

'I've been busy while you were away unearthing stuff about our Rector. Come on, Rosaria, I'll show you what I've found out. I can hardly call you 'Elena' when your children are here, can I?' he added seeing the expression on her face.

Rosaria sighed. 'You'd better call me plain 'Rosy' in that case. Everyone else in the family does!'

Sandro turned to the children again.

'Would you two like to help us in this investigation?' he asked them seriously. Two faces lit up with pleasure.

'Will it help us find Stella?' asked Riccardo.

'Well it might in the long run,' answered Sandro Greco, surprised by the directness of the question.

'What do you want us to do, Sandro?' asked Anna, more practical than her little brother.

Alessandro led them to the round 'conference' table and handed them each pens and sheets of paper.

'I would be very grateful if you could come up with some ideas, if you would be so kind, because I'm stuck. Here's my problem,' Sandro continued. 'Let's say there's a young man called Dario...'

'So it *is* to help Stella,' interrupted Riccardo with a delighted smile.

'Well done, Riccardo. Now, can you think of as many reasons as possible, both of you, why this young man called Dario would call somebody 'uncle' all the time when he isn't really his uncle at all?'

Anna and Riccardo sat pondering in silence for a time while Sandro and their mother went into his office to discuss what he had discovered.

'Our Rector has led a very interesting life,' began Sandro. 'Did you know he was the financial director at the University of Bologna for twelve years before he applied for the rectorship at Pavia University?'

Rosaria shook her head in silence. In the next room, they could hear the murmuring of the children's voices.

'He didn't last very long there before he escaped to the deep south of Italy. He allegedly had a number of affairs with younger women...'

'Shades of our beloved ex-prime minister!' said Rosaria sarcastically.

'There was one affair which nearly finished him off and certainly led to his wife leaving him. He had a brief but passionate relationship with a lady violinist from the *Orchestra Sinfonia di Milano* during a series of concerts they were giving in Pavia. He broke off the relationship suddenly and she threatened to denounce him to the media...'

'I think the fact that he was in charge of finances at Bologna University might have a bearing on the present, don't you, Sandro?'

They discussed the ramifications of the situation at length and were speculating fruitlessly about Stella's fate when Anna called out:

'We've finished, Sandro! This is what we have come up with,' Anna told them as soon as they were all sitting round the table. 'You go first, Riccardo.'

'Maybe Dario doesn't know this man's name so he just calls him *'zio'* because it's easier,' began Riccardo trying to decipher his own writing.

'Or the man has a long name which Dario can't pronounce, like Calogerino or something,' said Anna.

'Maybe Dario doesn't have an uncle and he just wants to call him *'zio'* because he misses having a real uncle?' suggested Riccardo.

'Or...we thought,' said Anna struggling to find the words that would express a more complex idea. 'We thought maybe this man doesn't really like Dario and he told him to call him 'zio' all the time because he doesn't want everyone to know that...'

'That's it!' exclaimed Alessandro, his eyes alight with amazement that he had not thought of it himself. 'Just a minute you three – wait there.'

Rosaria put her arms round both her children and hugged them tightly. She had understood what had occurred to Sandro.

'I think you two wonderful children have just done it again!'

'I'm not sure what we said, *mamma!*' Anna was pleased but puzzled by the adults' reaction.

Alessandro emerged from his office ten minutes later looking jubilant. 'The lady violinist had a son – just after her break-up with Mela,' he said. 'And guess what the son's name was?'

'Dario!' they called out in unison.

'Yes, Dario Fabbro,' confirmed Sandro. 'He must have kept his mother's surname.'

After celebratory drinks of coffee and Fantas, and murmurings that it was time to go home, Rosaria's phone finally rang. They all started in surprise, having momentarily set aside their anxieties about Stella. She set the phone down on the table with the loudspeaker turned on and said with a lump in her throat:

'*Pronto?*'

'I'm sorry this has taken all day to sort out, Rosaria. Well, they pulled the car out of the ravine. There was one body in the car burnt beyond recognition. The hands had been tied to the steering wheel before the car was set alight...'

Marco Scarpa had stopped in the middle of his narrative.

'Is someone crying?' he asked.

'Yes, it's Riccardo,' replied Rosaria. 'He's been worried about Stella all day. And when you said...'

'I'm so desperately sorry, Rosaria. I didn't realise you were all... Well, I must tell you immediately that it was a man's body. There are no signs of Stella. She's vanished!'

Sandro let out a sigh of relief. Riccardo dried his tears away with the back of his hand. He was smiling radiantly.

'I knew she was alright!' he said.

'No you didn't, Riccardo,' said Anna. But it was said with compassion for her little brother's feelings.

13: Vanishing Act

Rosaria felt too relieved herself to have the heart to tell Riccardo and Anna that the mere fact that Stella was not involved in this horrific discovery did not necessarily mean that she had escaped unharmed. The children would come to this conclusion by themselves soon enough. Alessandro, too, took one look at the joy on their faces and realised the devastating effect such a declaration would have. It would be better not to shatter their hopes as soon as they had been kindled.

Rosaria had arranged to meet Marco Scarpa the following morning at eleven o'clock at the Greco Agency to discuss what their next move should be. There was little else she could do – except hope and pray, and take the children home.

Adam was waiting anxiously for them when they arrived. Rosaria went up to him and hugged him warmly, kissing him sensuously on the mouth. Adam knew her too well after all the years they had been together – well enough to know there was a hidden message behind such an unexpected and spontaneous gesture of physical love. He knew better than to ask her what was going on in her mind. She would quite genuinely not have had the time to identify the hidden stimulus which had provoked the gesture. It was always a subconscious reaction to something which her mind was still in the process of mulling over. Adam was content that it seemed to express enduring love, whatever intrusive element was present. He might have to wait for several days before the cached message came to the surface.

Anna and Riccardo ran up to Adam for their hug and breathlessly began telling him everything that had happened.

'Where do *you* think Stella has got to, *papà?*' asked Riccardo. 'She seems to have vanished into thin air.'

Adam had to consider his answer carefully. He realised how deeply involved his children had become in Stella's disappearance. A facile or facetious reply would not go down well.

'Well, Riccardo, let's assume that Stella somehow managed to use that 'invisibility cloak' to fool anyone who was chasing her. At this point, she has to head for safety a long way from Matera. What do you think of that so far, Riccardo?'

'It makes sense, *papà.*'

Rosaria and Anna were listening intently to this exchange of ideas.

'So, if you were in Stella's shoes, where would *you* immediately head for, Riccardo?'

There was a deep frown on Riccardo's seven-year-old face as he thought about the problem, which Adam had deftly deflected from himself.

'That's obvious, *papa!* I'd come back here! I'd feel safe with you and *mamma.*'

'Then I think it's natural to assume that Stella would have thought in the same way as you. She will almost certainly try and find her way home to her parents.'

'*Bravo papà!*' said Anna clapping her hands. 'She'd head for Bologna, of course!'

It was Rosaria's turn to look pensive. Not only had Adam dealt with the sensitive question skilfully, he had also identified an obvious human reaction to the dangerous situation in which Stella must have found herself. Rosaria came up to her partner and gave him an appreciative hug.

'I'll run that idea past Marco Scarpa tomorrow, Adam.

The mention of the police officer's name jolted her subconscious mind. Her passionate kiss of a few seconds ago had been a reflex reaction to a hidden strand of guilt; during the afternoon, she had felt a pang of something resembling desire for the *colonnello* while he was talking to her over the phone. She walked quickly into the kitchen to cover her embarrassment. Her reaction did not escape Adam's notice.

* * *

The following morning, Rosaria drove to the *AltoTek* campus to pay her respects to Leonardo, Francesco and company. She was greeted like an old friend and colleague by the whole team. Luana had stopped her in the corridor outside Leonardo's office and thanked her simply for saving the science faculty from disaster. She succeeded in expressing precisely their collective feelings when she said how sorry she was that Stella had become fatally embroiled with the criminal elements that lurk like vultures on the fringes of decent society. Imprecise and contradictory details of Stella's disappearance had spread throughout the whole campus – like an elaborate game of Chinese Whispers. Rosaria had only felt obliged to contradict one version of events when someone expressed the hope that her kidnappers would soon release her on payment of the ransom money. Inventive conjecture had obviously been rife. Everyone except Livia Marchetti complimented 'Elena' on her success. The most that this particular lady managed was a curt nod of recognition.

Sitting round the table in Leonardo's office, both Francesco and Leonardo were looking grave.

'We mustn't give up hope,' said Rosaria. 'There's a good chance that Stella has escaped the fate that awaited Dario.'

All three of them secretly felt that Dario had got his just deserts even if none of them wished to dwell on the gruesome details of his last few minutes alive. No, they thought, it was Stella's fate that was close to their hearts.

Rosaria told them about the ingenuous solution on her son's part that Stella would have headed straight back to her parents. Leonardo pondered on this for a while. His first instinct was to dismiss the possibility as the wishful thinking of a child. But he remembered in time how often his own daughter, Emma, had revealed strands of thought that had left her parents open-mouthed in astonishment. He nodded sagely and said:

'I hope to God Riccardo is right, but...'

'I know exactly where Stella's parents live,' said Francesco smiling enough to raise one tip of his moustache a couple of centimetres up one side of his face. His lopsided grin was the first sign of a cautious return to optimism. Leonardo looked surprised. Rosaria regarded Francesco with a knowing smirk on her face.

'Bologna, surely?' said Leonardo.

'No, *capo,* they live outside Bologna in a village called Vergato,' Francesco informed them knowingly, pointedly but good-humouredly returning Rosaria's sardonic smile.

'Thank you, Francesco,' said Rosaria smoothly. 'Your outstanding relationship with your team members should stand us in good stead.'

This time, Francesco's smile raised both tips of his moustache high up on his cheeks as he made a bowing gesture with his head in acknowledgement of the jibe.

'*Grazie del complimento,* signora,' he said.

Leonardo smiled politely. As usual, he had failed to understand the subtle nuance behind their verbal exchange.

* * *

Later that morning, *Colonnello* Marco Scarpa, Rosaria and Alessandro were seated at the round 'conference' table in the Greco *studio.*

'On balance,' the senior police officer was saying, 'I think we should err on the side of optimism. I believe there is a reasonable chance that Stella might have evaded capture.'

'What makes you think that, *Colonnello?*' asked Alessandro hardly daring to raise his own hopes.

'In the first place, the mafia style assassination of Dario on his own would indicate that Stella was not present. The mob would never stage two separate murders when they could kill two birds with one stone.'

Rosaria nodded in agreement and looked at Marco in anticipation.

'And in the second place..?' she prompted.

Marco Scarpa smiled indulgently at Rosaria's customary impatience.

'In the second place, my colleague, the *commissario* in Matera – I told you he was thorough – reported that his team, asking questions back at the hotel, elicited from the hotel staff that they had seen three suspicious men in a black FIAT *Brava* in the early hours of the morning, nosing around the hotel. The night porter asked them if he could help. One of the men said they were looking for a friend – a dark-haired girl. She was supposed to be in Room 7. The porter was suspicious, but he was afraid to ask further questions because he sensed the men belonged to the mob. He told the officers that they didn't have local accents. He thought they were from Salento – from our part of the world.'

The sense of relief was tangible as the police officer paused before resuming.

'The strange thing was that, when the night porter went to check around, he found the room which Dario Fabbro had booked with its door wide open, all the lights on and a broken flower vase on the floor. When the police officers checked the room later, there was no sign of a woman's handbag or anything. But there was a man's bag with a few clothes in it still sitting on the suitcase rack. The door to the room leads directly outside on to a veranda opposite the car park.'

'So it looks as if Stella might really have escaped,' said Alessandro tentatively.

'And if my Riccardo's guess is right, Stella might have headed for home up north,' said Rosaria excitedly.

'But why would she have switched off her phone?' asked Alessandro.

'My guess would be she's so traumatised by what happened that she is scared to reveal her whereabouts,' suggested Marco Scarpa. 'Or her battery has run out and she can't recharge it.'

'Let's find out exactly where her parents live and go there to look for her,' said Rosaria.

Marco Scarpa smiled at her habitual impulsiveness and her desire to be personally involved in her investigations. She had been like that ever since he had first met her.

'I think we should guard against being *too* optimistic just yet, Rosaria. If you will allow me to,' he suggested diplomatically, 'I'll contact the local police in Vergato and get them to send someone round to see the parents first - much better to use the local police – just as we did in Matera. We don't want the *Carabinieri* charging about with sirens blaring, do we?'

'You don't seem to have much faith in your own organisation, sir!' commented Sandro smiling.

'Oh, we have our uses, Sandro. But very often, local knowledge and a soft touch are far more effective.'

Rosaria sighed deeply. She hated inaction at times like this. Marco Scarpa looked at Rosaria with something approaching affection, displaying a sympathetic understanding of how she was feeling.

'Don't worry, Rosaria. I'm going to keep you busy for the next few hours. We're going to see my nephew in the *Guardia di Finanza*. They are very anxious to hear what you have to say about a gentleman called Fabiano Mela.'

* * *

Their first port of call was the *Carabiniere* headquarters, situated on the busy ring road which squeezed the ancient city of Legano tightly in its grip like a noose around its neck. For the first time since her long acquaintance with Marco Scarpa, she found herself sitting next to him in the passenger seat of an *Alfa Romeo* bearing the insignia of the *carabinieri* and the number 112 in white lettering – to remind the population of this important emergency telephone number.

'I feel a bit guilty, Marco,' she said in jest, 'as if I'm being taken in for questioning.'

'I can assure you, Rosaria,' he said laughing, 'if that was the case, you wouldn't be sitting in the front seat with me! Think of yourself as an honoured guest.'

On arrival, Marco Scarpa summoned his colleague, Adriana Galante, into his office where she was surprised and delighted to find Rosaria Miccoli. She went directly up to her and gave her an affectionate *bacio* on each cheek. It was straight down to business after that.

'Adriana, I want you to look up the number of the *polizia* in a village in Emilia Romagna called Vergato. Tell the person in charge, whatever rank he is, that I want a word with him. Rosaria, can you fill Adriana in with the details of the case, please? You are more familiar with them than I am.'

The two women returned to Adriana's cubby hole of an office. There was no sign anywhere of the *Carabiniere* officer who had been so obstructive two long days ago.

'He's been banished down to Leuca, Rosaria,' explained Adriana. 'He's in disgrace!'

Obviously, *Colonnello* Marco Scarpa did not suffer fools gladly. Once again, Rosaria felt a frisson of excitement deep inside her at the notion of this man's authority. She dismissed the thought instantly, banishing it to the nether regions of her subconscious mind. Instead, she set about the task of putting Adriana in the picture before she made her phone call to Vergato.

To Adriana's surprise and pleasure, she was put through to a woman at the Vergato police station. The phone was in loudspeaker mode for Rosaria's benefit.

'Sonia Racanelli,' said a pleasant self-assured voice. 'How can I help you, *Signorina* Galante?'

It took a good ten minutes for Adriana to explain the complex situation to the police woman in Vergato. Only occasionally did she interrupt Adriana for clarification.

'There are three couples in Vergato with the surname Russo,' she said when Adriana had finished speaking. 'Unfortunately, it's a very common surname up here. Can you help us narrow it down?'

'I'm not sure,' said Adriana. 'We know that Stella Russo is an only child and that her parents had her later on in life…'

Sonia Recanelli said: *'Un attimo solo, Adriana.'* She cupped her hand over the receiver. Adriana and Rosaria could hear her asking someone questions rapidly.

'That's OK, Adriana,' said Sonia after a minute. 'We know who you mean. My colleague here went to school with Stella Russo. He tells me she was impossible to forget! All the boys doted on her.'

'Yes, I understand she is quite attractive!' said Adriana. 'Now, I'll pass you to our *colonnello,* Sonia.'

'With respect, *signorina…*Adriana, tell your *capo* that his colleague has explained the matter with admirable clarity. We'll deal with this immediately – in person. I'll phone you back as soon as we've been to visit the Russo parents.'

'Long live efficient policewomen!' said Rosaria in admiration of both Adriana and her 'colleague' in that far away village in the north of their elongated motherland.

* * *

Marco Scarpa, with Rosaria by his side, drove rapidly round the ring road with siren switched on.

'Is this an emergency?' asked Rosaria ironically.

'No, but on occasions, I do get impatient with the drivers in our city. I sometimes want to get to a place in a hurry – especially when there's something important to attend to.'

'Such as me meeting your nephew?'

'Precisely, and we are running a bit late.'

'Do you know how long it takes to drive round the ring road when there's no traffic, Marco?'

'No, I would imagine about fifteen minutes,' replied the *colonnello* amused. 'Don't tell me you've tried it?'

'I did it in nine minutes once, at night time, with all the traffic lights on green.'

'Without breaking any speed limits, needless to say!' said Marco sarcastically.

'No comment, *colonnello.*'

They had already arrived in front of the Legano headquarters of the *Guardia di Finanza* inside the city walls in an elegant old square called *Piazza dei Peruzzi.* Marco Scarpa parked his car among the grey *Guardia* cars with their bright yellow stripe down the sides. They all bore the number 117.

Marco's nephew was waiting for them on the steps and led them to a smart bar next to the *Guardia* headquarters. Marco introduced Rosaria to his nephew.

'I've heard so much about you from my uncle over the years, Rosaria. He threatens to write a book about you one day. I am delighted to meet you at last. My name's Giulio Pensiero, by the way.'

To her annoyance, Rosaria felt herself blushing. She attempted to cover her embarrassment with some modestly dismissive comment.

Once they had sat down with coffees in front of them, Marco invited Rosaria to go over the story of Stella and Dario. She talked at length about their certainty that Dario had been manipulated by Fabiano Mela.

'We found out yesterday that Dario is the Rector's illegitimate son, by the way,' added Rosaria casually to the two policemen, whose eyebrows shot up at this revelation.

Fabiano Mela, they believed, was using his position as Rector to sidetrack funds into his own accounts. Giulio, who held the rank of *capitano,* listened intently, only interrupting Rosaria's narrative occasionally to ask for clarification.

'So you are saying that Professor Molinari and his deputy, Francesco Zunica, are equally convinced of the Rector's involvement? This is important to know, you understand, Rosaria, if I am to convince my senior officer to open an investigation of this magnitude on a man who holds such a high profile public office. I am sure *you* understand that, *zio.'*

Marco Scarpa nodded. Rosaria went on to describe in detail the encounter the previous day between Leonardo and the Rector. Her *cappuccino* had long grown cold by the time she came to the end of her account.

It was after lunchtime before they could gain an audience with Giulio Pensiero's superior officer. Rosaria had had a conducted tour of the headquarters of the *Guardia di Finanza.* It had been an adolescent dream of hers to be able to wear that smart grey uniform with the yellow stripe down each trouser leg and spend all day tracking down fraudulent activities on an array of computer screens with free access to any bank account that existed. Being introduced to the young, uniformed men and women, whose lives were devoted to this kind of investigation, served to rekindle her dream.

'I know it's silly, but I've always wanted to be part of a *Guardia* team – ever since I was young,' she confided to Marco's nephew.

'It's not too late, you know, Rosaria,' said Giulio. 'We'll be recruiting new personnel in a couple of months' time.'

'You should think seriously about it, Rosaria,' added Marco Scarpa. 'You are admirably suited to this kind of work.'

'Are you being serious?' she asked with a gleam of hope in her eyes.

'Absolutely serious!' the uncle and nephew assured her.

* * *

The outcome of their discussion with Giulio's superior officer, *Maggiore* Matteo Rizzardi, had been predictable. He had listened attentively to every word they said. He had remained pensively silent for an alarming two minutes of suspense before saying:

'If you can prove collusion between this Dario Fabbro and the Rector of the University, I'll consider opening an investigation. The simple fact that Dario was his son is not enough by itself. The powers that be will not let me proceed without something more concrete. I really do appreciate what you have done, *signora...*' he said looking at Rosaria. 'It is quite remarkable what you have achieved almost entirely single-handed. We could do with someone like you on our side - but...well, you understand, I'm sure. We need a bit more to go on.'

Rosaria's disappointment was mitigated by the major's words. She carried away a secret hope that something positive might come of this encounter with the *Guardia di Finanza*.

In the car going back to the *Carabinieri* headquarters to see if there had been any news from Vergato, Marco Scarpa read Rosaria's thoughts accurately.

'They mean it, you know, Rosaria. You should think seriously about it.'

She smiled in recognition of his perceptiveness.

'I suppose your nephew is quite good-looking. He's certainly *in gamba.'* She felt the conversation needed redirecting.

'Being smart and alert runs in the family, of course,' replied Marco with feigned immodesty.

As soon as they stepped through the door, Adriana beckoned them into her office. She had a guarded expression on her face, not knowing quite what reaction to expect from the two of them when she told them about the phone call she had just received from the police station in Vergato.

'Don't get too excited, you two. Our colleagues in Vergato went round to the Russo parents' house – a tiny two bedroom affair in the village centre – and rang the doorbell. Their neighbour appeared immediately and told them the Russo couple had just left. She said she wasn't being nosey but *la signora* had asked her to look after her cat. They asked the neighbour questions and discovered they had gone off in the direction of the railway station on foot. She told them they reckoned they would be away for two days at the most...'

'Did they go and enquire at the station?' asked Rosaria with her customary impatience.'Yes, she's a good police officer. She found out that the couple had wanted to book a return ticket on the Intercity express to Pescara. The stationmaster knows nearly everyone in the village so he was quite sure it was the Russo parents. He had to explain to them that they would have to book their Intercity tickets at Bologna station.'

'But what about luggage? Were they carrying...? began Rosaria.

'My colleague asked them that very question. The stationmaster was quite categorical; they were each carrying a hold-all, nothing else. And he commented that he had the impression that their bags weighed very little - just enough for an overnight stay.'

'*Grazie, Adriana, sei stata bravissima!*' said Marco Scarpa to his young officer.

'Well, I don't know what it means, but...' began Adriana.

'I think we should go up to Bologna as soon as possible,' said Rosaria.

'I think it would be best if we waited for the couple to return to Vergato,' replied Marco Scarpa with annoying restraint.

'Don't worry, Rosaria,' Adriana reassured her. 'Our colleagues are going to keep an eye out for their return. They're good officers. They won't let us down.'

Rosaria sighed with suppressed impatience.

'You two have the patience of a spider!' she declared almost crossly to Marco and Adriana.

'Ah! You are thinking of that *Montalbano* novel by Andrea Camilleri, aren't you?' said Adriana. 'Believe me, in this line of work, you need that degree of patience.'

'Be warned in advance, Rosaria,' added Marco barely audibly.

'We'll be in touch with you the *minute* we hear anything,' Adriana reassured her.

There was nothing left for Rosaria to do. It was time to go home. She had an idea in her mind that she would have to mull over. She would try it out on Adam and the children when she got home. There was just one grain of hope contained in what Adriana had discovered thanks to a couple of alert police officers in an obscure village called Vergato, about seven hundred kilometres away.

'But why to Pescara?' wondered Rosaria. 'Why stop at a city only half way down the Adriatic coast?'

* * *

The frustration felt by a young captain of the *Guardia di Finanza* called Giulio Pensiero was acute. He was convinced that Rosaria's suspicions concerning the involvement of the University's Rector, Fabiano Mela, in illegal financial dealings were well-founded. Her account had the ring of truth about it. Yet, he knew that his superior would not budge until proof of collusion between Dario and Fabiano Mela had been formally established. He seemed to recall that the smart woman whom his uncle had introduced him to that morning had said something about having asked for Dario's phone number from the missing girl, Stella. He rang up his uncle again during the afternoon asking if he could have Rosaria's number. His uncle Marco seemed a little reluctant to part with it, he noticed with passing curiosity.

Rosaria was surprised to receive a phone call from Marco's nephew, Giulio, just as she was parking her Lancia Ypsilon in their drive. Anna and Riccardo, whom Adam had picked up earlier, were already running out to greet her. Their mother had that 'this-could-be-an-important-call' look on her face which prevented them from hugging immediately.

Instead they squeezed into the front passenger seat, sitting side by side, waiting until she had ended the call.

'It's not that *colonnello* who fancies *mamma*,' whispered Riccardo who could just make out a different 'official-sounding' voice on the phone. Anna admonished her little brother with a quick frown, puckering her lips in a silent 'Shhh'.

'Yes, Giulio, I did take Dario's number down as it happens. I thought it might become important. But that was before the burnt out Ferrari was discovered. I didn't think...'

More urgent words from Giulio...

'Yes, of course. It might well help us track down the connection between them. I'll text it to you immediately. Thank you, Giulio, for taking this so seriously.'

There were a few more words from Giulio. Riccardo thought he caught the words: 'And give that other matter serious thought, Rosaria.'

'I've been thinking of almost nothing else, believe me!' their mother was saying. '*Grazie di nuovo, Giulio, Ciao. A presto.*'

'You've been thinking about nothing else except Stella, haven't you, *mamma?*' asked Riccardo.

'That too,' said Rosaria. 'Let me send this text message to...'

'GIULIO!' the two children said in chorus, Anna managing to invest the word with a hint of *double-entendre* – much to her mother's amusement.

'Come on, let's go inside you two. I've got such a lot to discuss with you but I must have a shower and get comfortable first.'

Rosaria went up to Adam, who was preparing supper, and kissed him. 'Got a lot to tell you,' she said enigmatically, before disappearing in the direction of the bathroom.

Adam had long since realised that the food he was preparing would take second place to the animated conversations which would ensue about the latest developments concerning Stella. He had deliberately made his cooking as simple as possible, knowing that nobody would pay particular attention to the taste of the food in their mouths. Adam had been right. As soon as Rosaria started telling her family what had happened during the day, the taste of the simple pasta with shredded cauliflower, mozzarella cheese and tomato sauce became irrelevant.

'Those are the facts,' finished Rosaria ten or so minutes later.

'So they've gone to meet Stella!' declared Riccardo triumphantly.

'We mustn't jump to conclusions too soon,' cautioned Rosaria. 'They bought train tickets for Pescara, not Legano or Bari, as you'd expect.'

Riccardo was still too young to have developed a clear notion of where the various cities in Italy were located in relation to each other. He was still only half aware that, by travelling from Legano in an express train, by the time one reached the faraway boundaries of Puglia and entered Molise, the train had already covered one third of the length of Italy.

Anna got up from the table without permission and went to fetch a map of Italy which she spread out on the dinner table, pushing plates and glasses unceremoniously out of the way. She pored over the map, finding first of all, Bologna and tracing the coastline down until her finger arrived at Pescara. Riccardo was following the journey taken by his sister's index finger with rapt attention.

'I see what you mean, *mamma*,' Anna said. 'You'd expect them to go much further down than Pescara.'

'It's obvious,' said Riccardo, who simply refused to let go of the idea that Stella's mother and father could have any reason for travelling other than rescuing their daughter. 'They are very old and can't travel too far. Or they're poor and haven't got enough money to buy tickets all the way down here,' he stated, jabbing his finger on the bottom of the map where Legano was.

Adam knew what really must have happened as soon as Riccardo had uttered those words.

'That's the answer...!' he began. He caught the look of desperate appeal on his daughter's face. 'PLEASE let me tell them, *papà*,' her eyes were saying, filling with tears of joy.

'Go on, Anna,' said Adam. *'You've* understood as well, haven't you?'

'Understood *what?*' said Rosaria and Riccardo together. Anna was looking at Adam with a mixture of gratitude and a dawning insight as to the kind of man her unusual and rather older-than-average, English father really was.

'Thank you, papà,' she said quietly in English. She made a huge effort to find the correct English words to say the next sentence – just by way of saying 'thank you' to her father for letting her be the lucky one to impart the good news to the other two.

'It isn't Stella's mum and dad who have run out of money – it's Stella herself.'

237

There was an intense silence for a few seconds as the full implication of her words sank in.

14: An Important Journey

Nobody sitting round the kitchen table doubted for one minute that Anna's interpretation of events was anything but the simple truth. Stella was alive and had only had enough money left for a train ticket to Pescara. It had the ring of veracity about it.

'She wouldn't want to use her credit card for fear of her whereabouts being traced,' said Rosaria. 'She must be petrified of being identified for reasons which we still have to find out.'

'And the same must apply to her mobile phone, I suppose,' said Adam.

Rosaria stood up to hug her family. As if to reassert their unity, Adam, Riccardo and Anna stood up too and they joined together in a united embrace in the middle of the kitchen floor; a gesture of optimism to celebrate the survival of a precious human life.

'Now, I'm hungry! What's to eat next, Adam?' Rosaria asked.

Adam threw up his hands in mock despair.

'I didn't cook anything else tonight. You've been ignoring most of the stuff I've been preparing ever since Stella disappeared. But I suppose we could have takeaway pizzas?' he suggested.

The idea was greeted with enthusiasm. Adam took the car and drove into Legano while Rosaria prepared a mixed salad.

Forty-five minutes later, they were seated round the table devouring mouthfuls of the best pizzas that Legano had to offer with the stringy, hot mozzarella being wound round enthusiastic forks. A bottle of *Prosecco* had appeared on the table. Anna and Riccardo were allowed a generous half glassful of the bubbly wine to toast what at least one of the parents hoped was not a premature celebration of Stella's survival.

'You two children must be *in gamba* – really bright – well beyond your years,' said Adam, raising his glass in a second toast.

'I'll drink to *that!*' confirmed Rosaria.

'*Please* tell our teachers that,' said Anna plaintively. 'They might stop having a go at us all the time!'

Adam had long been convinced that the modern classroom did little to distinguish between the personalities of the pupils within it. 'If there are thirty students in one class,' he would often say, 'then you have thirty diverse people all of whom see life from a totally different perspective. No room for individuality there!'

There followed the usual amicable argument as to which of the two, Rosaria or Adam, had contributed most to the children's pool of brain cells. As usual, the result was more or less a draw. The same arguments about good looks were often dragged playfully into the arena – the outcome being weighted slightly in Rosaria's favour.

'I've got another piece of news, too,' said Rosaria with heart in mouth.

'You're not going to have a baby, are you *mamma?*' asked Riccardo in alarm.

'No, nothing as drastic as that, don't worry.'

She told them about the serious suggestion put to her by Marco and his nephew that she should consider applying for a job with the *Guardia di Finanza*.

'Of course, I shall have to submit myself to the usual *concorso,*' she added. 'There'll be hundreds of applicants for this competitive exam so I don't really stand a chance, but...'

To her delight, the idea was greeted by universal approval and cheers.

'Will you have to wear that cool uniform, *mamma?*' asked Riccardo.

'I would guess, Rosy, that for the first time in your life. You will have at least one person who will supply you with a guaranteed, steel-plated *raccomandazione!*'

'The *colonnello?*' asked Anna.

'It's a brilliant idea,' said Adam in total sincerity. 'Go for it!'

He often had more faith in his partner's abilities than she did herself.

Rosaria had not thought of the role which Marco Scarpa might be able to play in fulfilling this lifelong dream.

Nobody went to bed before eleven that night. In the end, the desire for sleep was overwhelming. Each one of them knew that the next day, or the day afterwards, would bring them news about the survival of Stella – or the shattering of their hopes.

And so a happy family retired for the night – a family whose strength and unity were soon to be put to the severest of tests.

* * *

The atmosphere around the breakfast table the following morning was more subdued as the family realised that they might well have to wait another twenty-four hours before Stella's survival was confirmed. Twenty-four hours filled with *school* and *homework.*

'If you hear anything during the day, *mamma,*' said Anna, 'you must promise to come and fetch us out of the classroom.'

'I promise!' said Rosaria smiling. She was still amazed that their children had taken the fate of a comparative stranger so much to heart.

Adam did the school run as he had an early English class that morning. The conversation on the way to school ranged over the subject of Stella to the ability of Adam's university students to speak English.

'Most of them *don't* have your advantage of having one parent to speak English to them every day,' said Adam, thinking that a bit of propaganda was in order. It was as a result of this statement Adam learnt from Anna and Riccardo that their English teacher at school, a middle-aged Italian lady, was afraid to ask them questions for fear of revealing her dreadful English accent.

'Be nice to her, kids! She's in a difficult situation.'

'Maybe we should put on a dreadful accent like all the other kids?' suggested Anna.

Adam was amused at this idea. 'As long as it doesn't become a habit,' he said.

Rosaria headed for the *AltoTek* campus at around ten o'clock, after she had downloaded all the documentation involved in applying for the *concorso* which might lead to her new career. The worst aspect for her was dealing with all the bureaucracy and paperwork involved in applying for *any* job. She sighed. It just *had* to be done. *'La pazienza del ragno!'* she kept reminding herself.

The first person Rosaria ran into at the university was, fortuitously, Giovanna Binetto. Rosaria took her friend to one side and told her about the unfolding events surrounding

Stella's disappearance and the discovery of her parents' inexplicable departure to Pescara.

'We should have some good news by tomorrow morning, Giovanna,' said Rosaria, determined to talk the situation up. Giovanna's face glowed with pleasure.

'Stella has been weighing on my conscience ever since she drove off in that car,' she said. 'I have hardly slept at night worrying about her.'

'Well, hopefully, we shall have something positive to report very soon, Giovanna.'

She told Francesco and Leonardo in much greater detail what had transpired in the faraway village of Vergato in Emilia-Romagna. Being men, they were far more cautious in displaying optimism, but both agreed that it was beginning to look 'promising'.

'By the way, Rosaria, Teresa wants to invite you and your family to dinner next weekend – and you Francesco, if you will. She's says it's been ages since you two met up. We want to thank you for all you've achieved in the last two weeks – well, nearly two weeks.'

'We would be delighted, Leonardo. Thank you so much.' She secretly wondered if she might not be on her 'rescue mission' by then. 'There seems to be a lot of activity this morning, Francesco – what's going on?' she asked.

'We're getting ready for our Open Days, Rosaria – you remember? We hope you'll bring your lovely family along to the preview. Your kids were promised a close encounter with our little robot, RIC6. I'm sure Anna and Riccardo haven't forgotten!'

'They'll be really excited, I'm sure. Just now, you wouldn't credit it, their hopes and fears are all for Stella. I've never known them so involved in someone else's fate.'

'They're good kids!' said Francesco, confirming the obvious.

Rosaria took her leave before midday and headed for the Greco *studio.* She was tempted to phone up Giulio, Marco Scarpa's nephew, to see if he had made any progress with Dario's phone. But the phrase about the spider came to mind again. It was time in her life to begin practising patience herself, in preparation for her new career.

'*Magari!*' she said to herself. 'If only…!'

* * *

Giulio Pensiero, at his desk in the headquarters of the *Guardia di Finanaza,* had easily isolated the phone numbers which Dario had called most frequently. It had been a matter of routine for him to obtain a list of the numbers dialled, from the Italian Vodafone network. It would have been too much to hope for that the Rector would answer the call and betray his identity by announcing his name. The number had rung for a few brief seconds before it was cut off abruptly. Subsequent attempts merely produced the usual sweet robotic voice announcing: '*La persona desiderata non è al momento…*' Giulio gave up. Most of the following attempts were answered by various owners of chemists' shops dotted around Puglia and Molise – plus one from Matera, who asked if he was the 'rep' from Menarini Pharmaceuticals, by any chance.

Giulio had explained who he was and the chemist had rung off abruptly. Giulio was disappointed but refused to give up.

There was just one number, which appeared three times on the list, that he had not yet tried calling. He did not know why, but he switched on the device which automatically recorded the conversation – maybe just because it *was* a last resort.

'*Pronto?*' said a woman's voice which sounded melodious.

'The voice of a musician, maybe?' thought Giulio hopefully, forgetting that the lady in question was purportedly a violinist not a singer.

'Dario? Is that you?' asked the woman.

'No, *Signora...?*' prompted Giulio, hoping the lady would supply her surname of her own volition.

'Fabbro,' she obligingly added to Giulio's joy. 'Francesca Fabbro. Sorry, I recognised the 0832 area code for Legano and I thought...'

Giulio was aware that he might get into serious trouble for this initiative that he was taking without authority. He would have to choose his words with care so as not to reveal more than he should.

'I'm from the police, *signora.* We need your son's help with an investigation. We thought he might be with you,' he lied with professional ease.

'Something has happened to my son, hasn't it?' said his mother, a note of anxiety tinged with resignation. 'I knew he was in some kind of trouble. I'm sorry I can't help you. You'd be better off talking to that man who calls himself his father...'

'You mean his natural father, *signora?*' asked Giulio with bated breath. He was treading on eggshells.

'Yes, of course! Who else? I knew that man would lead Dario astray sooner or later. I shouldn't have...'

'*Signora* Fabbro...Francesca,' said Giulio taking a gamble with the first name. 'We are very concerned about your son and feel it our duty to find out if he is in any trouble.'

'*Grazie signore.* I would be very grateful to you...'

The moment of revelation was retreating rapidly as Francesca Fabbro was preparing to hang up.

'Are you suggesting that I should start my enquiries by talking to his father, *signora?*'

'Yes, his father is bound to be in touch with him. Dario is always telling me how *helpful* Fabiano was being to him, she added.

One last chance! 'Excuse my uncertainty, *Signora* Francesca,' said Giulio ingratiatingly, 'but I need to be sure. We are talking about *Il Magnifico...*'

'Fabiano Mela, yes. That upright public figure who is playing at being Rector of the University of Legano,' she stated with bitter sarcasm.

'*Mille grazie, cara signora.* We shall be in touch with you as soon as possible.'

Giulio was jubilant. He had established a tenuous connection between the luckless Dario and the Rector, Fabiano Mela. Before going to his superior officer, *Il Maggiore* Matteo Rizzardi, it would be diplomatic to phone his uncle Marco and confess to him the ruse he had played. He would also ask why Dario's mother was still in the dark concerning the fate of her illegitimate son. The question might just spare him the full force of the verbal drubbing that he could expect from his uncle for acting without consultation. Ah well, he reasoned, nothing was ever gained in this life without taking risks.

* * *

Following a brief phone call from Giulio Pensiero, Rosaria was looking up information on the Internet about a violinist from Turin whose name was Francesca Fabbro, Dario's mother. She had had some reservations about Giulio's precipitous action. No sign of the proverbial patient spider there! Her main fear was that any subsequent contact between Dario's mother and the Rector might alert him prematurely to the fact that he was about to be in the public eye. Undoubtedly, Fabiano Mela would deny any involvement with his illegitimate son – if indeed he even knew about Dario's so far unreported fate.

Rosaria had phoned Marco Scarpa, who informed her that he had given his nephew a very severe dressing-down and an absolute injunction that he should consult his superiors in future before taking it upon himself to initiate investigations unilaterally.

'If I were to tell your *maggiore* what you have just done, he would demote you to the lowest rank – or even suspend you from duty, maybe permanently,' Marco Scarpa had thundered at his nephew. 'The only reason why we have not yet informed Dario's mother about her son's supposed death is that we do not yet have any post-mortem results on what is left of his body. It will take several days more to obtain dental records, which is about all that we can do to identify him officially...'

'Plus the fact that you did not have Francesca Fabbro's phone number,' Giulio had added, thereby deflecting his uncle's wrath very effectively.

Rosaria had smiled at the *colonnello's* account despite herself. Later on that day, talking to Rosaria again, Marco Scarpa had admitted that little damage had been done.

'Giulio has probably done more good than harm, since we can now proceed with an investigation against the Rector. But I certainly wasn't going to admit *that* to his face!' he declared. 'I talked to the *maggiore,* Matteo Rizzardi, and pretended that it was we, the *carabinieri,* who had made the call to his mother. But I told Giulio it was the last time I would cover his back.'

'No news from Vergato yet, I suppose?' asked Rosaria tentatively.

'Not yet. But don't be concerned, Rosaria. It's still too early. You will be the first to know when there are any developments, I promise you faithfully.'

Alessandro Greco was looking more relaxed than he had done in three days.

'I'm sure you are right about Stella. I think it's just amazing what you've done.'

'What my family have done, you mean, Sandro. They have played a big part in all this. The children have really adopted Stella as if she was their big sister. God knows, they will be devastated if our optimism turns out to be misplaced!'

'I believe Stella is alive,' said Sandro assuredly. 'But I suppose I *have* to believe that to stay sane,' he added quietly.

* * *

Rosaria was back at home with her children. Adam had had to attend a compulsory university faculty meeting and would not be back before nine o'clock. It was Riccardo who announced in a terrified yet excited voice: *'Mamma!* There's a police car outside.'

It had pulled into the drive quietly without the blue light flashing. The *colonnello* and Adriana Galante were getting out of the car.

'*O Dio!* This is it!' said Rosaria hugging Riccardo and Anna tightly, as much for her own comfort as theirs.

The two police officers looked far too solemn to be bearers of good news. Rosaria, Anna and Riccardo's hearts were beating fast, dreading the moment of truth.

'Don't look so scared, you three!' Adriana was the first to realise that the neutral expression on their faces must have caused the three family members to fear the worst. 'We don't have any *bad* news about Stella. It's just inconclusive.'

They sat round the kitchen table and Marco Scarpa nodded at his junior officer indicating that she should initiate proceedings.

'The two officers in Vergato took it in turns to wait outside the railway station well before the arrival of the first train that the Russo parents could have reasonably taken to get back from Pescara via Bologna. It was Sonia Racanelli, the police officer in charge, who was outside the station when the mother and father returned. She thought afterwards that she would have done better to put on civilian clothes, but she just hadn't thought about it.'

Three pairs of eyes were transfixed on Adriana's face. Riccardo and Anna's mouths were slightly open taking in extra oxygen.

'Well, the Russo parents came back at about four o'clock in the afternoon. But there was no sign of Stella. The police officer noted with interest, though, that they were only carrying one hold-all instead of the two they were carrying when they left. Sonia, the policewoman, was surprised that they took a taxi outside the station. Surprised because they only live a few hundred metres from the station – and the sun was shining, so it wasn't as if they needed to take a taxi...'

'Go on!' urged Riccardo, as Adriana had paused.

'Fortunately, Sonia Racanelli had the instinctive reaction to stay where she was to see if anything else happened. She was glad she did! Only ten minutes later, the Russo parents appeared again in their old black Peugeot and drew up outside the station entrance.

Another pause! Rosaria wondered if Adriana was simply waiting for dramatic effect, but her next words dispelled that notion. It was rather because she was not sure how her listeners would react.

'It all happened so rapidly,' continued Adriana. 'A girl with short-cropped blond hair jumped into the back seat and they drove off so quickly that Sonia Racanelli was left standing on the pavement. She thought afterwards that her uniform might have been spotted and that the girl had simply hidden in the station precinct until the Russo parents arrived in their car.'

There was a stunned silence round the kitchen table, which lasted for all of half a minute.

'Stella's dyed her hair,' said Anna finally. 'And had it cut short, as a disguise.'

'That's not quite all,' Marco Scarpa said, taking up the narrative. 'Sonia had come down to the railway station on foot from the police station. She walked as quickly as she could up the hill to the Russo's house. It was the neighbour who was looking after the cat – quite literally as it happens, since she was holding the animal in her arms – who came out when our colleague arrived.

'They just drove off again,' the neighbour explained, 'without saying where they were going. They asked me to feed the cat. They'd be back in about an hour, they said.'

'Sonia Racanelli asked her how many people there were in the Russo's car,' continued Marco Scarpa. 'This is the odd part about it – the neighbour looked surprised by the question and just said: 'Two of course!' as if the answer was self-evident.'

'Invisibility cloak,' muttered Riccardo under his breath.

Marco Scarpa and Adriana Galante had obviously not yet exhausted their account of what had transpired in Vergato. It was Adriana who took up the narrative again.

'This is where things get interesting,' she began. Adriana was surprised at the nervous laugh that her words produced in her rapt audience of three. The *colonnello,* of course, maintained a dignified silence.

'You mean you don't think what you've said so far has been *interesting,* Adriana?' said Rosaria drily.

'Well, just you wait for the rest,' she said mysteriously. This is going to have a happy ending, intuited Rosaria. They would not be taking so much pleasure in stringing this out if they didn't believe the outcome was positive. The tension in her body was beginning to lessen. Riccardo and Anna were still on tenterhooks.

'The two officers went back to the Russo residence an hour or so later – *un'oretta,* the cat-minding neighbour had said. Both Stella's parents were there. They looked surprised and a little sheepish as soon as they opened the door to discover two *poliziotti* on their doorstep. But, naturally, since they knew them well by sight, they invited them inside. Sonia Racanelli asked them politely where they had just been. Just to the supermarket, they claimed. 'What about the passenger in your car?' Sonia had asked. 'Just a neighbour of ours who we dropped off,' was the reply.

'Naturally, Sonia realised that they were desperately trying to cover something up, but she thought she would make assurance doubly sure. She's a bright lady, we get the impression.'

Riccardo and Anna were instinctively getting closer to Adriana as she was speaking. They felt the account was reaching its climax. This was better than a bedtime story any day.

'We have reason to believe your daughter has gone missing, *signori.* We are fearful for her life.' Sonia told me that, after the parents' next words, she was entirely convinced that they knew exactly where Stella was. 'Oh, Stella's always off somewhere or other. I'm sure nothing bad has happened to her,' the father said. 'I wouldn't worry about her yet.' It was such a bad cover-up act that the two police officers just took their leave, pretending they'd been taken in.'

Adriana had finished speaking. There was a brief silence before it was broken by Anna, Riccardo and then Rosaria breaking into noisy, uncontrollable cheers and tears of joy.

'Stella's alive! Stella's alive!' chanted the children dancing round the table. Marco and Adriana were smiling broadly at the scene before them.

'I've got to go up there and see Stella,' declared Rosaria when the excitement had died down. 'She's obviously scared out of her wits after what she's been through.'

'Correction!' said Marco Scarpa. '*We* have to go 'up' there, Rosaria. I will not sanction you deserting your family without proper police protection. Besides which, you seem to forget that Stella is my chief witness.'

'I think you should ask your partner first, don't you, Rosaria?' added a smiling Adriana.

Adam was greeted a few minutes later by the sight of a police car in their drive where he usually parked. 'Oh God, please let it be good news!' he said to himself. He was left in doubt for the space of a mere two seconds before two children ran towards him with a triumphant smirk on their faces.

'Stella's alive, *papà*,' they shouted hugging him.

'And *mamma* and the *colonnello* are going up to rescue her but the police lady, Adriana, says *mamma's* got to ask your permission first,' added Riccardo ingenuously.

Adam's Englishness allowed him to stifle the stab of fear that this revelation provoked inside him. He walked in with a welcoming smile on his face as he first kissed and hugged Rosaria before shaking Marco and Adriana warmly by the hand.

'So,' he said still smiling. 'You're taking Rosaria away with you, *mio colonnello?*'

'Only with your permission, Adam, but I fear she will attempt the journey alone if I don't insist on going too! Don't worry. She'll be safe with me.'

Adam managed a wry grin of good humour as he said quietly but distinctly:

'I'm not sure that it's *her* safety I'm worried about!'

* * *

It was the first time Rosaria had seen Marco Scarpa not dressed in uniform. The effect was to make him look shorter, more like a normal man.

'The last thing Stella, or her parents, want to see is a uniformed *carabiniere* appearing before them, I imagine,' he had explained.

It was the *colonnello* who had decreed that they should travel up to Bologna by train – an eight hour journey on the early morning *Intercity* from Legano. There seemed little point in delaying the decisive journey up north. 'We need to strike while the iron is hot,' said Rosaria. 'Besides which, it's Thursday tomorrow and I am still employed by Legano University until Friday. It seems a good way of earning my salary.'

Adam had not looked pleased about her decision to go off at such short notice but conceded that it was in a very good cause. He had refused to indulge in a display of Latin-style male jealousy about her travelling companion, deciding that events would unfurl as they were destined to. The famously succinct maxim, born in the cradle of the Italian language, *'Che sarà, sarà,'* enshrined a simple, inescapable truth, after all.

The sight of Adam with an arm round the shoulders of Riccardo and Anna standing waving 'goodbye' to her on the doorstep had brought tears to her eyes. Rosaria and Marco Scarpa had been whisked off in a police car at six in the morning to catch the seven o'clock train to Bologna.

The journey up north passed easily. They were travelling in luxury in an almost empty first class carriage. Rosaria and Marco Scarpa had known each other for more than ten years. They recalled their first encounter when Marco had held the rank of *capitano* in Rosaria's home town of Campanula. Rosaria had sought help from Marco after the tragic discovery of Rosaria's cousin's remains at the bottom of a well. Diletta had been murdered by her Mafioso husband as a consequence of Diletta belatedly discovering the true nature of the man she was marrying. Surprisingly, Rosaria had never found the occasion to relate in detail how she and Adam had tracked down Enrico Anacro in London and escaped death at the hands of this Calabrian *mafioso* by a hair's breadth. Marco Scarpa was enthralled by her narrative, often interrupting her to ask her for further clarification.

'One of us should write a story about your exploits, Rosaria. It would make a fascinating read.'

'Please call me Rosy. All my friends and family do,' Rosaria had slipped in at some stage. 'Rosaria sounds such a ponderous name, don't you think?'

The train had reached Pescara by the time they had filled in the details of the intervening years.

'Why did you never marry, Marco?' Rosaria asked cautiously as the train pulled smoothly out of Pescara station gathering speed on its way to Ancona. She was sure that she would never have asked that question, which had been niggling in her mind for ages, had Marco been wearing his imposing *Carabiniere* regalia.

He laughed at the directness of the question, only mildly embarrassed.

'I suppose I would have to admit that I am married to the job. But it's also true to say that I have never met the right woman – or rather, maybe I have, but it was not possible to see it through,' he added lightly. 'There have been a number of near misses but, really, nothing came of any of the relationships.'

Sitting opposite Rosaria, he had a nostalgic look in his eyes, but shrugged his shoulders and changed the subject.

'Now, let's talk about your future career with the *Guardia di Finanza,*' he said. By the time he had finished explaining what was involved in the application process and given her a brand new copy of the book which was designed specifically for those taking part in the *concorso,* Rosaria knew that she stood a very good chance of being *'assunta'* by this prestigious body of professionals. She might just become one of the 60 000 or so men and women of this élite force deployed throughout Italy.

'It would greatly help, Rosy, if you could really answer most of the questions in the *concorso* and the subsequent interview,' joked the *colonnello.* The word *'raccomandazione'* was, of course, never mentioned, but the implication had been clear. Rosaria let out a contented sigh and smiled at the man sitting opposite her.

'I'll do my best, I promise. I know that I would really love that kind of work,' she confided. 'If it happens, it will solve the one aspect of my family life that worries me most. Adam will have to retire in a few years' time and at the moment I still don't have a permanent job...or a guaranteed pension.'

The age difference between herself and Adam was not a problem on a personal level but she was becoming increasingly concerned about its financial implications.

By the time they had had lunch, not particularly because they were hungry but more to break up the long journey, the train had left Rimini behind and was on the last leg of the trek to Bologna.

* * *

To Rosaria's surprise, there was a hire car waiting for them outside Bologna station – an unobtrusive, dark metallic grey Fiat Brava. 'That'll do, I suppose!' said an unimpressed Rosaria.

'We don't want to draw attention to ourselves, do we?' smiled Marco Scarpa. They had been quite at ease in each other's company during the train journey and the sense of companionship continued during their forty-six kilometre drive southwards towards Vergato. Rosaria found it secretly reassuring to be in the company of someone with the sway to smooth the passage of every step they took.

'Do the police officers in Vergato know we are coming?' asked Rosaria as the car headed into the hills outside Bologna, with the irritatingly self-assured female voice of the *satnav* guiding them almost unerringly in the right direction.

'I certainly hope so by now,' said Marco with the quiet assurance that came with the authority of his rank, 'assuming that Adriana has done her job.'

'Then they certainly *will* know we are coming!' said Rosaria.

'Yes, she will rise quickly up the ranks, in my opinion,' said Marco with just a hint too much of male chauvinism for Rosaria's liking.

'As well as being an excellent example of womankind, you might have mentioned too!' she added with that sharp edge to her voice that the *colonnello* secretly admired and even feared. He took his eyes off the road for a brief second giving her a sidelong glance. It was long enough to appreciate the determined thrust of her striking profile as she eagerly studied the unfamiliar road and mountainous scenery unfolding in front of them. It was as if she was mentally trying to speed up the process that would bring them closer to their objective. Marco just stopped himself from placing an affectionate hand on her knee. He let out an audible sigh which attracted a quizzical look from his travelling companion. He had been right not to travel up to Bologna by car, he thought.

'And - assuming the efficiency of our two police officer colleagues in Vergato – we should have some information as to the whereabouts of your Stella.'

'*Che cosa?*' exclaimed Rosaria in astonishment.

'Just think about it from Stella's parents' viewpoint, Rosy. Where would you hide your daughter if you wanted to protect her from the outside world?'

Marco left the question hanging in the air, much to Rosaria's frustration.

'Well, aren't you going to tell me?'

'Good practice in lateral thinking to prepare you for your new career!' said Marco tantalisingly. It earned him a smart slap on his leg which stung him through the material of his trousers. Rosaria did not apologise for the assault on his person.

They arrived outside Vergato's police station to be greeted by two smiling police officers.

'Welcome to our part of Italy!' said Sonia.

Introductions were formally made.

'And this is *Commissario* Miccoli,' said Marco Scarpa with a broad smile as he introduced Rosaria. 'She might not have the rank officially but her investigative abilities are certainly a match for the real thing.'

Rosaria found herself blushing with pleasure. It had been the nickname that she had acquired a decade or so ago from grateful friends whom she had helped solve various problems. Sonia Racanelli took them to a bar for a coffee over which they discussed how to tackle the Russo parents.

'By the way, *colonnello,*' said Sonia, 'you were absolutely correct in your assumption. We found out this morning that the Russo parents *do* own another property. It's in a *frazione* of a village called Zocca, half way up a mountain some ten or so kilometres from Vergato. The rock star, Vasco Rossi, was born there. This is probably its only claim to fame!'

Rosaria was looking hard at Marco Scarpa. She was not sure whether she felt pleased or mildly annoyed that he had been one step ahead of her.

15: Turning Point

Sonia Racanelli handed a slip of paper to Marco Scarpa who immediately handed it to Rosaria. On it was written an address: *4bis Vialetto degli Angeli, fraz. ZOCCA.*

'You look after it for me, please, Rosy. I always lose bits of paper.'

'So do I Marco! But I'll memorise it instead.'

'It's the house where *Signor* Russo grew up,' explained Sonia. 'Well, shall we go and pay the Russo parents a visit?'

As soon as *La Signora Russo* opened the door and saw one uniformed police officer accompanied by two strangers whom she had never seen in the village before, she knew that their secret was out. However, she was not going to be the one to break the silence, so she called her husband to the door in a peremptory tone of voice. *'Arturo, vieni qua subito!'*

'Arturo' stood there with a mixture of fear and defiance – the peasant farmer of yesteryear ready to defend his territory against intruders. Rosaria was silently wondering how this plain looking couple, belonging to a rapidly fading generation, had managed to produce a beautiful daughter like Stella. It even occurred to her that Stella might have been adopted. She had a sudden surge of emotion as a picture of Adam, Anna and Riccardo came unbidden to her mind. She had to stifle the warm glow of comfort that the image engendered.

'May we come in, please?' asked Sonia Racanelli courteously, since it was evident that both parents had unconsciously taken a defensive stance in the narrow doorway, hoping thereby to repel boarders. Reluctantly, they stood aside, allowing the three visitors to squeeze past them in single file.

They were grudgingly invited to sit down in the living room. Sonia, wearing her uniform, remained standing – largely because there was no sitting space left by the time the Russo parents had sat down in their favourite armchairs, which faced the ancient television set with the nightly quiz game, *L'eredità* , still turned up loud. Sonia went over to the set and turned it off without asking permission.

'This gentleman is a *colonnello* from Legano and this is Rosaria who works with Stella at the university,' explained Sonia. 'They have come all the way up from Puglia to help Stella.'

'We don't know where she is,' said the Russo father looking stubborn.

'They need to talk to your daughter and help her get over the traumatic experience she has lived through,' Sonia persisted doggedly.

'We are friends. We are here to protect her, *signori,*' said Marco Scarpa adding weight to the proceedings. 'We know all about the events of the last few days.'

The Russo parents shifted uncomfortably in their seats but still refused to open up.

It was Rosaria who stood up and walked over to where they were sitting. She showed them the piece of paper she had been given by the *colonnello.*

'Do you recognise this address, *signori?* That's where Stella is hiding, isn't it?'

It was Stella's mother who caved in first.

'There's no point in pretending any more, Arturo. They know! I'm sorry,' she said addressing her visitors. 'Stella made us swear not to tell a living soul. I've never seen her so petrified in her life.'

After that, the Russo parents relaxed and seemed relieved that they no longer needed to keep up the pretence.

The visitors left half an hour later. Marco and Rosaria had agreed they would follow the Russo parents in their car early next morning.

'It's not easy to find my old house,' the father explained, smiling for the first time.

'Good,' said Marco. 'You will be able to ensure that Stella is happy to see us and that we are only here to help her. And *please, signori,* don't alarm her by telling her we are coming. She might worry that we are not whom we say we are and disappear again!'

'She hasn't got her phone any longer,' explained Stella's mother. 'And there is no landline, so we can't contact her anyway.'

* * *

'Stella?' said Rosaria with a note of alarm in her voice as she stepped into the kitchen of the little house just outside Zocca. It was not just because of the short-cropped blond hair, which she had been expecting, but the extent to which it made her almost unrecognisable compared to the Stella of a few days previously. 'You've lost weight too!' said Rosaria, shocked by the physical change to her body.

Stella had just looked at her parents with deep reproach and fear in her eyes when they had solemnly announced that they had brought along 'two people who are anxious to see you'. Her expression flashed from astonishment to pure delight as soon as Rosaria stepped into the rustic kitchen.

They had practically flown into each other's arms to the extent that the dimensions of the kitchen allowed such rapid displacement. A big pine table filled most of the intervening space.

'How did you find me?' asked Stella in wonderment. 'I never expected to see you up here in a thousand years!'

'Elementary, my dear Stella. You wait until I tell you how Anna and Riccardo – and this gentleman – put two and two together and worked out where you were.'

Marco Scarpa was introduced. Stella was worried when she discovered that this good-looking man in his late forties was a *colonnello* in the *Carabinieri*. She even looked guilty, as if she feared she had broken the law in some way. She needed reassurance that Marco was there to protect her.

'You are, however, my most important witness, Stella! But there's plenty of time for that. At this moment, we are all just so relieved that you are alive.'

'I'll make some coffee for us all,' offered Stella. *'Papà,* I think the *bombola* is about to run out of gas. I hope there's enough to make the coffee.'

Reassured and smiling by now, the Russo parents told Stella they would go and do some shopping and send someone up to replace the big blue cylinder.

Stella was visibly beginning to relax. She begged Rosaria to tell her all about how they had worked out where to find her. 'I thought I had thrown *everybody* off the scent!' she declared, seemingly disappointed at not living up to her own expectations of herself. A very 'Stella-like' characteristic, thought Rosaria.

Stella threw open the old blue wooden shutters and the mountain sunlight flooded into the house.

'Now tell me all!' begged Stella. Rosaria looked quizzically at Marco to make sure he did not mind going over events again. He waved a dismissive hand. He understood, as Rosaria had, that Stella wanted to delay having to relive the nightmare of those intervening days. Stella listened with amazement and amusement to Rosaria's account. She was moved emotionally by the childlike concern for her safety that Anna and Riccardo had manifested and horrified to learn how Dario had met his end – in a manner far more brutal than she had imagined. After almost an hour had elapsed, Rosaria finished her account. She said to Stella:

'Now, please Stella, don't leave us in suspense! Tell us how you escaped that night.'

She said she would make another lot of coffee – to give herself another minute or so to find the courage to tell her side of the story. Marco had whispered something to Rosaria, who nodded. She went outside to phone Adam and give her family the long-awaited news that Stella was *sana e salva* – safe and sound. *'Ti amo, amore,'* she concluded rapidly.

Back in the little two-storey house, Stella took a deep breath and closed her eyes as if reliving the scene in the hotel in Matera in all its vivid horror.

But she began by asking a question.

'Did you manage to listen in to that conversation with Dario?'

Rosaria nodded saying: 'Yes, I wouldn't have known where to start looking for you if you hadn't made that call.'

'I couldn't leave the phone on any longer because he would have noticed I was holding it up to catch his words. He isn't...wasn't stupid. And I was so afraid the battery would run low if I left it on any longer. Oh, Rosaria...'

Another pause, as Stella made one last effort to get going. Marco Scarpa offered to leave the kitchen if she wanted to be alone with Rosaria. She shook her head and began talking non-stop.

'After I switched off my phone, I accused him point-blank of colluding with the Rector and handing over the research material to him so that he could sell it on to a third party. I didn't know for sure that's what he was doing, but I guessed. I wasn't even totally certain that it *was* the Rector, even if I had recognised his voice on occasions. But Dario never denied it, so I assumed I was right. He had already told me some time previously that he was related to Fabiano Mela – in the beginning when he was still trying to impress me. I told him he was a fool, told him *I* had been a worse fool than him. After a time, he realised I meant what I said about not playing his game anymore. I could tell he was getting angry because he always fell silent. He never shouted at me but bottled up his rage until he could take it out on me – in bed usually...'

'Oh Stella! How could you...?' said Rosaria under her breath. Marco Scarpa stirred in his chair.

'Don't ask, Rosy. I know I've been reckless. It must have been my convent upbringing! I overdid it as soon as I had the chance. I blush when I think about how I allowed myself to be led...down that path.'

Rosaria, who had also been 'educated' by nuns, smiled bitterly and looked at Stella with greater compassion.

'But it was after I told him that I had been supplying him with incomplete information that I could see how deeply angry he had become. He just hissed at me: *'Una stronza sei! Me lo pagherai, Stella Russo!* If you knew who my father had been passing on that stuff to, you'd realise just how stupid you've been.' That's when I understood that he was *scared* too. I knew I would 'pay for it' as soon as we were alone in a bedroom. He even chose the most beautiful and expensive hotel in Matera just to reassert his wretched hold over me. I was terrified. He was totally ruthless and very strong. What scares me most, though, is that there was always a part of me that welcomed the punishment at his hands. Does that make sense, Rosy?'

Rosaria hesitated for an instant before nodding and saying almost imperceptibly under her breath: 'Of course it does, Stella!' There was a deathly silence in the peaceful, sunlit little kitchen.

'Please go on, Stella,' said a calm, persuasive voice in the background. 'It's important to get this out in the open once and for all.' Rosaria was glad she was not on her own to be a witness to what she was hearing from Stella's lips.

'I knew what to expect as soon as I got out of the shower in the hotel room. Well, it wasn't really a 'room' at all – more like a well-lit cave. And he was going to behave like a caveman, I remember thinking. But his violence took me by surprise. It was going to be rape, not just the usual energetic sex. He did it...from behind and he was forcing my face down into the pillow, Rosy. I was sure I was about to suffocate...'

Stella was taking in great gasps of air as she relived her terror. Rosaria came round to the other side of the table and held her tight. Marco got up to fetch a glass of the cold mountain spring water that came gushing from the tap. After a few moments, Stella picked up her narrative again.

'I was uttering my last prayer, Rosy, as the pain in my chest grew unbearable. I prayed for divine intervention. I thought of you, Rosy, telling me to be careful...and of Sandro. I was begging him to forgive me...'

Stella took in a few gasps of fresh air and drank a mouthful of water.

'I couldn't believe it when I heard someone knocking on the bedroom door. I knew it wasn't the police as soon as I heard that voice. I was just so glad my life had been spared – or at least that I had been given a chance to act. I am sure Dario would have killed me. I think he was too enraged to even notice what he was doing to me. I knew he would go and open the door – as soon as they said it was something to do with his sacred car. I shall never get into a Ferrari again, by the way! He began to put his clothes on again, fumbling in his haste. I knew I had barely thirty seconds to get some clothes on, grab my handbag – and that piece of material which I always had to hand...'

'Your 'invisibility cloak' as Riccardo always calls it,' said Rosaria.

'It saved my life as I knew it would. It's an amazing creation, Rosy, but it certainly does *not* warrant the word 'invisible' being attached to it,' said Stella, smiling nervously for the first time during her narrative.

'I had experimented with it while I was staying with Giovanna, bless her!' continued Stella without pausing to elaborate what she had meant by her last two words.

'I quickly realised two things, Rosy. Firstly, the 'cloak' does not make one invisible but, in the right light, it gives off a shimmering image that an observer might not look at carefully simply because they wouldn't expect it to be there. It works well on a smaller scale – like the vanishing photo of the President during Francesco's demonstration, but there's a definite *trompe-l'œil* effect even on a bigger scale. The second thing I realised in Giovanna's house was that I couldn't see *anything at all* when it was over my head! Do you know what...?' said Stella glancing at Marco Scarpa too for the first time since she had begun talking. 'I had to cut two eye-holes in it to see where I was going!'

The image conjured up was the first time during Stella's story that her audience of two let out a hesitant chuckle of amusement.

'As soon as Dario opened the door, I knew he was in deep trouble. I heard him gasp in fear when he saw those three men standing there. They frogmarched him out into the darkness, leaving me standing in the middle of the room. That was my only chance. I turned off all the main lights so there was only the soft glow of the cave wall lights, put the 'cloak' over my head and headed for the door just a few steps behind them. I nearly died when I knocked over that vase and it smashed to the floor. The mob, because I knew it was them, must have thought it was someone in the kitchen dropping a plate. One of them turned round but I was already outside moving along the terrace into the darkness. I couldn't believe it, Rosy! He just *couldn't* see me. Their chief, Max, they called him, ordered one of the men who had been trailing behind a bit to 'go back and get the girl!' When he came out of the room and told Max I wasn't there, he got his head slapped hard. Max sent the other man in. But by that time, I was out on the road, ready to head up the hill towards...I didn't *know* where I was going. I just had to put as much distance between me and those evil men as possible, because I *knew* they would be back to finish me off.'

'Didn't anybody see you?' asked Rosaria.

'Luckily, there were only a few people about. I went and stood in the road to avoid colliding with other pedestrians. One or two of them peered in my direction. There was one young couple walking arm in arm. The girl stopped and pointed at me saying to her boyfriend: 'Look, Pierluigi, I can see something moving. It looks weird.' I think they believed they had seen something supernatural because they hurried on without stopping to investigate.

I spent the worst night in my life, Rosy. I didn't know where to go. I didn't dare go to another hotel because I knew the mob would come back and search for me and I knew I would need what little money I had got in my purse to get me out of Matera in the morning and my vagina was so sore I nearly wept...Sorry, Marco!'

Marco made a gesture to show no apology was necessary. 'But where did you sleep?' he asked, as deeply involved in the narrative as Rosaria.

'Sleep?! I didn't dare go to sleep. I walked round the old part of the town where it was darkest. I heard the church clocks measuring out the slow passing of the night. It was just after two o'clock when I found that old church carved out of the rock face.'

'Santa Maria dei Idris,' said Marco quietly – as if to satisfy his own desire for precision.

'It's got a funny sort of crypt where there are old stone slabs. I was too tired to walk any further so I just lay down on the stone and waited, shivering, until dawn. I suppose I must have dozed off in the end because I was woken by a voice upstairs which seemed to be chanting. I realised it was the priest saying early morning mass.'

Silence fell over the group for a few seconds that seemed to stretch into minutes. Suddenly, Rosaria said out loud: *'O Dio!* Sandro doesn't know yet that you are safe. He'll be worrying himself to death over you, Stella.'

A smile of contentment spread briefly over her face at Rosaria's words. But she added quickly:

'I can't talk to him now, Rosy. You must understand. I feel deeply sullied – as if I've been unfaithful to him.'

'Nothing can be further from the truth, Stella,' said Marco firmly. 'But we understand how you must feel, don't we Rosy? Why don't you send Sandro a text message for now? That way he won't be anxious about her safety any longer.'

Rosaria sent a brief message, which was acknowledged almost immediately by a phone call from Sandro. Rosaria went outside to take the call. 'Everything will be fine, Sandro,' she reassured him. 'We just need to be patient for a time – Stella isn't ready to face the world just yet.'

She thought, ironically, how very good she was at counselling patience in others. Rosaria could tell that her 'boss' was hurt that Stella did not want to talk to him. She attempted to mollify him by explaining that Stella was feeling guilty about leaving him so abruptly – thereby sparing him from the harsh details of her ordeal at the hands of Dario. Back in the kitchen, redolent with memories of the last century, Stella smiled as she walked in and sat down next to her. Apparently, Marco Scarpa had, like a priest in the confessional, succeeded in persuading Stella that her non-existent sins would be forgiven. She carried on more willingly with the story of her long night on the run.

'Where was I?' she asked.

'You heard a priest saying mass in the church,' prompted Rosaria.

'I was so unbelievably frightened by then, chilled to the bone, with a dull pain down below, that even the presence of a priest saying mass was like an answer to prayer. I was paranoid about those three *mafiosi* pursuing me – even in that amazing church. I tiptoed up the stone steps with my *'mantello magico'* draped over my head. As I reached the top of the stairs, I tripped over the border of the cloak. I shall never forget that moment in my life, Rosy...Marco! The priest had got to the point during the mass where he holds up the host in midair and says the words, *Behold the body of Christ*. He must have heard the noise I made because he paused in the middle of his words and just stared in my direction with his hands in the air, still clutching the host. I stood stock still, but the priest was peering in my direction, trying to make out what he was seeing. He must have been nearly eighty but he had clear blue eyes. And then, God bless him, he shook his head gently as if he couldn't quite believe his eyes – and he *smiled* at me. He must have thought I was some spiritual apparition. There was only the altar boy with him, plus two elderly ladies in the congregation who looked up, wondering why the priest was still holding the host up in the air. The altar boy was half asleep and didn't notice anything. It suddenly occurred to me in my desperation that this old priest might be my salvation. So, I slipped my *mantello* off and revealed my human body as I knelt down at the back of the church and made the sign of the cross – just to show him whose side I was on!'

Rosaria and Marco were trying hard to suppress the desire to laugh out loud and failed completely. Comedy in the midst of what might have turned into tragedy is very hard to resist.

'Go on Stella! This is the most amazing story I've ever heard,' said Rosaria.

'Yes, I didn't appreciate the comical side of it until much later,' continued Stella. 'Well, the old priest finally lowered his arms and announced quite clearly: 'Mother of God, thank you for this revelation, and finished giving communion and his blessing at lightning speed. He didn't go back into the vestry but walked directly towards me. The altar boy had sleepwalked his way into the vestry thinking the priest was following him.'

'What did he say to you, Stella?'

'It was the first beautiful thing I had heard for days. He came up to me, his blue eyes alight with compassion, and said:

'Are you in trouble, my dear? I can help you.' I think I burst into tears of relief as he took me to the *canonica* and gave me a cup of hot coffee and a room of my own. I had a shower and he let me have an old tracksuit to wear. There was a younger priest there too. I knew I was safe while I was with them. They never plied me with questions but they understood without words that I had been in great danger. When I told them my story later that day, they sat there in amazement. But when I had finished, they just wanted to find practical solutions. I told them I wanted to go home to my parents and they set about making plans to disguise me and get me to the nearest big railway station. I phoned my parents from the *canonica* and warned them that I was coming home – and under what circumstances. They were sworn to silence. Rosy,

Marco, can you understand that I just couldn't ask those priests for money after they had saved my life? Plus the fact I didn't want to reveal my whereabouts to *anyone* just in case the wrong people found out where I was. So I didn't dare withdraw money from a *bancomat* because I knew any cash withdrawal could be identified geographically. I know I must sound paranoid but I was petrified by what happened that night...'

'We understand completely, Stella,' said Marco.

'So whose idea was it to cut your beautiful hair off and turn you into a blond?'

'That was my idea. It was the priests' housekeeper who took a not very sharp pair of scissors to my hair. I felt as if I was being prepared for a life as a nun – which I *was* in a way. I'll get to that bit in a moment. The housekeeper was despatched off to a chemist's shop to buy some blond hair dye – which, as you can see, didn't work too well.'

'And then what happened, Stella?' asked Rosaria, impatient for details.

'Well, I stayed in the *canonica* until the following day. The old priest offered to hear my confession if I felt there was anything on my conscience. He understood perfectly how I was feeling, you see.'

Stella blushed in embarrassment. Rosaria, too, understood how painful it must have been for Stella to reveal the darker side of her nature to the priest. She made no comment but waited patiently for Stella to continue.

'In the morning, the young priest offered to drive me all the way to Bari. It was him who hit on the idea of dressing me up in a nun's habit – I knew you two would find that amusing! But it was the perfect disguise, you have to admit. If we had thought of it the day before, it might have spared me having to cut and dye my hair. Well, that was it, I guess. I embraced that eighty year old priest as if he was Jesus himself. It was nothing short of a miracle meeting him. I phoned my parents and they offered to come down as far as Pescara to meet me and take me home. I knew I had only enough cash for a ticket from Bari to Pescara.

The young priest was as good as his word and drove me in a shaky old yellow Fiat Panda all the way to Bari. I don't know why, but have you two noticed how priests and nuns in Italy are the world's worst drivers? I reckon they believe they are protected by their faith! My heart was in my mouth most of the way – but, in the end, I would rather have run the risk of a road accident than running into *them!*'

Apart from minor details, that was the end of Stella's account of her nigh on miraculous escape. She had decided it was safe to take off her nun's habit as soon as she was on the local train to Vergato. 'I don't know how nuns can bear to wear such clothing in the summertime!' Stella had declared.

'The rest you know already,' she concluded with a profound sigh of relief and the sensation that she was safe – at least for the time being. How her life should continue was a matter that could be decided soon enough, she reckoned. Today, she could afford to relax, without being plagued by guilt and anxiety, for the first time in months. The blackest period of her young life was finally behind her and she could start all over again. Despite herself, she could only feel secretly glad that Dario could no longer harm her.

'*Grazie di cuore, Rosy!* And my deep gratitude to you too, Marco,' she added as a feeling of solace stole over her.

* * *

Lying in bed that evening, Rosaria was tired but over-excited by the events of the day. Sleep refused to come to her rescue. After Stella's account of her startling escape, all five of them had had lunch, paid for by Marco Scarpa, in an *agriturismo* high up in the hills above Zocca, where the purity of the air made them all comment on how much natural beauty has been destroyed by the paraphernalia of modern life. They had raised their glasses in a heartfelt *brindisi* to Stella and her survival. The afternoon had been spent back in Stella's kitchen. Marco Scarpa had been persuading Stella that her life must go on. He gave her endless reassurances that she would be protected from danger. He explained convincingly that she was absolutely essential to a successful prosecution of Fabiano Mela.

'He is the root cause of all your troubles, Stella. He must be brought to justice.'

Rosaria was able to offer further reassurance.

'We have a safe place for you to stay, Stella. Sandro has offered to protect you twenty-four hours a day in his apartment in Legano. He asked me to plead with you to come back – under escort.'

In the end, Stella had been persuaded that she should return to Legano. Rosaria had had a conversation with Adam – the children joining in – during which she was reminded forcibly that they had all been invited to lunch on Sunday *chez* Leonardo. In the end, she had agreed she would travel back to Legano on her own the next day, Saturday. Stella, accompanied by Marco, would make the journey on Tuesday morning, giving Stella time to go shopping for new clothes in Bologna on the Sunday and Monday – a treat promised her by her ever-loving father.

Did Rosaria detect a hint of quickly suppressed jealousy as she lay there sleepless in her hotel room in the remote village of Zocca? No, of course not! How could she feel jealous of someone like Stella? She missed her family. She simply needed the company of someone *simpatico* like Marco, her travelling companion, with his reassuring certainty about where his life was going. With these words, she succeeded in justifying her next act, which was to slip a dressing gown over her nightdress and knock timidly on the door of room 101.

'*Chi è?*' enquired his voice.

'*Sono Rosaria. Posso entrare, Marco?*'

She heard the tread of his bare feet walking across the tiled floor.

16: A Tear in the Fabric

Rosaria's solitary eight hour journey from Bologna back to Legano was accomplished in smooth silence as the *Intercity* train whisked her from station to station with effortless speed in yet another almost deserted first class carriage. The *colonnello* had accompanied her personally from Vergato to Bologna after a warm hug of deep gratitude from Stella, who had returned to Vergato to stay with her parents; a positive sign that her worst fears had receded.

'I'll see you as soon as possible after next Tuesday, Rosy,' Stella had promised.

On the concourse of Bologna station, Marco had embraced Rosaria warmly, holding her body tightly against his for half a minute, rocking her gently from side to side, in a gesture of reassurance.

'Now, remember everything I said last night, Rosy,' his parting words had been.

Rosaria spent most of the journey with conflicting arguments raging through her troubled mind. The book Marco Scarpa had bought her for her *concorso* for a post with the *Guardia di Finanza* lay open on the table in front of her at page five. It was difficult to concentrate on the complexities of financial law, even if her degree in economics rendered the language familiar.

What had possessed her to knock on Marco Scarpa's door the previous night? Above all, why should she be feeling so guilty? What had puzzled her about Stella's confession of guilt in respect of her supposed 'betrayal' of Sandro in Matera came back to haunt her. Ironically, the reassuring words designed to convince Stella that she need harbour no sense of guilt, now applied to *her*. How strange that those words of reassurance had lost so much of their plausibility! Not only that, but she was struck forcibly by the sensation that this whole business with Leonardo's science faculty had been too emotionally disturbing. She had become inextricably involved in the lives of too many people. Her hitherto tenacious refusal to let go of her 'professional' pseudonym, Elena Camisso, had been largely eroded by events. It seemed that only the Magnificent Rector himself remained in ignorance of her real name. That, in itself, was an alarming thought.

By the time the train had reached Ancona, her involvement with Leonardo's 'molecular troubles' simply indicated to her that a change in her working life was essential. As far as Marco was concerned, she had persuaded herself that the gesture had caused no lasting damage. It had been a passing moment of weakness, never to be repeated. No, she would simply pretend that nothing had happened and her life with Adam, Anna and Riccardo would continue as it always had done.

Her logical conclusions gave her sufficient peace of mind to concentrate on the book in front of her. She succeeded in absorbing the first section of the hefty tome. There was a multi-choice assessment at the end of each section, reproducing exactly the type of question she would have to answer in the first part of the *concorso* in September. She was delighted to find that she had scored 94% without really having to try too hard. But there was no room for complacency, she reminded herself. She would have to devote herself to study for three solid months.

But after the train pulled out of Brindisi, her resolve to bury her guilt seemed less convincing as the distance between her and Legano station diminished. In thirty minutes time, she would have to face Adam and her children standing waving cheerfully at her as she stepped off the train. It was all very well to pretend that nothing had happened. She knew how perceptive Adam was when something was troubling her. Her partner knew her inside out like nobody else had ever managed to do. Her heart was beating too fast as the train drew into the station.

And, of course, they were there waiting eagerly for her on the platform, with smiles on their faces, as if she had just returned from some remote part of the world after an absence of several months. Anna and Riccardo ran to greet her, dodging between the alighting passengers making their way to the station exit. Rosaria felt a sense of shame overwhelm her in that instant of time, followed quickly by the need to cover up any vestiges of guilt. She must, at all costs, conceal her fleeting departure from strict fidelity.

But Adam knew something had altered as soon as Rosaria embraced him and kissed him lightly on the mouth. The embrace was exaggerated and the kiss on the mouth a split second briefer than usual. And was there not the faintest trace of another person's scent lingering on her skin? Rosaria knew instantly that Adam was alerted to a change. She inwardly cursed his intuitive perspicacity. She continued beaming determinedly as she marched the children off in the direction of the exit. Her defensiveness made her slightly aggressive, which was confirmation enough for Adam.

He had turned very silent in the car, trying to suppress his encroaching unease. But it was as if the cold steel of a knife had been twisted in his stomach. He experienced that sensation of fear like a person who has just been told that he must undergo an unexpected surgical operation, bearing the unwelcome reminder that the fabric of life which holds us together can so easily be ripped open.

Anna and Riccardo sensed immediately that some invisible and disturbing change had altered the balance of love between their mother and father. During their evening meal, the atmosphere lightened as Anna and Riccardo winkled out every detail about Stella and her amazing exploits. Adam, too, could not fail to be caught up in the sensational events surrounding Stella's escape and her subsequent rediscovery by Rosaria and the *colonnello.* Perhaps his early suspicions had been unfounded? Maybe he was overreacting? He tried hard to convince himself that this was the case.

But as soon as the children had gone to bed, the tension between them was manifestly present. When they themselves had retired for the night, Adam's simple question, 'What's the matter, Rosy?' was met with a dismissive, 'Nothing's wrong, Adam!' From long experience, he knew that the protective shell she had created might remain clammed up tight for days.

'If you've been unfaithful, I want to know,' he added quietly, knowing that such a direct statement would serve little purpose.

'I haven't,' Rosaria replied abruptly and turned a stubborn back on Adam.

'So why are you acting so strangely?' he asked with a calmness he was not feeling. 'It has to have *something* to do with your journey up north!'

Rosaria sighed deeply but could not bring herself to answer the question. He lay awake for hours trying to determine how he should react, long after his usually loving partner had taken refuge in sleep. He felt keenly that his English reserve and self-control were inadequate in this situation. A fitful sleep overtook him sometime in the early hours of the following day; the Sunday when they were expected to have lunch with Leonardo, Teresa, his wife, and their daughter, Emma.

* * *

After a silent breakfast, Rosaria became immersed in studying the book which Marco Scarpa had given her. She opened her book on the kitchen table among the remnants of the breakfast things. Throughout the hastily eaten meal, Anna and Riccardo had looked apprehensively from their mother to their father, waiting in vain for an end to this inexplicable and unprecedented rift between their parents. Adam had led the children away to their bedroom for the weekly tidy up and change of pyjamas and bedclothes.

'What's happened between you and *mamma?*' asked Riccardo timidly.

'I wish I knew exactly, Riccardo. But don't worry. I'm sure things will be back to normal very soon.'

'It's to do with the *colonnello,* isn't it, *papà?*' said Anna with her customary knack of instinctive, child-like perception. Her words brought involuntary tears to Adam's eyes, which he instantly attempted to conceal by hugging his children even closer until he hoped his emotions were under control. A vain hope!

'Don't worry, *papà,*' said Riccardo, visibly upset.

'It'll be alright, *papà,*' his daughter reassured him in her special 'grown-up' voice.

'We love you both,' said Adam warmly and had to get up and walk away from them on the pretext of going to the bathroom.

The rest of the day, in the company of Leonardo and his family, went amazingly well and lifted Adam's little family out of the gloom that threatened to settle over them.

Almost as soon as they arrived at Leonardo and Teresa's vast fifth floor apartment in the modern district of Legano, just off the *Piazza Mazzini,* Riccardo and Anna disappeared with Leonardo's daughter, Emma. She was marginally older than Anna and took charge of her 'guests' with enthusiasm.

The adults sat around the kitchen table and talked entirely about Stella. They were all issued with a glass of a pale orange-coloured *aperitivo* as Rosaria launched into her now well-rehearsed account of the events of the last few days. Leonardo looked increasingly solemn as the account progressed. He only managed a fleeting smile at the description of Stella's encounter with the old priest and her subsequent escape dressed as a nun.

'People tell me I'm a clever man because I understand the behaviour of particles,' Leonardo commented with an ironic smile on his face. 'I have to say that the escapades of other human beings represent a far greater challenge to my understanding of life than the unpredictable nature of subatomic particles.'

Adam laughed quietly, realising that, for Leonardo, this was an expression of his somewhat ponderous sense of humour. Leonardo looked appreciatively at Adam. The two 'women' in his life were generally quite unaware when he was being humorous. The prevailing atmosphere of gravity around the kitchen table was broken by the sound of girlish laughter from down the corridor. Adam stood up to investigate, fearing Riccardo might be having a rough ride in the presence of the two older girls. His fears were groundless. Eavesdropping outside the closed door, Adam listened to Riccardo talking animatedly, giving his own version of Stella's escape.

'And Stella put her invisibility cloak over her head and crept up behind the old priest who was holding the bread... what's the word?... above his head.'

'Host, Riccardo.'

'That's it. Stella went 'boo' right behind him and he dropped the host, which rolled down the aisle and disappeared down the steps into the crypt. The priest and the altar boy had to run after it down into the crypt...'

'You're such a liar, Riccardo,' said Anna to her brother, laughing nevertheless at her brother's flight of fantasy.

'While they were down in the crypt, Stella was so cold after her night sleeping on the stone bench that she drank a bit of the wine in the big gold cup. She thought it was safe because it hadn't become Jesus's blood yet and...'

'Stop, Riccardo!' pleaded Anna. *'It didn't happen like this at all, Emma.'*

But Riccardo was on a roll. He was enjoying being the centre of attention in the presence of the two older girls. He was also trying to expiate the memory of the tears in his father's eyes a few brief hours beforehand.

'But the best part was that the two old ladies in the audience...'

'Congregation, Riccardo!' corrected Emma.

'…could only see the chalice, that's the word, raising itself in the air by magic. They ran out of the church screaming and crossing themselves.'

Adam left them to their mirth. He understood all too well what was going on in his son's mind, but he was smiling as he returned to the kitchen.

I had to come away,' explained Adam to the others. 'I think I was about to hear Riccardo coming out with something bordering on the blasphemous.' He considered it wise not to put Leonardo's belief in mankind to any further test by repeating the words he had just heard issuing from his son's innocent lips. Teresa was looking at him amusedly, wanting to be enlightened. Rosaria was struggling to resist the temptation of looking at Adam with affection – a slight thaw of the iceberg, he noticed with secret relief.

During the course of a beautifully prepared *antipasti* course, Adam learnt with delight that he would be teaching English at the *AltoTek* campus from September onwards. His status would be raised to that of an official university lecturer – with an Italian pension when he retired, at the age of seventy if he so wished.

'You seem to have friends in the right places, Adam,' said Leonardo. 'Your reputation as an English teacher has spread beyond the bounds of the *Beni Culturali* faculty. *Congratulazioni!*'

Rosaria had an enigmatic expression on her face which Adam could not interpret – as if he had somehow stolen a march over her. Adam and the children had been threatened with the direst of consequences if any of them dared to mention her bid to become a member of the *Guardia di Finanza* police force.

'It will bring bad luck if we tell anyone about it,' Rosaria had explained.

And so the conversation ranged over all sorts of subjects, mainly Stella's return to Legano and work and the impending investigation into the Rector's involvement in corruption and embezzlement – not to mention murder. All of this conversation was strictly confined to the four walls of the Molinari apartment, Leonardo warned them unneccesarily.

Rosaria commented in great surprise that there was a place setting at the table which was unoccupied. 'We never did that at my parents' home,' she explained. 'My mother used to say it was occupied by a dead person!'

Teresa was far less influenced by traditions and superstitions. She shrugged her shoulders and said:

'I hope not, Rosy. Francesco is supposed to be coming. He said he might be a bit late but that we should start without him.'

'Che bello!' exclaimed Anna and Riccardo together, delighted at the prospect of seeing their hero scientist again.

'And,' added Leonardo, 'he wants to invite Anna, Riccardo and Emma to the preview of our Open Door exhibition tomorrow after lessons – just for special guests. You remember we spoke about it BSD?'

'What does BSD mean, Leonardo?' asked Anna in her forthright manner.

'Before Stella's Disappearance' said Leonardo without the hint of a smile on his face.

'Just like BC – Before Christ, you mean!' Anna declared for which she earned a burst of laughter and a round of applause. Leonardo received no credit for his part in this verbal exchange.

Adam offered to pick up the children after school the following day and ferry them to the *AltoTek* campus. Francesco arrived in the middle of the meat course and instantly demanded that his wine glass should be filled – to Adam's great relief, since nobody had shown any sign of wishing to fill up the wine glasses from the bottle of *Salice Salentino* which had been standing, largely ignored, in the centre of the table. Francesco went round the whole table shaking hands and bestowing an expansive hug and a *bacio* on all the women and children present. The tips of his moustache spent a lot of the remainder of the meal in their upturned position. Inevitably, as the dessert and coffees arrived, the story of Stella's escape and rescue had to be replayed for Francesco's benefit.

'Without some of your own special inventions this time, Riccardo!' said Adam, smiling at his son.

Riccardo blushed and grinned sheepishly whilst the two girls giggled.

The group broke up around five o'clock.

'See you tomorrow, kids,' said Francesco. 'You'll finally be able to have a real meeting with RIC6 tomorrow, Riccardo,' he added, knowing how fascinated Riccardo had been with the DVD of the little boy-robot. 'You'll be our special guests, although there will be a small group of students from the *Liceo Scientifico* there too.'

'We'll look after you well, *ragazzi,*' added Leonardo. 'You'll love it!'

* * *

As soon as Adam's family drove off in the direction of home, Rosaria lapsed into sullen silence again. Anna and

Riccardo withdrew into their fragile shells, looking vulnerable once more. Adam sighed audibly but Rosaria did not react. 'This situation cannot be allowed to continue any longer,' Adam resolved silently. He would have to abandon his native English reserve, as he had had to do before on rare occasions since living in Italy. He would have to face the inevitable confrontation later on that evening, like it or not, even if he dreaded what he would hear. But he would not know how he was going to react until he knew for sure what had really transpired during Rosaria's visit up north. One thing was certain however – self-control and the stiff upper lip routine had run their course.

The moment came when they were lying side by side with that invisible barrier of tension slicing the bed into two distinct cold war zones – a barrier more effective than Riccardo's 'invisibility cloak', thought Adam ironically. Rosaria had erected the additional defence of her *Guardia di Finanza* exam preparation book, which she was studying with a concentrated frown.

She had led a couple of subdued children to bed some thirty minutes previously. She had kissed them both and wished them goodnight with a few rapid words of consolation. Back in the kitchen, where Adam was clearing up their meagre supper plates, she said to Adam: 'The children want to say goodnight to you, Adam. I'm going to bed. I'm tired.'

Adam hugged Riccardo and Anna warmly.

'Do you still love *mamma?*' asked Riccardo, deeply anxious about the sudden change that had taken place between his parents.

'Yes, I do, Riccardo, with all my heart.'

'So why aren't you talking to each other?' enquired Anna.

'Everything will be fine again very soon, children,' Adam reassured them.

'That's just what *mamma* said a few minutes ago!' said Anna accusingly.

Before leaving them, Adam had put an arm round each of them and said in a conspiratorial whisper: 'Listen, Anna, Riccardo – this is what I want you to do as soon as I have left the room...'

* * *

Rosaria was startled out of her wits by Adam's abrupt movement. She suddenly found the book she had been studying whipped out of her hands. But before she could protest her indignation, she was suffering the indignity of Adam sitting astride her just below the level of her belly. She protested loudly and squirmed angrily, her arms flailing. In two seconds flat, she found her arms pinned down helplessly by her side.

'Right, Rosy,' he said. 'Now you're going to tell me what the matter is whether you like it or not. Because I'll stay here all night if I have to.'

'There's nothing to tell you, Adam. I'm just...'

'*Non mi dire cazzate!*' he said in vulgar Italian, raising his voice and adding in English, for good measure, that the time for her idiotic prevarication was over.

Despite herself, Rosaria calmed down at the sight of her usually gentle partner's genuine anger.

'Don't shout, Adam, please! You'll wake Anna and Riccardo.'

'I very much doubt they are sleeping, Rosy. They are too desperately worried about us. They don't understand why their secure little world has suddenly been turned on its head. Do you remember more than ten years ago in London, just after we had nearly been murdered by that *mafioso,* you said to me, *I shall love you for ever, Adam* - just because I stood futilely between you and a bullet? Well you might have spoken those words in the space of a few brief seconds, Rosy, but the trouble with saying words like that is that they resound down the years and never go away again...'

'I *do* love you Adam. Of course I do!'

'Then you tell me what happened between you and...that policeman! And no more prevarication, because I'm going to sit here until you... No, first of all, I want you to come with me to the kids' bedroom. I want to show you something.'

By that time, Rosaria had been subdued sufficiently to be led docilely by the hand down the short corridor to the bedroom which Anna and Riccardo shared. Adam prayed fervently that the children had done what he asked. Yes! Anna was in her bed and her little brother lay curled up by her side with his sister's arms comfortingly round his shoulders.

'There, Rosy!' said Adam in a furious whisper. 'That's how they sleep at night now – because they just don't understand why their mum and dad suddenly appear not to love each other any longer. That's what your stubborn silence is doing to them.'

At last, Rosaria's tears began to flow. It was doubtful whether Anna and Riccardo were really asleep, but they feigned unconsciousness to perfection as Adam led Rosaria gently back to their bedroom.

Then, holding Adam tightly and with the lights turned out, Rosaria began talking unprompted about what had been troubling her since she had returned.

'When I told you I hadn't been unfaithful, Adam, I wasn't really lying to you. Not strictly speaking, at any rate. I don't know what came over me that night – a strange mixture of loneliness, missing you and the need to be with someone. I've been anxious about you growing old now for some time and leaving me without an income. I've never really told you that before because I didn't want to hurt you. I *do* love you so much, Adam, you know that. But we can't just ignore other factors...'

'I know all that, Rosy. But the fact remains that you wanted to be physically with another man at night time. You fancy Marco Scarpa, don't you?'

Rosaria let out a profound sigh before replying.

'I suppose so, just a little bit,' she confessed. 'And during those few days, he was always there, treating me like an equal. If he had been wearing his uniform, I don't think I would have had the courage to...' She left the sentence unfinished. 'It was me who went to his room in the hotel. I just felt drawn to be with him. When he saw me standing there, he asked me in. If he had sent me away, I would have been mortified, Adam. He asked me in and took me in his arms. I knew he wanted me because I could feel his... We just lay on the bed. Then he began talking softly to me for ages. He told me he had always been attracted to me because I was somebody special. He even told me I was the real reason why he had never got married – he had been waiting for someone like me but he had never found anyone. In the end, he held me tight and told me to go back to my own room – before we did anything we would regret. *You've got two beautiful children and a partner who is one of the best men I have ever met.* That's what he said, Adam, and I knew he was right.'

In the darkness, she could feel Adam shaking silently.

'Please don't cry, Adam. It will never happen again, I promise.'

But, moving closer to him in the darkness, she realised, disconcertingly, that he was not crying but shaking with silent laughter.

'ADAM!' she protested.

'I'm sorry, Rosy. It's the exact reverse of us ten years ago in London. Remember? When we had narrowly escaped being killed by that Calabrian - in the taxi, afterwards, I thought you were crying but, in fact, you were laughing at the memory of my feeble attempt at protecting you from being shot. I wasn't laughing *at* you, *amore*. It's just sheer relief that you've told me at last.'

'So, do you forgive me, Adam?' she pleaded.

Adam remained thoughtful for a few minutes, juggling with conflicting emotions and searching for the words to express them.

'Well, in the great scheme of things, I suspect there is nothing to forgive. However much we love each other, we sometimes need other people. Besides which, when I was your age, I wasn't exactly the world's most faithful individual. But then I found you, Rosaria Miccoli!'

Adam added, almost inaudibly, the words: 'To think I should be grateful to a policeman for saving us!'

Rosaria hit him smartly in the darkened room before they began, tentatively at first, to make love.

Outside their bedroom door, two pyjama-clad children had been listening attentively to the proceedings that would determine their future happiness.

'Why have they stopped talking?' whispered Riccardo innocently as he strained his ears to catch what was going on. 'Is *papà* punishing *mamma?*' he asked anxiously as his mother began uttering strange gasping noises.

Anna led her little brother by the hand back to their bedroom. 'No, Riccardo. *Papà* is making her happy again. They'll be alright now,' she added by way of explanation.

They slept in their own beds all through the short summer night. Riccardo dreamt he was talking to RIC6, telling him not to worry about his life as a child robot. Anna fell into a deep sleep, the feeling of dread and uncertainty of the last couple of days having magically been dispelled.

17: Anna and Riccardo in Wonderland

From the first moment that Adam, Anna, Riccardo and Emma stepped into the *AltoTek* campus, they felt as if they had entered another dimension of time and space. The team had constructed a bright yellow archway, looking convincingly 'stone-like', at the entrance to the laboratories, through which every visitor had to pass. Over the archway were written, in different colours for every letter, the words: ***Benvenuti nel Futuro – Welcome to the Future.***

Francesco, waiting at the entrance of the archway to greet all the guests and dressed up as a magician, told them that the archway had been constructed by their three dimensional 'bottom-up' photocopier. The group of seven students and their teacher from the *Liceo Scientifico* had just arrived too. Everybody present looked at Francesco, not sure whether to believe him or not. Enjoying the effect he had produced, Francesco grinned mischievously, sending the tips of his moustache high up his cheeks. The younger children giggled, but the seventeen-year-old students from the *liceo,* who had never witnessed this spectacle before, regarded this eccentric-looking scientist with fascination mixed with a touch of adolescent cynicism.

'Where's my *papà?*' piped up Emma, to the amusement of the other visitors.

'Waiting for you on the other side, Emma Molinari,' replied Francesco mysteriously. There were muttered comments about 'trying to be like Harry Potter' audible from the *liceo* group. Francesco Zunica had set the atmosphere for their visit, it appeared. The arrival of two local TV reporters, one armed with his shoulder video camera, plus a lady journalist from *Il Mezzogiorno,* who announced in a haughty voice that her name was Costanza De Santis, completed the visitors' party.

'Trouble - how had she got herself invited, I wonder?' thought Francesco. But it was too late to ponder on the issue.

'This way into the future, *signori!*' he announced in a clear voice as he led them through the parted black curtains behind the archway.

One of the proper classrooms had been transformed into a mid twenty-first century living room. A very large television set dominated one wall. Various standing lamps illuminated the rest of the space. Futuristic pictures showing Martian landscapes adorned the walls. In the centre, there was a low coffee table with a jug of water, a drinking glass and a wooden chess set on it. Behind the table, facing her 'audience' was a white-coated young scientist. Francesco Zunica, ever the showman, had donned his magician's hat with the golden stars on a blue background. More titters from the teenagers, but more out of amusement than cynicism by now.

'Ladies and gentlemen, boys and girls... May I introduce you to our youngest team member – Miky De Giorgi – who is a graduate in Robotic Biomechatronics, to give it its official title, from the Campus Bio-Medico University in Rome. But, more importantly, she is a local heroine from somewhere near Gallipoli.'

There followed a modest round of applause from everybody present – except of course Costanza De Santis, who was too busy studying the members of the group.

'Why have you got a tree growing out of your head, Miky?' asked Emma, unable to subdue her curiosity any longer. For the third time, Miky had opened her mouth to speak but shut it again as Francesco answered the question on her behalf. She grinned from ear to ear and threw up her hands in mock despair. Her gesture produced subdued laughter from her audience.

'I apologise, Miky,' said Francesco humbly. 'Miky has just graduated and it was my idea that she should put on her graduation laurel leaf 'crown' to celebrate her success...so she cannot be said to be resting on her laurels while she works here!'

Polite laughter from the *Liceo Scientifico* students and their teacher!

'*That's* why he interrupted,' thought Adam. 'He wanted to get his well-rehearsed joke in.'

'Now, Miky, I apologise once more. The floor is yours,' said Francesco with a bow.

'*Grazie, capo!*' said the good-natured Miky De Giorgi, without a hint of sarcasm.

The audience was treated to an explanation of the almost invisible wiring system that linked up the lights and the TV set.

'This is the wiring of the future,' explained Miky. 'The material is made of carbon nanotubes. This new material conducts electricity almost without any loss of energy. They are enclosed in a plastic material that has non-light-reflecting properties – rendering the cables virtually invisible.

'*Like Stella's cloak,*' whispered Riccardo to his sister.

The 'audience' found out that by calling out 'blue', 'yellow' or 'red', they could change the colour of the lighting. 'Simple voice recognition,' said Miky. Next, she called for a volunteer. Emma, Anna and Riccardo put up their hands – as did all the *liceo* students. Miky chose one of the older boys and put on his head a lightweight 'cap' whose material was inlaid with numerous invisible sensors, Miky explained.

'What's your name?' she asked the *liceo* student.

'Giovanni.'

'Now, I want you to switch on the television, Giovanni, just by thinking about it. We are developing this line of research to help handicapped people cope with simple tasks around the home. Giovanni's face became contorted with the mental effort required to switch the TV set on.

'It takes practice,' explained Miky. 'Some people can do it more readily than others – and girls find it easier than boys at first. This turned out to be the case as, on the fifth attempt, one of the teenage girls managed to turn the TV set on – amidst vociferous claims of female mental superiority.

'But now, ladies and gentlemen, boys and girls, I want to introduce you to the main occupant of this room. He's a little boy about five or six years old and he's called...'

'RIC6!' called out Riccardo in delight. By now, the *liceo* students and the three younger children were a united little group, sharing new experiences together.

'Riccardo,' said Miky, 'I understand this is the moment you've been waiting for.'

Riccardo, with his dark short-cropped hair, big brown eyes and beautiful face had already become the 'mascot' of the group.

'I was going to say, Riccardo, you should call out his name to wake him up, but I think you've already done just that!' said Miky, grinning.

From a curtained-off area next to the big TV, there was a stirring movement. The curtains parted and the little robot emerged amidst a collective gasp of surprise. He was attached to an 'umbilical' cable that he trailed behind him as he advanced towards the expectant group of human beings. He was wearing a green T-shirt bearing the words *I BELIEVE IN ITALY* written across the chest – in English, however.

'*Che carino!*' exclaimed one of the *liceo* girls, her latent maternal instincts aroused at the sight of the endearing, one metre tall boy-robot making its way towards them with steps which looked disturbingly natural. What made the little robot so cute, thought Adam, in admiration of what he was witnessing, was the fact that RIC6 had big, appealing eyes, like those Japanese cartoon children which Anna and Riccardo watched on the Rai *Gulp* channel. It was not just the eyes that gave the child robot such vulnerable appeal, but the addition of eyelids that closed and opened in a gentle blink. The robot's mouth and eyebrows were lit with lines of red LED diodes, giving the humanoid robot a surprising range of emotional responses.

'The name RIC is, of course an acronym. It stands for Robotic Intelligent Child,' explained Miky.

'What about the number 6?' asked one of the students.

'Six stands for his current mental age,' explained Miky. 'If he makes a lot of progress tonight, we shall have to upgrade him to a seven tomorrow,' she added jokingly.

'Our little robot is a humanoid child, as you see,' she continued. 'He is designed to act, react and learn like a child. He represents an important step towards our understanding of intelligence. He has 'artificial' intelligence, so-called – but, as you will see, the dividing line between *artificial* and *natural* intelligence and emotions is proving to be increasingly blurred...'

Miky quickly realised that her well-rehearsed semi-technical explanation was falling partly on deaf ears. Even RIC6 seemed to be paying more attention to the people looking at him than to Miky's description of him.

'I see it is time to introduce you properly,' she said, changing tack. 'I think it's only fair to let the youngest member of the group meet RIC6 first. So, Riccardo, would you like to step forward and introduce yourself to your namesake?"

Riccardo had already broken ranks from his post between Anna and Emma and was standing facing RIC6 with a shy smile on his face. He turned his head to look quizzically at Miky, as if to say: *'Now* what do I do?'

To everybody's amazement and amusement, his gesture was mimicked almost exactly by RIC6, as if they were both dependent on an adult presence to know how to proceed. Even Costanza De Santis seemed to be captivated by the scene, the hard lines on her face softening into a rare hint of a smile. The video camera was busy recording the scene for *Telenorba.*

'Introduce yourself, Riccardo,' Miky prompted him in a stage whisper. 'See what his reaction is! Don't forget, he can't speak – yet. By the way, we have given him a special name here – because there are about thirty RIC6s around the world. We've baptised him Santino.'

'The boy-robot reacted immediately to the sound of his name. His 'ears' were in the right place – one on each side of his head – and they looked for-all-the-world as if he was wearing a neat headset.

'Hello, Santino,' began Riccardo tentatively. 'My name is Riccardo.'

Santino's head looked up at the sound of his voice and the changing light patterns of his mouth and eyebrows registered surprise and pleasure. There was a murmur of astonishment as Santino's right arm began to rise up to a horizontal position, held out in Riccardo's direction. His five fingers began to unfurl gently.

Riccardo instinctively held out his hand and, to his surprise, he found the robot-boy's hand gently squeezing his and shaking his arm up and down three times before the fingers gently unfurled again.

'It felt weird,' said Riccardo, 'like touching a real child's hand. It was soft and tingly.'

'Yes, he has sensors in every finger – just like us,' explained Miky.

'What shall I do next?' asked Riccardo, who had obviously been moved by his first contact with a being that was supposedly only a machine.

'Two things, Riccardo – first of all, ask him to pour you a glass of water...'

'Excuse me, Santino. I'm a bit thirsty. Pour me a glass of water.'

It was instantly clear by the robot's reaction that he was puzzled. His eyebrows furrowed in what could only be described as a frown. His eyes looked expectantly at Riccardo.

'You forgot that little word beginning with 'p', Riccardo!' his sister chided him in a loud whisper. There were titters of amusement from the older students.

'PLEASE, Santino! May I have a glass of water?'

RIC6's red diodes gave a happy smile and he moved over to the table, where he picked up the drinking glass between the delicate fingers of his right hand followed by the water jug in his left hand. The enthralled spectators were whispering amongst themselves. It might well have been the case that RIC6 had been programmed to respond to requests only when the word 'please' had been added. But the expectation on his face had been so human. They began to grasp what Miky had meant when she had talked about the blurring of the distinction between *artificial* and *real* intelligence.

'Santino is ambidextrous,' explained Miky, who had picked up on the whispered comments among the onlookers about RIC6 being left-handed.

Riccardo's glass of water was passed to him without a drop being spilt. He reverentially drank it down as if he had been the priest drinking from the chalice during mass.

Santino was looking at Riccardo in expectation.

'Thank you, Santino,' he said carefully, not wishing to be found wanting in good manners for the second time in one evening. He looked at Miky in an interrogative way as if to say: 'What next?'

'Well, Riccardo. You are in the special position today of teaching Santino something completely new. Later on, we shall ask one of the others to test Santino to see if he has learnt what you teach him.'

There was a general murmur of interest and engagement from the spectators.

'Does anyone else want a go?' asked Riccardo. Only his father and his sister understood that he was dying to continue but that he was, at all times, a generous-spirited child who did not want to hog the limelight.

The unanimous opinion was that Riccardo should continue.

'Do you know the names of the chess pieces, Riccardo?' asked Miky.

Riccardo nodded.

'Well, pick up one of the pieces – black or white - and hand it to Santino, telling him clearly what the piece is called.

Riccardo did just that, holding out the white queen. Santino's hand stretched out slowly and took the piece delicately between his fingers. He studied it with an expression that mimicked exactly the curiosity of a young child looking at an unfamiliar object.

'Now ask him to put it back, Riccardo.'

With precision, Santino replaced the white queen on its square.

'Now do the same for some of the other pieces at random.'

When the process had been repeated, after a reluctant signal from Francesco jabbing a finger at his watch, Miky suggested that they all come back after their visit to see if Santino had learnt to recognise the pieces by name and where they belonged on the chess board. As they were gathering to leave, the TV reporter intervened.

'Can we just have a shot of Riccardo next to the little robot, please?'

'Of course,' said Miky.

There were only a few totally dry eyes, when Riccardo moved to Santino's side and took the boy-robot's hand in his own. Santino's head turned with a smile and a blink of his eyelids to look at the 'real life' child. The scene was quite uncanny. Anna turned round to look at her father with an expression of awe on her face, tinged with something akin to fear, as if Riccardo had formed an alien alliance outside the family circle. Adam understood immediately what his daughter was feeling. He smiled at her, shaking his head imperceptibly to imply that she need not fear that her brother was being abducted. Another tiny link was forged between father and daughter in that instant of time.

Reluctantly, the group prepared to move on to the next stage of their visit to the future, all of them aware that there had been a meeting between two worlds. Even Costanza de Santis patted Riccardo's head affectionately and murmured something quietly to him. Francesco thought he had noticed a glistening tear in the corner of her eye, quickly wiped away with the back of her hand.

'Can I just add one important thing, Francesco?' asked Miky pleading for a minute longer. It was plain that she could happily have gone on for hours if given the chance. A true lover of science, thought Adam. Francesco Zunica smiled and held up a single finger to mean 'just one minute'. There was no reluctance on the part of her audience to stay and listen. Even had they gone home immediately, they would have considered their visit deeply satisfying.

'I think it's important for you to know that all our research on RIC6 has ramifications beyond studying artificial intelligence; the way RIC6's body works will deeply influence our ability to make artificial limbs for accident or war victims. The tendons which operate Santino's limbs are 'natural' rather than mechanical. Our study of the brain – linking micro-chips to soft tissues will ultimately help to find the solution to degenerative diseases such as dementia. We are even developing a new skin just like our own skin. There is the fascinating prospect that your great grandchildren – or even your grandchildren - might well develop a friendship with Santino's descendants.' A discreet cough from Francesco stopped Miky in her flow. 'And with that thought...' Miky concluded smiling broadly, 'I had better let you get on.'

She was treated to a warm and appreciative round of applause before the group filed out through another curtain. Riccardo had to be prised away from 'his' RIC6 by Emma and Anna.

'I'll be back later,' he told Santino.

'Excuse me, *professore,*' an observant student asked Francesco on the way out. 'Hasn't your magician's hat just changed colour?'

'Ah, you noticed at last!' he laughed. 'It's all to do with nano-surfaces and the way they can be made to react to the photons which...' By the time they had reached the next exhibit, he had also told them about new nanotech materials for aircraft wings that can deflect lightning and a 3D photo-copier capable of replicating human bones.

'The Americans have manufactured a plastic revolver that fires real bullets,' added Francesco. 'We are learning to make things that will *save* lives instead!'

* * *

It was almost two hours later that the group arrived at the last port of call on their journey into the future. Their concentration was flagging as they were greeted in the 'Clean Room' by Leonardo himself, assisted by the lanky figure of Alessandro Agostini and the scientist with the five o'clock shadow at eight in the morning, Andrea Calvino. They were anxious to give their visitors a taste of the photon encryption machine before releasing them back to the present time.

They had spent too long with Giovanna Binetto, standing over an inflatable swimming pool looking at the wonders of an autonomous mechanical fish, which they had been invited to prod with long poles to see if they could touch it before it darted away from them, reaching the bottom of the pool where it found shelter beneath a rocky tunnel.

'The nano-sensors along the side of the fish were developed here in our laboratories,' explained Giovanna proudly. 'As you see, they allow the fish to avoid attackers. The fish is being developed to detect troubles in the deep ocean where it is dangerous or impractical for man to go. It can look for submerged wrecks, for instance, or even film life near the ocean floor.'

The group had been allowed to look through the lenses of the most powerful microscopes in existence at tiny creations magnified a million times. Francesco had shown them photos of everyday objects viewed through the microscopes' electronic lenses, inviting the audience to identify them.

'Can you guess what this is?' he asked.

'A big, fat cigar?' suggested Anna.

'Or a rusty old water-pipe?' said Emma.

'Is it a human hair?' asked the lady physics teacher from the *liceo.*

'*Brava, signora!*' Francesco had complimented her.

Inevitably, Francesco had demonstrated the apparent disappearance of the photo of the President of the Republic, being at pains to explain that this piece of science was still in its early stages.

'It only works when the light is not very bright, and on a small scale,' explained Francesco.

Riccardo and Anna glanced back at their father with a smug expression on their faces, as if to say: '*We* know all about *that!*'

'But how *does* it work, *professore?*' insisted some of the *liceo* students, their imaginations fired by the magical properties of the piece of material.

'Basically, if one can produce a surface that deflects the photons away from your eyes, then anything in the vicinity of the material will become invisible. Remember that the majority of the universe consists of 'dark matter' that does not reflect light. Thus, a big part of the cosmos remains invisible to us.'

There was a meditative silence from his audience.

'And let's think about colours and how we perceive them. It's all an illusionist's trick in reality. We perceive different colours only because different wave-lengths of light reach our eyes. It's an incredible universe we live in!'

'Here's another challenge to our naïve perception of the 'real world',' continued Francesco at a later stage. 'Miky?'

Miky produced a remote control car key and pointed it towards a car door that had been attached to a clamp and a car battery some six or seven metres away. She operated the lock a few times to show that it was a normal car door.

'Now,' she said, 'will one of you place this metal plate between me and the car door - yes, it's quite heavy, isn't it? Give him a hand someone.'

She handed the remote control key to Anna, who had not been involved in any demonstration so far.

'Now, Anna, point the key at the metal plate and see if you can still lock and unlock the car door through the plate – it's about the same thickness as a garage door.

Anna did as she had been asked and found the car door locked and unlocked as if the metal plate had not been there.

'So why does this happen?' asked Francesco.

'Invisible rays?' suggested Riccardo.

'Well, yes, Riccardo, *bravo*, that's true. The door lock is operated by an infra-red beam. But how does the beam pass through a solid metal plate?'

Even the lady journalist found the notion more taxing than anything she had come across in her life so far. She attempted to be facetious, offering the suggestion:

'The metal plate has got holes in it like a colander!'

The group members laughed politely, despite the fact that they did not consider Costanza's comment to have been either witty or helpful.

'It grieves me to admit it, Costanza, but of course you are quite correct!' conceded Francesco. 'What appears to us to be solid metal is not really solid at all. There are *spaces* in its constituent atoms that allow the beam to pass through it.'

'I never thought of it like that before, *professore,*' said Giovanni, the serious-looking, bespectacled student who had been unable to 'think' the TV into life.

Afterwards, the visitors had been treated to the sight of a vastly magnified robotic device seeking out impurities in a vat filled with fermenting wine. Emma Molinari had inadvertently provoked an outburst of mirth when she had suggested that one of the minute robots could end up in the drinker's stomach. The possibility was not convincingly denied.

The group had finally spent some time with Luana Palomba and her team, learning about the wonders of stem-cell research and its potentially life-saving implications for the future of medical science – particularly interesting to the *liceo* students who wanted to work in this field. What might have gone over the younger children's heads completely and left them bored was redeemed by a demonstration of one particular area of research.

'I shall need a volunteer,' said Luana.

Anna, Riccardo and Emma put up their hands eagerly.

'I shall have to cut your finger with a scalpel,' the scientist added.

Three hands came down again immediately. In the end, one of the *liceo* students bravely volunteered, holding his index finger over a glass dish while Luana made a quick incision in the tip of his finger. An almost universal gasp of horror could be heard as the scalpel blade sliced through the skin and an alarming amount of blood ran down the student's hand. Costanza De Santis seemed unmoved. The general reaction was nothing, however, compared to the gasp of amazement which followed as Luana sprayed what looked like spectacle cleaning fluid over the wound. When the blood had been rinsed off under a tap, there was no trace of a cut on his finger. He proudly showed his finger to everyone for their inspection – equally if not more surprised than they were.

'Natural, spray-on skin,' explained Luana. 'In the next few years, it will be generally available. Good-bye sticky plasters! And all thanks to our research here at Legano's university!'

* * *

The visitors were now standing in the Clean Room facing Leonardo Molinari who was preparing to demonstrate his pride and joy – the photon encryption machine.

As soon as 'Einstein', the physicist, began talking about the notion of the perturbation of quantum data and 'single photon cryptography', Adam felt his grasp of the words slipping away. He recognised the sense of individual words, yet they made no sense at all when strung together in a sentence. Adam was relieved when he saw Anna taking Riccardo by the hand and walking over to Miky De Giorgi. Anna whispered something into Miky's ear. Adam could easily figure out the nature of the request. Miky nodded with a smile and signalled to Adam with a gesture asking his permission to take his children back to the starting point of their journey. Emma was left behind hanging on to every incomprehensible word her father was uttering, openly proud that she was the daughter of her distinguished *papà.* Adam felt it would not be diplomatic to desert his post in light of the fact that Leonardo would soon be his official boss.

The *liceo* students must have been handpicked, since they all seemed to be following Leonardo Molinari's technical explanations without difficulty.

'So each part of the message is encrypted into a single photon which is then sent to a recipient with a similar device which, theoretically, could be anywhere. Today, the recipient will be one of these two gentlemen,' explained Leonardo, indicating his two colleagues, Alessandro Agostino and Andrea Calvano. 'By giving a specific property to a single photon – using the way or direction in which an electromagnetic wave oscillates – we can transmit a series of photons to the receiver, whom we always nickname Bob. The sender is usually nicknamed Adam,' explained Leonardo.

'Lucky Adam!' thought Adam, drowning intellectually in an ocean of mysterious scientific concepts.

'So,' continued Leonardo. 'I'm going to ask one of you to be 'Adam' and type in a key message into the computer.' Alessandro Agostino went off to receive the message in another part of the building. Andrea Calvano asked for a volunteer from the *liceo* students to be 'Adam', the sender of the key message.

To save arguments, the young *liceo* teacher chose one of her students to carry out the task. With a malicious smile on her face, a girl called Monica typed out a three word key message.

'Now,' instructed Leonardo. 'It is important, Monica – and Andrea - that you push this buzzer at exactly the same instant as you send the encrypted message. We will hear another beep from the recipient team the instant the message arrives at the other end.'

Monica typed out her brief message and sent it as instructed. Nobody could fail to notice that the beep from the recipient team could be heard simultaneously; some even thought they heard the receiver's bleep just before the sender's. Impossible of course! But it all happened in the blink of an eye.

Alessandro reappeared after a minute, holding a piece of paper.

"What does the key message say, *professore?*' Leonardo asked his colleague.

'It says: *Giovanni loves Donatella,* capo!'

'And what was your message, Monica?' asked Leonardo, oblivious of the amused giggles of the other students.

'Alright,' said Giovanni, with grudging good humour. 'Spare me the embarrassment, *prof!*'

'And of course,' continued Leonardo, who had just cottoned on to what was happening, 'any attempts to intercept the photons bearing the encrypted key message will result in the pattern being perturbed, because one single photon can only reach one unique recipient. So the message can only ever be decrypted by the recipient – thus sparing you any further embarrassment, Giovanni.'

On this occasion, it was not just Adam who laughed at Leonardo's dry humour.

'But just a minute, *professore,*' said one of the *liceo* students whose name was Davide. 'Why did we hear the recipient's bleep simultaneously with Monica's signal? It was even a split second before Monica buzzed, if I'm not mistaken.'

'Yes, Davide, it might have been as you say. We can't be sure, is the answer. We need to remember that we are now inventing things which are on the very boundaries of what we accept as part of our 'real' world.

Before Leonardo reluctantly released his captive audience, he had allowed other students to send their own encrypted messages using Monica's original key message. On the third attempt, he had led Giovanni to another terminal where he was going to intercept the encrypted photons. Andrea Calvano came into the Clean Room and announced that the message had arrived in a corrupted form, showing that Eve, the eavesdropper, had been at work.

'But how...?' asked Leonardo's audience in wonderment.

'It's a property of quantum mechanics,' explained Leonardo. 'If you attempt to measure one particle, it inevitably alters the state of other particles.'

'Pauli's Exclusion Principle?' asked the *liceo* teacher. 'Or is it Heisenberg's Uncertainty Principle?'

'The Principal Uncertainty of Adam's Brain,' thought Adam as a very thoughtful group of people filed out of the Clean Room and returned to the starting point, where Leonardo gave a short speech, rounding it off by inviting questions.

'*I* have one question, *professore.*'

It was Costanza De Santis. Francesco froze in mid-conversation with a colleague. There was something about her tone of voice which heralded trouble yet again.

'I've been looking at a list of your scientific staff, *professore.* It would appear that one of them, a certain Mariastella Russo, was absent this evening. Do you have any explantion as to her absence?'

Francesco looked at Leonardo, expecting to see a look of consternation on his face. To his shocked surprise, his *capo* was smiling engagingly at the provocative journalist. Leonardo announced calmly: 'You should go and interview our Magnificent Rector, *mia cara Costanza.* He should be able to furnish you with information on the matter.'

The video cameraman had caught the moment. Francesco looked white with shock. He would have to corner his *capo* in private.

The evening was not quite over. The *liceo* students were preparing to leave when one of them noticed the absence of their 'mascot' and his sister.

'We would like to say goodbye to your children, *signore,'* they said addressing Adam.

The result was that the whole group, excluding a noticeably shaken Costanza, trouped back to where they had started, to find Riccardo and Anna with Miky De Giorgi, saying goodnight to RIC6 with promises that they would return soon.

'Santino managed to absorb everything Riccardo taught him about chess pieces,' said Miky triumphantly. There were fond farewells as if they had all known each other for months rather than hours. It was nearly ten o'clock before they all went their separate ways.

'What on earth possessed you, *capo?*' asked Francesco with admiration all over his face.

'It was all staged, Francesco,' replied Leonardo. 'I was under orders from the *Carabinieri.* I think they've devised some scheme to open their offensive against our magnificent leader. Costanza was deliberately invited to ask that very question. I have the impression she was somewhat surprised by the nature of the reply, don't you agree, Francesco?'

Francesco thought his chief was becoming quite worldly-wise.

* * *

Back home, Rosaria greeted her family warmly. She had been becoming anxious about their protracted absence.

'I've missed you all so much today,' she said, holding Adam tightly before turning her attentions to Anna and Riccardo.

'Sandro has closed the studio for a week – he's getting his flat ready for when Stella returns tomorrow. I suspect that means he's ironing a month's worth of washing and giving the place a long overdue clean. Naturally, he has his mother with him, to give him a helping hand!'

After supper and a breathless account of their visit to Wonderland, Anna and Riccardo went to bed and slept soundly. They might well have dreamt about a future in which they formed friendships with androids which were outwardly indistinguishable from themselves, or about miniature robots which turned up in their glasses of red wine. But the peace of their slumber was primarily because the gash in the firmament that threatened to destroy their childhood security had been magically healed by a warm embrace and a loving kiss. The familiar planets, which had been on the point of flying off into the void of outer space, had resumed their steady orbit round the sun.

Adam and Rosaria were left to their own secret expression of love.

'Maybe we should get married after all,' suggested Rosaria in the intimate darkness of the room.

'For the children's sake, you mean?' asked Adam ironically.

'No,' replied Rosaria quietly.

18: L'esca (The Decoy)

The Rector of Legano University, *Il Magnifico Fabiano Mela,* had endured a very fraught couple of days. The house which he thought he had built on solid rock was showing distinct signs of crumbling in the shifting sands of changing circumstances. Matters appeared to be getting out of hand. Like all arrogant men with a modicum of power, he was convinced that his position was unassailable by ordinary mortals. He firmly believed that his misdeeds had been so skilfully concealed from the prying eyes of the outside world that he had become immune to attack.

Two days previously, he had received a disturbing phone call from a certain Francesca Fabbro from the city of Turin. He had been expecting to hear from Dario's mother and had been surprised that the call had taken so long in coming. When his secretary announced there was a distraught and irate lady on the phone, whose name was Francesca Fabbro, he had been tempted to ask his secretary to stall her. But there was little point in putting off the difficult moment, knowing as he did that Dario's mother was the sort of person to call up the university every ten minutes until she had achieved her objective.

'Put her through, Giorgina – and hold all other calls.'

'Pronto, Francesca,' he began with a tone of false bonhomie in his voice, designed to defuse the full force of her attack. The tactic had little effect, however.

'DON'T – whatever you do, Fabiano Mela – believe for one instant that you can hide behind your usual sugary, sycophantic charm. I have just attended the funeral of my son – *your* son.'

'What are you talking about, *mia cara...?*'

'And DON'T go through this charade of feigning ignorance, Fabiano. I have just lost a son in the most appalling circumstances imaginable. All that remains of him is a charred lump inside a coffin and you sit in your plush office trying to fob me off with your habitual lies and denials of responsibility.'

'I can assure you, Francesca...'

'You don't assure me *un cazzo,* Fabiano! Dario's only fault was that he inherited *your* corrupt and loathsome genetic make-up...'

The Rector of Legano University had been obliged to listen to a non-stop barrage of accusations and insults for nearly ten minutes more. He sidestepped every one of them, denying all knowledge of Dario's demise.

'All I can tell you, Francesca, is that Dario was in good health when I last saw him some four or five weeks ago. We really haven't been in touch since then. He had bought himself a blue Ferrari and obviously wanted to show it off to me...'

'I didn't expect to hear the truth from *you,'* concluded Francesca coldly. 'But know this, Fabiano Mela – your involvement in this will be a public issue within days.'

'If you say so, *mia cara,'* the Rector had stated with an irritating calmness that he was not feeling. Francesca had slammed the phone down before the Rector could formulate his insincere condolences.

Examining his conscience after the phone call, he was alarmed to find that he felt little guilt and even less remorse about the death – no murder – of his illegitimate son. He had succeeded in persuading himself that Dario had brought his

315

fate upon himself. If he hadn't drawn attention to himself by buying that very ostentatious car then business could have carried on as normal – at least for the time being. The technical information, emanating from the science department of his university, which he had 'shared' with that shadowy individual whom he knew as Don Augello, had been a useful source of income for a while. Fabiano Mela did not concern himself unduly with speculation as to where the information ended up. Once he had made the mistake of asking Don Augello over the telephone if the information remained in Italy. He had heard a rasping noise through the earpiece before Don Augello had cut off communication abruptly.

'That is none of your business, *dottore!*'

The local mafia boss had doubly insulted him by spitting out the word *dottore* – the lowest ranking title of respect possible – before cutting him off brusquely.

Fabiano Mela would have been entirely humiliated had he known, at that point of time, that the *mafioso* boss had sold the information on for roughly four times the amount he had paid the *Magnifico Rettore.*

That chapter was behind him. He would concentrate on diverting trivial amounts of the university's money into his own secret bank accounts – with the help of a well-remunerated minion in the finance department of Legano University. He had felt sufficiently insecure after the phone call from Dario's mother in Turin to feel the necessity to shore up his rearguard defences. He had invited Alfredo Mancini to his office, ostensibly to discuss the university's financial situation. Alfredo Mancini had followed the Rector down from Pavia. Mancini was a frail looking, bespectacled little individual whose wife had left him but who was constantly claiming financial support for their daughter. He had become dependent on the 'little extras' that he could procure on the side, thanks to Fabiano Mela's bold initiatives.

Alfredo Mancini was a man lacking totally in social graces but he was a wizard with figures and computers. He was so mouse-like in the workplace that the Rector knew nobody would ever suspect him of aiding and abetting his fraudulent dealings. After Mancini had left his office, Fabiano Mela felt reassured that, whatever assaults he would have to endure from his ex-mistress and the press, his covert financial manipulations were secure.

It was an unpleasant experience, the following morning, when he found himself confronted with that very forceful lady journalist from *Il Mezzogiorno,* asking him questions about the disappearance of one of his scientists from the science department. But he had had a number of run-ins with Costanza De Santis during his office and felt supremely confident that he could deal satisfactorily with her current verbal assault on his person.

'My dear Signora De Santis, of course I am aware of the disappearance of Mariastella Russo. Naturally, my colleague, *Professore* Molinari has informed me of the matter. She is very young and is probably undergoing some emotional crisis over a boyfriend. How should I know? She is sure to reappear on the scene before long.'

The Rector had succeeded in stone-walling the journalist for over twenty minutes. To her annoyance, Fabiano Mela had doggedly refused to be goaded into showing any signs of unease or embarrassment. But the Magnificent Rector was a past master at evasion. It was a question of survival.

He was sitting behind his desk on the Thursday morning of the week in which the Science Faculty was holding its Open Door exhibition. He reluctantly came to the conclusion that he ought to put in an appearance at some stage. His hand was actually stretched out to pick up the intercom telephone to his secretary when an agitated Giorgina phoned *him.*

Her next words shocked him out of his complacency within a couple of seconds.

'Excuse me for disturbing you, *Magnifico,* but there's a young woman in my office who is demanding to see you. She says her name is Mariastella Russo.'

Fabiano Mela experienced a shock wave of panic shooting through his nervous system. His brain told him that the words he had just heard were impossible. They represented a stark contradiction of what he held to be true. Mariastella Russo had been dispatched into eternity at the same time as his illegitimate son. He had paid a large sum of money to ensure that this bane of his life had been removed for good. Mariastella had been a regrettable but necessary part of this process. He swallowed hard before replying to his secretary. He felt as if there was an impediment in his throat preventing him from talking naturally. His usual suave tones emerged in a strangulated knot of vocal chords.

'That's impossible…'

His secretary, Giorgina, could be heard remonstrating in a desperate bid to control the situation.

'No, *signorina!* I'm afraid the rector cannot… *SIGNORINA!* You can't just barge in like that. You must make an appointment.'

The complete failure on the part of his personal secretary to stem the tide of events was self-evident as the double doors were flung wide open and a striking-looking young woman with black shoulder-length hair strode determinedly into his office.

'It's alright, Georgina,' the Rector managed to stammer. 'I'll see her for a few minutes.'

'I expect you are somewhat surprised to see me, *Magnifico!*' announced the young woman, infusing his title with a degree of contempt that was truly awe-inspiring. His mind was attempting to assimilate what was happening to him. He had the distinct impression that he had seen the girl somewhere before. Yes, it must have been at the *Hotel Europa* during the fund-raising conference. She looked remarkably alluring standing defiantly in front of his desk. No wonder his illegitimate son had been attracted to her, he thought. What did not tie up, however, was Dario's description of her as a reserved young woman who could be easily manipulated.

'Won't you sit down, *Signorina* Russo?' he managed to say.

'No, *Magnifico,* I won't. What I have to say to you is better said standing up. Besides which, I have no wish to remain for longer than a minute in the presence of the criminal lunatic who ordered my assassination at the hands of the local mafia!'

'*Signorina,* I really must protest...'

'Save your breath!' snarled the young woman. 'Are you so absolutely stupid as to assume that Dario did not tell me *everything* about you? He hated you, you know. You refused to acknowledge him as your son. What kind of a father makes his son call him 'uncle' – just because he is too ashamed to admit the truth?'

'*Signorina* Russo, I am glad you are no longer missing. Your colleagues have been anxious about you. How did you manage to…?'

Fabiano Mela had begun the sentence without realising that saying anything further would be tantamount to an admission of personal involvement.

In any event, the young woman calling herself Mariastella Russo did not allow him to complete the sentence. She placed her hands on the edge of his mahogany desk and leant forward angrily towards him. The Rector found himself staring, mesmerised by a beautiful cleavage and the insistent presence of two firmly rounded breasts straining forward through the material of a low cut top. To his discomfort, he felt an erection stirring in his trousers.

'Try to concentrate on what I am about to tell you, *Magnifico!*' the contemptuous voice was saying. Fabiano Mela did his best to avert his eyes from temptation and tried to outstare the forceful Fury who was standing in front of him, spelling out his fate.

'Tomorrow evening, I have a televised interview with *Telenorba.* There is also a very determined lady journalist, whom you know I am sure, who is eager to hear the whole story of my ordeal in Matera. I shall be able to tell them how your son was driven off by three of the local mob and burnt to death in his car with his hands bound to the steering wheel. That will go down well with the public, won't it? I shall make your involvement perfectly clear, *Magnifico.* You're finished!'

With those words, the young woman turned her back on Fabiano Mela and strode out of the room, walked past a stunned secretary and out into the ancient courtyard of

Legano University's administration building. Surprisingly, once out of the building, she stopped in the tree-lined avenue leading back to the main road and began talking urgently into her mobile phone. She might even have had a smile on her face.

The Rector was out of his office in a trice. Giorgina was pretending to study her computer intently. Fabiano Mela snapped his fingers at a young man occupying another desk.

'Daniele, get after that mad woman and follow her. I want to know where she goes.'

'But if she has a car...?'

'See what car she drives off in. Get going!'

The minor employee of Legano University scuttled off to do his master's bidding with a sinking feeling in his stomach. This irregular mission was doomed to failure, he reckoned. He had never known the Rector to be so rattled. To his surprise and relief, he found the beautiful young woman standing obligingly under a tree, talking into her phone. He lit a cigarette and tried to look nonchalant as he waited for the woman to make a move. She was a looker alright!

The Rector returned to his office, looking furious, and slammed the double door shut behind him. He realised with horror that they had remained open during Mariastella Russo's tirade. His secretary would certainly have heard every word. He sat and pondered over the pitifully inadequate alternative courses of action that remained to him, which included bribing the media into silence and phoning the education minister, begging her to impose a news embargo on the affair. Short term solutions, he concluded pessimistically.

Twenty minutes later, he heard a timid tap on the door.

'*Avanti!*' he shouted irritably.

The minor clerk, Daniele, was standing shuffling his feet nervously.

'Well?' snapped the Rector.

'Nothing, *Magnifico.* She crossed Via Gallipoli and walked back to a block of flats just off Via Degli Abruzzi. She let herself into number 13. About five minutes later, she came out again and drove off in the direction of Monteleone in a blue Twingo, registration number...'

'*Basta! Grazie* Daniele. You can go,' said the Rector dismissively. The address coincided exactly with the one he had given his illegitimate son six months ago. Mariastella Russo had almost certainly driven off to the *AltoTek* campus. That was all he needed to be sure of. He knew what he had to do next and he wasn't looking forward to it one little bit.

* * *

His fear of the mafia boss, Don Augello Parzanese, was absolute. He had dreaded the man's reaction when he made the reluctant call on the mobile number that he had been provided with – for emergencies only – at precisely 12.45. When the rector had begun explaining the reason for his call, the rasping voice of the old man on the other end of the line soon silenced him.

'We don't discuss business over the phone, *signore.* We'll meet at four o'clock this afternoon at the Bar Alvino near the Roman Amphitheatre. Be there on time – or else you'll only have yourself to drink coffee with!'

Yet again, the Rector, his title reduced even further down the ranking, was left feeling fearful and humiliated by this man, who wielded power like a medieval executioner.

At four o'clock sharp, he was sitting on the crowded pavement terrace of the Bar Alvino, drinking a solitary mineral water. Don Augello kept him waiting in suspense for twenty minutes before he arrived with no hint of an apology. He was accompanied by a young man in his mid-twenties, who looked as mean as Don Augello himself.

'My nephew, Augusto,' was the only introduction that was offered. Both of the men had arrived wearing sunglasses despite the weather being cloudy, threatening summer rain. As soon as the Rector began talking, it was evident that Don Augello was having difficulty hearing what the Rector was saying. When he raised his voice, Don Augello treated him to a furious scowl.

'Tell my nephew what you have to say – and be quick about it,' snarled the *mafioso* boss.

Fabiano told the nephew about the visit he had had that morning with a girl who was supposed to be dead. He even dared to suggest that there had been a catastrophic failure on the part of the mob. The nephew looked at his uncle, accusingly, the Rector thought. The rector handed him a piece of paper with the address in Via Degli Abruzzi written on it. The two mobsters, young and old, stood up to depart, Don Augello walking with a pronounced limp, Fabiano noticed. The nephew was being groomed to inherit his uncle's throne, he supposed.

'We'll deal with the problem, *signore,*' the nephew said abruptly, with a sinister confidence which sent a shiver down the Rector's spine.

'*Ci penso io, zio,*' Augusto said to his ageing uncle as they got into the rear seat of an illegally parked black Lancia Delta

– the younger man, assuming responsibility for the simple task of murder that would become his stock in trade.

As soon as the Rector stood up to leave, a young couple, sitting at the neighbouring table to the Rector's, looking like a hundred other summer tourists in Legano, stood up in their turn and left. As he made his way back to the University on foot, Fabiano Mela meditated on the fact that no waiter had come over to their respective tables to take drinks orders. Strange!

* * *

Augusto, the up-and-coming leader of the local mafia clan, 'took care' of the problem in draconian manner. The three mobsters who had turned up that evening in Matera were standing in front of their *capo's* nephew with a look of terror on their faces.

'You were given the simple task of killing one man and one girl,' Augusto said, speaking entirely in the old Salento dialect which was their first language. 'You told me, I seem to recall, that you carried out your mission without a hitch. You lied to me!' he snarled.

'Honest, *capo!* There was no girl there! We went back afterwards and went round the whole of Matera all night. She wasn't anywhere, I swear!' said Max, the ringleader.

'So how come she turned up as large as life in Legano today, accusing our client of being party to the murder of the one with the blue Ferrari?'

'I dunno, *capo.'*

Fearing retribution, Max and Manny shifted the blame on to the weakest member of the trio – the simpleton called

Antonio, who had had his head slapped for failing to find the girl.

A revolver had appeared in Augusto's hand. He shot Antonio between the eyes with a total lack of compunction.

'Get rid of him!' ordered the nephew with chilling indifference. 'Now, this is what you're gonna do this evening…'

* * *

'This is it, *capo!* They've arrived.'

The two *Carabinieri* officers, dressed in civilian clothes, were sitting in an unmarked car outside Mariastella Russo's flat in Via Degli Abruzzi. The officer in the passenger seat had relayed the message to Marco Scarpa, waiting inside the studio flat on the second floor.

'OK. Here we go. Best of luck everyone. You'll be alright,' he said reassuringly to the girl with long, dark hair, who was looking white-faced with tension, sitting on the edge of the bed.

Somebody was knocking loudly on the solid door of the flat, calling out in a loud voice:

'Signorina! Signorina Russo! There's a fire in the flat below. We've all got to evacuate the building.' The man's voice sounded harsh, uncouth, as if he was not used to speaking Italian. To the surprise of those waiting in the room, a cloud of acrid smoke was coming into the room through the gap between door and floor.

'That's a new trick!' muttered one of the police officers. *'Merda!'*

'OK, NOW. Go and open the door!' said Marco Scarpa to the young woman in a furious whisper.

She got up from the bed, gave the key a double turn and took two rapid paces backwards towards the bed.

She was taken completely by surprise at the speed of the attack. Afterwards, she said the mobster moved with the speed of a cobra striking its victim. Max felt the perfectly honed blade slip on the bullet proof jacket that she was wearing under a sloppy jumper. He heard her cry out in pain as the lethal blade cut her arm. But he also knew that it was a trap in the same instant as two burly police officers brought him to the ground and twisted his arms painfully up his back. For the first time in his life, he felt the metallic grip of handcuffs round his wrists. Manny, his accomplice, fled towards the stairwell pursued by a third officer. Marco was on the phone immediately to the waiting officers down in the street.

Then he turned his attention to the young woman sitting on the bed. She was looking appealingly at him – with an expression of deep gratitude on her face that his reaction had been so swift. Without thinking, he sat down beside her and gave her an affectionate hug.

'I don't think I'll volunteer to be a decoy in a hurry again,' she said, her voice trembling.

'You've been truly courageous, Adriana,' he said. 'And your acting this morning must have been impeccable.'

It was only then Marco noticed the blood running down her arm.

'Call for an ambulance!' he shouted at one of his officers. 'That bastard has got her!'

He made a makeshift bandage and tied it tightly round the wound. He helped her down the stairs supporting her weight with his arm as soon as the ambulance's siren could be heard approaching.

'Get these scumbags down to the police station,' he ordered his men. 'I'll join you later.'

Marco Scarpa sat near Adriana in the ambulance on their way to the A and E unit of Legano's main hospital. She was looking at her *capo* in a particular way. Why had he never noticed how beautiful she was before, he wondered - astonishment at his own blindness being the sensation uppermost in his mind.

From that moment on, he determined to forget all about the unwritten rule which discouraged members of the *Carabinieri* to form intimate relationships within their ranks. It was as bad as forbidding Catholic priests to marry! This was the twenty-first century - and he had remained unattached for too long. He lifted her up gently in both arms, being careful not to squeeze her newly dressed left arm, and they hugged affectionately. Evidently, it wasn't just *him* who felt this way. For Marco Scarpa, the journey through the solitary wilderness was over.

19: Sandro Greco's Altered Perspectives

Unlike Adriana Galante, the real life Stella Russo was not exposed to any danger at that particular moment in time. If anything, it was Alessandro Greco whose well-ordered existence was under threat. He was lying on his back naked on the bed while Stella was sitting astride him. She was very far from being passive. During the four long years spent with his former *fidanzata,* whose notions of love-making had been infinitely more staid and predictable than Stella's, he had never experienced anything as exciting as this. He had rather come to assume that all women must behave more or less the same way in bed as his former girlfriend. Looking up at Stella, he was being treated to the living proof that this was not the case. In the first instance, Stella wore a beatific smile of erotic pleasure on her face as she moved up and down, alternating this with a rocking motion of her pelvis which was excruciatingly pleasurable.

Not knowing what to do with his hands, he cupped them round her breasts, which rose and fell in time with her whole body. After a few seconds, she brushed his hands aside as if their presence impeded her concentration.

In the end, the growing pressure inside him broke his fascination with the visual image of their love-making which this perspective afforded him. He pulled an unresisting Stella down on top of him and rolled her over on to her back without leaving her body. His restraint was thrown to the winds as she gasped out the words: 'Oh yes, Sandro.' Her intense and joyous cries of ecstasy were ringing in his ears as he released all the pent up sexual passions of the last few years. After they had reached their more or less simultaneous climax – a 'first' for Sandro – he was thrilled by the physical and emotional feeling of Stella's hands on his spine pulling him into her as hard as she could. 'Don't leave me yet, Sandro!' she said. Amidst the sheer joy of absolute sexual release, he had time to recall that his former *fidanzata* would have been well on the way to the bathroom at this stage – to wash away the inevitable stains of carnal intercourse.

As they lay speechless and breathless together, Alessandro became aware of the muted sound of a vacuum cleaner being frantically dragged backwards and forwards across the floor of the flat above. The flat was inhabited by a middle-aged couple. He assumed it must be an attempt on Nicoletta's part to drown out the unwelcome reminders of long-forgotten passions emanating from downstairs. He said nothing to Stella, snuggled up by his side – the voluptuous pressure of her firm body all the way down his body, threatening to arouse him again.

'Please, Sandro, will you come to California with me?' she asked out of the blue.

At first, he assumed that going to California was merely an expression of a desire to have a holiday in America, so he laughed and said it sounded like a brilliant idea, and that it was a place he had always wanted to visit.

'No, Sandro. I mean would you like to go and live there for six months with me?' she stated in total seriousness.

'What are you talking about, Stella?'

'I was talking to Leonardo yesterday after you took me to the *AltoTek* campus,' she explained. 'I told him I was still scared of the mob finding out that I'm alive and back in Legano. And I *do* feel so guilty about what I did. All my colleagues are being very understanding but I still feel that I betrayed them. That makes me feel very uncomfortable in their presence.'

'I'm sure you have very little to fear, Stella. Just as I am certain your colleagues understand the difficult situation you were in. But why California? It's a brilliant idea but...'

'It was Leonardo's idea. The University of Los Angeles wants to second a scientist to develop nanotechnology projects over there – we are truly ahead of the field here in Legano. I know it sounds crazy that I was involved in...you know what I'm saying. But now we have the chance to openly share what we have developed with the rest of the world. It's ironic, don't you think? Leonardo himself will be travelling to Beijing sometime soon, he tells me.'

'But have you already agreed to go to Los Angeles?' asked Sandro, fearful that he was about to lose Stella before their relationship had got under way.

'I told him I would only go if you agreed to come too,' she answered simply.

The ability to shock him and keep him on his toes reminded Sandro very poignantly of Rosaria Miccoli. She had the same ever active mind that seemed unable to rest for more than a short period of time before looking for a new challenge. The thought made him consider the responsibility he had towards Rosaria, who depended on him for gainful employment. He mentioned this aspect of the matter to Stella.

'I think you will soon discover that you might be doing Rosaria Miccoli a favour by giving her a holiday, Sandro. I am sworn to secrecy by the *colonnello* – you know him of course, don't you? But I am pretty sure that, if you talk to Rosaria, you will discover that she has a secret career project that she has been dreading telling you about. I think she will be relieved.'

All attempts to prise information out of Stella failed completely. He only desisted when Stella began to make love to him again, more slowly but equally passionately.

Sandro's neighbour upstairs was in despair. She could hardly hoover the carpets again, so she put on her CD of famous arias from Puccini's operas instead, and turned up the sound as high as she dared.

20: A Magnificent Downfall

Rosaria's predominant feeling during that week was one of relief that she could spend time at home. The occurrences of the last few weeks had proved more emotionally draining than she could have possibly imagined since the day she had first set foot in the *AltoTek* campus. She had unwittingly unleashed a tide of complex events, any one of which could so easily have ended in tragedy. Her own family had become embroiled in the investigation in totally unexpected ways. Now she should be able to draw breath and relax, letting others shoulder the responsibility for seeing that justice was done. The only thing which troubled her was the thought that she would, sooner or later, have to face the embarrassment of confessing to Alessandro Greco that she was intending to desert him and try for a drastic career change. She was, at this point, unaware that Sandro's own circumstances had also dramatically altered.

'You don't need to feel guilty about it,' Adam had repeatedly reassured her. 'He may well not react in the way you fear, Rosy.'

Perhaps this was also an aspect that secretly troubled her; that Sandro Greco would simply let her go without any qualms.

'Best to get it over with as soon as possible,' Adam urged her at roughly the same moment as Stella was broaching the subject of going to America with the new love of her life.

Adam and the children's long academic summer break would soon begin. She would have the time and the necessary peace - she hoped – to prepare herself for her preliminary written exam for the *Guardia di Finanza,* even if this entailed lugging the book to the beach, where Adam would give her a *viva voce* test in between swimming and playing with the children in the sea. They had shelved plans to get married until the outcome of her job interview was known. Once again, she secretly thanked her invisible gods for her partner's support and understanding for her desire to acquire a 'real' State-paid job.

She had barely managed to pluck up the mental courage to continue studying the heavy volume which should guarantee that she got to the first interview stage, when her mobile phone rang. She would have ignored it had it been her mother, father or one of her countless cousins, aunts or uncles, but perhaps not her sister, Martina. But, to her surprise, it was Giulio Pensiero, Marco Scarpa's nephew in the *Guardia.* In light of her renewed determination to get down to her studies, his phone call bordered on the portentous.

'Ciao, Rosaria,' he began. 'Are you very busy at the moment?'

'I was about to sit down and study for my exam, Giulio.'

'Never mind about that for now - we could do with your help. *Il Maggiore Rizzardi* would be very grateful if you could come over and clarify a few aspects of a case we are investigating at the moment. I hardly need to say which one.'

Rosaria felt a secret thrill, even though she could not imagine how she might help the *Guardia.*

A quick phone call to Adam to make sure he was able to pick up Anna and Riccardo. Adam detected the excitement in her voice. She was parked outside the *Guardia* headquarters within twenty minutes and felt uncannily at home walking through the main entrance door to be greeted by Marco Scarpa's nephew.

'Thanks for coming so promptly, Rosaria. We've got five of the team, including myself, working on the case of our Magnificent Rector. There have been a number of developments that you might not be aware of. He's in custody at the moment, protesting his innocence. But my uncle's team intercepted a phone call he carelessly made to the local mafia boss, Don Augello, whose phone has been tapped since the beginning of the week.'

'How incredibly stupid of him!' commented Rosaria. 'Why should he do that?'

'Because he was in a state of total panic, Rosaria; a young lady by the name of Mariastella Russo turned up at his office and accused him of murder. He was quite surprised since he was convinced she had been eliminated alongside his illegitimate son, Dario.'

'But...surely, Giulio, Stella wouldn't have dared...'

'Ah, but it wasn't the real Stella, just a decoy. And it worked to perfection. As well as the couple of mobsters who carried out the killing of Dario Fabbro, we have arrested Fabiano Mela for collusion in murder and finally succeeded in pinning a murder on Don Augello. We even had two plain clothed officers sitting in the Bar Alvino, where Don Augello arranged a rendez-vous with the Rector. We've got it recorded. It's watertight this time.'

There were so many questions that Rosaria wanted to ask, but Giulio didn't want to keep his *capo* waiting any longer. Rosaria was asked about many aspects of the disappearance of Stella and Dario the week before. But what the *Guardia di Finanza* were particularly interested in was the source of considerable sums of money that had arrived in the University's coffers over the last few weeks – and where they had ended up. Rosaria was able to enlighten them to a large extent.

'The science department held a fund-raising conference at the *Hotel Europa* the other week. I understand that several million euros were promised. Professor Molinari received about five million from the Rector for research,' explained Rosaria.

'The University received nearer five and a half million in sponsor money, *capo,*' added Giulio Pensiero. 'So he certainly didn't hand it all over!'

'We suspect strongly that the Rector has managed to channel some of it into his own bank accounts,' continued Matteo Rizzardi. 'Now we've got Fabiano Mela distracted by the murder charge, we have raided the University's finance offices and confiscated all their hardware without his knowledge,' said the major with sinister glee. 'We are certain that he has a man on the inside.'

After *il maggiore* Rizzardi had finished plying Rosaria with further questions, he thanked her profusely for her help.

'I'm quite certain we shall be meeting again, Signora Miccoli,' he said looking meaningfully at her with piercing grey eyes. Rosaria felt a thrill of excitement at the promise implied in his words. A new frontier was opening up before her, she felt.

Rosaria spent almost another hour with Giulio's team, looking in wonder at the Rector's bank accounts on the computer screens and at the various sums of money that had been paid in over the past months. None of the payments was excessively large but they must have added up to half a million euros in total, she reckoned. Making sense of it all was a painstaking operation. Just as she was thinking she ought to make a move homewards, an officer called Valentina said to the team:

'Look at this. The Rector paid out €4700 just over a week ago. I can't make any sense of it.'

Rosaria asked if she could have a look. The sum of money had been paid into a deposit account in a small bank in Campanula. Rosaria looked at the information on the screen for several minutes, her eyebrows knitted in a concentrated frown. In an instant of inspiration, it came to her.

'I think I can guess what that's all about,' she said trying very hard to keep the triumph out of her voice. 'The date of the payment coincides precisely with the murder of Dario Fabbro and the disappearance of Stella Russo. I would say the €4700 is the payment to Don Augello to eliminate the two people who knew too much about what the Rector had been up to. There are a number of payments coming out of the same bank account in Campanula into the Rector's account. I wouldn't mind betting they are payments for the falsified information that Stella Russo was supplying through Dario. That's what Stella herself suspected anyway.'

There was a stunned silence before it was broken by a round of applause and cries of *'Brava Rosaria'* from the small team of *Guardia* officers, looking in admiration at Rosaria. The rapturous response clinched it for Rosaria. This was decidedly where she belonged.

'So Stella Russo was secretly on the side of the angels,' stated Gilberto, one of the team of five.

'I wouldn't go that far,' replied Rosaria smiling grimly at memories of Stella's confession. 'But she was certainly more sinned against than sinning. And there is no doubt she redeemed herself afterwards.'

On the way out, Giulio Pensiero accompanied Rosaria to her car.

'One question I wanted to ask you, Giulio,' said Rosaria pensively.

'Go ahead, Rosaria.'

'Who was the decoy? Who played the part of Stella Russo?'

'One of my uncle's officers, Adriana Galante – you know her, I imagine?'

Rosaria nodded.

'It appears my uncle has fallen in love with her.'

Rosaria experienced a little stab of pain at this news and her heart missed a beat. She quickly stifled the spasm of irrational jealousy and asked in a voice more cutting than she intended:

'Reciprocated, I assume?'

'It looks that way, Rosaria.'

* * *

Rosaria arrived home to find her family waiting anxiously. Her jubilance was apparent. Adam had prepared a meal and a bottle of *Prosecco* was self-evidently called for to celebrate Rosy's first investigative success under the flag of the *Guardia di Finanza*. Anna and Riccardo were developing an alarming taste for the sparkling wine, thought Rosaria, the concerned mother. Adam shrugged and said something about it being preferable to drugs.

I still haven't told Sandro yet,' said Rosaria anxiously. 'Tomorrow, without fail...'

At that moment, there was a ring on their door bell. Anna and Riccardo had a race to see who got there first.

'STELLA!' Adam and Rosaria heard them cry out in delight. 'You look so funny with short blond hair!'

Stella showed them her roots, bowing her head forwards.

'Look! My real colour hair is beginning to grow again now,' she said proudly.

Riccardo and Anna led Sandro and Stella into the spacious kitchen. Stella gave Rosaria an effusive hug, and a *bacio* to Adam. The remainder of the *Prosecco* was shared out, thereby reducing the children's share of the contents of the bottle.

Some thirty minutes later, Sandro looking very sheepish, said to Rosaria:

'Rosy, there's something I have to tell you...'

On hearing what Sandro was intending to do, Rosaria treated him to a spectacular display of histrionics which would have done credit to a professional actress.

'How could you abandon me to my fate in this way, Sandro Greco...?' she began in mock horror, crocodile tears appearing in the corner of her eyes.

Alessandro Greco could not understand why Anna and Riccardo were giggling uncontrollably whilst Adam was looking superior. Even Stella's eyes were sparkling with mirth.

'I told you that you didn't have to worry about Rosy!' she said to Sandro.

'Mamma's going to join the *Guardia di Finanza!'* announced Anna proudly – even if a trifle prematurely.

'And wear a uniform!' added Riccardo.

'And Adam is going to be teaching English to the scientists,' explained Rosaria.

'Well, it rather looks as if the future has been decided for us all!' conceded Sandro with a grudging smile.

'Including that of the Magnificent Rector of Legano University, I trust!' concluded Stella vehemently.

After what must have been a covert signal between the pair of them, Riccardo and Anna sidled up to Stella and, behind cupped hands, held a whispered conversation in each of her ears.

Rosy and Adam looked puzzled until Stella laughed and looked affectionately at both of the children, saying:

"I'm quite sure Leonardo isn't going to let him out of his sight ever again but I'll ask Francesco if you two can make a special visit to meet Ric6 again. I'm sure he won't say no!"

"I hope he hasn't grown up too much," said Riccardo anxiously.

"Well," added Stella,"we *are* beginning to work on his little brother who will also be able to speak – in English, by the way!"

"That'll please my *papa!*" Anna added *sotto voce.*

Epilogue

The population of Legano followed the trial of Fabiano Mela, the ex-Rector of the University, with curiosity rather than surprise; corruption amongst public officials sometimes appears to be endemic in Italy, to the extent that it arouses little astonishment. Costanza De Santis had a field day before the reading public began to lose interest. Rai news reported the trial briefly on the national network. An insignificant little man in the University's finance section, named Alfredo Mancini, seeing that his benefactor had dug a deep hole for himself, turned State's evidence, thereby helping the Guardia di Finanza and saving his own neck. Fabiano Mela was condemned to a period of imprisonment for embezzlement, corruption and collusion in the act of murder and attempted murder. It was presumed that the information acquired through his illegitimate son had found its way to Beijing – although this was largely conjecture. The subsequent opening up of the international frontiers of science made the Rector's financial venture seem farcical.

Don Augello Parzanese fared worse. His two henchmen had been arrested for the murder of Dario and the attempted murder of Adriana Galante. Realising that he would be condemned to a lengthy prison sentence, Don Augello became a 'latitante' – a fugitive from the law – and went into hiding for the rest of his natural days, holed up in a cramped flat owned by the mob somewhere in the back streets of Foggia. His nephew, Augusto, son of Rosaria Miccoli's convent classmate, took up the reins of power for a short while, until his clumsy excesses got him assassinated by a rival section of the mob in Nardò. Augusto had ordered 600 ancient olive trees to be cut down overnight with a chain saw – all because some farmer had refused to pay his 'pizzo', it was claimed. There was, however, an element of conjecture surrounding the whole affair.

Confusingly, the eminent lady journalist, Costanza De Santis, propounded the interesting hypothesis that Augusto Parzanese's assassination revealed the hand of the Chinese Triad clans, angered by the fact that they had paid out considerable sums of money for worthless information. Having failed to identify the whereabouts of Don Augello, they took their revenge on his successor. Costanza's theories steadily gained credence in some well-informed quarters.

Stella Russo and Sandro Greco went to California, where they remained for the best part of three years – until family ties and nostalgia for the homeland brought them home again, with a young son in tow. Their departure from Legano had been delayed because Stella's testimony at the trial of Fabiano Mela was crucial. Stella worked for the Nanotechnology Faculty at Los Angeles University whilst Sandro went into partnership with a realty agent who specialised in selling run-down Puglian farm houses and 'truli' (those strange, conical-roofed houses found in parts of Puglia) to rich Americans beguiled by the fascination of the Old World. On his return to Legano, Sandro specialised in property sales in collaboration with his American counterpart. He had to find new premises. Sandro's uncle had been delighted at his nephew's departure since it meant he could finally make money by renting out the Greco studio, which he had rashly allowed Sandro to use, free of rent. (See 'The Demise of Judge Grassi') Stella felt that she had done her penance and returned to work under Leonardo

Molinari with a clear conscience. Her fears of three years ago had subsided.

The team of scientists settled down again to their research into the magical world of stem cell development and nanotechnology, under a new Rector. Francesco Zunica was intrigued to notice that Giovanna Binetto often left work in the company of the pretty secretary, Renata Colombo. But as Stefano Pellegrino often accompanied them, his animated words accompanied by graceful sweeps of his hands, Francesco did not attempt to draw too many conclusions.

And last but not least...Rosaria waltzed through both the written exam and the viva with no difficulty. She was initially disappointed that she could not become a fully-fledged officer because of her age and family commitment. But she became a highly valued investigator behind the scenes. Riccardo was delighted that his mamma was allowed to wear a uniform.

It took Adam nearly six months to resolve the bureaucratic labyrinth that had to be negotiated before he and Rosaria could get married. Even getting married in the town hall was fraught with red tape. Divorce still remains an obstacle to remarriage in Italy. To Adam's eternal surprise, Rosaria's parents were present at the ceremony, alongside a host of cousins, aunts, uncles and friends. Her loyal sister, Martina, was there too – as Rosaria's one-and-only bride's maid. Rosaria's father, Umberto, solemnly shook Adam by the hand. Adam remembered clearly his first encounter with Umberto in an orchard attached to the family's country house, looking down on an ancient stone well – the symbolic beginning of Rosaria and Adam's long romance. ('Dancing to the Pizzica') Anna (with beautifully manicured, bright pink finger nails) and Riccardo were dressed up as pages at the wedding reception

*and stole the show – the link between their parents and the
hitherto estranged mass of Rosaria's kith and kin. Anna and
Riccardo accompanied their parents on their 'honeymoon'
much to Anna's amusement; a long-awaited trip to see Big Ben
- or Big Bang, as Riccardo pronounced it - and the rest of
London in the hectic space of five days. It was an exciting
experience, but for Riccardo at least it did not quite match up
to the magic moment when Francesco had draped a cloak over
their heads in a darkened corner of the AltoTek laboratories
and, one after the other, brother and sister had vanished into
thin air.*

"It's so cool!" Riccardo had declared.

"It's too scary!" Anna decided...

Glossary and cultural notes:

Prologue:
Non ci resta che piangere *(Nothing to do but weep)*
A remarkable comic film starring Roberto Benigni and Massimo Troisi

Chapter 1:

capo
chief : head
amico mio
my friend
Magnifico Rettore
'Magnificent Rector' – the correct official title of a university dean

Chapter 2:

Forza!
"Go for it!" - used to exhort a person to show strength or courage.
caro : cara
dear : (also) expensive
Il Sole 24 ore
The Italian eqivalent of our Financial Times

Chapter 4:

Benvenuto da noi
Welcome (to our group)
In bocca al lupo
Best of luck! (Lit: In the mouth of the wolf)
penne
a pasta shape – in the form of a tube
buon lavoro
said to wish someone a good day's work

Chapter 5:

fidanzato/a
fiancé(e) : can also mean simply boyfriend/girlfriend
superstrada
One step below a motor way – a super highway

Chapter 6:

CGIL
Confederazione Generale Italiana del Lavoro – a left-wing union.
Disturbo?
Excuse the intrusion
fave e cicoria
A dish from around Lecce – mashed broad beans and chicory. Delicious!
A dopo!
See you later
C'è una collega
I'm with a colleague

Chapter 7:

Il Mezzogiorno
Here, the name of a newspaper. 'Midday' or 'The South of Italy'
grazie mille
a thousand thanks
d'accordo?
agreed?
Montalbano/Camellieri
The fictional chief inspector of police created by Andrea Camilleri
amore mio
my love
Ti voglio bene
I love you – to a friend or family member.
cf 'Ti amo' to an intimate partner
tesoro mio
my little treasure – a form of endearment
ragazzi
lads (and lasses)
una talpa
a mole – in both senses
buonasera
good evening
Ci vediamo domani
See you tomorrow
scusami
sorry : pardon me

che schifo!
How disgusting!
bravissimo/a/i/e
Well done!

Chapter 8:

Dai! Forza!
To exhort courage – 'Come on! Be brave!'
grazie infinite
my eternal thanks
Pronto
What you say when picking up the phone – 'Ready'

Chapter 9:

patate al forno
baked potatoes – potatoes in the oven
Principe azzuro
A knight in shining armour (Blue Prince)
Grazie di cuore
Thank you from my heart
Le Cantine Due Palme
A wine producer from Cellino San Marco.

Chapter 10:

campanile
bell-tower
mannaggia (la miseria)
a mild expletive expressing surprise or irritation
un bacio
a kiss
zio
uncle - cf 'zia' meaning aunt

La Guardia di Finanza
The financial police

Chapter 11:

Apra la porta
Open the door
un attimo
just a minute
cazzo puttana
A vulgar expression of anger by the mobster.
adesso muoviamoci
now let's get moving
merda!
shit!

Chapter 12:

Certo...a prestissimo allora
Certainly...see you very soon then
il peculato
embezzlement
buon lavoro
good work!
Non dire sciochezze, Riccardo
Don't talk nonsense...

Chapter 13:

in gamba
clever : smart : alert (lit: 'in leg')
a presto
see you soon
un concorso
a competition for a job
La pazienza del ragno
The patience of the spider   *(Also the title of a Montalbano story)*
magari!
If only!
La persona desiderata non è al momento disponibile
The person you are calling is not available at this time
Che sarà, sarà
What will be, will be

una raccomandazione

Cynics in Italy will tell you this is the only way to get a job – by recommendation.

Che cosa?

What!?

Chapter 15:

Arturo, vieni qua subito!

Arthur, come here at once!

L'eredità

Inheritance – a popular quiz game on Rai Uno.

una bombola

a gas cylinder

sana e salva

safe and sound

Una stronza sei! Me lo pagerai!

You're a bloody fool. You'll pay for this.

una canonica

the Catholic church's equivalent of a vicarage

un brindisi

a toast

simpatico

nice : friendly : kind

Chi è?

Who is it?

Posso entrare?

Can I come in?

Chapter 16:

Beni Culturali

A university subject devoted to the study of Italy's vast artistic heritage

Che bello!

How lovely!

Salice Salentino

A grape variety native to Salento

Liceo Scientifico

High school specialising in science

Chapter 17:

laurel leaf crown
worn by new graduates at their induction ceremony. A *laurea* is a degree.
Che carino!
How sweet!

Chapter 18:

un cazzo
a vulgar word for penis
avanti
Come in! (lit: Advance)
basta
enough
Ci penso io, zio
I'll take care of it, uncle.

About the author

Richard Walmsley lived, loved and worked for eight life-changing years in Puglia – the 'heel' of Italy. From 2002 until 2005, he taught English at the University of Salento (Lecce) until age forced him reluctantly into retirement. At present, he spends his time writing novels and short stories. His novels and many of the short stories are born of his vivid experiences during the years spent in this contradictory region of Europe. Apart from writing, the author loves Italian cuisine and wine, cooking the aforementioned cuisine, walking and classical piano jazz. He has a marked preference for life in the countryside.

Although written ostensibly as tales of intrigue, mystery, suspense – even romance – and the influence of the mafia, the stories have other themes running through them. For example, 'Leonardo's Trouble with Molecules' explores the destructive power of sex when not linked to love and the often undervalued contribution of the wisdom of children. The stories are laced with humour - it is impossible, he maintains, to live in Italy without being struck by Italians' anarchical relationship with the world around them.

(Revised version – January 2019)

Printed in Great Britain
by Amazon

66802078R00208